Coolstone Takes Flight

Flying Without Feathers is not Easy

Roger G. Crewse

© 2023 by Randall A. Crewse

All rights reserved. No part of this book may be reproduced, stored in a retrieval system, or transmitted in any form or by any means without the prior written permission of Randall A. Crewse except by a reviewer who may quote brief passages in a review to be printed in a newspaper, magazine or journal.

Randall A. Crewse grants the final approval for this literary material.

First Printing

This is a work of fiction. Names, characters, businesses, places, events, and incidents are either the products of the author's imagination or used in a fictitious manner. Any resemblance to actual persons, living or dead, or actual events is purely coincidental.

Cover design by MarkGelotte.com

ISBN:979-8-218-22487-5

Printed in the United States of America

Table of Contents

Foreword · v
Dedication · vii
About the Author: Roger G. Crewse · ix
Coolstone Take Flight Glossary · xiii

Stories

Routine Passenger Pickup · 1
Cool Ones with Coolstone · 9
Coolstone Gains Experience · 19
Coolstone Convenes the Board · 27
Long Day, Short Trip · 41
Coolstone Does a Pitchelmann · 51
Another Real Good Deal · 61
Commercial Air · 73
Violations, Violations · 85
Weather Strains a Friendship · 93
Coolstone Chickens Out · 103
That's a Wet Runway · 117
Coolstone Plays Pick a Chart · 127
Scram Bell · 139
Holiday At Delta Dump · 147
A Routine Formation · 163
Coolstone Slides Again · 173
Coolstone Tries a Six Pack · 183

"Special Twelve" 193
Coolstone and the Weatherman 205
The Fox and the Falcon 215
Weekend Cross Country 225
Rumors, Rumors, Rumors 237
Decisions, Decisions 251
Snowbunny Go Home 261
Coolstone Meets the Mustang 271
Experience Wills Out 283
Ferry Flights are Not Easy, Either 291
Coolstone Plans? A Flight 301
Coolstone Beats the System......... 311
You've Got It Coolstone 321
Coolstone Ends an Era 331
No Lace on Coolstone 349
Coolstone Lights a Stogie 357

Foreword

Roger Crewse –

How do you define a legend – author; artist; humorist; mentor!

But, best of all – friend!

I first met Roger when I was assigned as the F-106 Safety Project Officer in the Air Defense Command at Ent AFB, Colorado. But I had known him for several years before that through his insightful visions as "Coolstone One" in the *"Interceptor"* Magazine – the Safety Magazine he founded and edited in 1958 for the Air Defense Command (ADC) where he was the Chief of Safety Analysis. I had the education branch at the F-106 Combat Crew Training Squadron at Tyndall AFB, Florida, prior to reassignment to ADC and was amazed by the number of "Coolstone" stories that defined flying the "Delta Dart." His investigation into F-106 post-stall gyrations/spins and inverted spins led to him developing spin recovery techniques which he briefed to each F-106 squadron. And similar efforts were equally effective for modifications and improvements to the F-101, F-102, and F-104.

Roger left ADC for the Air Force's "Air Force Inspection and Safety Center" (AFISC) at Norton AFB, California, where he was the Chief of the Reports and Analysis Division of the Air Force. I followed Roger as the Editor of the *"Interceptor"* for a brief period and, after a tour in Southeast Asia, rejoined him at AFISC. My job at AFISC included defining new programs to build safety into USAF operations. Roger's innovative analysis programs were instrumental in helping develop a program to combine the four European Air Forces accident/incident data for the F-16 with that of the USAF, thereby doubling the rate we learned to fly the "Fighting Falcon" safely.

So – "Author" – Roger wrote with incredible clarity. You would actually feel his emotion when you read his many works!

And "Artist" – your mind's eye could see the pictures he painted with his words!

"Humorist" – "Coolstone One" was the "coolest" pilot who ever flew a jet fighter. Read the episodes in this book and fly to a special place with a special guy!

And "Mentor" – you would have to be "me" to understand how much I learned from Roger!

"Friend" certainly needs no further definition!

Roger is, indeed, a legend in the US Air Force!

Richard "Dick" Henderson
Lt Col, USAF (Ret)

Dedication

This book is dedicated to my dad, Roger G. Crewse, the author of these stories, and my mom, Dorothy A. Crewse, who supported him throughout their 40-year marriage.

My dad joined the Air Force in 1942 and flew in the South Pacific during World War II. He joined the National Guard after the war and was activated in 1950 for the Korean Conflict, and remained in the Air Force until he was medically retired in 1961. He worked for the Air Force as a civilian until he retired in 1982.

In 1958 he became the originator and first editor of the Air Defense Command's Interceptor magazine. From 1963 until 1982, he worked as the Chief of Safety Analysis for the Air Defense Command, then later as Chief of Reports and Analysis for the Air Force.

Beginning with the early days of Interceptor magazine, he created and authored his Coolstone stories. As far as I can tell, he wrote about 45 Coolstone stories, 34 of which are compiled in this book.

My dad's intention when he and my mom retired and left San Bernardino, CA, for Rockford, WA, was that he would put the stories into a book himself.

Unfortunately, as they headed to Rockford, WA, my mom ended up in the hospital in Winnemucca, NV, with the first manifestation of her cancer.

They fought their health issues for the next five years before dying in 1987, six weeks apart.

After my brother's passing two years ago, I came across my dad's file containing all his stories, with the beginnings of his effort to organize them for his book.

Working on bringing these stories to life was like having my dad in the room with me again. I grew up with his sense of humor and his way with words.

These are light-hearted flying stories, often with a safety message intended for pilots but with a sense of humor that any reader can enjoy.

I hope you enjoy them as much as I have enjoyed bringing them to you.

Randy Crewse

About the Author
Roger G. Crewse
Major, USAF (Ret)
"Coolstone One"

Roger Crewse joined the Army Air Corps on December 2, 1942, and entered cadet training in March 1943. He graduated from pilot training in April 1944 and served 22 months in the South Pacific from New Guinea to Okinawa, flying C-47 troop carrier missions.

From 1946 to February 1950, he was a member of the 116th Fighter Squadron, Spokane National Guard. In 1950 he was recalled to active duty with a 12-month tour in Korea with the 319th Fighter Interceptor Squadron flying the F-94. He flew with Air Defense Command units until 1958.

Roger flew the B-25, C-47, F-51, F-84B, F-84C, F-84G, F-89, F-94, F-101, F-102, F-104, F-106 and T-33. He was a Command Pilot with over 4,500 flying hours.

Roger was assigned to Air Defense Command Headquarters, in Colorado Springs, in March 1958 as a project officer for the F-106. He became the first editor of the highly regarded Interceptor magazine in October 1958. It was at that time that he originated and authored his infamous Coolstone stories.

Roger G. Crewse

Roger was medically retired in 1961 but returned to the Headquarters of the Air Defense Command in April 1963 as Chief of the Safety Analysis Division until 1974.

In October 1974, Roger served as Chief of the Reports and Analysis Division of the Air Force at Norton Air Force Base. He was personally involved in forming the analysis capability for the entire United States Air Force. He revolutionized how airplane accidents were evaluated, leading to the development of a one-of-a-kind, forward-trending accident prevention capability.

Roger was a true Safety Warrior. During his career in safety analysis, he was directly responsible for modifications and improvements to the F-101, F-102, F-104, and F-106. Most notably, Roger was known for his in-depth study of the F-102 compressor stall problems, which resulted in aircraft modifications, tech order changes, pilot handbook changes, and a drastic reduction in F-102 compressor stalls. Additionally, Roger pinpointed and investigated F-106 post-stall gyrations/spins and inverted spins. By applying his findings in terms of understandable aerodynamics, he was able to isolate the cause of unsuccessful spin recoveries. He developed new spin recovery techniques, which he personally briefed to each F-106 squadron resulting in a marked reduction in this type of accident. His spin recovery techniques are still being taught at the Air Force Academy today.

Roger may be best known for his Coolstone series. Coolstone is the quintessence of all the fighter pilots Roger had ever known. Coolstone could be counted on to get himself regularly into some variety of trouble or mischief. Since Coolstone's adventures and misadventures were based on actual events to which Air Defense Command aircrews could readily relate, they received instant recognition and served an important role in accident prevention. Roger's smooth writing style and brilliant character portrayals further enhanced the forcefulness of the safety messages delivered to his eager readers.

Roger's service to the United States Air Force spanned 38 years on active duty and as a civilian. During his service to our country, Roger earned numerous medals and awards, including the Bronze Star, the Air Force Air medal, the Air Force Meritorious Civilian Service Award, and the Air Force Decoration for Exceptional Civilian Service, the highest award granted by the Secretary of the Air Force to a civilian employee.

Roger earned the well-deserved reputation of "Mr. Safety" for the Air Defense Command.

Coolstone Take Flight Glossary

The Coolstone stories are flying stories written in the 60s and 70s by a pilot for pilots with Acronyms that were in use at the time. I could not find all of those used in the stories, but here are many of them. For us nonpilot types, they will help bring the stories to life.

ACM-Air Combat maneuvers
ADC-Air Defense Command
ADF-Automatic Direction Finder
ADIZ-Air Defense Identification Zone
AFM-Air Force Manual
AG-Adjutant General
AIM- Air Intercept Missle
ANGELS-Altitude in Thousands of Feet
AO- Air Officer
APU-Auxiliary Power Unit
ATC-Air Traffic Control
BOQ-Bachelor Officers Quarters
CAA-Combat Aviation Advisors
CAMRON-Consolidated Aircraft Maintenance Squadron
CAVU- Ceiling and Visibility Unlimited
CCTS-Combat Crew Training Squadron (at Tyndall AFB, 4756 CCTS)
CO-Commanding Officer
COC- Combat Operations Center
CRT-Cathode Ray Tube
DASH ONE- Aircraft "Owners-Manual"
DF-EWO-Direction Finding Electronic Warfare Officer

DME-Distance Measuring Equipment
DNIF-Duties Not Including Flying
EGT-Exhaust Gas Temperature
EW Electronic Warfare Officer
FAC-Forward Air Controller
FEAF- Far East Air Force (WWII)
FIVE SQUARE- Loud and Clear
FORM 175- Military Flight Plan
GARS-Guided Aerial Rocket
GCA-Ground Control Approach
GCI-Ground Control Intercept
IFF-Identification, Friend or Foe
IFR-Instrument Flight Rules
ILS- Instrument Landing System
IP- Instructor Pilot
IWS-Interceptor Weapons School
MA- Mission Accomplished (successfully intercepted a bogey)
NOTAMS- Notice to Airmen
OHR- Office of Human Resources
OHROIC-Officer in Charge
OMNI- Omnidirectional Radio
OPS-Operations
ORI- Operational Readiness Inspection
PARROT CHECK- Identification Friend or Foe Check
PE-Personal Equipment
PIGEONS- Bearing and Range to Base
PIO-Public Information Office
RAPCON-Radar Approach Control
RC-Radar Controller
RCR-Runway Condition Report
RIO-Radar Intercept Officer (later changed to WSO)
RLS-Remote Light Sensor
RMI-Radio Magnetic Indicator
RO- Radar Officer

RON-Remain Over Night
RT-Receiver/ Transmitter
SOP-Standard Operating Procedure
TACAN-Tactical Air Navigation
TCM-Theater Containment Manager
TDY-Temporary Duty
TPT-Tactical Petroleum Terminal
TVOR- Terminal-Very High-Frequency Omnidirectional Radio
UHF- Ultra High Frequency
VFR- Visual Flight Rules
VOODOO- F-101
VOR-VHF Omnidirectional Radio
VORTAC-VHF combine with TACAN
WAG- Weather Officer/Wild Ass Guesser
WEAPON-Radar
WSO-Weapon Systems Officer

Routine Passenger Pickup

Coolstone was scheduled to make a passenger pickup – he was going from Selfridge to Colorado Springs to pick up one each one-star general. The Ops officer was briefing him.

"Look, the Old Man has just had a physical. I have no idea what all he has gone through, but I do know that he'll be ready to come home pronto, so don't pull one of your infamous RONs in Chicago, Kansas City, or any of those other fat spots. Just fly directly over there and back. General Wild Bill never was the patient type, and I know he'll have your flight planned better than you will. Within five minutes of when you should be there, he'll be in Base Ops at Peterson. You be there!"

"No sweat, Major-it'll be a piece of cake. I'll go from here to Kansas City, refuel, and whip over to Pete."

"Okay, Coolstone, but make it. Remember, the General will be waiting."

Coolstone, with his usual aplomb, filed his clearance and preflighted his aircraft. He posed just a moment for the crew chief to snap his picture - the crew chief always did this when Coolstone flew, not because he wanted a keepsake, but because he wanted a record of what the aircraft looked like *before* the flight.

At Richards-Gebaur, Coolstone checked the TV weather and found that Peterson was excellent. Without further ado, he filed his clearance.

As he flew along, he couldn't help but speculate on how many points he could make with Wild Bill if he played his cards right. "Get there on time," he thought. "Show him what a professional pilot I am. Personally, mix his martinis if we should RON someplace. I might even fix the Old Man up with a - no, maybe I'd better forget that part."

Coolstone passed over Salina, figured his ETA for Goodland, and gave his position report. When he had that completed, his thoughts returned to the general. Rumor had it that the Old Man was a real terror-that he didn't just happen to come by that "Wild Bill" tag by accident. They said he had lopped off so many heads that he kept a red rug in his office so that the blood wouldn't show. They also said that the one thing which upset the General most was an incomplete mission. He considered an abort a crime more heinous than any other thing a man might do. Coolstone's thoughts were interrupted.

"Hello, Coolstone One-Coolstone One. This is Salina radio. Come in, please."

"Roger, roger. Salina. This is Coolstone One. Go ahead."

"Coolstone from Salina. I have a Flight Service advisory for you. Colorado Springs is now reporting 400 feet and one-mile visibility in fog. They are forecasted to go below minimums in the next half-hour due to an up-slope condition. What are your intentions?"

Coolstone Takes Flight

Coolstone stood straight up in the cockpit. The 400 and a mile wouldn't have bothered him normally, but with all that real estate sticking up 12- to-14,000 feet, you couldn't afford to make just a little mistake on the approach, and Coolstone had been known to make slightly more than little mistakes.

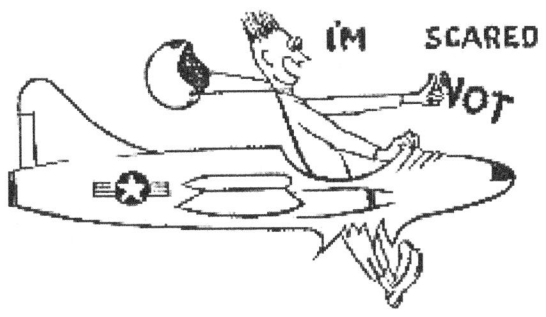

"Salina—er—ah—er, what is the weather at Denver?"

"Coolstone from Salina. The weather at Denver is high broken, with 15 miles vis. Do you wish to change your destination?"

Coolstone thought for a minute. His only chance would be for Colorado Springs to go below minimums.

"Hello, Salina-this is Coolstone. I guess I'll proceed on to Colorado Springs and see what the weather is when I get there."

"Roger, Coolstone," said Salina. "I'll advise Flight Service."

Coolstone dug out the Central letdown book and thumbed rapidly through it. When he finally found the right page, he was relieved to see that the minimums shown were 300 and three-quarters of a mile for the ILS.

Shortly thereafter, he found himself over Goodland and called in his report.

Goodland came back. "Roger, Coolstone One. Have your position report okay. Flight Service has an advisory for you. Colorado Springs is now 300 and three-quarters. What are your intentions?"

"Boy, oh boy!" thought the Cold Rock. "They're really putting the pressure on now. If the weather doesn't get worse, I've had it."

This was probably the first time in Coolstone's flying career that he had found himself wishing and hoping for the weather to get worse.

"Hello, Goodland," he said a little weakly. "I'll proceed to Colorado Springs and check the weather there. If it isn't below minimums, I'll make an approach. Otherwise, I'll go to Denver."

"Roger, Coolstone. Call Colorado Springs Approach Control five minutes east."

Coolstone once again picked up the letdown book, took a look at the chart for the Colorado Springs penetration, got the headings in mind, and sat there, worrying. When he was about five minutes out, he called for the weather.

"Roger, Coolstone," said the Springs Approach Control. "The weather at Colorado Springs is now 200 obscured and one-half mile in fog."

"Roger, roger, Boy," said Coolstone. "Guess I'll just have to go to Denver."

"Boy!" he thought. "It didn't look so good for a minute. Wild Bill may be mad at the weather, but he knows I couldn't break regulations. I'll send a car down for him from Denver. You never know; he might just want to RON, and Denver isn't such a bad town."

Coolstone's thoughts were interrupted by Colorado Springs Approach Control: "Hello, Coolstone One. Continental 342 just landed at Peterson

Field and reported that the ceiling is actually 300 feet and the visibility on the approach three-quarters of a mile."

The color drained from Coolstone's face. Leave it to a smart-alec airlines pilot to go into a field that was reported below minimums. A picture formed in his mind-Wild Bill pacing Operations, knowing full well the field was above minimums and waiting, waiting for Coolstone, who was in Denver. He couldn't stand the thought.

"Springs Approach," said Coolstone, very faintly now. "I'll make the approach at Peterson. Could I have an approach time, please?"

Once again, a new emotion came over Coolstone. He was praying for a delay-any delay.

"Roger, Coolstone. No delays are expected. You are cleared for a penetration off the Springs omni. Give Colorado Springs a call when departing the high station."

"Roger," said Coolstone, and as he turned back to the Springs omni, he was barely straightened out before he got station passage, and he wasn't ready, but he dumped his boards, picked up the outbound heading of 160 degrees, and started the descent. As he passed through 16,000, he looked again at the book. "Missed approach!" he thought. Frantically, he grabbed the book with both hands, flying the aircraft with his knees, and held it up close to his face to read the fine print covering the missed approach.

"Let's see – it says right turn, climbing to 8000 on a track to 'ELL' R-BN. Boy, I'll never find out what that ELL is," he thought. Then he read on. "Proceed to intxn R-109 'COS' VOR and R-350 'PUB' VOR." That did it!

"Oh, Lordy!" he thought. "I'd better not miss this approach." As he hit the penetration turn, he suddenly remembered the "real estate" to the west. He increased his angle of bank to almost 90 degrees in an effort to stay well to the east of the ILS center line. He rolled out, leveled at 7300, and noted that the center line was well to his left. That suited him fine. He babied up to it 10 degrees at a time and got his gear and flaps out somehow. Then he got a call from Springs Approach Control asking for his position.

"I'm inbound at er – ah 83, no – 7300 on the ILS," he answered.

"Roger, Coolstone. Give us a call at the outer marker."

Just as Coolstone turned ten more degrees toward the ILS needle, he hit the outer marker. The ILS center line needle jumped from full left to a full right deflection and the glide slope went to a full down deflection. Coolstone's stick actions were like the rapid stirring of a giant bean pot-all the way down, he mixed the beans. When he approached ILS minimums, a horrible thought crossed his mind he didn't have a current altimeter setting.

Quickly, he called, "Springs Approach, I'm over the outer marker; what's the altimeter?" But Coolstone couldn't continue the conversation-it took his full attention to fly the center line and glide slope and, at the same time, try to force himself below the minimum reading on his altimeter – and he was still in the clouds. Instinctively he pulled back on the stick and dumbly stared as the ILS glide slope needle slowly worked its way to full down.

"Tombstone from Colorado Springs-altimeter setting is 3000. Where did you say you were?"

All that Approach Control heard was an "er-ah-er I am–" because Coolstone couldn't talk. It was all he could do to fly the airplane. Rather than try the missed approach, he gritted his teeth and let the bird down farther, adding power to obtain 150 knots, with some vague notion of zooming up and ejecting, getting on top, or something. Then he began to see, out of the corner of his eyes, dark splotches of ground. He gave the beans another stir and looked out. Sure enough, out the side, he could see the ground through some scud. He welded his attention to the ILS and brought the plane down to the glide slope. He was doing 160 now. He looked out the sides again; he was out of the clouds. He looked out the front; he was still in. He looked closer; he had an iced windshield. No defrosters!

Coolstone was so low now that he knew he must be near the field. He kicked the rudder vigorously until, out the side, he could see a runway. But he could also see another runway-there were two runways at about a 45-degree angle to each other. Which one to land on? With lightning calculation, he took the one closest to him and set her down at 140.

"His Stick Actions Were Like The Rapid Stirring Of A Giant Bean Pot"

His braking techniques were a marvel to modern science, but he got stopped. As he turned off the taxiway to park his bird in front of Base Ops, his knees were shaking so that the turn was accomplished in 10-degree jerks. He got the airplane stopped, stopcocked the engine, and sat and shook. Finally, he raised the canopy and up-bounced the AO.

"Man, Coolstone, you're really an ILS pilot. Man, oh man, not many people could have made that approach. That was really something."

Coolstone rolled his eyes over toward the AO and mumbled, "It's really nothing-really nothing to it," and shook a little more.

"By the way," the AO added, "the weather was so bad the General decided you wouldn't be able to get in and took a car to Denver."

Cool Ones with Coolstone

Coolstone enjoyed flying target missions. One reason was that from his lofty perch at the headquarters, it was very easy, he found, to lose touch with operational problems. He wouldn't admit specifically that he might need to go to the well occasionally to get pumped back up, nor would any of his cohorts at the headquarters. They felt that with their broad and long experience in air defense matters, any gaps in currency which might exist could be spanned. They assured themselves of this daily over coffee.

Coolstone also enjoyed the target mission for another reason. He usually flew them with his boss. He could demonstrate his skill and cunning as a pilot, his quick wit, and his general affability at the bar. And, of course, while he had the boss trapped in the front or the back seat, as the case might be and the case was usually the front seat-he could expound on current problems graphically without paper and without intermediaries interjecting their thinking. He was sure he made all sorts of points during discussions of these types.

When the Rock received a call inquiring as to his availability for a target mission, he quickly agreed to take it. He contacted his boss, who was a light colonel, and the boss also agreed quickly. The colonel enjoyed these missions (in spite of Coolstone) if for no other reason than to escape from his windowless cubicle for a day or two.

On the morning of the flight, they were briefed in detail. The mission was to be flown out of Mountain Home AFB, an easy hop from Pete. The two departed with a forecast indicating weather could be a problem all over Idaho later in the afternoon and early evening. Ceilings, the forecaster indicated, would be about 1500 feet with good visibility at their ETA, and the fog shouldn't set in until several hours after they had landed.

Their flight had progressed normally for about an hour with Coolstone's constant comments from the back seat. He made little jokes, discussed business, and when he had time, he took care of the navigation and the RT.

Center called, "Hello, Coolstone One, Coolstone One from Salt Lake City Center. We have you 100 miles out of Mountain Home. You may reduce your altitude to FL200. Advise passing through 250 and level at 200."

"Roger, boy," said the Rock. "We are departing 310 at this time."

Up ahead, they could see the weather was solid. The colonel suggested getting a weather check just in case the forecast wasn't holding up. Coolstone quickly checked with the center. They gave him 500 and 2 in light rain and fog for Mountain Home and 600 and 2, in rain and fog at Boise. The center cleared them to reduce their altitude further to 12,000 and advised them that they would be making a radar approach to Runway 30.

"Maybe we had better check with Metro," said the colonel, "Just in case."

"Roger," said Coolstone.

Coolstone Takes Flight

He advised the center, contacted Metro, and was horrified to hear that Mountain Home weather was now 200 and 1/2 in rain and fog. He tried to keep the panic out of his voice when he said to the colonel, "Man, that weather changed quite a bit in the last hour or so. I'll check Boise, too." He found that Boise was 500 and 2 in rain and fog.

Now Coolstone didn't like ceilings lower than 1,000 when he was flying himself, and he wasn't sure what the colonel could hack. He would rather take 500 and 2 with an ILS than 200 and 1/2 with any kind of radar approach. At that point, they received a call from the center. "This is to advise you," said Salt Lake City, "That there will be a slight delay. A B-52 has missed an approach. Climb to FL220, and you are cleared present position direct to Mountain Home TACAN. Hold southeast inbound on the 111-degree radial between 35 and 45 nautical miles. Expect further clearance at 45."

"Roger, boy," said Coolstone; then to the colonel, he said, "It takes quite a while to get one of those flying towns back around. That's 15 minutes delay. That weather must really be lousy, and we'll never get the missions off. Probably we'll just sit there for two days."

Coolstone had an idea. How to avoid 200 and 1/2 at any cost was primarily on his mind. So, he decided to use the oblique approach.

"Say, colonel," he said, "How about going to Boise Municipal? As long as we are going to sit on the ground someplace, we would be a lot closer to a town if we land at Boise, and let me tell you, colonel, that Boise is not bad, not bad at all. We could change our destination, and they have 600 feet, so far as I am concerned, that would beat RON-ing at Mountain Home."

"Sounds good," replied the colonel. "Give the center a call and change our destination." The colonel had been mentally searching for some honorable way out himself.

Quickly, before his boss had a chance to change his mind, Coolstone called the center. He changed their destination, received a clearance to Boise, and soon they were on ILS final. When they broke out, they found that it was indeed raining, and there was, indeed, fog at Boise Municipal Airport. After landing there, Coolstone had to admit the colonel did a fine job. They taxied over to the guard area, disengaged themselves from the airplane, and became thoroughly soaked while sprinting from the aircraft to base ops.

The colonel checked in with the division just to be sure that the instructions hadn't changed. They had. He was advised that he and Coolstone were to proceed to Hamilton Field for target missions out of there. They would be briefed as to the details after they checked in at Hamilton. The two filed their clearance, went out to the aircraft, and preflighted it in the rain. They were thoroughly and completely soaked by the time they finished.

The trip from Boise to Hamilton was uneventful, and other than being very damp and soggy, the two arrived in reasonable condition. The target briefing officer indicated they had about an hour and a half to get refueled, preflighted, and make the mission. The pair decided they would go to the BOQ, check in, then fly the mission before they had anything to eat.

"Sir," Coolstone said to the colonel. "I'll take care of the reservations."

"Fine," replied the colonel. "Go ahead. I'll make out our clearance, so all we'll have to do is just preflight and go when we get back."

Coolstone went over to the phone, called the BOQ office, and in a tone of voice that automatically denied any resistance at all, he said, "I would like accommodations for Colonel White and one other, please, a suite with two beds will be just fine."

"Yes, sir, colonel," the clerk answered Coolstone. "Yes, sir, we'll fix you right up. That will be VIP suite 127. Stop by here and get the key, if you will, please, sir, and we will also sign you in."

"Roger," said Coolstone, "I appreciate your timely and efficient action. Speaks well for your operation!"

The pair found a car and proceeded to the BOQ office. "I'll handle it. You sit right here, sir," said Coolstone. "There is no point in your coming in at all." Coolstone got out of the car and trotted over to the BOQ office. He signed them in, very carefully leaving off the "Lieutenant" from the colonel's rank.

They arrived at their quarters, and as the colonel entered, he said, "These are excellent accommodations. Rarely have I seen BOQ rooms quite as plush as this for transient troops. What did you tell that guy, anyway?" Coolstone didn't answer.

As they looked around, each noted the TV set, refrigerator, thick beautiful carpeting, finely upholstered and very expensive appearing chairs, and a large coffee table that looked as though it was made from mahogany, no less. Coolstone went to the refrigerator, opened the door, and sure enough, it was well-stocked.

"Hey," he called to the colonel. "Look at this. They knew we were coming, apparently."

"Roger, boy," answered the colonel. "That looks great. Tell you what we should do. We should plan ahead. Let's make up a bowl full of martinis, fill the glasses, and put them up in the freezer compartment so they'll be ready when we come back."

"Excellent idea, said Coolstone. "Excellent. Shows great foresight and that type of planning worthy of a senior officer of your status."

They mixed their martinis, decided four - two apiece - should be about right for a start, filled the glasses, and placed them in the freezer. The car was still waiting outside, so back they went to base operations.

It was dark out now, and as they preflighted their bird, the two discussed the martinis they would have as they were cleaning up and then the large steak they would have at the club.

"Man, that was real thinking," Coolstone said, "putting those martinis on ice."

"Yeh," replied the colonel modestly. Then he added, "This Hamilton really has fine BOQs. Makes a person feel like a VIP or something."

Coolstone swallowed rather nervously - "Yes, colonel, it sure does. Well, we'd better get in and get ready," he said. "Don't want to rush you, but on the other hand, we want to be sure and make our takeoff time."

Approximately 30 minutes later, 150 miles due west of Hamilton, they were advised to reduce their altitude to 3,000 and that the fighters would be coming in. This they did. They were low-altitude targets for F-101s, and Coolstone, from his back seat position, kept a constant watch for attacking aircraft. He didn't see a one. He did notice, however, that with the reduced altitude out over the water, they no longer had their TACAN operational. They were vectored around rather aimlessly, Coolstone thought, for approximately 20 minutes. Of course, he didn't know their specific position, but he was pretty sure of their approximate location.

A big bright yellow light showed up on the instrument panel. Coolstone, with a forced calmness maintained only because of years of experience, shouted, "What's that, what's that?" He took out his flashlight and carefully read "Generator Out." "We'd better climb," he declared to the colonel and noting that they were already in a climb, called for pigeons. He received "Zero-eight-five, 150 miles."

Coolstone Takes Flight

"That's quite a ways out," said the colonel.

"I want to tell you," answered Coolstone. "I hope that battery holds up."

They ran the checklist for electrical failure, turned off all hard-to-get equipment with the exception of the TACAN, and headed for Hamilton.

The lights of San Francisco were visible in the distance, and as these lights became brighter, the cockpit lights became dimmer. With only a full fuselage tank for sure, they made a straight-in approach to Hamilton from over the bay, but both pilots were rather quiet during the latter stages of the approach, excluding their heavy breathing on the interphone. The landing was a success, and the two were met by an impressive group of firemen, ambulances, maintenance personnel, and the SOF. They shut down, explained their problem to the maintenance people, went into base operations, and arranged for transportation once again.

Coolstone called the driver aside and said, "Take us to the VIP quarters if you would." The colonel, in the meantime, was talking to the SOF. He came back over to Coolstone.

Say," he said, "There's not a thing open for chow. We're too late for everything but early breakfast, which doesn't begin until 3 a.m."

"Oh boy," replied Coolstone. "That's what we need at the end of a perfect day. At least we've got the martinis on ready."

They flushed a couple of candy bars from the machine and returned to their lush quarters on the hill.

They stripped from their soggy and by now slightly smelly flying suits, turned on the TV set, retrieved their martinis from the freezer compartment, and sat down in the fine chairs with their stockinged feet on the mahogany table. They sipped their martinis while watching color TV.

Coolstone had removed his pen-sized flare pistol from his flying suit pocket and laid the pistol on the mahogany table. He picked it up idly as he was watching the TV and unconsciously fingered the trigger. He flipped at it a couple of times, and finally, it fired. Immediately one, each ball of fire began to ricochet around the room. It bounded off the lush chairs and the lush tables; it rolled on the lush rug; it careened off the finely decorated walls. If the specifications were right, the flare had five hundred feet to go, and it could only accomplish this by moving ten feet in one direction.

"Trap it, trap it!" yelled the colonel.

"I am trying to," screamed Coolstone.

Wildly they chased it around the room. They knocked over the plush chairs and the fine table. Then the flare turned on them and chased them. They both ran like yellow dogs until, looking over their shoulders, both charged into the wall and fell – one-tenth of a second behind the flare. The flare reversed its direction as it slammed into the wall above them, and the two again were on the offensive. But the ball was moving at or very near the speed of Mach 1. Finally, after its energy was spent, it slowed. The colonel grabbed his hat and tried to trap the flare under it. He missed several times but was able to herd it into a corner. He threw his hat over it quickly and poured his martini over his hat. Coolstone added his martini, also, just in case. They waited to be sure, and then carefully, the colonel peeked under his hat to see if the fire was out. It was. Together they heaved a great sigh of relief.

"That was pretty bad," said the colonel. "How did it happen? What was it?"

"Oh - uh - sir, I believe it was a flare from my pen gun. It just went off, I guess." Coolstone added quickly, "What we need is more martinis."

Coolstone Takes Flight

"Trap it, trap it"

They retrieved their two extras from the freezer compartment and surveyed the jumbled, lush mess. There were small round burned spots well distributed over the entire room and its furnishings.

10 or 12 seconds of their frenzied activity - shouting - hollering - running - pouring - had not gone unnoticed by the other tenants using the VIP quarters. Soon there was an impressive, half-dressed group in the room, each one of which required a personal briefing as to what had transpired. The briefing was augmented by considerable liquid refreshments.

Coolstone and the colonel awakened the next morning, and as they faced once again their somewhat battered quarters, the colonel advised Coolstone that he had better call the BOQ office and tell them what had happened. The Rock reluctantly did so. Within minutes a knock came at the door before they had had a chance to tidy up the room at all. The colonel (light) opened the door and was faced with a colonel (bird) who had with him a fire marshal.

Coolstone had to admit that the shock registered on the colonel's (bird) face was not altogether unwarranted. The lush mahogany table was spotted, the fine expensive chairs were spotted, and the thick beautiful rug was spotted. The motif was complete with the spotted walls. Twelve martini glasses were also on the fine spotted table, and the whole room smelled like gin.

The colonel (bird) asked no questions. He merely stated, "These are VIP quarters, and I don't even know what you two are doing in them. However, you are here." He glanced at his watch. "You now have exactly 5 minutes to get off my base."

He turned around and slammed the door. The colonel (light) looked at Coolstone. "VIP quarters!" he shouted, with awareness dawning in his eyes. "I have been had!"

But he said nothing further, and on the flight back, Coolstone, in the rear seat, also had no comments.

Coolstone Gains Experience

Coolstone was about to set up for alert. He and his flight leader had the night shift. The weather was clear. This Coolstone had confirmed at least seven times during the day, and it was forecasted to stay VFR all night.

It always made Coolstone just a little bit nervous to pull alert with his flight leader, for he felt that he was probably undergoing a quiet examination during the entire period.

"Coolstone," said his flight leader. "You go ahead, relieve No. 2, and when you finish, take No. 1. Then let me know, and I'll set up. OK?"

"Yes, sir," said Coolstone and headed for the alert shack.

About 30 minutes later, Coolstone and his flight leader had finished pre-flighting the 106's and officially relieved the other two pilots from alert duty. It was about 1900 hours, and the sun had just gone down.

When they were alone, the two pilots settled down to the alert routine. They would pull the duty from 1900 to 0700. The flight leader and Coolstone decided to switch No. 1 every three hours. The flight leader said he would take the first shift, 1900-2200, then Coolstone would take the 2200-0100 shift, the flight leader would take 0100-0400, and Coolstone the last one. They would only fly scrambles; the training flight had taken the evening missions.

While the flight leader watched TV, Coolstone made a big show out of studying 55-5. When he saw the flight leader was paying little or no attention to his studious attempts, Coolstone also started stealing glances at the TV. Of course, he kept the manual in his hand. He'd rather play cards if he had his own way, but the flight leader was a TV fan.

At 2200 hours, Coolstone said, "I've got it," and his flight leader nodded. He added, "I guess I'll go out and give the bird a once over again-check out the cockpit lights, and so on."

Coolstone was always just a little excited when he was No. 1 to go. From experience, he knew that everything must be just right-his parachute, helmet, mask, ladder placement, switches, and so on-for when the horn blew, he had a tendency to go to pieces. Often, he found himself at 5,000 feet, wondering what he'd forgotten.

Coolstone had pulled alerts so long that even a slightly abnormal-sounding telephone bell would launch him. In fact, during one exercise, when he was standing cockpit alert about No. 8 to scramble, the horn blew, and before anyone could stop him, he cranked up and went off. To make matters worse, the rest of the pilots sitting cockpit alert, amazed at his reaction, had decided that Coolstone must have received instructions they hadn't and also scrambled. The crushing blow came when the ops officer found out there wasn't any target, and COC had decided to put one up on cap. They got back to the ground in an hour or so, and Coolstone was told later that the ops officer was a sight to see, standing at the window watching the afterburners cut in, waving his arms about and shouting, "Stop them, somebody; stop them."

They were in the midst of turn-around when, sure enough, the exercise targets started coming through, and not one bird could be scrambled from the squadron. The next day the general came down and gave a little talk. The squadron commander gave a little talk, and the ops officer gave a little talk to Coolstone in private. Even with this experience to his credit, Coolstone was a hard man to stop when the bell rang.

Up at the alert barn again, Coolstone found that the flight leader had sacked out. The TV was still on, and the late movie had started.

About five minutes before the next shift was to begin, he awakened his flight leader *very carefully,* and they swapped the No. 1 position. The weather was still clear, and Coolstone, who had been spring-loaded to the scramble position, now relaxed, removed his boots, stretched out on the sack, and soon was asleep.

The flight leader went down to his bird, gave it a good check, then glanced out of the hangar for a weather check. The weather was good but a little hazy.

He came back up to the ready room, strolled over to the telautograph, and noted that the spread was only 4°. He called the duty forecaster. "Say," he said, "I notice that the temperature-dew point spread is only 4°. There is just a little bit of wind, and if I remember my weather course right, the temperature wouldn't have to go much lower for fog to form. What do you think?"

"Roger, boy," said the forecaster. "We're just about to revise our forecast. There's a good possibility of fog forming here in the next hour or so. We have advised the COC."

The flight leader thanked him, then called the duty controller at COC.

"Look, boy," he said, "Better put us on mandatory. According to Weather, this base will be below minimums in fog before too long."

"The forecaster has already called us," said the controller. "No sweat. We have an alternate planned for you about 200 miles away, so if we scramble you, we know where the recovery will be. The alternate is out of this air mass and is forecasted to stay up all night."

"That doesn't sound too peachy keen," said the flight leader. "I don't care to make a 200-mile trip tonight. How about using your head, giving us a little warning?"

"Will do if we can," said the controller.

The flight leader settled down and picked up a slightly racy novel (the only kind available at the alert hangar) and worriedly read. He wasn't worried about the scramble, but if he didn't get home in the morning when he was supposed to, his wife would kill him. She had a big day planned for him.

At about 0145, the phone rang. The flight leader answered. It was Weather.

"Have you looked outside lately?" asked the forecaster.

"No," said the flight leader. "Has the fog hit already?"

"Has it ever!" said the forecaster. "We're carrying an obscured ceiling, ¼ mile, and fog. What are you planning for an alternate if you should scramble?"

"Well," said the flight leader, "what do you have that's good? COC gave me one, but it's about 200 miles away."

Coolstone Takes Flight

"It's your best bet," said the forecaster, "even though it's kind of far. The rest of our bases are under the influence of this cold air mass. They might go down in fog, also. You better plan on using it. We'll keep you posted."

Disgustedly, the flight leader put down the phone. Now I'll probably get scrambled, he thought. It always happens to me. He poured himself a cup of coffee and settled down with his book again.

About five minutes later, the hotline rang. The flight leader picked it up. "Alert shack," he said.

It was the duty controller. "It looks like we have one coming. It's north and will be in range in about ten minutes. If we can't identify, you'll have to launch.'"

"But the weather ..." said the flight leader.

"Yes, we know what the weather is, but your alternate is still fine."

Here we go again, thought the flight leader, but, wait a minute, why shouldn't Coolstone get some of this experience? He needs it; it makes for a well-rounded alert pilot. No point in hogging all this experience myself. In fact, the more the flight leader thought about it, the nearer he came to the conclusion that he would be remiss in his duties as a flight leader if he withheld this experience from Coolstone.

Finally, after just the briefest of struggles with his conscience, he went over to where Coolstone was happily sleeping and called to him. No answer. He shook him. No answer. Then he both called and shook him.

At this point, the Cold Rock raised up quickly and said, "OK, OK, I've got it. Boy, what a short three hours!"

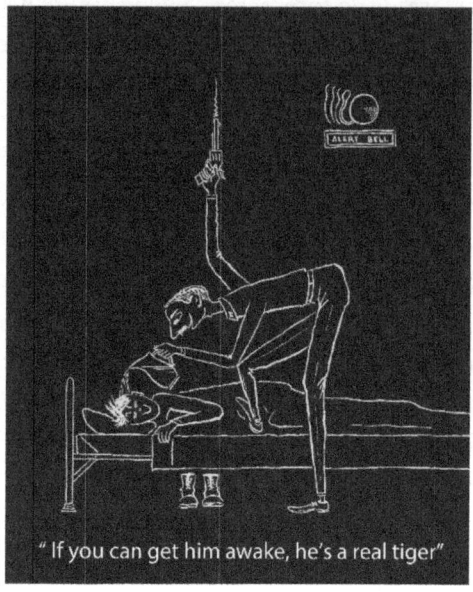
"If you can get him awake, he's a real tiger"

Coolstone slowly put on his boots, got up, and stretched. He was starting for a cup of coffee when the buzzer sounded.

The flight leader stopped him just momentarily and said, "Look, I'll monitor the radio here. There's fog out there."

But it was too late. Coolstone was scrambling, and you know what that means. In the cockpit now, Coolstone was frantically strapping in and, at the same time starting the 106 as the hangar doors were raised. He got the start, signaled for the power disconnect, hooked up his zero lanyard, and with a big flourish, advanced the power and rolled out of the hangar.

For the first time, he became aware that he had a visibility problem. In fact, he figured either he was blind or it was terribly foggy. He soon discovered that he wasn't blind. He had to stop his aircraft immediately. He didn't even know where the runway was. He let it roll very slowly while with nose wheel steering, he turned the nose wheel both left and right. Very faintly, he could see the broad yellow stripe that would take him from the alert hangar to the runway.

Over the radio, he heard his flight leader saying, "No sweat, Radar is waiting. Your recovery base is 200 miles away, and it is clear."

"Roger," said Coolstone weakly. "If I can't find the runway, I won't need a recovery base. Do those guys know what the weather is like here? It looks like zero-zero to me."

"Roger, Coolstone," said the flight leader. "It's mandatory, but you can handle it."

Sure I can, said Coolstone to himself as he inched his way out to the end of the runway.

"Tower," he said, "am I clear to take the active? And please turn your lights up full bright."

"Roger, boy," said the tower. "Full bright they are, and you're cleared for the takeoff."

Coolstone turned to the runway heading, and he could see just one light up ahead. This was going to be a real instrument takeoff, no matter how you cut it. He locked his brakes and ran the engine up. Carefully and thoroughly, he looked at each instrument. As his eyes passed by the clock, he backed up again. 0205! Is the clock wrong?

"Tower from Coolstone. What time do you have?"

"Coolstone from tower. We've got 0206."

"0206," said Coolstone. "Alert hangar, are you still on? How come you're not taking this one?"

"No sweat, buddy," said his flight leader. I'll monitor the entire flight here on the ground and watch out for you. It's good experience."

Coolstone took a deep breath, released the brakes, picked up his steering, and selected afterburner. In the roll, just as he passed one light, he could barely pick up another, and then, as his speed increased, he went to instruments and became airborne. As he gained a little altitude, he brought up his gear (breathed for the first time since brake release) and went to departure control frequency. The tops were fairly low-about 1500 feet above the ground. He broke out and now contacted GCI.

"I'm turning north," he said, "Squawking normal, climbing buster, passing through 14 angels."

"Roger," said the controller. "The target has been identified, Coolstone. Take up a heading of 140 for your alternate. Pigeons are 140, 200 miles away. And, by the way, the senior controller says it will be necessary for you to send a letter up to the sector explaining your seven-minute scramble."

Coolstone Convenes the Board

Coolstone had just taken off on a test flight in an F-101B. While climbing out, he experienced some lateral control problems. He held at 35,000, and as the aircraft slowed down after the climb, he experienced an uncontrollable roll tendency to the left at around 270 knots. Even with full right aileron below 270 knots, he couldn't hold the aircraft level. He knew he was in serious trouble.

"Hello, McCoy Tower, McCoy Tower. This is Coolstone One, over." There was a certain amount of urgency in Coolstone's tones.

"Roger, Coolstone. This is McCoy. Go ahead."

"This is Coolstone. I'm having control difficulties with this aircraft. Please call our squadron Ops and ask the CO to get on the radio. I'll pick him up on the tactical frequency."

As Coolstone waited, he began to weigh all the factors in this situation. He was pretty sure he couldn't land the bird without an accident in its present condition, but he certainly didn't want to bail out. What do you suppose the Accident Board would say? If he bailed out, he probably wouldn't be open to much criticism, but it seemed such a shame to leave a bird in this kind of shape. If he tried to land and goofed in the slightest, well, he'd seen the results before - GCI.

...she kept trying to roll..

Then on the radio, he heard, "Hello, Coolstone One. This is Surefire Ops. Do you have a problem?" Coolstone recognized the voice of his commander.

"Surefire from Coolstone. You bet your boots I have trouble. I can't control this bird under 270 knots. It seems as if the aileron control craps out or something. I let it go to 260 just a few minutes ago and got into a roll before I could get the speed up enough to stop it. What do you recommend?"

"How much fuel do you have, Coolstone?"

"Well, if I hold it here at 270 to 275, I'd say I have about one plus 45."

"Roger, boy. Stand by."

At this point, a thought began to take form in Coolstone's mind - an insidious, sneaky, dirty thought that only could gain birth in a devious mind. I know what I'll do, he thought. I'll give the accident board my problem. I'll do precisely what they recommend, and no matter what happens, it won't be my accident. Let the experts investigate this one before it happens. For once, they can do their famous second-guessing on the first go.

"Hello, Surefire. This is Coolstone One. Over."

"Roger, Coolstone. This is Surefire." It was the commander still.

"Roger, Skipper. I've got a problem here. I don't know whether to bail out or try to land this thing. In any case, I'm sure I am going to have an accident of some type. I can't control the bank under 270, and I can't stop it with full right aileron or rudder. I've turned off the autopilot, and I've pulled the circuit breaker, so that shouldn't be the trouble. What I was thinking - how about getting the Accident Board members together there in the squadron and give me the expert advice before I have the accident? I'll abide by their judgment on whether to bail out or try to land this thing and have my accident then. I'm pretty sure I'm going to have one."

"Well, now, Coolstone," said the CO. "This is unusual, indeed. Actually, it is up to you - the pilot's discretion and all that type of thing. It's really your deal."

"Yes, sir, I know it is my problem, and at my discretion, but if my discretion isn't the Board's discretion, I'll get tagged with a pilot error accident, and you know what that means. Unless you'd care to advise me what to do yourself?"

"No, no, er, ah, I wouldn't care to do that right now, and you have a point. I'll tell you what I'll do. I'll get the Board down here as quickly as possible."

The CO called the tower and activated the crash circuit, as there is nothing that will scare up an Accident Board quicker than the activation of the crash circuit. Therefore, 15 minutes later, an impressive-looking puffing group was standing around the squadron radio. This group was composed of the Board president, the accident investigator, the flight safety officer, the doc, the tech reps for the aircraft and the engine, the weatherman, the group maintenance officer, and, of course, the squadron operations officer and the CO.

The Board president took the microphone. "Hello, Coolstone One. This is the Accident Board president. I understand you are having a little problem. How much fuel have you remaining?"

"Yes, I might say I have a little problem. I just can't control this bird under 270 knots. I have about one plus thirty remaining. I could use some advice. How about holding a board and right now, based on the information we both have available to us, advise me on what to do. Shall I get out, or shall I try landing? I figure I have an accident cinched both ways. I might save part of the bird at least if I landed."

"Mmm, ah, yes. Let's see," said the Board president. He looked inquiringly at the group surrounding him, and surprisingly enough, none were anxious to talk. At normal Accident Board meetings, the president couldn't keep them quiet. They all knew exactly what the pilot should have done and didn't, but now they were strangely silent.

"How about you?" The president looked at the aircraft tech rep. "What would you suggest under the circumstances?"

Well, let's see," said the rep. "I really should have my dash two to look at, so I can check out the circuitry. I would hesitate to say without my books. I wouldn't be a bit surprised if this wasn't an engine problem anyhow." He looked slyly at the engine rep.

"Oh, come off of it," said the engine rep. "You airframe people stay up nights trying to hang us. Now you can't get out of this one."

"Well," said the Board president. "I'm still waiting. What do you think? Should he come in and land, or should he bail out?"

"Well," said the aircraft rep, "offhand, I'd say he is probably exaggerating his problem somewhat and undoubtedly could make a safe landing. Our equipment has double-safe circuits, with failsafe failsafe devices provided to you only by my company." He broke off as the president handed him the mike.

"You tell the pilot all this information and whether you think he should land or not."

"Oh, no, no, no," said the tech rep, handling the mike like it was smallpox. "No, I didn't say for him to land. I just said...."

"Well, to sum it up," said the president. "What you said was that you don't know what he should do."

"Well, now, I didn't say that either," said the rep, "but look, I'm just an advisor. I'm really not a member of this Board."

"OK, OK," said the president. Looking around once again, he said, "Who's got something to say? How about you, Wag?"

"Yeah, yeah," said the irrepressible weather prophet. "I'd say about 5,000 broken and 15 miles, just as I forecasted."

"Sure, you would, Wag. How about it, Doc? What do you think?"

The Doc looked thoughtfully momentarily, then said, "Is he hypoxic? And ask him if he had breakfast. You might even ask him if he's having any personal problems."

"No, Doc. He's not hypoxic, and I doubt if personal problems or the lack of breakfast have anything to do with the aileron."

"Well," said the Doc, "Obviously, I can't contribute."

At this point, the maintenance officer spoke up. "I've been thinking," he said. "Maybe if he came down to a lower altitude and tried it there, the temperature difference might improve the operation of the aileron control. Now, I don't mean that this particular problem right here is caused by temperature. Still, on the other hand, wide temperature changes can sometimes cause even the best-maintained equipment to operate strangely."

The Board president recognized this pitch from the last accident board. "Here's the mike," said the Board president. "Go to it."

"Hello, Coolstone; this is the maintenance officer. I wonder if you have considered coming down to, say, 5,000 feet or so and seeing if the temperature change will solve your problem. It's just possible it might clear it up."

"Roger," said Coolstone. "I understand you're recommending that I come down to 5,000 feet."

He was interrupted by the maintenance officer. "I didn't say I recommended that you do that. I just wondered if you had thought of it."

"Yes," said Coolstone. "I thought about that and lots of other things, too. Now just what is it that you recommend? Shall I come down and land, or shall I stay up and bail out, or is there something else you'd like me to try?"

"Well, now, let's see. Mmm ... I recommend ... no ... stand by."

The maintenance officer wordlessly handed the microphone back to the Board president. The Board president addressed the Flight Safety Officer. "What do you say? What should he do?"

"Well," said the Flight Safety type. "He obviously is experiencing a malfunction. I'll be sure and put it in my next Safety Officer's Report. But as to what he should do right now, it looks like it's a decision he'll have to make for himself. But I sure would like to get the bird back so we can find out what's wrong."

"You tell him that," said the Board president, and the Safety Officer found himself holding the microphone.

"Hello, Coolstone; this is the Flight Safety Officer. Do you read me?"

"Roger, boy," said the Cold Rock. "What do you recommend? Do you have something?"

"Well," said the Flight Safety Officer. "I recommend that you do whatever you think is right. It's up to you, the way I look at it."

"Wait a minute," said Coolstone. "I want to do the right thing as you people see it, not as I see it. Now it would appear that you and the rest of the experts there, standing with both your feet firm on the ground, could do a little first-guessing for me and give me some suggestions. What do you recommend I do? I'll follow through."

"Stand by," said the Safety Officer.

"Let's call the division," someone suggested.

"Excellent idea," said the Board president.

A priority rush, rush call was placed. After a second or so, the division Safety Officer was on the line.

"This is the Accident Board president here at McCoy. We've got a problem," and he went on to explain the situation in full to the Safety Officer at the division. Then he said, "What do you recommend Coolstone should do here? He is insisting that we give him some assistance in the form of recommended action. Would you suggest that he land, or should he bail out?"

"Stand by one," said the division Safety Officer. After a long delay, while the president could hear much loud discussion in the background, the Safety Officer came back on the line. Then he said, "Being that far away from the problem, we don't have any firm recommendations at this time. However, we think you'd better check with ADC."

"Roger," said the president. "That sounds real good."

The lines to ADC were promptly cleared by the emergency call. Soon the Director of Flight Safety at ADC was on the phone. "This is the Director of Flight Safety. Can I help you?" he said.

"You certainly can," said the Board president, and then proceeded to explain the whole situation, ending with the fact that Coolstone only had about 30 minutes of fuel remaining and asking him for recommendations.

"Well, let's see," said the Director of ADC Flight Safety. "Ah... mmm... I sure wish I had this on paper; I would definitely recommend that the pilot... Ooops, there goes the blue phone. The general is calling. I'll have to hang up, but be sure and let me know how it comes out."

The Board president had the problem back in his lap once again. At this time, Coolstone came back on the radio.

"Come off of it, you guys. I'm going to have to come in now if you recommend that I land. Otherwise, I'll fly over the field and eject. I'm at the end of my fuel. I've tried flying the airplane with gear flaps and speed brakes down, but I still can't hold it below 270. What do you recommend? I have to have it right now."

Sweat broke out on each and every board member's forehead. The moment of truth had arrived. The president stared thoughtfully. The rest of the members shuffled their feet and cleared their throats but said nothing. Then the Board president had an idea. He called the squadron CO and the Ops officer over. "Look," he said. "Let's tell him to come on in, and if he can't keep it in control all the way through to the final, have him eject. Is that OK?"

"OK," They all nodded in agreement.

"It's a real good idea," said the maintenance officer. "The temperature might help, too."

"OK, Coolstone," said the Board president with a sigh. "Here's what we recommend. Come on in. Keep your speed no higher than necessary, make a high pattern, and make a long, long final. If you have trouble anywhere in the pattern, eject before you get below 1,000 feet."

"Roger," said Coolstone. "I'll give it a go. Thanks a lot."

He brought the airplane down, entered a high downwind, put out his gear, flaps, and speed brakes, and kept his speed above 270 - right on 275, as a matter of fact. He turned a long, long base and, trying to keep his altitude, allowed the speed to bleed off. The bird, already in a left bank, increased its angle of bank uncontrollably. Coolstone frantically brought in both afterburners, and he was ready to eject. It looked like he'd had it. Then the speed came up slowly, and he regained aileron control once again.

There were ten separate sighs of relief - nine board members' and Coolstone's. At this point, all the board members were yelling instructions at the president.

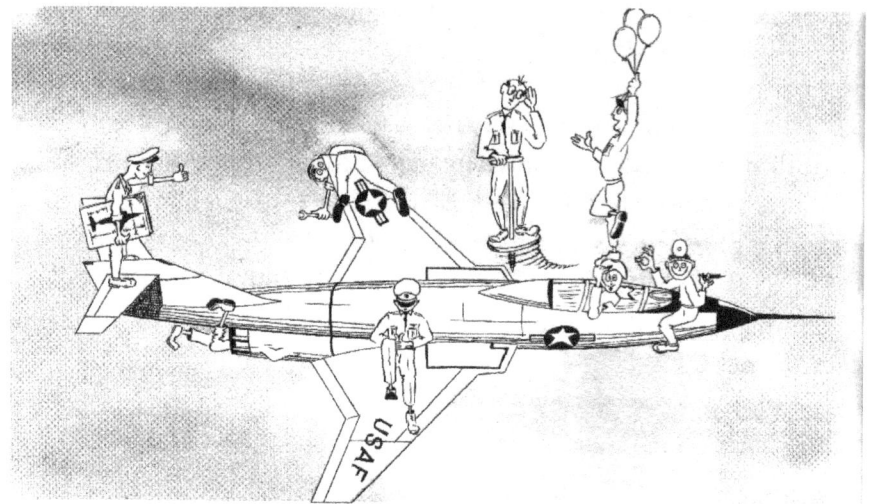

The second guessers lend a helping hand

"Tell him to eject," one said.

"Tell him to turn without banking," another said.

"Tell him to hold it straight up," said another.

"Make a longer final."

"No, a shorter one."

Coolstone heard none of this. The president of the Board remained silent.

On final now, Coolstone held a good, solid 275, with the stick full right. He even had some rudder in to hold the wings level. This caused a slight skid, but Coolstone was planning on releasing it as soon as he touched down. In fact, he had all of the steps firmly in mind. The runway was

9,200, including overrun. It had a barrier. He figured he'd pull the chute just as soon as he landed, use aerodynamic braking until 110 or so, and then lower the nose and really get on the binders. With luck, the barrier would catch him with little or no damage. If he missed the barrier, he'd be going off the end slowly enough so that there would really be no serious damage to the aircraft.

Over the threshold now, he let the bird down, and then pulled the drag chute and felt it catch, and then was horrified to feel it release again. He saw his airspeed was about 250. He held the nose up as far as he could without getting the main gear off. He felt the aerodynamic braking take over, and then he saw the end of the runway coming up at a remarkable pace. At 115 or so, he placed the nose gear on the runway and really clamped on the binders. The antiskid went into action.

Coolstone could see he wasn't going to get stopped. At the last moment, he released the brakes and steered for the center of the barrier, then just held on. He glanced at his airspeed and saw he was doing 60 knots. The barrier did not catch him. He went off into the boondocks and, just before he stopped, hit a small ditch that collapsed the nose gear. That was all. The bird stopped.

Whoops, he thought. I made it, and I did a pretty good job, even if I do say so myself. He got out of the airplane and surveyed the damage. Sure enough, all that was really dinged was the nose gear itself.

A week later, Coolstone attended the Accident Board for his accident. The president reassured him that it was merely a formality, just to satisfy the records. After Coolstone was sworn in and had sat down, the president said, "Now we have a few questions, just for the record. For instance, what speed did you hold on final?"

"About 275," said Coolstone. "I couldn't hold the airplane level at any less. I tested it several times, and you saw what happened when I turned base."

"I'll say we did," said the president. "It took a good bit of flying to recover from that. When did you deploy the chute?"

"Well, right at touchdown, of course," said Coolstone. "But it came right off because I was going too fast. For just a bit, I thought it would hold."

At this point, the maintenance officer spoke up. "Just for the record, here's what we found wrong with your control. It was a maintenance error, and there was nothing that you could have done to correct this problem in the air. And, just for the record, the chute did not malfunction. It was packed correctly and deployed correctly, but on account of the high speed, it sheared from the aircraft. That's just for the record," he repeated.

The Board president took over once again. "I think that's all we'll need, Coolstone. Thank you very much. It looks like you did a real good job."

Coolstone left the room and decided to wait outside. He felt good. Everyone said he did a good job, and they had found the failure. But he wanted to hear the words - the actual Board findings - from the horse's mouth. About an hour later, he was still waiting. He wasn't particularly concerned, for he knew of the many details and paperwork involved in an aircraft accident report. Finally, the door opened, and the Board president led the group out.

Coolstone rose to greet them, all smiles. "Well," he said jokingly. "What's the verdict?" Never doubting for a moment what he would hear.

"Sit down, Coolstone," said the Board president, placing a fatherly arm around Coolstone's shoulders. "Here's what we found - pilot error."

"Pilot error!" shouted Coolstone. "I did just what you said. You knew I was going to have some kind of an accident. I told you I would. You recommended that I land. I did just what you told me to do."

Coolstone Takes Flight

"Yes," said the Board president, "but how could we know you would deploy the chute at 270? The maximum drag chute deployment speed we find in looking at the dash one is 215. Also, by our figures - we have just spent an hour with the charts - if you had waited until you did have 215, it would only have taken about 5,100 feet of runway to get stopped."

"But ... but ... but," said Coolstone.

"Don't worry," said the Board president. "This is just a fact-finding committee. No disciplinary action will be taken."

Coolstone started to protest, but he knew better. He knew it would be no use. He walked dejectedly out of the room and said to himself, "Oh well, maybe I'll like GCI."

Long Day, Short Trip

Coolstone was in trouble. He had just departed Norton AFB in an attempt to fly to Colorado Springs. The weather at Norton was such that an IFR climb-out was necessary, using one of Norton's handy little departure cards. By the time Los Angeles Center had gotten through with him, he estimated his position was somewhere south of Tijuana at 29,000 feet. The departure had gotten away from him-he had to admit it. In fact, as near as he could figure, he had been two radios, one arm and one head short of having enough equipment to handle the climb instructions issued to him from Los Angeles Center. Now, even with 100-knot tailwinds and the distance remaining less than 600 nautical, he didn't have enough fuel remaining to make it. And, on top of this, he knew he was going to be the proud owner of a violation.

The cockpit was a shambles. Low-frequency charts were wadded up on either side of him, and big pieces had been torn from some. Coolstone couldn't rightly remember just how that had come about, but it was probably when they gave him that Julian intersection jazz. Before takeoff, he had briefed himself as well as a man could be briefed; he had studied the departure sheet until he had it memorized. But L. A. Center had pulled Julian right out of the hat and the rug right out from under him.

At 20,000, in the soup, going south, 180 degrees from his route but with everything reasonably well under control, he was cleared to the Julian intersection to climb in a holding pattern on Red 65. This was the first time in all his life that Coolstone had heard of Julian. He had looked at the diagram on the climb-out - no Julian. He had wildly scanned the low-frequency chart for the area which, up to that time, had been carelessly draped over his knees.

While he was scanning the chart, Coolstone's flight instruments presented a picture the likes of which had rarely, if ever, been seen. When he glanced up at them, he stared in amazement. Needles were going in all directions. It took him 5000 feet of altitude - down - to get them all sorted out and reading steadily again. If the Center controllers had known this, they would have fallen right out of their chairs.

His first act, after he got the T-33 flying in the right direction, right side up, was to turn off the IFF. Double jeopardy was the way he looked at it. Coolstone admitted to the Center that he just couldn't find Julian, and, after much Coolstoning and Tombstoning, they finally came right out in plain English and told him where it was. But in the meantime, the T-bird had proceeded south at seven miles a minute, and all of those minutes were directly off-course at a very uneconomical altitude.

He had to do something. He had to change destinations. "Las Vegas is always good," he thought. "I'll change to Nellis." He had just passed Hector.

"Hello-Needles Radio, Needles Radio-this is Coolstone One, over."

"Roger, Coolstone One, this is Needles-go ahead."

"Roger, Needles. This is Coolstone. I want to change my destination from Colorado Springs to Nellis. Are you ready to copy?"

"Roger, Coolstone. Ready to copy."

Coolstone proceeded to change destination according to the book. Nellis was always clear, and he could just shoot over the mountains into Colorado Springs-no sweat.

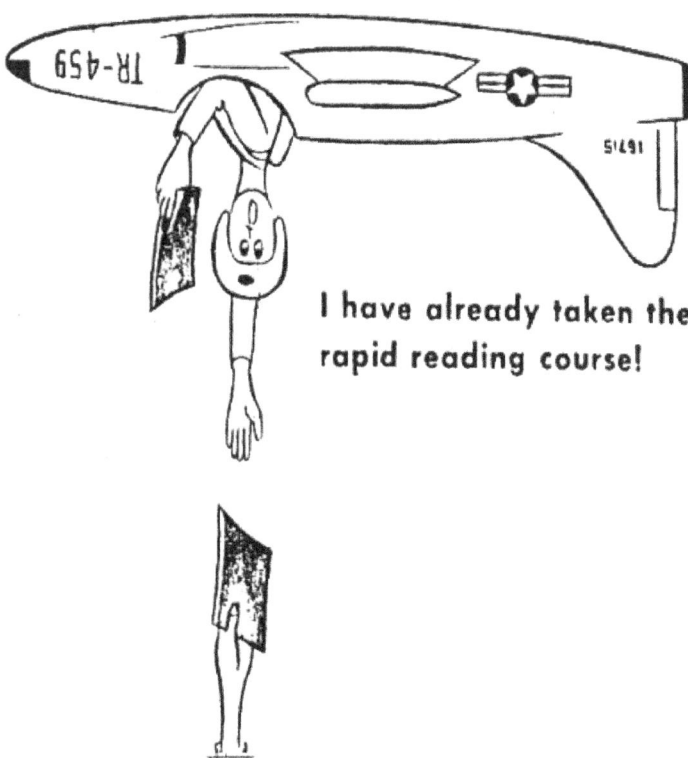

After a brief pause, Needles came back again. "Coolstone from Needles, Los Angeles Center wants to know if you are having trouble. Will you proceed on your original routing until clearance comes, or are you orbiting?"

"Needles from Coolstone. Look-the Center gave me one of their fancy climbs, and I just can't make my destination because of the fuel it took. I'll proceed along my route to Peach Springs. At that point, I'll orbit for a clearance. Tell them to snap it up because I'm only going to hang around Peach Springs for ten minutes or so. Then I'm going to Las Vegas. Over."

"Roger, Coolstone, understand."

Less than five minutes later, a clearance came through for Coolstone to proceed direct from his position to Las Vegas, maintaining a flight level of 290. Coolstone eyeballed the course, turned to the heading, and all was well.

Somewhat to Coolstone's surprise, he was still on top of the overcast when he arrived at Las Vegas. The report he had received previously was 16,000 broken. But when he queried Approach Control, they told him that the weather was actually just lower broken with a higher overcast. He made the penetration and broke out at 5000, canceled his IFR, and landed at Nellis.

Coolstone filed his clearance and was advised by the airdrome officer that there might be a slight delay in obtaining his ATC clearance because of the weather in the Las Vegas area. The AO had no idea what kind of a climb Coolstone might receive because they rarely had weather at Nellis.

Coolstone went out to his T-33, pulled the preflight, got into the cockpit, and strapped himself in. Then he called the tower. "Hello, Nellis Tower. This is Coolstone One. Standing by for ATC clearance, Over."

Coolstone Takes Flight

"Roger Coolstone. This is Nellis. You might just as well go back into Base Ops. Salt Lake Center advises there will be an indefinite delay. We will call you in Base Ops when the clearance comes through. Over."

"Roger," said Coolstone and unstrapped himself from the bird. He walked wearily back to Operations and found the AO again. "Say," he asked, "How many are there ahead of me, anyhow? The tower told me there would be an indefinite delay."

"Well," said the AO, "Looks like you will be number four. There are two T-birds and a flight of Navy Cougars ahead of you. There is no use for you to worry about a clearance until the Navy gets theirs. We have a problem here when there is weather. The airlines' Tunnel of Love runs right over the base, and unless you can climb, VFR, Salt Lake Center hesitates to let jets take off because there is so much traffic overflying Las Vegas. And, of course, they've been pretty nervous, you know, since that mid-air occurred."

Coolstone thanked him and strolled outside. He quickly scanned the skies for a hole. To his chagrin, not only was there no hole, but a terrible, big black line of clouds was slowly moving in on Nellis from the southwest. There was lots of rain coming from these clouds, too. Mothers all over Las Vegas were probably calling their children out to show them the first rain of their lives, thought Coolstone.

Four hours later, Coolstone was maintaining his number four position nicely and had become friendly with the other pilots who were waiting. The Navy boys were on a round-robin, and Nellis never has weather. The pilots of one T-bird were from the east coast, CRT flying. Nellis never has weather. The pilots of the other T-33 were en route to Sacramento. One of them was on emergency leave, and Nellis never has weather. The rain was really coming down now, and the ceiling at Nellis, which never has weather, was 800 feet with two miles of visibility.

An hour later, the T-33 pilots in the number one slot were alerted. They literally scrambled out to their bird. They got a clearance. Everyone in Base Ops cheered. They heard the engine start, but the T-bird didn't leave the line. The engine was stopped. Two dejected, wet pilots trudged slowly back to Operations, oblivious to Nevada's annual rain. Their mike button had broken, stuck in the *transmit* position. They canceled, and Coolstone was number three.

Minutes later, the pilots of the next T-33 were alerted. The clearance was transmitted to them, and the engine started. Once again, a little cheer went up in Base Ops. Then the engine was stopped because the tower told them to disregard. There would be an indefinite delay. The pilot, who was on emergency leave, came into Operations on the double. He called the airline ticket agent at the civilian field serving Las Vegas. "Delays?" the agent asked. "We're not having any delays. All flights are departing on schedule." The pilot paled visibly but made reservations on a flight to Sacramento.

Coolstone was now number two.

Two hours later, he was still number two. It was getting dark. The Navy pilots decided they had better go out and check their formation lights. When they came back, their faces reflected great sorrow. Two of the aircraft had been found to have defective formation lights. The Navy canceled. The pilots had no clothes other than their flying gear. They were forced to reconcile themselves to a night in exciting, romantic Las Vegas, as seen from rooms in the BOQ.

Now the Cold Rock was number one. He had a couple of aces up his sleeve and was just looking for an opportunity to use them; he'd played some games with ATC before. "Can you get me a line to Salt Lake Center?" he asked the Ops clerk.

Coolstone Takes Flight

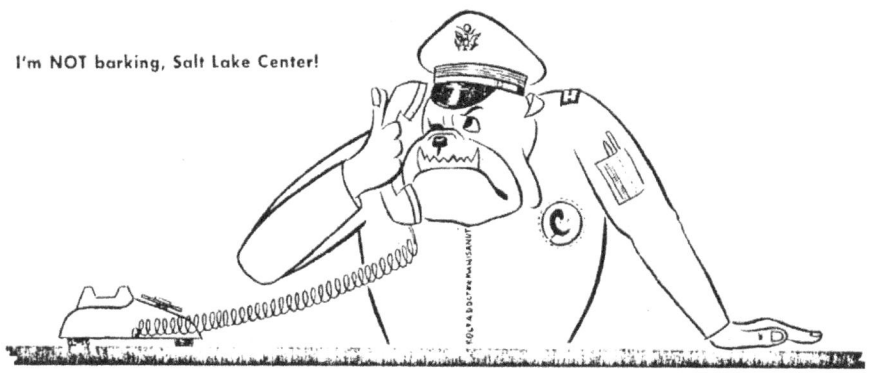

"Sure thing, Sir; just step back to the switchboard, and I'll ring them for you." The sergeant rang the Center and handed the phone to Coolstone.

After a short pause, "Salt Lake Center on." It was a controller.

"This is Coolstone, Salt Lake. I've been waiting nine hours for a clearance here at Nellis. What seems to be the trouble?"

"Yes, Coolstone, we know you've been waiting, but the inbound traffic here has been very heavy, and we have to have a clear route through all altitudes before we can send you up through the positive control air-way."

"Yeah, yeah, I know all about that. But suppose you let me take off. I'll climb off the airways and then reenter at any altitude you want, wherever you want. Okay?"

"You'd have to have 8000 feet for minimum terrain clearance, Coolstone, and I can't get you eight."

The Coolstone's temperature was rising steadily. "Look, you give me clearance, and I'll worry about the mountains. The airliners seem to be getting through 8000 without any trouble."

There was silence on the line for a moment; then, "Can you get off in 12 minutes, Coolstone? I think we can get you out to the south and then, after you climb, bring you back in at Mormon Mesa."

"You bet your boots, Center. I'm practically airborne."

"Okay, Coolstone. Go on out to the plane, and we'll give the clearance to the tower."

Coolstone rushed wildly out to his bird, strapped himself in, and when the power came on, he called the tower. "Hello Nellis-Nellis, I say." There was a lift in Coolstone's voice that had been sadly lacking all day. "Would you please give me my long-lost clearance? I'm ready, Boy."

The tower came in. "Go back to Ops, Coolstone. The Center called the whole thing off. There is an…."

"Yeah, I know. Indefinite delay."

Back in Operations, Coolstone was foaming at the mouth. "Give me that phone," he snarled at the Ops clerk, who was quick to react, for rarely had he seen such magnificent fury.

"Hello, Center? I want to tell you something. It has been nine and one-half hours since I filed my clearance. During that time, not one soul has received a clearance at this base. I've lived on dispenser coffee and candy bars. When can I expect to get out of here? I want it straight this time."

"Tombstone, old boy," the Center replied, "you can expect to depart from Nellis whenever you can make a VFR climb. Suggest you try in the morning. Good night."

Coolstone had nothing to say. He hung up the phone and walked slowly over to the Operations counter. The clerk held up his clearance and looked questioning. Coolstone nodded. The clerk ripped the clearance into shreds.

Coolstone began to fill out a RON form. When he got to *Reason*, he wrote *Weathered in at Las Vegas*. He stared at that momentarily. "The Old Man will never believe it," he thought, so he scratched over it and wrote *Aircraft out of commission*.

As he turned to leave, his eyes rested on a large map of the United States. He shook his head. It had been 11 hours since he left Norton, with 100 knots tailwind. In those 11 hours, he had gone 200 miles.

"I could have driven twice that far in my car," he thought, and the Cold Rock joined the others at the BOQ.

Coolstone Does a Pitchelmann

Coolstone was one of the favored. He was on alert. It had been so long since he had been through an actual scramble that he really wasn't worried about pulling it. All he knew for sure was that he was going to sit in the alert hangar for 24 hours. He was looking forward to catching up on his reading, his writing, and his ping pong. Right now, he was just sitting with his fearless WSO, Two, and the other crew, who were on alert with him.

As usual, they were in a highly technical discussion about the F-101's capability. The other alert pilot was telling the Rock, "When I first started flying the 101, I was very, very careful. My breaks were cross-countries in themselves. Needed 1500 pounds from initial to final. Now that I have considerably more experience in the machine, 150 hours, I have found that it's a real good aircraft, a real performer."

Now the Rock didn't quite have 100 hours in the 101, and he still was very, very careful. But he had talked to many of the old heads, and they, too, were favorable in their comments about the 101.

"Probably nothing will beat it to 20 grand," one of them had said. And Coolstone believed it. It was difficult not to if you had ever made a burner climb on a cold day.

"Yes, I know what you mean," he told the other alert pilot. "I used to be very, very careful with it also. But now that I have had some experience, I have been able to do most anything in the 101 that anyone else can do in any other aircraft."

"Ever try an Immelmann?" the other pilot asked in a whisper. The WSOs overheard, however, and both of them became completely attentive to the conversation.

"An Immelmann?" said the Rock incredulously. "No, and I don't think that I will either."

"They're a cinch," said his friend. "Just get it up to 450, 20 thou and pull it up and over. You don't even need burners. You finish up wings level, 280 knots, maybe even 300."

"I don't think we're supposed to do Immelmanns," said Coolstone. "I thought they were prohibited."

"Yeah," said his friend, "but what do the old folks know anyway? I'll bet they've never even tried one."

"Have you tried one?" said Coolstone with a great deal of awe showing through. "Have you really tried an Immelmann in this bird?"

Coolstone Takes Flight

"One," snorted his friend. "I've done dozens. Absolutely no problem. Four-fifty, 20 thou, no burner, pull it up at about four Gs, let it kinda come on over till the nose is falling through, and just roll it upright. End up at 280 minimum."

His friend's WSO looked just a little green as he said, "I've never been with anyone who even did a loop in a 101, let alone an Immelmann."

"Yeah," said Coolstone Two, "neither have I, and I want no part of either one."

But Coolstone One's eyes were shining in admiration. He said to his friend, "You've made loops, too, I gather?"

"Naturally," said his friend. "Loops are easier than Immelmans. Now that I've done a few of them, I go in at 20 and come out at 20. A perfect circle."

"Now that I've done a few of them, I go in at 20 and come out at 20. A perfect circle."

"With burners?" asked the Rock.

"No burners," said Friendo. "Who needs them with 450 at the start?"

"Wow!" said Coolstone. "What a machine!" To himself, he thought, "I didn't know that Friendo was that good."

The two WSOs, who had been extremely quiet during the last portions of the conversation, also didn't think that Friendo, or Coolstone for that matter, was that good, and both mentally noted that whenever the schedule paired them with either of these pilots again, they were going to try a trade at all costs. Rumor had it that one WSO paid $50 to get out of a flight with a specific pilot. That's what it cost him to make a trade.

The flying talk dwindled, and routine alert duties took over. The 24 hours passed very slowly. There were no scrambles on this tour, either.

About three days later, Coolstone was scheduled for a high-altitude intercept sortie, and he was paired with Two, the same WSO who had pulled alert with him. It seemed they would probably be a crew as long as they were assigned to the squadron.

Coolstone One had absolutely no objections to this. He had flown with Two enough to know that he was pretty good on the scope and he was a good companion on a cross-country. As they sat drinking coffee, waiting for the briefing to begin, Two was attempting to talk One into a cross-country for the following weekend.

"Look," he said, "you get the airplane. We'll leave Friday night, come back Sunday night, get a few hours in, and if we stop at the right places, I'll practically guarantee you..."

"Look," said One, "I'm not really interested this weekend. I've got a few things lined up for myself. And besides, I'm a little short. We don't get paid until next week."

"Look," said Two, "if you put in for the airplane and we get it, I'll even lend you some money, and you'll never regret it if we go to the right places. And besides that, you'll be a big hit with ops. They try to scatter these 101s all over the country on the weekends to get flying time, and our maintenance doesn't have to work on them."

"Well," said One, "I might, but if I borrow the money from you, then I'm going to have to pay it back."

"All right, all right," said his WSO. "I'll pay for the trip. It's on me."

"Boy, you really are eager to go, aren't you?" said One. "I'll have to think it over. I just can't see it right now."

"You won't regret it," said Two. "I promise you that."

The two of them went into the briefing room and met with the other crew that they were paired with. The mission was for a front snap, then high co-altitudes, followed by a formation recovery. The alternate mission was instruments. One and Two preflighted, got strapped in, and cranked up. When One checked in, he found that the other 101 was going to abort. One contacted the SOF and was told to go ahead and fly the alternate mission. One and Two were all for that since the worst part of the mission was already over (they thought) - the briefing, the preflight, and the strapping in. They got airborne in a minimum of time. One decided to climb to altitude and burn down some fuel prior to shooting a few GCAS. He checked in with the controller and was cleared to do most anything that he wanted to do at most any altitude he cared to do it. He leveled at 30 and was immediately bored.

"Not much of a set," said Two. "Even the altitude line is weak. Good thing we didn't have a target."

"It must really be bad," said One. "Usually, when we don't have a target, YOU have the best set you have ever seen and can't believe your bad luck in not being able to run a few."

They groaned along for three or four minutes, then One told Two, "Guess I'll do a few rolls just to keep my hand in."

He turned the RLS off in preparation because he didn't want anything to interfere with his tricky stick action.

"Roger," said Two, and he immediately began storing loose objects, tightening straps, and checking his seat pins. He had rolled with One before. Sometimes the rolls became pretty spectacular.

One pulled it up sharply and rolled once (to the left, of course). He hesitated, wings level, and rolled it again. He climbed back up to 30 and tried to figure out how he had lost 5,000 feet and 50 knots.

"Pull harder and roll faster," he told himself. "That must be what's wrong."

Around they went again, hesitated, did another. Then he climbed back up to 30. He decided that chandelles were his thing anyway. He dove the airplane, honked back, got the horn, released a little, and ended up at about 37.

"Not bad," he said to himself. "Not bad at all."

Over the interphone, he heard Two. "You're pretty hot today," said Two. "A Tiger all the way."

Two immediately regretted his remarks, for One said, "By golly, I believe I'll try one of those Immelmanns. We'll do it just like Friendo told me. Twenty thou, 450, three and a half to four Gs, let it come over real good and roll it up. No burner."

"You know," said Two, "some of us have been talking over that Immelmann business. There are lots of people that don't think that it's possible without burners and a lot more airspeed and a lot lower altitude at the beginning.... And besides, you shouldn't do it anyhow."

"Oh, come on," said The Rock. "Friendo has done dozens of them. He says that it's easy. He ends up at 280 on top, no problem at all."

"Yeah," but said Two, "you've never done one, and he may be ... just may be exaggerating a bit."

"Look," said One, "I've got it in the old arm. If Friendo can do one, I can do one. If we get in trouble, I'll just zero G it around and fly out of it. The book doesn't say you can't do an Immelmann at all. It doesn't say anything about it. If you were going to have trouble, it would say so. The book doesn't cover a loop, either. If the Immelmann works out okay, I'll try a loop too."

"Oh boy," said Two. "Oh boy, oh boy, oh boy."

"Here we go," said One as he advanced the throttles to military and dove for 20 thou. As he leveled at 20, he saw that he had about 480 knots, even more than he needed, which he pointed out to Two. One loaded the airplane up to almost four Gs. Then he caught what looked like a pretty good airspeed bleed. "Better use the burners," he said to himself and plugged them in. As he was approaching near vertical and at about 35,000, he saw that the airspeed, to his horror, was at 200 knots, going down rapidly, with no indication that it was going to slow down - let alone stop. He experienced a sinking sensation, a quick lessening of the G level,

"We've pitched up," he shouted to Two.

"Forward stick," said Two as One firewalled it. The resulting negative Gs were pretty spectacular. Both One and Two came out of their seats a lot, but Two was better off because of his preroll preparation. The nose was definitely headed for the horizon, but as it passed through about 20 degrees, nose up, the aircraft did what had to be a quick snap roll (flip, for our Canadian friends) to the right. The snap roll was so fast that both One and Two's gyros tumbled. One lost the stick for a moment, but, fortunately, he got it right back again.

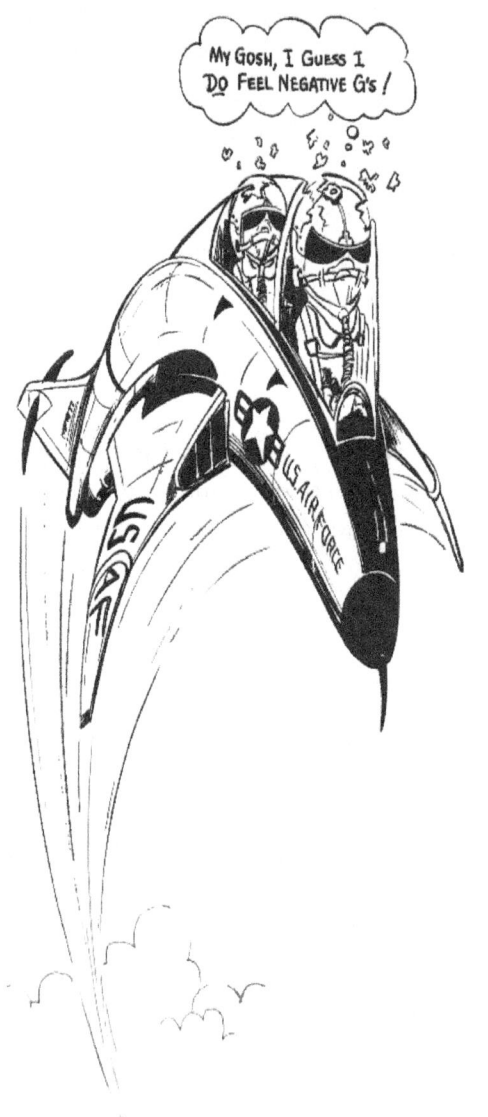

"Full forward," said Two.

One already had it there. The aircraft quit rolling, and the nose had dropped to about 45 degrees below the horizon. The airspeed was building up and was at about 150, but One felt no negative Gs. He pushed the stick forward harder, if that was possible. At 170 knots, the bird snap rolled again.

"What was that?" said Two. "Why did it do that? Didn't you neutralize when you felt the negative Gs?"

What negative Gs?" said One. "I didn't feel a thing."

"I did," said Two, "and I'm beginning to feel them again. Get the stick back."

Sure enough, the bird was again nose down with the airspeed building and over 150. The Rock was still holding the stick full forward.

"My gosh," he thought, "I guess I do feel negative Gs," and eased the stick back.

"Ten thou," said Two, getting himself ready to go.

"Don't go. Don't go," said One. "I've got it now. I've got it now." One let the airspeed build up to over 300 before he even started a pull-up. He leveled at about four, took several deep breaths, turned the RLS back on, and called for clearance to enter the GCA pattern.

"Did you get the chute out?" asked Two. "I didn't say anything about it."

With a quick glance at the handle, One saw it was still in. "Nope," he said, "I guess I just didn't get around to it."

"It's not surprising," said Two very dryly. "You've got to be fast to pitch up twice and recover twice in 20,000 feet. Boy, what was it with you on that first recovery? Didn't you feel those negative Gs? I was hanging by the straps, something terrible."

"I was numb," said One. "I didn't feel anything." Then he started to feel something - but it was more of a burn. "Dozens of them, Friendo said he had done. Nothing to it, huh? Four-fifty, 20 thou, no burners. I even used burners. No way."

"Look ole buddy-buddy," the Rock said to Two. "Let's kinda keep this quiet. As a matter of fact, let's not tell anybody about it at all."

"Well-l-l-l-l ..." said Two uncertainly, "Well-l-l-l-l-l, I don't know. Friendo might have told someone else the same thing he told us, and some other stup... er, pilot, may believe him and try it himself."

"I'll take care of Friendo," said One. "I'll politely mention to him that I'll personally kill him if he doesn't backtrack and admit to everyone that he has never done a loop, an Immelmann, a steep turn, a roll, or a climb of over 10 degrees, and he's probably the biggest pussy cat who ever flew a 101."

"Well, okay," said Two, "but I'm still not certain we shouldn't tell. I think that maybe I'll ...»

"Okay, okay," said One. "Where do you want to go this weekend, and how much is it going to cost me?"

Another Real Good Deal

Coolstone had been chosen! It was another one of those real good deals. A T-bird target mission. It was for the middle of the night, medium to low altitude, out over the Atlantic, in what looked like very marginal weather. Coolstone had been chosen often for these real good deals - deals which always seemed to gravitate toward Blue Three and below. Filling his back seat had been a problem for a while. So many pilots suddenly went on sick call, and the Flight Surgeon came down to the squadron to see what was happening. He ran into Coolstone right off in the squadron lunch room.

"What's going on down here?" asked the Doc. "I've had more people on sick call these last two days than all of last month. They're all pilots, and they're all from the squadron."

"Must be a virus," answered the Rock. "Everyone I've asked to fly with me in the T-bird has developed it shortly afterward."

"Hey," said the Doc, "I could use some of that T-bird time if you need a back seat filled; I'm your man."

"Great," said the Rock, "that solves a problem for us. It's a target mission; we stage out of Westover, recover at Andrews, then come back here."

"I've been meaning to go on one of those," said the Doc, obviously not understanding the problem. "When do we leave?"

"Wheels up at 1000 hours tomorrow, Doc. Briefing at eight-thirty. Can you make it OK?"

"Sure," said the Doc, "if this darn virus outbreak slows down some."

Now the Doc was not only the Flight Surgeon but also an experienced private pilot. He regularly flew with the squadron in the B model and the T-33. He generally kept himself well abreast of the flying operation. Coolstone, therefore, was not a bit reluctant to have him on board, and besides, he wouldn't have to split the front seat time.

The following day at about eight, the Doc showed up. He found the Rock, who was flight planning the mission. "I got away earlier than I thought I would," said the Doc. "You know that virus I was talking about yesterday that only affected the aircrews? Well, it must have been a 24-hour bug of some type. Nobody was on sick call this morning. How about that?"

"Strange," said the Rock, "I noticed a lot more people around this morning, myself."

They arrived at Westover a little before noon, as did the rest of the six target airplanes from other participating ADC units. The aircrews gathered around the flight planning table in Ops and planned their individual target routes. They checked the forecast weather, which was still a bit marginal, but mission take-off time was still almost eleven hours away.

Coolstone Takes Flight

As they finished their preliminary planning, Coolstone found the Doc and said, "Let's have lunch." The Doc readily agreed to this. However, it wasn't quite that simple because the dining facilities were closed for cleanup. The Doc was then introduced to the standard target pilot's lunch-potato chips, beer nuts, and cokes - after which the two of them departed for the Q for their mandatory eight hours of restless sleep.

At 2200 hours, the Rock awoke. "Come on, Doc, get your rompers on, and let's get something to eat."

The Doc grumbled unintelligibly about beer nuts ruining his digestive system, but he finally got moving. They went down to the Q office to call for transportation. While waiting, Coolstone asked the clerk on duty where the best place would be to get a meal. After shuffling through his bulletins and staring off into space a bit, the clerk allowed that the last dining room closed for cleaning at 2100 hours.

"No sweat," said the Rock, "We'll get a candy bar down at Ops."

The Doc paled visibly.

At Base Operations, suited up now, Coolstone called target control for the final go, no go on the target mission. The target control officer told him that there was a weak cold front stretched from Canada down the eastern seaboard causing low ceilings in the northeast, but the weather at the target area and the recovery bases was good. The word was Go.

Coolstone then strolled over to the base forecaster for just a bit of preplanning on the trip back to Loring from Andrews.

"What do you think Loring will have about four or five this morning?" he asked.

"Well," the forecaster said, "it's a weak front, it's not moving, and there are no buildups of any magnitude. Loring is VFR now and probably will stay that way until around sunrise. Their forecast calls for a possible 400 scattered, 700 overcast, with 3 miles, between 0500 to 0900."

"Sounds like about normal," said the Rock. "No sweat." He walked over to the candy machine and got a Snickers and a Coke.

The Doc tried to ignore the whole operation, burped gently, and mumbled, "Beer nuts."

They launched for the mission at 0030 as scheduled, and it was completely routine and as planned. While they were recovering into Andrews, Coolstone remarked to the surgeon, who had held the stick a lot, "You know, Doc, you do good work. You should have been a fighter pilot instead of a doc. You have a good feel for an airplane."

"That's the only good feeling I've got," said Doc. "My stomach is in terrible shape. I need to eat a regular meal."

"No sweat," said the Rock, "Andrews has a great snack bar. They'll have anything you want."

At 0250, the by now slightly bedraggled crew entered Andrews Operations.

"We'll be going out as soon as we eat," Coolstone told the Ops clerk.

"Sorry, sir," said the clerk, "the snack bar is closed between 0230 and 0430 daily for cleanup. We have some candy and coke machines if you're interested."

The Doc groaned. The Cold Rock said, "Look, Doc, I still feel real good. We're well within crew rest limits, and if the weather at Loring is still

OK, let's make a quick turn and go home. We can always get something to eat at the squadron dining room when we get back."

Reluctantly the Doc agreed, and they both headed for the candy machine.

The route of the flight home was as familiar to Coolstone as the road to the alert barn. It was simply: radar vectors to J-55, J-55 to the handoff point for Loring approach control, then down the chute to the runway. With the preliminary planning out of the way, the crew moved over to the weather desk, and Coolstone pushed the night buzzer. When the forecaster appeared, obviously awakened from a sound sleep, the Rock said, "Get me your best VFR to Loring," making a little joke that the forecaster totally ignored.

"Let's see," said the WAG, "at 29,000, you will have a 30-knot crosswind, no buildups en route, and the Loring weather will be about 5,000 broken with 11-mile visibility. VFR conditions will prevail in the entire Loring area. No alternate required." And he set about filling in all the blocks.

Back out to the aircraft, the intrepid crew went. The Doc strapped in while Coolstone preflighted. Then the Rock climbed in, started it, and called for his clearance while taxiing out. It was given to him just as he had filed: Loring, flight plan route.

With the wheels in the well at 0400, the Rock and Doc settled down for the routine conclusion for another one of "those real good deals." The routine was broken slightly when Departure Control handed them off to the Center.

"Coolstone One from the Center. We have a change in your flight plan. Are you ready to copy?" "Roger, Center, go," said the Rock, expecting nothing more than an altitude change. "Roger, Coolstone One, you are cleared to Loring direct J-121, J-581, direct, direct. Read back, please." The Rock's voice went up slightly.

"Aah, would you, aah, give that again? You say direct to J-121 Instead of J-55?"

"Roger, Coolstone, direct J-121, J-581, direct, direct. Have you got that?"

Coolstone scribbled on his kneepad, which he really couldn't see, repeated the clearance, and dived for the High-Altitude Chart. He was still climbing in weather, flying with his knees. He also noted that the DME had not locked in. He needed to figure out where he was going, how he was going to get there, and how far he was from it.

"Hold the airplane a minute, will you, Doc? I've got to sort out this new route."

"Rog," said the Flight Surgeon, "but my instruments are nothing fancy."

"Neither is mine," said Coolstone, "when I'm flying with my knees. Just keep the wings level."

Coolstone Takes Flight

The noise level in the interphone increased noticeably with the associated increased breathing rate of both parties. While Coolstone picked out the new route from the jungle of routes in the east coast area, Doc was valiantly herding the bird in a climb through the weather. A rather rhythmic oscillation in pitch, bank, and yaw was noticeable, and it corresponded exactly with Doc's crosscheck as he corrected each instrument as he went. But the Doc was content; the airplane was flying within acceptable limits as far as he could see. He burped, not so gently, this time. That last Coke had almost done him in.

The Rock finished his new flight planning and, much relieved, told the Doc, "That new route is OK. We'll still have 180 gallons at the initial approach fix, and our only requirement is 100 gallons on the initial for a VFR approach. We're still fat, fat, fat. I've got it," said Coolstone. "Thanks a lot."

"You are entirely welcome," said the Doc, with sweat now dripping slightly into his eyes.

The DME was definitely out, Coolstone saw, but who needed it? Once again, they leveled at 29,000 and settled down to a routine flight.

"Boy," said the Doc, "can I ever use something in my stomach besides cokes and candy bars!"

"I'm with you, Doc. I think I'll have bacon, eggs, and a lot of milk when we get to the squadron," said Coolstone. "These target missions are hard on the stomach."

"Rog," said the Doc, "and you know, I think I'm beginning to understand that 24-hour virus, too."

They were cleared en route to descend to 18,000, and as they neared Loring, the Center turned them over to Approach Control for recovery.

"Hello, Loring Approach Control; this is Coolstone One. Forty miles south descending to 18,000."

"Roger, Coolstone One, from Loring Approach Control. Continue your descent to 2,500 feet, and be advised that a B-52 has just made a missed approach to Runway Zero One. He reported visibility is less than one-quarter of a mile on the approach."

"What's that again?" said Coolstone. "What happened to that 5,000-foot broken?"

"Be advised," said Approach Control, "the weather has deteriorated rapidly, and the field is now 300 obscured, one and one-quarter mile visibility, with one-quarter mile on the active approach."

"Kee-rist," said the Rock to the Doc, "let's see what we can use for an alternate."

As he looked through his charts, he saw that Chatham would be OK. They'd get there with about forty gallons or so, but if the weather was anything approaching VFR, that would be enough.

"Loring Approach Control, this is Coolstone One. Would you get me the Chatham weather, please, and I'll continue this approach."

Loring Radar continued to maneuver Coolstone for the precision final, and while doing so, he called the Rock and told him the Chatham weather was 600 foot overcast. The Rock ran this information through his now weakened computer and said to the Doc, "Forty gallons and six hundred feet! Never happen!"

"Approach Control from Coolstone One. How is Presque Isle? And I'll continue this approach." Presque Isle was a small private field some twenty miles away, was 7,400 feet of uncontrolled runway, and had a VORTAC.

The Rock leveled at 2,500 feet, was seven out, and was ready for a precision final.

"Keep your eyes open, Doc. If you see the runway, holler. It's going to be close. The minimums are a hundred and a quarter, and the weather is a hundred and a quarter, but if we don't make it, we'll try Presque Isle, providing the weather's OK."

"Sounds just great," said the Doc weakly.

"Coolstone One from Radar. Turn zero nine zero, climb to 3,000 feet -- precision radar is unable to pick you up."

The Rock drug his feet something terrible. "Look, Radar," he said hastily, "how about letting me continue on the ILS and see if the precision radar can pick us up as we get in closer?"

"What a revolting development!" said the Doc.

"Negative, negative," said Radar. "The field is below ILS minimums."

"OK," said the Rock, "I'm turning zero nine zero, but make it a short pattern, Radar, and I'm at minimum fuel."

He really wasn't there yet, but that was the only thing he could think of at the time. He damn well would be at minimum fuel when he got to the field, however. That was for sure. As they came around to final again, the controller announced that they had him on the precision radar this time. The Rock took a deep breath and settled down to run as good a GCA as he ever had in his life.

At minimums, they were calling him on centerline and glide slope, and he had the ILS localizer centered. He looked out - absolutely nothing ahead.

"I see something," said the Doc. "Right below us."

Sure enough, Coolstone could see those great big flashing strobe lights, "Got it made now," he mumbled to the Doc with little conviction for where the end of the runway should have been. There was nothing.

He eased down a bit. He could see no overrun, no threshold lights, no runway lights, no nothing.

"It's down to your socks," he exclaimed to the Doc, then added just a bit of power. He was fresh out of strobe lights, still nothing. For a second, he got a glimpse of the runway centerline. He lifted the brakes, called Radar, and said, "We'll try a circling approach. Maybe that mile and a quarter is on the other end."

He banked right, checked the airspeed, and looked back out to where the runway should have been. It had disappeared.

"Approach Control, we're making a missed approach. We have emergency fuel, and we're headed for Presque Isle. Have you got that weather yet?"

He dug out the Low Altitude Approach Chart he had been carrying around in his pocket for two years. It was creased and greased-stained, but he had checked it for currency a couple of weeks before, and it had still been good then.

"Tombstone ... er ... Coolstone One," said Approach Control, "Center advises us that runway one nine is under construction. You will be required to circle to runway two eight. Two eight has no approach lights, no overrun, is 5,900 feet long, and has no barriers."

"Roger, Approach Control, Tombstone One . . . er . . . Coolstone One, understand. It will have to do."

The Rock was on the VOR radial, headed in, and radar was supplying range almost every mile. At about ten out, Coolstone started letting down. Fifty gallons on the liquidometer.

"Tombstone One from Approach Control. The Presque Isle weather is reported as eight hundred overcast with two miles."

"That's Coolstone One, not Tombstone, and I'll make the VOR into runway one nine. My DME is out, so keep me advised of the range."

"If we ever break out," said the Doc, "I think I can find the field. I fly light planes out of here all the time."

The Rock let down lower and lower. Minimums came and went. Finally, they broke out of a ragged ceiling at about 400 feet above the ground.

"See that lake ten degrees to port," said the Doc excitedly, "that lake is right at the end of runway one nine."

Quickly the Rock turned towards the lake. Sure enough, as he neared the lake, the runway appeared. But it was one nine - two eight was not in sight. When he was about halfway down one nine, he could finally see two eight. He could also see thirty-five gallons on the liquidometer. He got on a short downwind, very close in. Then, just as the field was about to go out of sight, he cranked around on a very, very short final, and touched down right on the end of the runway. He could see the runway was wet, but braking action was reasonable. At the last taxiway, he was slowed down enough to get off the runway, but the turn was very erratic. The Doc noted that the rudder action in his cockpit was extremely quick and oscillatory in nature.

"Fighter pilot's weather syndrome," he briefly opined.

The aircraft was parked and shut off with slightly over ten gallons remaining.

"That was pretty close, wasn't it?" said the Doc. "That's not much fuel, even in a Mooney."

"Close, close, close," said the Rock, and just sat a spell.

The base taxi from Loring finally arrived (with more fuel than the T-bird had), and on the way back to the squadron, the target crew began to relax from rigid to tense.

"Boy," said the Doc, "these target missions are rough. I'm ready for that breakfast and about twenty-four hours of sleep."

"Rog," said the Rock, "bacon and eggs and lots of milk still sounds about right."

They pulled into the fighter area, got out of the car, and headed for the squadron kitchen. Yep, you guessed it. It was closed for cleanup.

Commercial Air

Coolstone had ferried a 101 to the East Coast from St. Louis. It had been a terrible ordeal. The weather was lousy all the way, and minor maintenance was necessary at every stop. Delays, delays, delays. He had been gone from his home base, which was Oxnard, for over ten days already. He had been out of money at least three times, and it had been necessary to get pumped up at the various officer's clubs he visited across the United States by floating a little paper.

He was now at the Kansas City Municipal Airport on the road home, waiting for his flight time. He had precisely $1.38 in his pocket.

He checked his ticket over once again. He was routed from Kansas City to Denver, from Denver to Los Angeles. He would hitchhike from Los Angeles to Oxnard if necessary.

Typically ferry flights weren't too bad a deal. You got to meet some very interesting people, very, very interesting. One in St. Louis was so interesting, Coolstone wasn't sure he could ever go back there. Oh, well, there were lots of other cities with other interesting people, a whole U.S. full of them.

An announcement came over the P.A. system. "Imperial Jet Flight 709, Diamond-crusted Mink Carpet Service, with Napoleon brandy, filet mignon, and hot and cold running stewardesses, will be delayed an hour due to weather in Chicago. All passengers for this flight may use the facilities of the Imperial Excellency Lounge upon presentation of their tickets to the attendant at the door."

This was Coolstone's flight, and it didn't surprise him a bit that it was delayed. It was the story of his life for the last ten days.

Well, he thought, I might as well soak up a little of that Imperial Excellency business, and besides, it gives you an opportunity to meet some new interesting people. I'll have to watch it, though, for I could hardly get across the country without landing at either Kansas City or St. Louis.

As he got up, he glanced into a large mirror on the wall opposite him. He saw that his uniform was very crusty, in fact, quite a mess. He decided to forego the Imperial Excellency Lounge and to be as inconspicuous as possible in the waiting room. At least that stale beer odor was fading. He had been rather liberally doused with Pabst in a perfectly innocent accident three days earlier at a highly technical meeting attended by the cream of Chicago's South Side. What happened was that a stripper kicked over his glass of beer while doing a very intricate maneuver on the bar.

About two hours later, the P.A. system blared again. "Imperial Jet Flight 709, Diamond-crusted Mink Carpet Service, with Napoleon brandy, filet mignon, and hot and cold running stewardesses, will be delayed indefinitely due to the engineers' strike. Passengers should make arrangements for overnight accommodations. Limousine service is available to

Coolstone Takes Flight

downtown Kansas City at the front door of the terminal. Passengers, please leave your phone numbers at the passenger service desk. Don't call us; we'll call you."

It was about 2200 hours, snowing nicely outside, 10 degrees or so above zero.

Coolstone wearily picked up his shaving kit and started for the terminal door. Engineers' strike! What else could happen to him, he thought. Then he remembered $1.38. Where was he going to stay with $1.38? It would probably cost at least a dollar to go to town. He'd have to have more money, no questions about it.

He went into the washroom and emptied his pockets, and sure enough, all he had was a buck thirty-eight. He straightened his tie, hitched up his pants, and tried a confident, carefree smile out on the mirror. It didn't quite come off.

He left the washroom and headed for the airline ticket counter.

"How do you do; how do you do?" said the affable Coolstone to a clerk who was plainly busy with some paperwork.

The clerk glanced up annoyedly and grunted, "I'll be with you in a minute."

Coolstone softly whistled a little tune. He was very casual, very suave, he hoped.

After a minute or so, the clerk looked up and said, "Now, what can I do for you?"

Coolstone said, "Er, ah, I'd like to float -- er, cash a check, please."

"For your ticket?" asked the agent.

"No," said Coolstone. "Not exactly. I have a ticket, as you see here." The Cold Rock held the ticket for the clerk's examination. "But these delays are running me a little short of cash."

"Sorry," said the clerk, "we only take checks for the exact amount of tickets. No others are allowed."

"But, look," said Coolstone. "I'm hurting."

"Sorry," said the clerk. But he clearly wasn't, and then he dismissed Coolstone by becoming very, very interested once more in his paperwork.

The Rock walked over and sat down. He tried to plan another course of action. I suppose he thought there is a chance a hotel would cash a check for me. Everything is against it; however, no baggage, only a shaving kit, and I look like the devil. It'll cost me a dollar to go downtown. That'll leave me $0.38, and then I can't even get back out here if I can't get a check cashed—serious trouble.

He dug out a pack of cigarettes, lit one, and noted that there were only three remaining. Got to cut down anyhow, he thought.

Well, to town it is, I guess. I'll try a check-cashing trick on a hotel.

He didn't even have a checkbook, and he'd used the three spare checks he always carried in his billfold during the days before. This wasn't going to be easy, but hell, you're always reading about people who cash bum checks. It must be easy, and Coolstone had money in the bank.

It was almost midnight by the time he got into town. Coolstone now had thirty-eight cents, no cigarettes, and a big appetite. He had to make a move and make it quick.

He walked up and down the streets, trying to decide which hotel he'd honor with his check. It was cold, bitterly cold. The snow had increased, and of course, Coolstone did not have a topcoat. His ears, nose, and face were becoming numb. He was thoroughly chilled.

He saw a large sign indicating a hotel. He walked up to the front of the building and saw that it was a fancy one. He made up his mind. This would be the one he'd try. He stood for a moment in front of the hotel and rehearsed a little pitch that he would give the manager in his efforts to cash the check.

With shaving kit in hand, in he walked. His steps were brisk, his demeanor all business. As he approached the desk, he tried out his old smile, but his cheeks hadn't thawed enough to allow it. The clerk looked up.

"I wonder if I could speak to the manager, please," said Coolstone.

"Why, certainly, sir," said the clerk. He left the office for a moment and returned with the manager.

"Can I help you?" asked the manager, all smiles.

"Well, yes, you can. Would you cash a check for me?" the Cold Rock blurted out, blowing his entire sales pitch.

The manager looked him over carefully up and down. Under his close scrutiny, Coolstone's color, which had been a rather dark blue, changed to a light purple. He shuffled his feet a bit.

"You mean," the manager said slowly, "that you walk in cold, off the street at midnight, and want me to cash a check? I suppose you want to do it without getting a room either."

"No, no," said Coolstone quickly.

"I need a room. I'm stranded because of the airline strike and just don't have any money." He trailed off. It didn't sound like much of a story, even to him.

"I don't suppose you have any baggage," said the manager. Coolstone shook his head mutely.

"Well," said the manager with a sigh. "I'm probably a sucker, but you take a room. It's $10 a night, and I'll cash a $15.00 check. It's against my better judgment."

"That's fine," said Coolstone. "Fine. I thank you ever so much."

The manager gave him the register to sign, and after Coolstone made his X, the manager stood waiting for the check.

"Er -ah," said the Rock. "Do you have a counter-check?" For a moment, he was afraid he had blown the whole deal.

Slowly the manager brought out a counter check, staring fixedly at Coolstone, then asked, "What bank is it on?"
"California bank," said Coolstone weakly. "Bank of America." He would have whistled the Star-Spangled Banner at that point if he thought it would have done any good.

"OK," said the manager. "Fill out the check."

The chore completed, Coolstone raced over to the cigarette machine, got a pack, opened it, lit one quickly, then went up to his room, dodging bellboys all the way.

He stood in a hot shower until he got rid of the chill. Then he cleaned up, went downstairs. And was back in business.

Coolstone Takes Flight

"You mean, that you walk in cold off the street at midnight, and want me to cash a check?"

Well, now, he thought, a couple of long, tall ones, and I'll be as good as new. Thirty minutes later, he had $3.13. Then he went into the dining room, ravenous, and had the $1.75 chopped sirloin special. For a man whose mouth was watering for the diamond-crusted carpeted fillet mignon - chopped sirloin did nicely.

When he finished, he went upstairs and hit the sack.

The next morning, he called the terminal. "How's the strike coming along?"

"It looks good," he was told. "We should start operations about noon. Your flight isn't scheduled yet. Suggest you come on out and check in. Then you'll be sure to get on the first one going."

Coolstone counted his money once again. Now he had $1.38. He'd been this route before.

Coolstone noted that he had to check out at noon and had at least 24 hours or so to go before he could possibly be back to Oxnard. He wasn't feeling too good either, with sniffles and an upset stomach. That hour-long stroll in the cold the night before hadn't done him any good.

He didn't dare try to cash another check, and 2,000 miles to go didn't add up. Of course, they would serve food on the plane. That was one worry he didn't have to consider. The good old airlines, with their diamond-crusted service, they take care of you.

He glanced at his watch and saw it was ten o'clock. I've got to get moving, he thought. But wait a minute. How about that old hack watch? He'd pawn it. Now, he'd had the watch for years, but it worked very well and should be worth at least a buck or so. The Air Force wasn't going to like it, but with the exigencies of the service as they were, who had a better, right? He kind of hated to part with it, but you have to make sacrifices sometimes.

With a spring in his step which had been lacking for days, he started for a pawnshop. It was still cold out, but it didn't bother him at all. Four blocks from the hotel, he found a pawnshop. He entered and was met by the clerk.

"Can I help you?" asked the clerk.

"Yes," said Coolstone. "I would like to hock my watch and redeem it by mail when I get home. I'm in a bind for dough on account of that engineers' strike."

"Let's see the watch," said the clerk.

Coolstone Takes Flight

Coolstone took it off his wrist and launched into a highly flattering description of the watch's many merits.

"That's fine," said the clerk, "except for one thing. It isn't running."

"Sure it is," said Coolstone. "'It's just that it's very, very quiet."

"It isn't running," said the clerk. Coolstone took the watch from him, listened to it, shook it, wound it, pounded it, but it had stopped.

The clerk shook his head very slowly. "Nice try," he said. "Nice try."

Wordlessly, the Rock left the shop.

At the airport, now with thirty-eight cents, he checked in at the ticket counter. "Have you got me scheduled?" he asked.

"Yes, sir," said the agent. "We're very pleased to say that by using some of our supervisory personnel as engineers, an aircraft will be available for your flight, which will take off at 3 a.m. It's a DC-7, with a 45-minute stop at Denver, then direct to Los Angeles."

"Three a.m.," said the Rock. "Is that the best you can do?"

The agent's face showed considerable disappointment. He had thought he was doing such a big favor for Coolstone. "But, sir," he said, "You're one of the lucky ones. Others aren't scheduled to leave until late tomorrow night. You can swap if you like with one of those."

"Oh, no," interrupted Coolstone. "No, perish the thought. I'll take this one."

Thirteen hours to go, thirty-eight cents, three cigarettes, and he felt lousy. Two hours later, he was reduced to cadging newspapers left behind by his more affluent passenger cohorts.

At 2000 hours, Coolstone was hungry and out of cigarettes. Thirty-eight cents left! Should he eat, or should he smoke? This was a major decision, a problem to which careful thought must be given. Once on the plane, he could eat, but cigarettes were another thing.

He made a snap decision. He would buy cigarettes. He now had thirteen cents remaining, was starved, and had picked up a whale of a headache.

At midnight he began to anticipate in detail the meal which he believed would be served in flight. They really went all out on some of these flights - champagne first, then some hors d'oeuvres, steak, baked potatoes with lots of butter, and probably some exotic dessert. Boy, was he ready!

At about 2:30, Coolstone got into position at the gate. At 3 o'clock on the dot, they called the flight. The Rock was first on board and went well to the front of the aircraft to find a seat, for he had learned by experience that most of the time, they served meals from the front to the back.

After becoming airborne, one of the two stewardesses came by his seat. Coolstone stopped her.

"Say," he said, beaming. "If it's all right, I'd like to have my meal now. I'm really not hungry, you understand, but if you can serve me now, then I can get a little sleep. You know how it is."

"Meal?" said the stewardess. "We don't serve meals on this flight. I can bring you doughnuts and coffee, cookies and milk, or crackers and juice."

"No meal?" said the Rock weakly.

She shook her head. "No meals."

Bring me the doughnuts and coffee, please," he said resignedly.

The first hour out, he had three orders of doughnuts and coffee, three of cookies and milk, and three of crackers and juice. He just couldn't hold any more liquid.

The flight to Denver was uneventful. Just before landing, the stewardess announced a 45-minute stop for breakfast. Coolstone pretended to be asleep when they landed and remained in his seat as the rest of the passengers unloaded.

He was awakened gently by the stewardess. "Time to unload for breakfast," she said cheerfully.

"Thanks," said the Rock disgustedly and struggled to his feet. His head was hurting, his mouth was dry from the cigarette diet, and he was generally a mess.

They were airborne an hour later on the last leg, and Coolstone was finally able to nap a bit. At first, he was very restless; then, he slept soundly. As he slept, he dreamed. He dreamed that the big bird was on fire and they were going to crash-land. There was panic in the cockpit. He, with years of flying experience, knew that the safest place, if there was one, during a crash was the tail section. And now he saw the fire more clearly in his dream. They were obviously going to crash.

Wild-eyed, he jumped over his startled seat companion and raced down the aisle for the tail, the only safe place. About halfway down the aisle, he became fully awake and saw the two stewardesses in the aft section of the aircraft rising out of their seats as one, with incredulous expressions. He brought himself up short. Quickly he searched for something to say, "Where is the restroom?" he finally choked out.

Wordlessly, they pointed to the other end of the plane. Then, as he stared at them, "Up front," one of them said.

He turned around, and now, to keep up the pretext, he had to run the entire length of the airplane to the restrooms in the front. Once inside, Coolstone figured he would never come out. Finally, he had to. Most of the passengers were asleep as he walked back to his seat, and they hadn't even noticed. His seat companion had, and remarked dryly, as Coolstone sat down again, "Pretty close one, wasn't it?

They finally got to Los Angeles, and Coolstone knew for sure now he had the flu. He was running a temperature, was sick to his stomach - the works. He had only thirteen cents remaining, and with ten of it, he made a collect call to a friend at Oxnard.

"This is Coolstone," he said.

"Coolstone?" said the friend. "Where in the world have you been? You should have been back a week ago. The Old Man's been wild."

"Never mind," said Coolstone. "Go over to the dispensary and get an ambulance. Then come down to Los Angeles International for me."

"Why? What's wrong with you? said the friend.

"Look," said the Cold Rock. "Lots of things are wrong with me, but the most pressing right now is that I have the Kansas City flu."

Violations, Violations

Coolstone had been chosen because of his wide and varied flying experience to transport a two-star to a conference in a T-33.

They landed at their destination successfully, and the general then released Coolstone to return from whence they came. He was to come back in about four days to pick up the stars again.

It was on the return trip that Coolstone gained even more experience. He filed into his destination from a base about 700 miles out. His destination was reporting low ceilings and visibilities, and he knew delays would be most probable at this busy base.

He looked for the nearest alternate he could find and came up with one about 70 miles away. However, the weather at his alternate was nothing fancy either, but he figured he would arrive at his destination with over 270 gallons of fuel if the winds held at all. He could then hang around for 20 minutes or so until he got down to about 200 gallons, at which time he would have to make a move.

The flight was uneventful until he reached a point about 15 minutes out from his destination. Here the Center directed him to descend to 26,000 and cleared him to the penetration omni. His estimate for the omni was ten past the hour.

On the hour, he was advised to enter the holding pattern when he arrived at the penetration omni, to expect approach clearance at 20, and to contact the Approach Control immediately. At 12 past the hour, as Coolstone read the clock, he arrived at the omni on instruments in the weather. He had 264 gallons as the station swung.

He called Approach Control and told them that he was entering the holding pattern.

"Roger," said Approach Control. "Your new expected approach time is 31. Expect clearance to a lower altitude at 25."

Using a rule of thumb - four gallons a minute, Coolstone figured he would be right at alternate fuel requirements at approach time. Really he would be below the 200 gallons he had planned as alternate fuel, but upon refiguring, he decided that 180 would be rock bottom minimum which, by great coincidence, would be about what he would have remaining at 31.

He made two circuits of the holding pattern before he solved it. This had been rather exciting. Four minutes remained until approach time. He figured a 360 would just about do it.

He called Approach Control. "This is Coolstone One. How does the approach time of 31 look?"

"Coolstone from Approach Control. Stand by one."

This wasn't too heartening. It sounded to Coolstone like they might extend it once again. He then called Approach Control and asked them what the weather was at his alternate.

"Roger," said Approach Control. "Stand by one."

Maybe, thought Coolstone, about a third of the way through his 360, I'd better look at that alternate approach; 180 gallons might not do it if they have an involved penetration.

Flying the aircraft with his knees, he thumbed quickly through the letdown book, attempting to locate the plate for his alternate. He ruffled through the book rather quickly at first and was unable to locate it. Then he backed up and started down page by page in the general area. At this point, the aircraft had assumed a rather interesting attitude and required Coolstone's undivided attention for a second or two.

He was about halfway through his 360, and once again, he gave his attention to the letdown book.

It wouldn't surprise me one bit, he thought, not to have a plate under the field name. He didn't know what else it could be under, but he was sure the book-makers could think of something.

Then he tried the index, dividing his attention between the fine print and the instruments without doing justice to either. He was about 40 degrees from the inbound heading when he had made it through the index, and now he was willing to bet that the alternate just didn't have a penetration.

Then it dawned on him! He looked at the back of the book again, and sure enough, his alternate was shown to be about an eighth of an inch beyond the book's coverage. He was starting to fumble for the letdown book, which covered the area of his alternate when Approach Control called.

"Coolstone One from Approach Control. You'll be cleared for a penetration at 33. Weather is reported to be 400 foot overcast, three miles, and rain."

The Approach Controller went on to tell Coolstone that his alternate weather was reported at 800 foot overcast, two miles, and rain.

"Roger, boy," said Coolstone. "Is that approach time firm?"

"Coolstone from Approach Control, it looks good now. Give us a call departing the high station."

Coolstone was at a loss to figure out how he could get to the station at 33 since he was already over the station at 31, but, game to the core, he cranked his bird up into a 45-degree bank, and around he went. He noted his fuel was 170 and accepted the fact that the alternate was out the window.

Well, he thought, at least that's one problem that's behind me. Even with the good try, it looked like he was going to be a minute late for his arrival over the station. This he was quite proud of, considering the shape he was in at the last extension.

He was about to call "Beginning penetration" when Approach Control called him.

"Coolstone from Approach Control. This is to advise you that this base is on official business only. If you land without orders, you will be violated."

But Coolstone didn't hear, for while he was attempting to roll out on the penetration heading, he noted his slave gyro had ceased turning. He increased his bank automatically and checked the horizon. He was already over 45 degrees, but the compass wasn't budging.

Then, before his very eyes, it began rapid 360 gyrations. Quickly he checked the inverter light, and found it out, then the horizon flag, which was not showing. Then he noted his No. 2 needle, which was holding steady, although the compass card was rotating with the slave gyro.

"Er, ah, Approach Control. Coolstone One here. I'm having a little trouble with my gyros. What channel is radar?"

"Coolstone One from Approach Control. Did you get the transmission about the violation?"

"Violation?" said Coolstone. "What violation? I need radar. My slave gyro is out."

"Roger, Coolstone. Operations advises that this base is for official business only, and even with orders, you need prior approval for landing. You will be violated if you land here."

Coolstone had devoted every brain cell he could spare, three, to Approach Control, and the remaining millions were all busily engaged in a maximum effort trying to remember and apply the omni procedure to be used when the gyros were out.

"Roger, Approach Control. I need radar. Have started my penetration, but my gyros are out. What channel for radar?"

"Assume you understand the information on the violation, Tombstone. Radar is on 268.3. Over."

"Look, Approach Control, that's Coolstone One, not Tombstone. I'm going to radar now." He switched channels.

"Radar, this is Coolstone One, somewhere in the penetration. I need a no-gyro approach, but quick."

"Coolstone from Radar. I read you five square. How me?"

"Radar from Coolstone. Five by, but my gyros are out. Do you have me?"

"Coolstone from Radar. Squawk two. And this is to advise you that if you land at this base, you will be violated. Do you understand?"

"Roger, boy, I understand, but I need a gyro-out approach. Do you understand?"

"Roger, Tombstone. Squawk three. The AO just called and said to tell you that you are directed to proceed to your alternate. You cannot land here. What are your intentions?"

"Look, Radar," said Coolstone, very deliberately and enunciating very clearly. "My compass is out. I don't know where I am in the penetration. Give me a steer and tell the AO that I'm not going to my alternate. I intend to land at your base if I don't have to bail out, and that's Tomb. . . , er, Coolstone One. Have you got the message?"

"Roger, Tombstone. You intend to land here in spite of the violation, and your gyro's out."

"That's Coolstone, not Tombstone, and do you have me on your weapon?"

"Squawk two again for ID, Tomb ... er, Coolstone, and turn right to 40 degrees. You have badly overshot the final turn. Do you wish a gyro-out approach?"

"Do I ever?" said Coolstone. "My gyro is out."

"Tomb ..., er, Coolstone from Radar. Turn right now." And then, with his mike keyed, Controller added, "Roll out now. And the AO advises that there is no parking space, due to a big high-level conference involving lots of generals. Refueling will be delayed by at least four hours. There is no BOQ space. What are your intentions?"

"Keep running this approach, Radar," Coolstone said, almost pleadingly. "I'm hurting. I understand the AO's message. That will be fine."

The gyro-out approach was continued to where the descent was to be started. At this point, GCA had Coolstone on centerline, and called once again.

"Coolstone from GCA. The AO advises that you will not be able to take off from here until tomorrow. Start your radar descent now if you still want to land."

"That will be just fine," said Coolstone weakly, and added, "Starting descent now."

Coolstone broke out at about 400 feet with the windscreen full of rain which seemed to be freezing on contact. He finally picked up the runway lights and, looking out the side panels, he got a visual on the runway. It wasn't much of a visual, but enough to make a touchdown of sorts. He raised his flaps, gave a big sigh of relief, and tapped his brakes. Immediately the bird did a little trick to the left.

Quickly Coolstone tromped on the right rudder.

The nose remained left, but the bird was skidding down the runway in the general direction of the runway heading.

Slowly, as he jabbed both the right brake and the right rudder, the nose began to come back. As far as braking action was concerned, he had nothing.

With about 4,000 feet to go, Coolstone, in desperation, stopcocked the engine, opened the canopy, and with full rudder deflections, worked mightily to keep the bird any place on the runway. His braking action was just full of technique. He tapped them softly; the bird skidded and veered. He jammed them both on hard, and the bird skidded and veered. He pulled the stick back and tried it; the bird skidded and veered.

Then, as he entered the overrun, doing about 30 or 40 knots, he now began to get some deceleration on the slightly rougher surface. As the nose went off the overrun into the mud, he got the bird stopped.

Coolstone sat still for a second, quite thankful to be in a minimum number of pieces, then called GCA. He said, "I appreciate greatly all the information on the parking space, refueling delay, BOQ space, violations, the news item on the generals' conference, and the personal interest taken in my flight by the AO. But did anyone advise you today about the braking action on this runway? I'm off the end and need a tow."

"Negative, Coolstone. We have no information on braking action. However, this is a new runway, and you might expect it to be slick when wet."

"Roger, Radar. Tombstone One out."

Weather Strains a Friendship

Coolstone's old buddy buddy had managed to set up an F-106 ferry flight for himself and had cleverly talked Coolstone into tagging along behind him in a T-33, carrying their clothes and shaving kits, so that he could provide the transportation back to their home base. The two of them arrived at Ogden and picked up the F-106, which Coolstone's buddy buddy was to ferry to Kelly.

The weather had been forecasted to be really stinking in the afternoon. Therefore, they had planned to start out from Ogden for the first stop at Albuquerque at 0400 hours the next day. The only trouble was that the F-106 was bent, and it was almost 1000 before they finally got airborne at Ogden.

When arriving at Albuquerque, the F-106 had developed pneumatic problems and, while Coolstone had tried to convince his old buddy

buddy that Coolstone should take on off and wait for him at San Antone, he was not able to persuade his buddy that it was a good idea to get separated by four or five hundred miles from his clothes.

It was, therefore, a little after 1500 before they were able to file for San Antone. The two of them checked the weather and found that Kelly was in good shape - just some middle-scattered clouds - but the route was miserable - severe weather warnings, tornadoes, the works. They talked to a pilot who had just landed and had flown over their proposed route from Kelly. He said with an air of superiority that he had topped everything at 38,000 without trouble. However, he did say that thunderstorms were almost solid and were building very rapidly.

Coolstone then began a foot-dragging campaign. "Look," he said to his buddy. "This T-33 I'm flying is a real dog. With the baggage rack, I'm not sure I can even get to 38,000 feet. Maybe we'd better wait until tomorrow morning. You know what the ferry regs say."

"No sweat," said his buddy. "I'll go on ahead of you and call back the tops. That way, you can see how it's going, and if the tops are just a little bit above you, you can fly through them. I'll keep you posted, buddy buddy. If the tops are way up there, I'll let you know, and you can turn around and go back."

"Well," said Coolstone reluctantly, "OK, I guess. You keep me posted good. For this weatherman says, we might run into a cow or a barn up there. Tornadoes are forecasted all over the place. If it doesn't look good, you tell me, and I'll turn around and go back and meet you tomorrow morning."

With that, they both filed VFR on top with a VFR climb.

As Coolstone was preflighting his bird, he could see to the east that there were indeed severe high buildups, but his better judgment was discounted, and he hurried his preflight.

Coolstone Takes Flight

The F-106 took off first, and Coolstone followed. As Coolstone turned out on course, he could see up ahead that the VFR climb was going to be very, very difficult to accomplish in a T-33, especially his.

As he changed to the Center frequency, Albuquerque asked him for his Roswell estimate, and as it was about a 150-mile leg, Coolstone figured 30 minutes and gave the Center an estimate of 45.

As Coolstone neared the weather, he could see that the storms were gigantic, and on his present course, he didn't have a chance of topping them without circling. He noted his rate of climb at 27,000 feet was about 600 feet per minute. A real dog. He could no longer avoid the storms, so he started a slow orbit to the left. As he did so, he saw that there was a crack between two of the large storms about 45° to his right, in which a VFR climb could still be made.

He turned toward the crack and continued his climb. At about 35,000 feet, well to the right on course, climbing at about 150 to 200 feet per minute, he ran out of crack. He still was not on top. He reversed his course, as the only alternative was to penetrate.

Since the crack had narrowed alarmingly, he lost 2,000 feet in the turn, trying to stay in it. He called to his old buddy buddy from whom he had heard not one word.

"Roger, Coolstone," said his buddy. "I'm on top at 38,000. No sweat. I top everything up here."

"Roger," said Coolstone and took some hope from his news, but boy, was his ETA going to be off! He called the Center and told them that he was circling to stay VFR and extended his Roswell estimate by 20 minutes.

The Center called him back shortly afterward and said, "Coolstone, from Albuquerque. Would an unrestricted climb help?"

"Roger, roger, boy," said Coolstone. "I sure would appreciate an unrestricted climb."

Coolstone had nosed the T-33 up to about 37,500 and was sure that he would be OK now.

"Roger," said the Center. "You are cleared to climb unrestricted to VFR on top. Report reaching VFR on top and over Roswell on this frequency."

Coolstone turned on course. Well, what he really did was home on Roswell, and some of the tension which had been building up in him was relieved. As he approached the weather, he could see that the clouds were just wispy cirrus.

Undoubtedly he was almost on top. Hadn't his old buddy buddy said he cleared everything at 38,000?

His airspeed was about 190 knots. He tried all sorts of airspeed combinations, trying to get the T-bird to climb further, but 38,000 looked pretty much like the limit.

Coolstone Takes Flight

Suddenly the clouds became denser, and the Cold Rock was favored with severe turbulence. He struggled to keep the T-bird from stalling out and right side up. He lost several thousand feet of altitude. There was even hail way up there. He worked like a Trojan trying to nurse that T-bird back up to 38,000 feet between bouts of turbulence.

He called his buddy again and asked him for his altitude.

"38,000 feet, Coolstone, old boy, tops everything," was the reply.

Then in the midst of this chaos, he received station passage from Roswell. He took up a heading of sorts to Wink. He gave his position report.

"Albuquerque Center from Coolstone One. Over Roswell at 15 (one hour after takeoff), climbing IFR, estimate Wink at 35 San Antonio."

"Roger," said the Center. "You say you are still climbing? What altitude are you passing through?"

"Well," said Coolstone, "I have passed through several both directions. It is pretty turbulent up here. Is there any traffic?"

"No," said the Center, "Not where you are. There is some on-top traffic. Most of them are reporting on top at 40 to 46,000 feet. Please advise when you are on top."

"OK," said Coolstone. Then with some grounds for suspicion, he asked, "What altitude is F-106, 414 reporting?"

"Well," said the Center. "He was at 38,000, but he is under San Antonio's control now. We don't have contact."

"Roger," said Coolstone, and then he was extremely pleased and relieved to break out of the weather. He wasn't on top, but he had come out the side of the storm, which appeared to go at least 50,000 feet. Up ahead, directly on course, he was faced with another, and it looked just as formidable.

He nursed the T-33 to 38,500 now. The reduction of fuel load must account for it, he thought. Then inevitably, he found himself back in the weather. This time not only did he have turbulence and hail, but there even was lightning. In spite of his best efforts, he found himself back down to 34,000, descending almost uncontrollably.

Then over the radio, he heard, "Coolstone One, this is San Antonio Center. We have a weather advisory for you. Over."

"Roger," said Coolstone. "Go ahead." There was a noticeably jerky quality in his voice.

"Coolstone from San Antonio Center. We have received a weather bulletin to the effect that seven separate funnel clouds have been reported in the Wink area. What are your intentions and altitude?"

Coolstone suffered a yellow-out. He was in the weather and also in the vicinity of Wink.

"I'm nearing Wink," he stammered, "and the turbulence is quite bad, but I'll try to go on through. I'm at 35,000 feet, still climbing." He didn't dare try a 180. He was fighting just to keep the bird under some semblance of control.

"Roger, *Tombstone One,* from San Antonio. You state you're still climbing. We had one report that you were climbing through 38,500 feet. What happened?" ·

"That's *Coolstone One,* not Tombstone One, Center, and I have climbed through 38,000 feet several times, but when I hit turbulence, I lose altitude."

"Roger, Tomb - - er, Coolstone. Understand," the Center replied dryly. "Give us a call when you're on top."

There was about a ten-minute lull in the turbulence. He was still in the clouds but evidently out of the heart of the thunderstorm area, and Coolstone was able to get back up to about 37,500 feet. He could see that he must be almost on top, for it had become very bright.

Then, as he watched, horrified, the RPM started down. It went from 100% to 99%, then 98, 97, and 96.

Alcohol, his thoughts shouted. I forgot about alcohol.

He toggled the switch wildly, and the pressurization dumped nicely. Wrong switch! He finally got to the alcohol switch and held it. He couldn't be bothered about pressurization now. The RPM was down to 84%. His altitude was back to 34. He was also back in the turbulence.

As he fought to hold the aircraft approximately in level flight, he watched the RPM continue down to 82%, 81, and 80. He still held the alcohol switch. Then there was a sudden blurp, and the alcohol did its work. The RPM returned abruptly and almost painfully to 100%. The compressor stalled all the way.

For the first time since the RPM began descending, the Rock breathed. He also noted that the canopy was rapidly frosting over, and in spite of the auxiliary defroster, which of course, he was late in turning on, it appeared to him that he was entombed in ice.

He selected the safety switch on his oxygen regulator and manfully tried to regain his altitude. It was hopeless. All he could do was ride out the turbulence and hope that he didn't run into a tornado like the weatherman intimated he might.

He had passed Wink some time back but hadn't noted the time. What he would have liked to have done was to throw in the towel, declare an emergency to San Antonio and anybody else who would listen, just to commiserate.

Then he received another radio call. "Tomb - - er, Coolstone One from San Antonio Center. What is your position?"

"Roger, San Antonio. This is Coolstone One. I was over Wink at about 40 (it was now 55), climbing IFR, er, ah ..." He didn't have a San Antonio estimate nor any idea what his ground speed had been, but he came up with one anyway. "Estimate San Antonio at 22 Kelly."

His tone of voice prompted the Center to ask, "Is everything OK, Coolstone?"

"Roger," said Coolstone manfully. "Everything is just dandy."

The turbulence ceased, and Coolstone, sometimes off of the alcohol switch for two or three minutes at a time, relaxed from rigid to tense and started nursing the T-33 up again. The canopy was completely frozen over. He couldn't see a thing, and he worked and worked for the altitude. He was almost up to 39,000 feet, and he had never been this high before.

Then it dawned on him. Maybe he should peek out. He rubbed the side of the canopy with his warm hand until he had a spot about two inches square and pasted an eyeball to it. To his amazement, he found he was in the clear. He scratched another spot on the windscreen, and up ahead, he could see it was completely clear. He could even see San Antonio.

Almost triumphantly, he called, "San Antonio Center, from Tombstone One, er Coolstone One, that is, cancel my IFR."

"Roger, Tombstone, you're canceled."

Coolstone Takes Flight

After circling for 20 minutes at low altitude, which was as much time as his fuel would allow, Coolstone could see well enough to land. After he parked the aircraft, he entered Base Operations and found his old buddy buddy waiting impatiently for him, with clearance in hand.

"What took you so long?" said his buddy. "I've been in here for almost an hour waiting for you. Come on, let's file out of here."

"Buddy," said Coolstone. "I'm not filing anywhere today."

Buddy buddy replied, "What's wrong with you, anyway?"

"First," said Coolstone, "what altitude did you come over here at?"

"Well," said his buddy, scuffing his foot a bit. "I started at 38, but I had to go up to 46 at Wink to top thunderstorms."

"Why didn't you tell me?" said Coolstone accusingly. "All I ever heard from you was 38,000 two times. Do you know what I went through there? It was terrible," Coolstone said, shuddering at the thought of his recent flight.

"Well, you made it all right," said his buddy. "What's all the sweat?"

Again, Coolstone said, "Why didn't you tell me what the tops were? You knew that bird of mine couldn't get over 38,000. I doubt if it would with rockets on it."

"Well," said his buddy, "I was afraid if I did tell you, you'd turn around, and you had the shaving kits and the clothes."

"Had is absolutely correct," said Coolstone. "The travel pod came off sometime during the flight."

Coolstone Chickens Out

It all started when Coolstone moved to the country. He rented a place that had about forty acres, horse corrals, pasturage, and, unfortunately, a chicken pen.

First, he bought himself a couple of ponies for his boys, and then he contemplated the great savings that could be his if he raised chickens. Fryers seemed to be the best way to go, so he located an old Sears farm catalog and looked up poultry and found, to his great surprise, that you could buy 100 white Leghorn day-old roosters for $8.50. $8.50 per hundred was so cheap he ordered 200.

The catalog stated that the purchaser would be notified two weeks prior to the shipment of the day-old chicks. The Rock knew that he had to have an incubator with heat, waterers, and feeders, but he figured with two weeks' notice, he would have plenty of time to think of something before the chicks arrived.

Sometime after Coolstone had placed the order, long enough so that he had completely forgotten he had even ordered 200 chickens, about 0700 on a Saturday morning, the phone rang. Coolstone answered out of a sound sleep, and he heard a voice say, "This is the North End Post Office, and your 200-day-old chicks have arrived."

In the background, Coolstone could hear considerable peeping.

"But they said they would give me two weeks' notice," he told the postman.

"I don't know what they told you," the postman said, "but you had better get down here and take care of these chicks because if they ever start dying, they go like flies."

With that, Coolstone threw on his clothes and headed for his car, trying at the same time to figure out how he was going to take care of those 200-day-old chickens.

"I'll put them in the furnace room to start," he thought to himself, and as he drove down to town, he constructed a brooder of sorts in his mind, made up of wallboard with an extension cord and a heat lamp. He figured he would get the waterers, the feeders, and the heat lamp before he got the chickens from the post office.

The salesman at the farm equipment store gave him some real good advice on how to handle day-old chickens. He should have thermostatically controlled infrared, non-shock, martini-proofed heat elements, he was told, and an automatic heater and waterer. The total bill for all was well over $100.00.

Coolstone settled for the $2.00 waterer, the $1.50 feeder, and a $1.25 heat lamp and continued his race to the post office.

As he entered the post office, he could hear the peeping right off.

The postal clerk at the window couldn't get the chickens out to him quickly enough. They came in two cardboard boxes, complete with numerous holes, from every one of which a chicken head stuck out with its mouth open, peeping. He could only guess what the other end was doing.

On the trip home, he drove 10 to 15 miles an hour faster than he would normally have because the constant peeping generated an adrenalin level and a sense of urgency he just couldn't handle.

When he arrived home, he brought the boxes of chickens into the furnace room and, with his wife's help, stacked some wallboard so that a rectangle was formed about three by four feet. He hooked up the heat lamp on an extension cord, filled the waterers and feeders, brought the chicks in, and turned them loose.

Very quickly, he was pleased to see they began to eat, drink, and perform those other biological functions for which chickens are so well known.

Unfortunately, Coolstone's Siamese cat did not exactly understand the chicken operation. The peeping she did understand. While Coolstone and his wife were congratulating themselves over a cup of coffee, the Siamese leaped over the wallboard and into the 200 chicks. The cat, with this unexpected wealth, didn't exactly know how to handle it. She batted the chickens around, mouthed them, laid on them but killed very few before Coolstone was able to get her out of the incubator and then out of the furnace room.

Chickens grow quickly. Their appetites vary directly with the square of their growth. What began with five pounds of feed a day and a little water soon was up to 100 pounds of feed a day and lots of water.

The chickens were finally removed to the pen – the same pen which was responsible for the whole idea. And the losses were extremely low. In fact, Sears had sent about 215 chickens to make up for any attrition that might occur, and at the end of two months, Coolstone still had 208 chickens - all roosters.

In the third month, they began to crow, and the mornings were very interesting indeed. Coolstone, much to his surprise, found that roosters begin to crow *before* sunrise. A good bright porch light would also launch them. But he was resolved to hold out until the 4th of July before he killed the first chicken for food.

When the 4th came, it was a drizzly, dark day, but undaunted, Coolstone advised his family that everybody had fried chicken on the 4th of July, but they were going to have their *own* fried chicken on this 4th of July.

He got himself a knife, heated some water, and went out to the pen. With one tremendous lunge, he had a chicken in each hand. Quickly he wrung their necks. After they were well bled, he went back into the house, got his bucket of hot water, took it out to the pen, scalded the chickens well, and began to pluck them.

The first one plucked just great. However, during the second plucking operation, Coolstone accidentally inhaled a small feather. This set up a fit of coughing that watered his eyes and those of anyone else in the same county. During this tremendous coughing fit, he managed to finish his plucking and began the gutting. The gutting operation was one that he was very poorly prepared to perform. He ended up completely splitting the chicken open so he could get everything that was important.

The gutting completed, the Rock proudly presented his two chickens to his wife, at the same time coughing so much that he couldn't explain to her the joys of a killing-plucking-gutting chicken operation. He went to the front room, sat down, had a tall cool one, and managed to control his coughing to mild fits spaced from five to ten minutes apart.

After an hour or so of this, the Rock figured he would bring up that feather with one gigantic cough. He performed the coughing act and immediately experienced what he was sure was a heart attack. He had a sharp pain in his chest; when he tried to inhale, the pain became worse, and he advised his wife to take the kids downstairs because he didn't want them to see him die of a heart attack and, for God's sake, call the flight surgeon.

Now the flight surgeon was an unusual type in that he seemed to have a genuine desire to keep his pilots flying. Up until this flight surgeon, it had been Coolstone's experience that, at the first complaint to a flight surgeon, a DNIF slip would be written out, which might change and get worse before the flight surgeon even knew for sure what was wrong with his pilot patient.

But this one was different. The last thing he did was ground you. Therefore, he built much confidence in the minds of his pilot patients, who then would tell him their real symptoms so that an accurate diagnosis could be made.

When Coolstone's wife called Doc and told him she thought the Rock had had a heart attack, the flight surgeon was on his way. Even though he had 20 miles to drive in an ambulance, he did so in far less than 20 minutes.

He arrived breathless, poked, listened, felt, and finally looked up with a smile and said, "You damned fool. You collapsed a lung."

"Now," the Doc said, "what we have to do is cut a little hole in the lower back of your rib cage and insert a tube to bleed off the air that has escaped into the chest cavity. Then you will be all right. It isn't much of an operation," he said. "In fact, I could do it right here, but I think that it would be better if I took you to the hospital where it can be a little more closely controlled."

Now, the Rock was much relieved to find out he hadn't had a heart attack, but he wasn't overjoyed with the collapsed lung. "What about flying, Doc? Am I going to be able to fly again?"

"Sure," he said. "Nobody will ever know but you and me exactly what happened. A feather, huh?" Doc said. "You sucked one right in?"

"I sure did, and I have been coughing ever since," the Rock said.

"Well, no problem. The ones I worry about are when the lung collapses for no reason at all. Then we have to take a good look."

He loaded the Rock into the ambulance with the medic's help and took him to the hospital. By the time they arrived, it was after normal duty hours. Coolstone was propped up in the bed so he would be as comfortable as possible and was told the operation would take place the next morning.

"Now, don't worry about this," said the Doc. "It's just a little slit. We put the hose in, and immediately, you can breathe again with that lung. No pain, no problem. I could do it myself tonight," he added, "but it would probably be better if they took an X-ray or two and then performed it under a little more controlled circumstance."

"Okay," said the Rock. "Thanks a lot, Doc," and watched him leave.

After a very fitful night, where no position Coolstone was able to get into was really comfortable, breakfast was served. He wasn't that hungry.

At about 0800, he was taken up for X-rays, blood tests, and an examination by an absolutely uncommunicative chest doctor. He was then taken back to his room. About an hour later, four doctors came in - a lieutenant colonel, two majors, and a captain. It was evident that the lieutenant colonel was the spokesman. He introduced himself and the other three, who were residents, and stated that they were from the thoracic clinic. He said they wanted to talk a bit about how the lung collapsed.

Coolstone explained how, while plucking a chicken, he had sucked a feather in and, after an hour or so of continuous coughing, he had made one last gigantic cough, and the lung collapsed.

"Sucked a feather in?" said the colonel. "Are you sure?"

"Of course, I'm sure," said the Rock. "I told you I sucked a feather in and started coughing right off."

"I hardly think that sucking a feather in would cause a collapsed lung," said one of the residents very knowingly.

"I agree with you," said the colonel. "It is obvious that he had a bleb on his lung which ruptured."

"A bleb?" said Coolstone. "I don't think so. I sucked a feather in. I coughed a lot."

"Nooooooo," said the colonel. "You just think you sucked a feather in. The bleb ruptured, and that caused the coughing."

"Well, maybe," said the Rock, who didn't know what a bleb was anyhow and was having difficulty saying more than four words because of his inability to breathe well. "But how about fixing me up?"

"Okay," said the colonel. "Now, this isn't much of an operation. We make the incision from the breast bone around to the backbone. We then put in a rib expander, and we expand the ribs open so . . ." he demonstrated with his hands.

It looked as if he was trying to spread the bars in a prison window. The Rock thought he also had a nasty leer on his face.

"Then we scruff up the chest wall, and we scruff up the lung until they both bleed a little bit. Then we stick them back together. They grow together, and you'll never have another collapsed lung."

"Wait a minute," said Coolstone. "What happened to that little bitty operation the Doc was going to do on the dining room table?"

"We then put in a rib expander and we expand the ribs open so......"

"Oh," the lieutenant colonel said, "you don't want to do that. You want us to go in there and make this incision. This isn't much of an operation either. And you spread these ribs . . ."

"Wait a minute, doc," said Coolstone. I want you to understand right off that you're dealing with a coward. Now," he added, "What do you think I should really do?"

Coolstone Takes Flight

"Well, the first thing," said the colonel, "if you're a smoker, quit!"

Coolstone had been worried about the cigarette bit too, mentally he had begun to throw cigarettes away.

"The second thing," the colonel said, "is to be sure that that lung won't collapse again. Now, if you do what I told you, with the scuffing up of the chest wall and the lung surface, they will grow together, and this will never happen to you again."

"I don't think I want to do that," said the Rock, "Let's just say that we will put a hose in the back there, drain off this air so I can breathe again, and then I'll think it over."

Very disappointed, the four went back out in reverse order of their entry.

Lunch came. Nothing happened. During mid-afternoon, the lieutenant colonel, the two majors, and the captain entered his room again. The colonel spoke.

"Now, we think that if you have thought this over rationally, you will know that what you need is this little simple operation that opens up your chest cavity, stretches the ribs . . ."

"Hold it," said the Rock. "There ain't no way. I've thought it over. There's no way at all that you're going to do that operation. Just give me a little hole in the back, and let's get it over with."

Wordlessly the four filed back out of his room. Nothing happened. Dinner came. At this point, the Rock was perfectly miserable. He couldn't breathe. He couldn't smoke. No martini hour, and he was in a certain amount of pain if he got in the wrong position. About seven o'clock that night, a resident, making his rounds, entered the Rock's room.

"Did they get that tube in?" he asked the Rock.

"No, doc, they sure didn't. They're talking about some other kind of operation, and, in the meantime, they haven't done a thing."

"Well," the resident said, "I can take care of that. At least give you some relief. We'll just put a needle in there and draw off some air."

"That sounds better than nothing," said Coolstone and accompanied the resident to his office.

"Give me the syringe," he told the nurse. "Now," he said, "we will take off your pajama top, lean you over the desk, and I'll put the needle in the back portion of your chest cavity and draw off that air."

At about that time, the nurse came in with a mahogany box approximately 16 inches long, 5 inches wide, and 4 inches high. When she opened it, Coolstone was horrified to see the biggest needle and the biggest syringe he had ever seen in his entire life.

"You're not going to stick THAT in there?" he said to the doctor.

"Of course," he said. "You won't even feel it."

"I'll feel it. I'll feel it," said the Rock. "I know I'll feel it."

"No," he said. "We'll put a little novocaine around the edges there, and when the needle goes in, you won't even know that it has."

"I think I'll know," said the Rock to himself as he leaned over the desk. He felt a slight prick and the needle going through various levels of tissue and gristle. All of a sudden, Coolstone could take a deep breath once again. The doctor had removed the air in the chest cavity, and as he did so, the lung inflated fully. Coolstone turned around and said, "You cured me doc. I won't need any kind of an operation now."

"Well, I wouldn't say that," said the doctor. "I suspect they will still want to put that tube in there. But at least you can sleep tonight."

Right away, Coolstone wanted a cigarette, and he wanted it bad, but he didn't dare smoke. They had certainly scared him out of that.

The next morning, he got up, went to breakfast on his own, and felt just fine except for needing a cigarette very badly. He was back in his room reading a magazine when in filed the lieutenant colonel, the two majors, and the captain.

"I don't need anything now," Coolstone said to the colonel. "They took care of me last night with a needle. Just drew that air right out of there."

"Oh, you can't count on that," said the colonel. "That lung may collapse again at any time. Now what we need to do is this very simple operation where we start at the breast bone and go back around to the . . ."

Coolstone interrupted him. "No way, doc. I've told you already. I'm not going to do that. What's the matter with you cats? Is the chest surgery business that slow around here?"

His question was ignored. "Well, if you insist," said the colonel. "We'll go ahead and put a tube in there for a day or two to be sure the lung has time to heal. If it does collapse again, the air will be drawn right out of the tube."

Well, okay," said the Rock very reluctantly. "I'll go along with that."

"We'll put the tube right in the front of your chest on the left-hand side next to the breast bone, high," said the doctor.

"Wait a minute," said the Rock. "What happened to that little bitty slit that was going to be cut in the back of my chest cavity with that little bitty hose slipped in it that my flight surgeon was going to do on the table?"

"Oh," the doctor said, "we don't want to do it that way. We'll do it up front on account of we don't want to disturb that area in the back. You still might want us to do that other operation."

"I don't think so," said the Rock firmly. "But you can put the hose in any place you want to. Let's get it over with. I want to go home."

That afternoon Coolstone had that simple operation with that little tube placed in his lung and attached to what looked like about a gallon jug. He was wheeled back up into the ward, and as the anesthetic started wearing off, the Rock was aware of a lot of pain. His whole left side hurt. Right from his shoulder down to his littlest toe.

"A little simple operation," he saw, obviously was going to wipe him out for more than one or two days.

After three or four days of lying pretty much on his back, he finally was able to get up and walk around some, carrying his jug. On about the fifth day, the "group" entered his room again.

"Oh, no," thought Coolstone. "I don't think I am strong enough for this."

"All right," said the colonel, "we are going to take the tube out tomorrow. Now, what we think you ought to do is have the other operation now, scruff up those lung and chest walls so that they will fuse, and then you won't have to worry about this happening again. These blebs are unpredictable, and the operation will allow you to return to flying status while otherwise, you may not be able to."

Now, for the first time, Coolstone was really concerned. He longed for a cigarette. "Are you telling me," he asked the doctor, "that you don't think I can be placed on flying status like I am without that other operation? Did you find something bad on my X-ray? Is that why I can't smoke?"

"No," said the lieutenant colonel, "I tell everyone to stop smoking on general principles. But I doubt you will be released to fly again unless you have that operation."

"Get my flight surgeon," said Coolstone. "Get him up here, and if he says to have it, I'll have it. If he says not to have it, then I'm not going to have it. He's the one that decides if I am going to be on flying status or not." Coolstone was pretty sure that the Doc hadn't even taken him off yet.

"And another thing, has anyone got a cigarette?"

One of the residents fumbled in his smock pocket and silently handed a crumpled pack to the Rock.

The next day, the four from the thoracic surgery department entered his room along with Coolstone's flight surgeon. They explained to the flight surgeon what the problem was. Coolstone told his flight surgeon through a cloud of smoke that he would do whatever he thought was right.

The flight surgeon studied it for a moment or two and then said, "I'll tell you what I think you ought to do. I think you ought to get that tube out, get your clothes on, and come on home with me."

With that, Coolstone leaped out of bed, handed one doctor his jug, and to another, he said, "Get that tube out of there."

The tube was very gently removed by a very disappointed resident, and Coolstone went home.

Unbeknownst to Coolstone, while he was in the hospital, the people from his office had decided that they would assist by killin', pluckin', and guttin' the 200 chickens. Consequently, because of this great effort, above and beyond the call of duty, Coolstone could see there wasn't chicken one in his pen and that his freezer was completely full of chicken.

Two days later, he finally got back to his office and to work. A delegation came in to see him. All sections were represented. His commander led. Coolstone was advised by formal proclamation, on behalf of the killin'-pluckin'-guttin'-freezin'crew, that he was never, never again, to raise chickens unless he got their unanimous approval first. Coolstone agreed wholeheartedly.

That's a Wet Runway

The Cold Rock had just finished an exhausting, unexciting, and completely unsatisfactory two weeks in his airline job. He had read checklists, snatched and extended gear, and raised and lowered flaps at some of the finest airports in the country, all at the whim of his captain. Now he was on the way to his Guard Squadron. He was ready to do some flying himself, make all the decisions, and do it in a machine that would just flat streamline your ears when you plugged in the burners. That's what it's all about.

"Yep, pretty lucky," he thought. "And you got paid for it too." When he checked in with OPs, he was told that they had a bird that needed to be replaced at Great Falls. He would ferry one up and then bring the other back to the Squadron for an inspection. Coolstone was pleased. He would get about four hours of flying, and that would pretty much take care of the day.

"Look," said the SOF, "get up to speed on the AIF. It's been a while since you've been around. And be sure you read that new message on not landing the 101 on a wet runway."

"What do you mean?" said the Rock. "Why can't you land on a wet runway? That doesn't make sense at all."

"I guess there've been a couple of accidents and all sorts of hairy incidents since we put three-groove tires on the bird," said the SOF. "Read the AIF, and then we'll brief. OK? "

"OK," said Coolstone, and he strolled over to where the Great Book was kept.

The Rock eyeballed all the paper for a moment before he started reading. "More paper makes it safer," he said to himself. "At least someone must think so."

Sure enough, as he plowed through all the new no-nos, he ran across the one pertaining to "No 101 landings on wet runways." He finished and went for a cup of coffee. There in the coffee bar, he met Two, his fearless, irrepressible WSO.

"Understand we are headed for Great Falls and back today," said Two. "I've got the Form 70 all filled out. I've checked the charts, NOTAMS, and weather. Everything seems to be fine. There may be a few scattered showers in the area when we get there, but other than that, it looks OK."

Now, while Coolstone was somewhat thankful for the assistance, on the other hand, this was hardly "doing the whole thing himself." "What about the runway?" he asked two. "Was it wet?"

"Darned if I know," said Two. "I didn't check."

"Well," said Coolstone with a faintly superior air, "we can't land on it if it's wet, you know. New message."

"You're right," said Two. "I remember that now."

"Come on, both of you," said the SOF. "Let's get the mission briefing over with."

The pair followed him into the briefing room. The briefing was standard until they got to the weather. "Looks like you will have to find an alternate where you know the runway will be dry. Check in before let down at Great Falls and be sure that no water is on the runway there. If there is, divert right then. Have you looked for a good alternate yet?"

"Negative," said One. "Two looked at Malmstrom, but we don't have a good feel for an alternate right now."

"Well," said the SOF, "find one with good turnaround facilities, like Glasgow or Minot and have a good flight."

One and Two got the forecaster on the horn and found that Glasgow had rain, but Minot would remain loud and clear all day. They determined that it would take about 4,000 pounds from Great Falls, and, with the winds they were given, they should arrive at Malmstrom with over 6,000 pounds. "No sweat."

Preflight, start, and taxi was uneventful. They cleared last chance and lined up. As the tower released them, One was aware of that small thrill of anticipation always present when he flew fighters and which was completely absent when he was driving "the bus." He released the brakes, picked up the nose wheel steering, and plugged in the burners. "An airplane that takes off like this can't be all bad," he grinned to himself.

Two had taken over the navigation chores without being told and kept up a constant chatter on the "how goes it" information. Ground speed and fuel flow consumption were pretty much as planned, and these Two pointed out several times since he had accomplished the majority of the flight planning.

When they were about halfway to Malmstrom, One decided he had better get a check on Malmstrom weather just to be sure that the runway was still dry. The Center advised him that there was no rain reported in the area and, therefore, the runways would be dry.

As they swung another station, Two remarked again, "Right on the old money. Fuel and time. In other times I would have been navigating for Magellan or Columbus."

Coolstone Takes Flight

"Probably Columbus," said One. "I understand he got his crew out of the prisons and didn't know where he was going or where he was when he got there."

About 100 miles out of Malmstrom, One could see some pretty fair-sized buildups ahead, typical thunderstorms, even though they were pretty well isolated. He advised the Center he would hold his altitude for a while and check weather. He set up the Metro frequency, made contact, and requested current Malmstrom weather and runway conditions and Minot's weather and runway conditions.

"Thunderstorms south of Malmstrom," he was told. "No rain at the field, and the runway is dry. Glasgow is reporting showers, runway is wet, winds are high, and visibility is down in rain."

Minot was still loud and clear.

He went back to center frequency, started his descent, and switched to approach control.

During descent, he found himself well embedded in a small thunderstorm, and when he leveled at 7, he was in what had to be heavy rain.

"Approach control from Coolstone One. Check Malmstrom's weather for me, please, and get the runway conditions."

"Roger, Coolstone. Malmstrom's weather is 4500 broken, 15 miles, runway dry, thunderstorm south of the field."

Coolstone pressed on.

At about 2 to 3 miles, they broke out. One saw the runway up ahead. It was wet, wet, wet ... it glistened in the sun. Got to get out of here, he thought.

"Going around," he told radar. "Heading for Minot. Requesting flight level 370.

What's the heading?" he asked Two. "We're going to Minot."

"You've got to be kidding," said Two. But as they passed over the runway, he could see it was wet. "But it's not raining now," he told One."

You know what the message said," answered One. "What's the heading?"

"OK," said Two. "Try 060 for a starter, and I'll get you a more exact one in a minute."

One established a mil climb on 060 and saw they had about 5,800 pounds remaining.

The Center called. "Coolstone One from Great Falls Center. Level at flight level 240. You will be given a higher altitude in about 60 miles. There's an airspace reservation for refueling, and it's active at the present time."

"Roger," said One, "but I need a higher altitude ASAP. Requesting 420 when I can get it."

"How's that heading?" he asked Two. "060 about right?"

"Roger," said Two. "I'm measuring it right now. 060 looks pretty good, though."

After what seemed like an eternity, and with that little thrill of anticipation now developed nicely towards pure panic, Coolstone finally received clearance to climb to flight level 420.

"How's the fuel?" said Two. "It's going to be pretty close, isn't it? I figured that 4,000 pounds without a descent and climb."

"I won't know until we get level," said One. "And get a ground speed check and the fuel flow." He leveled at 420 and set power. Fuel flow was 4,500, fuel on board 4,500, and fuel required 4,500.

"It is going to be close," said One to Two. "The way I figure it, we will flame out on the runway ... if we're lucky."

"That's pretty close," said Two.

"Let's see if we can find something closer." said One. "Check the charts."

"Roger," said Two, and he immediately had a problem. Southwest - right side up, northwest - upside down. Southwest - upside down, northwest - right side up. Let's see, Two said to himself, we're about here. We could go to... no, too far. Ah-h-h, how about... no, that's too far. "Now that we've come this far," he told One, "Minot is about as good as anything."

One had been going through the same exercise with the charts. When he finally did get on the right side, right side up, he couldn't see a thing that looked like it might work as a 101 airport. "In fact," he thought to himself, "if I were trying to pick the most isolated spot in the United States for airports, it would be in this area." But the fuel was low so, why not Minot?

He checked the fuel again. It was going down at an extremely alarming rate.

"Hello, Great Falls Center. This is Coolstone One. I'll have emergency fuel when I arrive at Minot. "I hope," he added to himself. "I'll need a straight in and will have to land first crack."

"Roger, Tombstone One, from Great Falls. Understand you are declaring an emergency for fuel. Is that correct?"

"That's Coolstone One, Center, not Tombstone One, and, no, I'm not declaring an emergency." Then he checked his fuel again. He couldn't believe the rate it was going down.

"Center from Tomb ... er, Coolstone One. I am declaring an emergency for fuel."

"Roger, Tomb ... er, Coolstone. Descend at your own discretion. Minot is 85 miles, 065 your position. We have advised the tower of your difficulties."

As the fuel quantity passed through 1,000 pounds, One pulled off the power and started down. He saw that he was still using about 2,400 pounds per hour.

"Not going to make it," he mumbled to Two, who had become extremely quiet ..... except for his breathing. "Going to stopcock one," he said.

"Roger," said Two weakly.

The fuel quantity seemed to hold at about 800 pounds. One convinced himself that it was right and was just playing catch-up because it had been going down too fast up to the point they had started to descend.

"Look," he said to Two. "Check pins out, tighten your harness, and run through your ejection procedures. If the engine quits, go. Don't wait for me to tell you because when it quits, we are going to be right out there on final."

"Roger," said Two, "but I'd rather land with the bird on the runway if it's just the same with you," trying a weak little joke.

One checked his pins out, tightened his straps, and glanced quickly down to ensure that nothing loose was going to get in the way of an ejection.

Coolstone Takes Flight

"Boy," he thought to himself, "the way I have screwed this one up, if I do eject, the chute probably won't open, and I don't even have a will."

Center turned him over to the tower, and the Rock checked in.

"Minot from Coolstone One, about ten out on final, will be coming straight in. Please keep the active clear. I won't be able to take it around."

"Roger, Tombstone One. You are cleared straight in, and do you want the emergency equipment standing by?"

"If I get that close, I won't need them," said the Rock with ersatz bravado.

It was coming up on decision time. First, when to put the gear out. Second, when to really start descending for the actual landing. He had leveled at about 300 feet. He had the whole thing to himself now. Two was very quiet. He was approaching the field boundary, and he started down again. He glanced at his fuel. It was still 800 pounds, but that had to be wrong. He dropped the gear and, through habit, dropped the flaps also. He was horrified. He had to bring the power in all the way before he got the flaps back up. He was over the overrun. Now he dumped the flaps, flared, and landed. He got the chute out and looked at the fuel gauge. It was reading flat zero. He turned off the runway, and his last engine flamed out. He rolled to a stop and sat there for a minute before he had nerve enough to try his voice.

"Tower, this is Tombstone One, flamed out. Would you send someone out to put the pins in and tow us to the ramp?"

"Roger, Tombstone," said the Tower. "Transient alert is on its way." Then the Rock had a horrible thought. The nose gear will collapse; you aren't supposed to shut down before the pins are in.

He remained fully tense until the transient alert people finally got the nose pin installed. Then he and Two just sat in the cockpit for a few minutes. They enjoyed the sunshine and the beautiful view of Minot Air Force Base. With his adrenalin level slowly subsiding, One thought to himself, "That 727 is looking better all the time."

Coolstone Plays Pick a Chart

"Just give me Operations," Coolstone hummed softly under his breath, "way out on a lonely atoll." He looked out the window again for about the tenth time, and the volume of his voice increased slightly as he added, "For I am too young to die, I just want to go home."

He was worried. Eight 106's and their intrepid crews were standing by for a division exercise. The rain was not mainly on the plain but right here on the old home patch. Showers had been passing over the base as forecasted for the past three hours.

The Old Man was on leave, and as Operations Officer, the Rock was holding a rather soggy bag. Everyone knows that paper loses its strength alarmingly as it becomes damp.

Specifically, the problem that kept nagging away at his peace of mind concerned the condition of the runway. He had played "pick-a-chart" until he really didn't know how much runway it would take to get stopped with a bag failure. Before the last supplement had come out with all the James jazz on it, he had had no problem. He could have just used the dash-one, and that would have been the end of it.

Just for kicks, he tried it again. With a thousand-foot touchdown, zero wind, a wet runway, and no chute, using the dash-one chart, he came up with a total requirement of 9,100 feet.

I've just got to quit fooling with that chart, he told himself and burped gently. It must be acid indigestion, no doubt. The runway was 8,700 feet to the barrier. He turned back to the front of the book and the supplement with the James Brake Decelerometer readings. This is better, he told himself. Let's see ... with a dry runway, the rollout would be 5,000 feet. Then I run up to the 11-13 line on the chart, and it looks like about 6,700 feet. With 1,000 for touchdown, I've still got 1,000 feet to spare.

It sounded fine to him, and the supplement stated that it should be used, but the chart had been available for only a couple of weeks, and this was the first time the runway had been anything but dry. The numbers the chart came out with looked good, but unfortunately, his experience on this runway when it was wet led him to expect a rollout in excess of any 6,700 feet. In fact, with a drier runway than they had right now, birds with drag chute failures had performed all sorts of interesting tricks on the runway before the pilots had finally acquiesced and taken the barrier.

Technique, maybe, but into the barrier, they'd gone. He went back to his seat by the window, looked out, and hummed again, "Just give me Operations..." It was really pouring now. The odds were that there wouldn't be any chute failures, but if they did occur, well, at least he had one chart on his side... "way out on a lonely atoll."

His rendition was interrupted by one of his flight leaders. "It looks pretty slick out there," he said. "A drag chute failure would probably put us right into the barrier. The book says . . . .."

"Hello, Sector? This is Coolstone One. I'm Ops Officer over at Nervous Hotel. Say, we've been checking our landing roll charts and we don't think we'll be able to get the bird... What's that? Scramble? But... but... but..."

"I am reasonably familiar with what the book says," snapped the Rock, "but if you will look and see what the supplement says, we would be just fine."

"How about those barrier engagements last month?" asked the flight leader. "The runway wasn't even wet." Then he added, more to himself than to Coolstone, "You can find a chart for anything these days. Just pick one."

"Well," said the Rock, making a decision that he had been playing with for some time, "I'll call the Group Commander." He walked over to the hot room and said to the operator, "See if you can get the colonel on the phone."

He waited a moment, and the operator handed him the receiver. The colonel was on the line.

"This is Coolstone, Colonel. I don't think we should take this one with the runway the way it is. If we have a bag failure, I'm pretty sure we'll probably have a barrier engagement. If we have two bag failures in a row, I'm pretty sure we'll have an accident. What do you think about canceling out until the showers get by and the runway dries out a skosh?"

"What does the book say?" asked the Colonel.

"Well," Coolstone answered somewhat reluctantly. "One chart says we are all right, but the other one says we'll go off the end. You know, Colonel, the last time it rained, we had two chute failures and a barrier engagement with both of them. Of course," added the Rock, "I guess we could recover somewhere else, but that always causes lots of problems."

"I agree," said the Colonel. "We don't want to get scattered out. Stand by, and I'll check with the Sector."

If Coolstone could have had his say at this point, he would have scratched all flying until the squadron commander returned, regardless of runway condition.

"What did he say?" asked the flight leader.

"Stand by one was the word," said the Rock.

"Coolstone," called the Duty Officer. "We have just been moved up to five…"

"All of the birds?"

"Rog. All of them on five."

The announcement was made over the squadron P.A. system. Pilots interrupted Ping-Pong games, television viewing, and other endeavors designed to improve the mind long enough to get their equipment together so that they would be ready to go.

The Rock was Number One to go, so he decided he had better tidy up a bit also.

"Phone," someone said to him.

"Coolstone here," he said into the instrument.

"Rog," said a strange voice to him. "You are the commander, I presume."

"Just in his absence," emphasized the Rock. "Just in his absence. I am really the Ops Officer."

"Understand that you don't want to fly them today. Is that right?"

"Yes, sir, that's right. To whom am I talking, please?"

"This is the Weapons Director. What's your problem?"

"Well," said Coolstone. "With a drag chute failure and the runways as wet as they are, I don't think we can get them stopped. I guess you had better cancel us out until the showers pass. Weather says we should be getting clearing conditions in about four hours."

"It sure takes the heart out of our exercise," said the Weapons Director. "The targets should be coming in any time now, and we were counting on taking tactical action with you people first. Are you sure you can't go?"

"I don't think we had better," said the Rock reluctantly, and he knew there was a subtle aura of pressure in the Weapons Director's remarks. Then he firmed up his refusal, straightened his shoulders, and said, "No, count us out. I'm sorry."

"Look," said the W.D. "How about standing by for a moment before you go off readiness?'

"Well," said the Rock. "Well... O.K. We'll stand by for a minute or two."

He had barely replaced the receiver when the Group Commander came into Operations. "I talked to the Sector,'" said the Colonel as he approached the Rock. "They were mad as Hell, but I told them it was your show." (Coolstone couldn't help but notice the emphasis on the phrase, "your show.")

"You know," added the Colonel. "According to the new Safety of Flight Supplement in the front of the dash-one, you should get stopped just fine, even with a drag chute failure on ice. The James reading is 11 today."

"Yes, sir, I know, but I am convinced that that chart for all configurations is generally optimistic. Our experience is that the dash-one chart, while perhaps too pessimistic, is more accurate because there is usually a directional control problem associated with a really slick runway. You just can't brake all the time like it says in the book. Besides, the last time it rained, we had ..."

But he was interrupted by the hot room operator. "Sector on, Major." said the operator.

"Coolstone One," he spoke into the instrument.

"This is the Battle Staff Commander," said a rather authoritative voice in his ear. "I have the dash-one for the six in front of me. Now, you have 9,000 feet, the winds are variable, but let's use zero wind, three thousand pounds ... it's about 75 degrees there, isn't it?"

Coolstone quickly answered, "Yes, sir, it is."

"I come up with 6500 feet, using the RCR of 11. What's the problem?"

"Well," said Coolstone rather weakly, "in the first place, I have to figure at least 1,000-foot touch down; that leaves me with 8,000, and then, if you use the chart in the back of the book for a no-chute landing, actually it shows about 8,100 feet for the roll-out. I feel this is a more reliable figure simply because the last time it rained, we ran a couple into the barrier with chute failures, and I don't believe the runway was as slick as it is right now."

"Well," said the Colonel. "It says right here in the Safety of Flight Supplement that this is the chart to use. Why are you using the other one?" Then he added rather quickly, "Now, don't get me wrong. It's your show. I'll go along with whatever you decide. I just wanted to know if your squadron doesn't participate in this exercise, it will be a great disappointment. The targets are already committed."

"I know that, sir," said Coolstone. He hesitated for a moment. "Let me run it over one more time and see what type of distance I can come up with. Maybe," he added, hedging a bit, "the true distance is somewhere between the two figures."

It was a compromise that he didn't want to make. Oh boy, he thought, I've had about all the squadron commanding I can use right now.

"Well," said the voice on the phone. "See what you can come up with, and in the meantime, we'll continue to show your eight sixes on five."

"Well, sir," said the Rock, dragging his feet, "I'd rather not," and he looked pleadingly at his group commander, who was just as intently studying the slightly stained ceiling tiles above the Rock's head, as if he was considering some rather extensive staff action concerning it.

Coolstone gave it up. "OK, sir, I'll call you right back and let you know."

He handed the receiver to the hot room operator, reached for his dog-eared, dirty dash-one . . . and at this point, the world of Coolstone became unglued.

The scramble horn blew... the loud speaker was calling off the scramble information... his pilots were on their way... and he, who was supposed to be their leader, was standing there holding his dash-one.

He fought an inclination to scream at them, "Come back, come back." But the horn finally got to him also. Just too many years on alert had conditioned his reflexes.

As he ran for his bird, he rationalized, "Our drag chute failure rate is good anyway."

About an hour and a half later, the Rock was recovering his flight on GCA. He felt pretty darned good. There are quite a few MA's left in the old boy yet, he told himself. He had salvaged one that was real tough. He knew the troops couldn't have missed seeing it. As near as he could tell, the whole squadron had done really well.

Coolstone Takes Flight

The flight was turned on final. As they let down to their approach altitude, they broke out. While the rain was definitely still there, the visibility wasn't bad. At GCA minimums, he started his flare and brought the power back. He touched down just fine at about 1200 feet. He had carried a few extra knots for his wingman, and he waited until he heard Two call drag chute.

Coolstone then deployed his chute. "One potato, two potato, three potato," he counted to himself, as he always did, as he waited for his chute to deploy. "Four potato, five potato." He started saying the words loudly to himself as he waited to feel the chute's decelerating force.

Then, over the radio, he heard, "Coolstone from Mobile. You have a streamer."

He dropped the nose, hit the idle thrust switch, and brought the brakes in real lightly, he thought.

The bird did one of its tricks to the left immediately. He got off the brakes, and with elevon, rudder, and nose wheel steering along with right brake, he tried to get the bird straight with the world.

Slowly .. ever go slowly ... the bird began to straighten. He hit the brakes again. The drag to the left which followed was identical to the first.

He came off the brakes, and this time, even with a fully deflected nose wheel, the six did not respond. Hook, he thought, wildly pressing the button. The end was coming, and all too quickly.

He hit the right brake, held it to the skid point, then into the skid. Slowly the nose started to come around. Then, as he overcontrolled, the bird showed him a trick to the right. It showed it to him so rapidly that he couldn't get the nose wheel steering in phase. He was approaching the barrier, so he released the left brake, still sliding straight but pointed to the right, and engaged the barrier at about 80 knots. As he did so, the aircraft straightened itself out real fast, and the right wing started dropping.

"Major Coolstone... Your drag chute didn't work eh? Looks like you were on the right chart after all. Too bad you could not make up your mind."

The Rock finally came to rest, sitting at a list of about 10 degrees. Must have blown the tire, he thought.

He stopcocked, unstrapped, got the canopy opened, and tried to deplane in some semblance of an orderly fashion since an impressive group of fire troops were congregating around the aircraft.

He hit the ground, tried to recover his composure for a moment, then reluctantly looked at the right main gear. It's crumped, he thought, because he saw it was spraddled outboard, way out of shape, resting against the drop tank. But then his blood pressure became normal again, as he saw that there was no real damage to the bird.

The staff car was coming across the field, and Coolstone really wanted to hide. Then, shuffling his feet slightly, he waited for the Colonel.

Coolstone Takes Flight

All too soon, the Old Man arrived. "It looks like you were right," offered the Colonel. "That other chart was the one you should have used and stuck to."

"Sir," said Coolstone, his voice reflecting little of the temperature rise he felt, and only the most discerning would have noticed it, "It was almost worth it to get us all on the same page."

"I could just scream"

Scram Bell

♦

Coolstone was on alert. He had just received the 2100 weather - they gave him 200 feet overcast, one-quarter mile visibility in rain and fog, and no suitable alternates within 300 miles. He figured it was going to be a pretty quiet night.

Coolstone got himself a cup of coffee, picked up a rather racy pocketbook, and slouched down comfortably in a big, overstuffed chair. He hadn't finished the first chapter of his book before the telephone rang. It was the GCI site.

"Coolstone, this is Fallout. We have an aircraft executing an emergency pattern approximately 100 miles to the northeast. He's squawking "Mayday," and we're checking with ATC now to see if they have someone overdue."

"That's nice," said Coolstone. "Be sure and keep me posted. I hope he makes it."

"You're not getting the idea, Coolstone," said the Fallout controller. "We are also getting scramble clearance for you. He's probably on top, and after you make the intercept, bring him back into your base. It's the nearest one to him that has adequate recovery facilities."

"Hold it a minute, Fallout. Don't you know what our weather is? How in hell can I bring him back in here? I'm not too sure I can get myself in. Isn't there any place else we can take him?"

"Look, Coolstone - the nearest place we can take him where there is good weather is over 300 miles away. Bring him back to your own base. We'll have to take a chance on making it. Okay, the boss has approved the scramble, and we have clearance for you. Get going."

The loud, continuous honk of the scramble horn began, accompanying the controller's last words. It was his conditioned reflexes, Coolstone guessed, because, whether he wanted to go or not, he found himself climbing into the cockpit of his F-106, wildly strapping in, then making the start and pulling out of the hangar. He lined himself up on the runway, took a deep breath, released the brakes, and hit the burner. Fifteen seconds later, he was in the murk, cursing the pilots of the aircraft he was after. The Cold Rock switched to the GCI channel, made radio contact, and picked up his first vector. The controller called him again.

"Coolstone from Fallout. ATC advised that they have a T-33 they haven't heard from in about an hour. They figure that, with the time involved, this should be our boy. He filed for 33 Angels, so level at 33 and remain at Buster."

"Roger, Fallout. This is Coolstone. Will level at 33 Angels and continue at Buster. I was on top at 26,000."

Coolstone Takes Flight

Coolstone leveled at 33, and the controller continued to give him slight heading corrections and called off the range periodically. Finally, the range was 20 miles at 12 o'clock.

"No joy," said Coolstone as he concentrated his attention on his radar scope.

At 12 miles, Coolstone got contact and locked on. He advised the controller and, at the same time, noted he had over 200 knots of overtaking speed. He dropped the boards and throttled back, glancing out of the cockpit periodically as he tried to pick up the navigation lights of the emergency aircraft. He got a visual, finally, and slowly moved in. As he neared, he saw it was a T-33, flying very slowly. He joined up on the wing of the T- bird and reported to GCI. He could see two heads in the cockpit, but they weren't looking in his direction. He turned his aircraft slightly away and moved ahead. Then the pilot saw him and promptly joined up on his wing.

"Fallout from Coolstone. Got the T-bird on my wing. Give me pigeons to home plate and advise the base that I want a minimum-fuel GCI- GCA, which includes a minimum of turns. There's no telling how much fuel this T-33 has remaining."

"Roger, Coolstone, nice work. Weather tells us that the ceiling is now 300 obscured, with about one-half mile viz. We've already checked with

ATC on the T-bird's fuel. They tell us that, according to his flight plan, he should have about three-quarters of an hour remaining."

About 40 miles out, GCI gave Coolstone instructions to start his penetration. The T-33 stuck like glue to his wing. In fact, the Cold Rock figured he couldn't have lost the T-33 if he had done an Immelmann. They made it down to the GCA pattern and, with a minimum of gyrations, Coolstone found himself on the final. He slowed the wedge to 170, which he knew was way too fast for the T-33, but that was as slow as he could go. At GCA minimums, the approach lights came into view, and as Coolstone looked, he saw that the T-33 was taking spacing, so he added power and made a missed approach.

"Hello, GCA. This is Coolstone. When the T-33 has landed, how about bringing me around for a full stop."

"Roger, Coolstone. Climb to 4000 and give us a call when steady on 130."

Coolstone was about to answer when he was suddenly jabbed with a red light - AC power failure. Quickly, he reset the AC generator. The warning light was still on. Without hesitation, he selected the emergency AC power and called GCA.

"I've had an AC power failure, and I'm working on emergency AC power now."

"Roger," said GCA. "Do you wish to declare an emergency?"

Coolstone didn't answer, for an oil warning light had just come on. With his luck, he wasn't surprised. In fact, he had rather suspected that the AC power had failed because the engine was losing oil.

"GCA from Coolstone. I'm declaring an emergency. I've got an oil warning light on. Give me as tight a pattern as you can."

"Okay, Coolstone. Turn to three zero degrees for dogleg to final. Perform landing cockpit checks at your discretion. We have advised the tower to alert the crash crew."

"Roger," said Coolstone. "If the engine starts to get rough. I'll pull up and eject."

GCA was fumbling for words --- he really didn't have a reply to that. Coolstone watched his engine instruments almost as much as he was watching his flight instruments. In fact, he found that weather flying wasn't bothering him one bit - the gauges were followed automatically. But that pair of red lights was giving him fits. He was sure that he would never make it to the runway - his luck just wasn't that good. He cursed the pilots of the T-33 once again and fumbled for his low-level lanyard. He found that it was still connected from the takeoff. He then felt for his leg straps to be sure they were connected, for he had been known to forget them and find them only after he was unstrapping at the end of a flight. His seat pins were out, and he figured that if he kept his speed up now, he would have as good a chance as anyone if he had to eject.

He didn't even remember getting on the final, but he was there somehow and decided to hold his gear until he started to descend - he just couldn't bring himself to put it down. He knew he'd have to add power, and he didn't want to touch the throttle. He started his descent and still held the gear. At one mile out, he threw it down and held his breath as he brought the power back in. Nothing unusual at all. The engine was still smooth, and the temperature was normal. He picked up the field visually, finally pulled off power to lower the airspeed, saw he had it made, heaved a sigh of relief, and stopcocked the throttle. The landing wasn't the best he'd ever made, but it felt like the best.

They towed the aircraft off the runway, and it wasn't far, for he'd used most of it. Then he got a ride back over to the alert hangar. He went upstairs and poured himself a cup of coffee, having much difficulty getting the coffee into the cup rather than on the floor. He made several attempts at lighting a cigarette and found that he was using the wrong end of the match.

Two lieutenants came into the alert hangar and asked for the pilot who had brought the T-33 in. Coolstone was pointed out to them. As they came up to him, one of them said. "We sure thank you. We lost our radio and didn't know what to do, so we decided we would circle and get intercepted."

"You lost all your radios?" Coolstone asked, with anger creeping into his voice. "You couldn't talk to anyone, but your navigation radios were working okay, I suppose."

The lieutenant backed up a bit. "Well, yes - we had our navigation aids, but we couldn't talk to anyone."

"You couldn't have gone to your destination, I suppose," said Coolstone. "You couldn't have gone to your destination and made a letdown there - oh, no! - you had to come down right now, with me bringing you, because you couldn't talk to anyone. There are provisions for radio loss, you know."

"Yes," said the lieutenant, "but the ceiling at our destination was forecast to be down maybe to 1500 feet and five miles with rain, and..." but Coolstone cut him short.

"What do you think it was here?" His voice was almost a shout.

"Well, I didn't really notice - it was pretty low, but I was busy flying your wing. It worked out all right - I picked up the lights okay."

"GET OUT OF THIS BUILDING -- NOW!" Coolstone roared.

As the two stumbled down the stairs, they were talking. "There's no figuring some guys," said one. "You try to thank them, and they get all upset."

"Oh, well," said the other. "Let's forget it. If he doesn't want to be thanked, he doesn't want to be thanked. Say, where's town, and what time does the floor show start?"

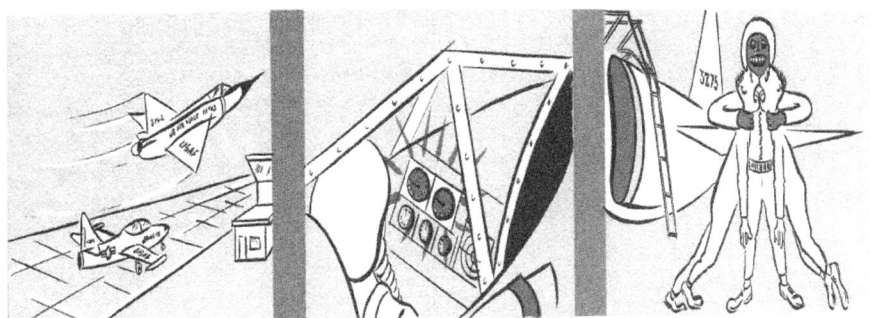

Holiday At Delta Dump

"Tann, this is Pete; how's it going, boy?"

"Fine, Pete. How goes it with you at Bombers' Roost?"

Oh, so-so. Say, the reason I called - did you see the paper this morning? Our PIO types had a little news in ... thought you might be interested."

"Not really, Pete. What was it about?"

"Well, heh, heh." (A real nasty note to that laugh, thought Tann.) "Well, one of our bombers landed at one of your fighter bases down the road a piece, and you'll never believe this, but they kidnapped one of your personnel right out of your max security area."

"What's this?" said Tann, coming out of his seat. "Who was it?" he shouted into the phone, "and where is he now?"

"It was a Lieutenant Curtiss LeMoose, and he's in our max security area right now."

"What do you mean, LeMoose? What kind of a name is that?"

"That's what the boys call him. Actually, he's just an old moth-eaten moose head, but we've got him. Pretty funny. It just confirmed what we always knew about you fighter types - a little light-headed. Short of a gas attack, you couldn't get it away from us, no matter what you did. We've got security, boy, security with a capital 'C.' But you're welcome to try any time. If your pilots have any esprit, that is."

Tann was reduced to a quivering eagle; he was choked with rage. He had to wait a moment before he could talk; then, with his voice carefully controlled, he said, "You mean that moose is on your base right now, just next door to us?"

"Right, Tann. In fact, you can read all of the details in this morning's paper. As I said, our PIO had a lot of fun with the item. Even mentions your name as commander of the wing that got robbed. Kinda offsets that PIO release your people made on the Community Chest - you 100%, us 70%, and with the fact left out that we gave 15,000 bucks, and your small group just gave twelve hundred. I had to wait a little while, but I think we're even now."

The line was silent.

"Are you still there, Tann?" Again, there was silence.

Then Tann said, "We'll get that moose, Pete, right out of your mole hole if necessary, and we'll do it within two weeks."

"Sure you will, Tann, sure you will. When I capture your troops trying, don't write me; write the Pentagon for their return. Heh, heh, heh."

Coolstone Takes Flight

Tann slammed the receiver down.

"GET ME A MORNING PAPER," he roared to his secretary.

The Colonel had called him and told him that he wanted to see him immediately, and Coolstone knew this to be an ominous portend. His fears were further confirmed when the secretary told him to go right on in, that Colonel Tann was waiting for him.

He entered the room, threw a salute, and started to report, but Colonel Tann said briskly, "Shut the door, sit down, and listen real good."

"Yes, sir; yes, sir," said Coolstone.

The Colonel dropped his voice, leaned across his desk, and his steel blue eyes pierced Coolstone's as he said, "Have you ever heard of Lieutenant Curtiss LeMoose?"

The Rock shook his head wordlessly, but the small hairs on the back of his neck raised slightly.

"The enemy has it," whispered the Colonel. "He is gloating about it, and you have exactly two weeks to get it. Use all of the resources of this command you need, but get LeMoose."

Coolstone wanted to ask questions, but from the Colonel's attitude, he could see that he had just been dismissed.

Back at the squadron, the Rock called for all the pilots. When they were settled in the briefing room, and the doors were closed, he looked at them and said quietly, "What goes on in this room during this meeting is highly classified. Now, do any of you know a Lieutenant LeMoose?"

There were a few snickers, but no one looked real enlightened. A voice from the back of the room said, "I know a General Le ...."

"Never mind," said the Rock. "It's a lieutenant I'm talking about. Colonel Tann is somewhat disturbed about this young man, and he wants him, wants him real bad."

But to himself, Coolstone wondered for the first time, didn't the Colonel use the word "it" in conjunction with the "lieutenant?"

"Look," said Coolstone to the pilots. "I'll lay it on the line. I need help. He gave me just two weeks to get LeMoose back. He said the enemy had it."

There was a moment of silence while the pilots looked at him as if he had lost his mind.

Then one of them jumped to his feet, knocked over an ashtray, and said, "I've got it; I've got it. It was in the paper this morning. The boys from the Wobbler Squadron across the way stole some moose head from one of the fighter squadrons. They made a big issue about it - PIO releases, the whole bit."

"You mean the bomber squadron got a moose head, and now it's over at their base? Well, we have two weeks to get it out of there. Boy, we are in trouble. We don't even know for sure where it is."

One of the captains got up. "Say," he said, "One of those Wobbler Squadron commanders lives right across the street from me. I'll work on him. Maybe I can find out where old LeMoose is."

"That would help," said Coolstone weakly. "We should at least know where he is if we're going to get him." Then he added, "We've got to come up with some ideas, fellows, and I'll be the first to admit I don't have any. The Colonel gave me access to all of the resources of this command to get that moose head back."

Now, the Flight Surgeon was also attending the meeting, and this was a very fortunate occasion because the Doc was extremely intelligent. In fact, he had the only real idea that the 17 or 18 of them could come up with. "Look," he said, "I've got kind of a plan. It's still a little sketchy, but let me run it by you."

"What, what, what?" said Coolstone, ready to accept anything.

The Doc briefly outlined what he had in mind. Then he said, "It will take four or five of us, but once we find out where old LeMoose is, we can give it a try."

"Terrific idea," said Coolstone. "Now, I'm looking for volunteers. Let's face it, fellows, if we get caught, we are going to be in serious, dire, deep trouble. From what I have heard about their security, we might even get shot, so I can't tell anyone to take this trip with me. I'll just have to ask for volunteers, preferably single men."

Coolstone was pleased to see that to a man, the squadron pilots all raised their hands. He picked out three of the single ones and then said, "O.K. As soon as we find out where that moose is, we'll work out the details of our plan."

It was three days later that the captain who was attempting to locate the moose reported back to Coolstone that he had found it. "It's hanging on the wall of the aircrew lounge in the max security area," he said. "It looks like an impossible deal. We'll never get it out of there. I almost got captured going in, and I was with the squadron commander."

Coolstone groaned. "Worse than I ever suspected," he said. "Draw me a map. Show me exactly where it is and how we get there."

He then called the select little group together, three of his pilots, the Doc, and himself. "Look," said Coolstone. "This is going to be a little harder than we originally thought. The first thing we've got to do is quit using names. As of right now, we're Stoned One, Two, Three, Four, and Five. We'll always call ourselves by our numbers from now on."

"How about using Tombed?" said one of the men.

"No, that gives it a nasty connotation." Then the Rock continued. "All right, fellows. Here's where LeMoose is, right in the middle of the max security area."

"I quit," Three, Four, and Five said as a man.

"Come on now. We've at least got to try." He discussed the details of the plan and the physical layout of the bomber base security area. "We'll do it at night at about 12:30, so it will be dark."

The group quailed as they heard the details.

"We'll never make it," one of them mumbled.

Coolstone continued, "Leave all personal effects at home, rings, watches, billfolds, shot records, prayer books, dog tags, and so on. We'll get flashlights from Supply, and Doc'll take care of the uniforms."

At the end of the discussion, it was noted by some that Coolstone was tending to talk out of the side of his mouth, slouch his shoulders, cast his eyes about furtively, and assume some of the other less desirable characteristics of the pocketbook secret service heroes. The Doc also noted the phenomena and identified it as a "Bond" syndrome.

At Midnight Wednesday, the group individually and quietly gathered at the infirmary. Not a light was showing. Coolstone checked each one in as he arrived - Stoned Two, Three, Four, and Five. They were all there. Doc was "Two."

"Look, Two," said Coolstone, "Are you sure the uniforms will fit?"

"No sweat," said Doc. "We've got about 25 to choose from here."

The uniforms they were talking about were obviously medical jackets, shirts, and so on.

"Now, look," said Coolstone, as he saw Three, Four, and Five putting their rank on their jackets, "we can't all be Docs. Somebody is going to have to be corpsmen."

There was a little grumbling, but finally, they convinced Three, Four, and Five that they were going to have to be the corpsmen.

They went out the back of the infirmary, got in an ambulance, started it up, and headed for the nearby bomber base. With just the red light flashing, they were waved through by the AP at the main gate.

They turned off the flashing light and cruised slowly while following the map provided to them by their undercover agent until they approached the first security gate to the flight line.

At this point, they took a deep collective breath, turned on the flashing red light and the siren, and headed for the gate. They were waved through, to their great relief, without any hesitation, but they still had almost two miles of driving to go yet before they would arrive at the max security area, and there was something about sneaking around in the middle of the night with the siren on and a red light flashing that was very trying.

While they were driving along parallel to the taxiways and parking areas, Five, who was at the wheel, glanced in the rear-view mirror and gasped. "They're forming a convoy behind us."

Sure enough, when they looked out the back window, they saw that a convoy was indeed forming behind them.

"How many cars?" squeaked Coolstone. "It looks like two trucks full of men, a staff car, a couple of Air Force pickups, and, yep, just now, one of those great big cherry pickers joined up."

"We've had it," said Coolstone.

"Had it," echoed Three, Four, and Five in unison.

"Do you suppose they'll let us smoke before they shoot us or get a last meal at least?" said Four.

But the Doc wasn't quite so willing to give up. "Look," he said, "This could be SOP. Let's stop. Let me do the talking, and you four don't let a word out of you."

He stopped the ambulance and got out. The staff car drove up beside them, and a bird colonel got out of it.

"Where's the crash?" asked the colonel excitedly. "What kind of aircraft is it? I'm the Base Commander."

"Crash?" said the Doc. "There was no crash, sir. We just had a report that there was a man injured near the readiness building. We haven't been able to get that confirmed, but we started down immediately."

"Fine," said the colonel. "I like the way you medics operate fast and timely. I'll lead you down there." He bounced back into the staff car and raced off with the ambulance behind him, two AP vehicles behind the ambulance, two trucks full of men from the crash squadron behind the AP cars, and one large mobile crane behind the two trucks. Numerous red lights were flashing, and all vehicles with sirens were using them very well.
"You're a genius, Two," said the Rock, "a real genius. This way, we'll get led right into the area."

"And then what do we do?" said Three.

"How are we going to shake this convoy? I wish I was home."

They arrived at the max security gate and stopped. The guard told the colonel, who in turn told the Doc that no one required an ambulance thereabouts. "It might have been over at the shops," said the colonel. "We'll head for there."

They went over to the shops -- the whole convoy, but for some strange reason, they were also unable to find anyone who was in need of medical attention.

At this point, the colonel apologized to the doctor. "Apparently, it was just a false alarm," he said, "and I'll tell you one thing, Doctor. I'll see that it doesn't happen again. I run a tight base here, and I'll trace this down."

"Yes, sir," said the Doctor. "You are really on your toes; I can tell that." Without incident but with considerable high-pitched conversation, Coolstone and his group returned to their base. Back at the infirmary, once again, they discussed their failure.

"Our basic plan is solid enough," said the Doctor, "but apparently, the bomber boys make up a convoy at the slightest sound of a siren, so we've got to work something else out."

"You mean do it again?" gasped one of the members of the raiding party. "Not me; I've had it. Find yourself another boy."

"Oh, come on now," said the Doc. "That wasn't so bad."

"No, no," said Coolstone, trying to muster up some strength in his own voice. "It was close, but it wasn't so bad." They were all quiet for a moment.

"I've got an idea," said the Rock, and he outlined his plan.

Even the two or three who had become rather cool to the operation had to agree that this new modification to the original plan was indeed brilliant.

"Tomorrow night then, fellows; 2330, same place. Our diversion will take place at 0130, which will allow us time to get in position."

Coolstone Takes Flight

The next night there were few words as the group formed up and changed uniforms, not even an argument about who was to be the doctor. They knew what to do; they were well-trained, experienced, and cool. Their actions were quick and limited to only those absolutely necessary. It was an efficient group, with obvious confidence in their ability and their plans.

They moved the ambulance quietly off the base and proceeded as they had done the previous night. Only this time, after they had entered the bomber base, they proceeded to a warehouse area near the first flight line security gate. There they parked behind one of the warehouses, turned off their lights, and waited. At precisely 0130, over the emergency radio, they heard the crash alarm sound. They saw the crash trucks and ambulances come out of the barns, form up, and start for the flight line.

As the convoy pulled past them and entered the gate, they tacked onto the rear. Coolstone's group couldn't help but admire the efficiency of the bomber crash rescue operation. After moving through the gate, the convoy turned left and headed for the flight line, where obviously an aircraft emergency was in progress. As Coolstone and his group went through the gate, they turned right with their lights off.

"It must have been some emergency he declared," said Coolstone.

"He said he was going to tell them he had a fire in the cockpit," said Two.

"It's working, whatever he said, and I told him to keep airborne as long as he could, so that crash convoy would stay in position and out of our hair," said the Rock. Then he added, "every time they look at one of those Sixes, they think it's going to explode anyhow, so they won't be paying much attention to us."

They drove along in silence until they reached the maximum-security area. As they neared it, they turned on the siren and red light. To their relief, it was a different guard from the night before. He took a quick look at them, then waived them through without comment.

The Doc got out of the ambulance, two of the pilots followed him with the stretcher, and Coolstone followed the stretcher carrying an impressive-looking medical kit with red crosses all over it. Five remained in the ambulance driver's seat. Although the guard watched them curiously, he made no effort to stop them or even question them.

Following their map, they entered the building, went upstairs, and found the lounge, which was totally black. With judicial use of their flashlights, they examined the walls. Sure enough, there was LeMoose, moth-eaten, scarred, and obviously the victim of many wars, but to them, it looked beautiful. They went to work. In less than two minutes, they had removed the moose from the wall. They put it on the stretcher, covered it with sheets, and started out of the room. But to their extreme horror, the horns wouldn't go through the door. There was a moment of supreme panic. They turned it sideways, they turned it backward, they turned it slaunchwise and diagonally, but the horns would not go through the door.

"Get a saw," said Coolstone, "Or break them off." And he wasn't talking out of the side of his mouth now.

"Wait a minute; wait a minute," said the Doc. "Let's not panic now. We're in too deep."

Coolstone Takes Flight

"Too late," said one of the pilots. "I'm panicked."

"Now, look," said Doc. "Let's take the door off the hinges, and maybe it will go through then."

Coolstone fished out a screwdriver, and the job was accomplished in just 30 seconds. With a slight turn, the moose head came through the door. Carefully they put the door back on its hinges.

"Cover him up now, fellows," said the Doc, "and kind of walk to the side of him when we go by the guard, so he can't see that rack."

Downstairs they went out of the building, quickly loaded the moose, and as they passed through the gates with the light flashing and the siren on, Coolstone shouted to the guard, "He hurt himself going through a door."

They headed for the first security gate, and the guard waved them through, obviously thinking that they were part of the earlier emergency. They turned off the light and siren and successfully passed through the base entrance and out on the highway. Not a word had been spoken since they left the max security gate.

Finally, the Doc lit a cigarette, exhaled a great cloud of smoke, and said, "You know, I didn't sleep too well last night."

Colonel Tann had been invited to attend the morning briefing. He had just entered the room, and all the pilots were still standing at attention.

"At ease; at ease," he said and walked purposefully to the front. As he approached the briefing platform, the group of five standing on it moved apart so that LeMoose was visible. The Colonel stopped in mid-step. A smile slowly manifested itself across his features. Some said later that they had never seen him smile before.

"You got it!" he shouted. Then doubts possessed him for a moment. "Are you sure it's the right one?"

"Yes, sir," said Coolstone. "Are we ever sure. You can't imagine what we went through, but we didn't get caught."

The Colonel threw back his head and roared with delicious laughter. No one had ever heard him do that before. Tears ran down his face. "You got it; I can hardly believe it." He turned and addressed the group in general, "Fighter pilots are fighter pilots. I was pretty sure you'd think of something." Then he said to Coolstone, "Tell your hot room to get the Bomber Base Commander on the phone and put the call on the debriefing squawk box, so we can all hear it."

There was a second or two of delay, then Coolstone told the Colonel, "He's on, sir."

"Pete, this is Tann. How's it going, boy?"

"Fine, Tann, fine. And how goes it with you at Delta Dump?"

"Oh, so-so. Say, we have a friend of yours over here – I thought you might be interested. Heh, heh."

"Is that right? Who is it?" said Pete, mildly curious.

"LeMoose is ours," said the Colonel dramatically.

"Sure he is," said Pete. "This is a figment of your imagination. What are you trying to do? Use psychological warfare on me or something. Tann, you couldn't get that moose, no matter what you tried. It's in our max security area."

"We got it, Pete. We got it. I'll hold the line, and you just check with your boys."

"Only to humor you, Tann, I'll call, just to humor you, but you couldn't possibly have that moose. Hold on a second." The line was silent, and then in the background, they could hear Pete yell, "What do you mean it's gone? It can't be."

There was a delay of two or three minutes. Then he came back on the debriefing line. "Look, Tann, I'll call you back. I have an emergency developing here." He hung up the phone.

The Colonel turned around and spoke to Coolstone, "Get the PIO types going. And keep that darned moose in the vault unless you check with me." Then he said, still laughing, "Take the rest of the day off, boys; it's a holiday at Delta Dump."

A Routine Formation

It was just a routine cross-country formation flight. Coolstone was carefully latched onto the wing of his fearless leader. He was demonstrating once and for all that, as a formation pilot, he could scarcely be equaled. He hummed a little monotone tune just to keep his RO from becoming worried as he waved his wing in the general vicinity of the leader.

They had just finished a weather penetration, and the flight had leveled at 4,000. Coolstone hadn't found time to hook up his lanyard as yet. To his RO, he said, "Let me know when we are in the clear, so I can move out and get my lanyard hooked."

"Roger," said the RO. "I'll let you know."

His leader had called Approach Control and had been told to change frequencies and then check in with radar. Because several aircraft were being worked by the controller, the flight leader was unable to make contact.

"OK, now," said Coolstone's RO. "We're between layers if you want to hook up."

"Roger," said the Rock and moved out a bit. He reached for his lanyard, and as he did so, he noticed that the attitude indicator was rolling gradually off to the right while at the same time indicating a climbing turn.

Fumbling with the lanyard, Coolstone fed in the necessary control actions to level the aircraft. He found the lanyard and was about to hook it up when he glanced at his leader and saw that he was in a diving turn away from him. He rolled back quickly, looked in the cockpit again, and now saw that every gyro instrument he owned was in motion.

They had just re-entered the cloud, and Coolstone lost his leader. "We've had it," he told the RO. "My gyros are gone, and I've lost the leader."

At this point, the flight leader made contact with Approach Control radar. Coolstone really didn't hear the conversation. His immediate problems demanded every bit of attention he was able to devote to them.

His initial panic subsided a bit; Coolstone tried to interrupt the conversation between the leader and the Controller but was unable to work a word in. His leader was being given clearance for a back course ILS, and he was arguing a bit with the Controller, trying to get a front course clearance, but could not do so. The Controller had explained that the traffic was such that it would require the flight to hold 20 minutes or so before they could be cleared for a different approach.

"Negative, negative," said the leader. Then, in a startled voice, he asked, "Two, where are you? I don't have you in sight."

In a rush, Coolstone transmitted, "I've lost my instruments; I don't know where I am. All I have is the needle and ball. I'm in a shallow right turn away from you."

"Roger," said the leader. "Keep turning and climb away from me. And is your master warning light on?"

Before Coolstone could answer, radar broke in and advised them that the field had gone below circling minimums. Weather was now 300 foot broken, 2,000 overcast.

"It will be necessary," the Controller added, "to hold 30 minutes or until it is possible to get you in for an ILS."

A certain amount of darkness entered Coolstone's cockpit, and it couldn't all be attributed to the denseness of the clouds. He started to call Approach Control. However, the Controller was in the process of breaking several aircraft off from their penetrations. He was giving them various holding instructions, and as he did so, each pilot declared minimum fuel, regardless of what holding times they were advised would apply. The Controller was hard-pressed to find sufficient holding points to keep all of the aircraft separated without climbing them back up on top.

"Hello, Approach Control," Coolstone once again tried. "This is Coolstone One."

"Roger, Coolstone One. This is Approach Control."

"Approach Control from Coolstone One. I also have a little problem here. I've lost all my gyro instruments. I'm at 4,000 feet. This is an emergency. I need an immediate vector for an approach."

"Coolstone One, this is Approach Control," and it was obvious by the tone of his voice that the Controller was at the breaking point. "Go hold someplace on the TACAN at 8500 feet and give us a call."

"Roger," said Coolstone weakly.

"This is to advise you, Coolstone," said Approach Control, that you are number four or five in the emergency pattern. We haven't got them all sorted out yet."

The Rock started to climb and get to the TACAN at the same time. He couldn't help following the horizon, which was now making a rather interesting pattern to the right, slowly rolling off and undulating up and down. Instinctively he would allow his eyes to bring that instrument in his crosscheck, then force himself to look away and get on the needle and ball again.

Indications on the needle and ball were enough to gag a buzzard. Coolstone's digestive system was much more delicate than this. The needle flopped from side to side every time he made the slightest stick application.

"Average it out ... average it out," he told himself. He was trying to average it out, but it was pretty tough to do when the needles hit the peg on both sides, and sweat was running off the end of his nose.

"Coolstone One from Approach Control Radar. I have a clearance for you."

"Roger, roger, boy," said Coolstone. "Ready to copy."

"Coolstone One, hold on the 130 radial of the TACAN between 20 and 30 miles out. Right-hand turn and call when established in the holding pattern. Maintain 8500 feet."

"Roger," said Coolstone, "but I need an approach pretty soon. Can't you feed me in on the radar? I'm in trouble here."

"Stand by one," said the Controller. "How is it going?" asked the RO with a studied calmness to his voice. "I've got the charts out for the area, and 8500 feet should clear everything. You want me to take care of the TACAN for you?"

"Roger," said Coolstone. "You navigate us in there, for it's all I can do to fly this thing. It's a bit tight," he went on, "but if we can make these turns without pranging or pitching up, we'll probably make it. But run through your ejection procedures, just in case. Now remember, if something happens and I say go, go!" And then he remembered once again that he still needed to hook up his own lanyard. Too late now, he told himself.

Approach Control called him again. The Controller told him his approach time was 58, and he would be cleared for an ILS approach.

Coolstone glanced at the clock and wouldn't have been a bit surprised to see that it had also stopped. But it was going. However, he would have to hold for 33 minutes. On needle and ball in rough air? He was in real serious trouble, if not in an impossible position.

"Approach Control from Coolstone. Look, I don't think I can hack it. I want down as soon as I can there. I need radar assistance with a no-gyro approach. I don't think I can even find the localizer. I need help."

"Look," said the Controller. "We have four aircraft that are in the emergency pattern now. We just can't work you in any quicker than that. Suggest that you go to your alternate. It's 37 miles away from your present position. We'll notify their radar."

"Understand," said Coolstone. "But what is the weather at the alternate?"

"Coolstone, from Approach Control, weather is 1500 broken, 2000 overcast, lower scattered conditions, visibility two miles in rain and fog. I have another clearance for you. Are you ready to copy?"

"Roger," said Coolstone. "Ready to copy."

"You are cleared to your alternate direct from your present position. Maintain 8500 feet and give radar a call on 279.4. Over."

"Roger, Control. I have it."

"Tune in alternate TACAN," Coolstone told his RO. He saw the course line needle come over again. He herded the aircraft around by using the needle and ball and swinging mag compass that he hadn't looked at for at least five years.

Let's see, he said to himself, when you turn east, it lags, and when you turn west, it sags. No, no, that isn't it. I'll never remember, he said to himself. He concentrated on the course line indicator and needle and ball.

He made contact with radar, and the Controller was handling him well with gyro-out techniques. Coolstone, while still tense in the cockpit, had relaxed from that edge of panic he had approached earlier. Without radar, he knew an approach would have been impossible with the weather conditions he faced. In an attempt to keep up some semblance of outward control and remembering his RO in the rear seat, he hummed a faint little tune.

"I've got her hacked now," he told the RO. They were on the base leg, and he got his gear and flaps out with a minimum amount of gyrations. In fact, as he used the needle and ball more, he found he was able to keep it rather well under control.

The GCA Controller, who was a fine one, turned him on final in three increments. Coolstone established himself on the glide path approximately ten feet low.

"You're on centerline, but you're ten feet low on the glide path, Coolstone. Do you read?"

"Roger, GCA, understand. Holding ten feet low on the glide path." Mentally Coolstone was congratulating himself for being only ten feet low. He wasn't about to change anything.

"You're still ten feet low," the Controller advised as he talked him on down.

The Field elevation was 540, and Coolstone noted he was approaching 1,000 feet on his altimeter. Where is that 1500-foot ceiling, he wondered.

"Do you see anything?" he asked the RO.

"Not a thing," said the RO. His stick action would have churned butter now. Once again, the needle was pegging both sides of the instrument, and the rate of climb indicator couldn't keep up with the bird.

They were down to 300 feet now, and he advised his RO, "We're going to have to pull up and eject if we don't break out soon."

"Hold it," said the RO. "I can see straight down. Hold it. Don't do anything rash."

Coolstone gave the butter one more good stir and looked out. He could barely see the ground beneath him.

"You are still ten feet low," advised the Controller. " Tombstone One, if you don't have the field in sight, take it around and execute a missed approach."

"Negative, negative," said Coolstone. "Keep talking."

(The Rock didn't have the vaguest idea what the missed approach procedures were.) In a guts play, he let the aircraft down a bit further, and there in front of him was the field, wet, snow-covered, and barely visible, but the most beautiful runway he had ever seen in his life. He hummed a little tune for the RO's benefit.

At Base Operations, he was greeted by a rather warmed-up Base Operations Officer. "Where did you come from?" demanded the major. "We have no clearance on you. You can't just go to an alternate without making some kind of arrangements," he continued sarcastically.

"But, sir," said Coolstone. "I was in an emergency, without instruments. It was terrible."

"I'm sure it was," said the Base Ops Officer. "Fill out a report."

I'd better call my flight leader, Coolstone thought to himself. What a story he had to tell. There'd be no question in anyone's mind about the skillfulness of his instrument flying, that's for sure.

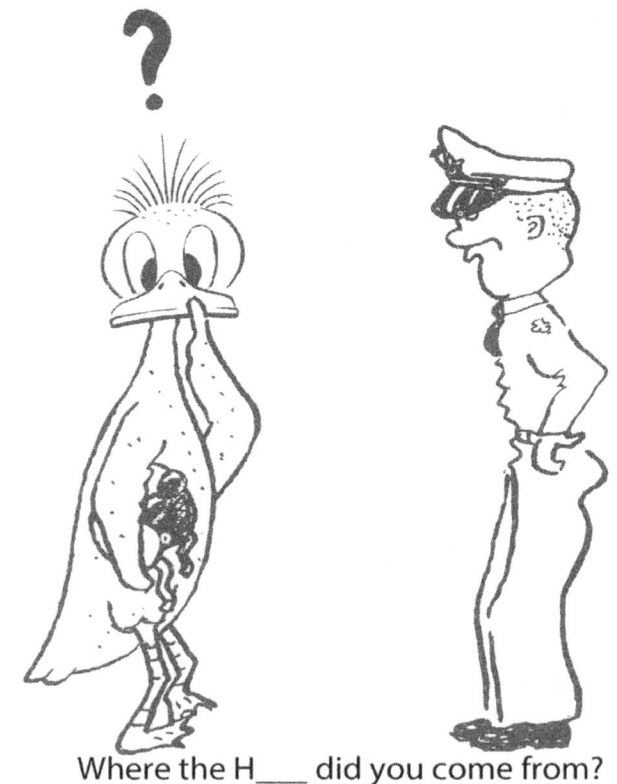

Where the H___ did you come from?

He put in a call to the base where his leader had landed. It was a moment before he could get him on the phone, but finally, he came on.

"Boy," he told his flight leader. "I really had a rough one. Everything left … no gyros, no nothing."

The leader interrupted him and said, "Did you make it OK?" "Roger," said Coolstone. "I made it OK, but here's what happened. It was terrible."

The leader interrupted him again. "Don't bother me with details. I'm in so much trouble here that I may never get out. I have about five violations against me. It seems that they advised me that the field had gone below circling minimums right in the middle of your gyro problem. I missed the transmission and ran a back course ILS. About four of us ended up about head-on out there someplace. It was terrible. I'll tell you about it when I get back if I get back. Right now, the Base Operations Officer has got me collared here, and I've got to get everything on paper."

"Roger," said Coolstone. "Don't worry about me. I made it all right. No sweat. And I have a little paperwork to do also."

Coolstone Slides Again

It was Rock's turn. He had been selected to be the board president for an F-106 accident. To qualify as board president, you needed to be a bird colonel and to have flown the aircraft involved in the accident at one time or another. Coolstone had many hours in the 106 and was still current in the T-33, even though paper was his bag at the present time.

The inevitable happened. He received the call and was advised very respectfully that he had been *selected* over a good many of his contemporaries because of his broad and extensive experience in the F-106. The accident had occurred on the West Coast. Coolstone was on the East Coast.

"You couldn't find anybody closer; I don't suppose?" he told the very respectful major who had fingered him.

"No sir. Even the next colonel on the list was at Tyndall. Er... that is, the next colonel on the list with anything approaching your broad, vast..."

"Never mind," said the Rock. He knew he had been had.

"When should I get there?" he asked.

"Well, sir," the major told him, "tomorrow morning would be just fine. And, by the way, the Investigator will be waiting for you at his base. If you are able to get a T-33 or a T-39, we would appreciate it if you could pick him up en route."

"Okay," said Coolstone. "I'll see what I can line up. I'll get in touch with the investigator. But I won't get there until tomorrow afternoon, at the very earliest. The weather is lousy here. In fact, it is lousy everywhere east of the Mississippi."

"Certainly, sir," said the major. "I'll tell the general that we will expect you out at the accident tomorrow."

"Okay," growled the Rock. He recognized gentle pressure when he heard it. He had used the same technique many times himself. The following day, early, Coolstone was jousting with the forecaster. He had a T-33. He had the investigator standing by at his base about 600 miles west, and now, with the weather just given to him, he was trying to figure out how to get to the investigator without a major crisis of some sort. Not only was the destination terrible, but he couldn't find an alternate that was much better.

"Okay, 400-1 in rain and fog. That's about as far as I am going to be able to go. I'll file for FL 280. There's no point in going any higher."

"Well," said the forecaster, "you could use Terre Haute. I think it will probably stay about 1500 feet, and it shouldn't get any worse until maybe early this afternoon. On the other hand, if the front should get organized and start moving . . ."

But Coolstone had quit listening. "Terre Haute it is," said the Rock and left for the flight planning room.

He filed, went out to his bird, and pre-flighted it in a drizzle. He was nicely damp as he climbed into the cockpit. The thought crossed his mind that he might be getting too old for the whole thing.

He received his clearance, cranked up, and with little or no delay, was airborne under radar vectors, of course. He couldn't help but remember the long delays for clearances and the wrong-way climbs he'd encountered not too many years ago.

"No question about it," he told himself. "We've come a long, long way."

The T-bird hadn't come too far, however. It was hell to be the slowest thing in the sky over 20,000 feet, and this particular T-bird gave every indication that anything over 20,000 feet was going to be a real strain.

"De-rated engines," Coolstone growled. "All of them have to be," he thought.

About 30 minutes after takeoff, he finally leveled at 28,500. He let the bird descend gradually, allowed the airspeed to build to about 270, and then pulled the power back to 96 percent. The airspeed held at 250. He would rather have had 260, but he wouldn't have been surprised had it been 240.

He took a quick ground speed check and found that he was making about 280 knots. "I hope the WAG was as sharp on the weather as he was on the winds," he thought.

The flight was routine. About 90 out, Center started him down. Coolstone asked to leave the frequency for Metro, but before he received approval, the Center controller advised him that his destination was reporting 400 and 2, freezing rain, and a slick runway. The RCR was six.

"What are your intentions?" he asked Coolstone.

"I intend to go to my alternate," said the Rock without any hesitation at all. He leveled right where he was. "But I believe I'll check with Metro first," he added.

He was cleared to leave the frequency.

"Metro, from Coolstone One. Request existing weather at Terre Haute and a forecast for about thirty minutes from now."

"Roger," answered Metro. "Stand by, please." After a short delay, the forecaster came back on.

"Terre Haute is carrying 800 overcast, three miles in freezing rain and fog. And they report an RCR of eight. I expect little or no change for the next hour or so."

Coolstone had a problem. His destination runway was 13,000 feet long. Terre Haute was 9,000 feet. The 13,000-foot runway had an RCR of six. The 9,000-foot runway had an RCR of eight. He didn't like either one. He didn't like his fuel either. He was right at 220 gallons. About 100 miles was as far as he would be able to go for an alternate.

He brought out a slightly crumpled FAC chart. He located himself and then identified several bases that he might be able to get into. He called Metro again and asked for the weather at Lockborne, Patterson, and Fort Wayne.

"Stand by," said Metro, "but I think they are all about the same." The Rock searched the chart for other bases that might hold him. "Boy," he thought, "they are making the letters smaller and smaller. You used to be able to read them real easily. Now, even by holding the chart near the Instrument panel, I'm still having trouble with the names of the fields."

Metro came back. "Tombstone One from Metro. None of those fields you have asked for are any better than Terre Haute or your destination."

"That's Coolstone One, not Tombstone One. What *do* you have that is not in freezing rain?"

"Just a moment," said the forecaster. "Now let's see. Blytheville looks great. High broken, good vis, no precipitation."

"Blytheville, Arkansas?" asked the Rock. "That's over 300 miles away from here. What do you think I am flying anyhow? This is a T-33. I can make about 120 miles with the required minimum fuel, and that's it."

"Roger, Tomb . . . er, Coolstone. Of the bases around here, Terre Haute is the best."

The Rock went back to the Center and advised them that he was going to proceed to his original destination. The Center controller immediately descended him to 9,000 feet and turned him over to Approach Control. He checked in.

"Approach Control from Coolstone One. Forty miles out, passing through 18 for 9."

"Roger, Coolstone. The base operations officer advises that you should proceed to your alternate. There is ice on the runway; the RCR is six, and freezing rain is falling at the present time."

"Negative, negative," said Coolstone One. "I have already checked my alternate, and it is just as bad as it is here, and the runway is a lot shorter. I'm coming on in."

"Coolstone One from Approach Control. The base commander advises that you should not land here. The runway is extremely slick. He has suggested that Blytheville, Arkansas would be a suitable alternate for you."

"Negative, negative," answered the Rock. "I can't make it to Blytheville. I'm in a T-33, and I just don't have the fuel."

There was another slight delay, then . . .

"Tombstone One from Approach Control. The wing commander directs you to proceed to *any* alternate. The field is closed."

"That's Coolstone One, not Tombstone One, and you tell them I'm coming in, so they had better get the field open."

Coolstone Takes Flight

On the ground, in base operations, an exciting series of events was taking place. Two colonels, a lieutenant colonel, and the major Coolstone was going to pick up were huddled around the operations desk.

"What did he say that time?" one of the colonels asked the dispatcher who was on the phone to Approach Control.

"He says that he's coming in, no matter what, and to get ready."

"He wouldn't come in here after what I told him," said the colonel.

"Yes, he would," said the major. "He is coming in. He said so, and he'll do it. He just hasn't got any place else to go."

For the first time, the base commander realized that the Major was probably right. Coolstone was going to land at their base despite his instructions and probably *would* have an accident on his base. With this realization came several immediate actions.

"Get the urea on the runway," he shouted to the base operations officer. "Alert the crash equipment. Get it in position." To the dispatcher, he said, "Ask him what his skill level is. We should know that."

There was a slight delay as the dispatcher contacted Approach Control and received an answer back from Coolstone. When he got the answer, the dispatcher hesitated and looked at the colonel for a moment.

"Well," asked the colonel, "what did he say?"

"He said," the dispatcher answered, "that his skill level is good enough to get it on the ground, and would you please get off his back?" The dispatcher had edited Coolstone's remarks considerably and added the "please."

"Tell radar to hold him out until we can get the urea on the runway," the colonel said. "I see the trucks are on their way out now."

He could also see the rescue equipment beginning to move into place. The colonel was now completely resigned - there was no way they would prevent Coolstone and his accident from happening on his base.

Back in the air, Coolstone had been descended to 1,300 feet and had been held out of the GCA pattern. He was right in the middle of the freezing rain. The windscreen was so bad that he couldn't see out of it at all. He looked at his wings and wished he couldn't see out of the side either. The wings were icing up so badly that constant power increases were needed.

"Look," he told radar, "get me down as quickly as possible. I can't stay up here much longer."

"Tombstone One from Approach Controller. Are you declaring an emergency for fuel?"

"Negative, negative, negative. I do not have a *fuel* problem. I am icing up. I am going to fall right out of the sky if you don't get me in pretty soon. And that's Coolstone One, for your information."

"Roger, Tomb . . . er, Coolstone One. I am turning you on final right now. You are cleared to make the approach. You will be starting down in two miles."

The Rock ran a real tight GCA. At about 400 feet, he could see that he was out of the weather by looking out of either side of the canopy, but he couldn't see a thing up front. Very reluctantly, he kept his speed up so he could slip the bird first to the left and then to the right while looking for the runway. When he did, he saw the runway lights. He also noticed that the weather people were slightly optimistic about the visibility.

Coolstone Takes Flight

As he was approaching touchdown, he noted an area in the middle of the runway where there was no ice. Every place else in the field was ice-covered. He sat the bird down right in the middle of the urea strip. It wasn't the best landing he had ever made, but, at this point, he was happy with any landing. With no braking problems whatsoever, he slowed the T-33 until it was almost stopped. When he attempted to turn off at one of the taxiways, the bird became completely uncontrollable. He headed the bird back into the urea strip and stopped it completely. Very carefully, using the brakes as little as possible, he finally exited the runway. He was amazed to see the display of emergency equipment that had been following him.

Very slowly, he began to taxi back to base operations. The emergency equipment maintained a loose formation but kept him under close scrutiny. He parked, and as he shut down, he saw a group of people approaching. The base operations officer, the base commander, the wing commander and, of course, his investigator were waiting for him at the bottom of the ladder as he deplaned.

The wing commander looked him over very carefully, noted his eagles, the gray that tinted his temples, and finally, without saying a word, he shook Coolstone's hand. Then he spoke for the first time. "Yes, I guess you could handle it all right. Now, what can I do for you? A car will be available, and we have excellent quarters on this base. Is there anything else?"

"Yes," said Coolstone. "As a matter of fact, there *is* something you can do. I need a quick turn because I must be on the West Coast this afternoon."

"I told them that would be what you would want," said his investigator with a smile, "but they didn't believe me."

The wing commander shook his head. He still didn't believe him. Followed by the group commander and the base operations officer, he strolled slowly back to base operations.

"What's with those guys?" the Rock asked his investigator. "Let's get in and file."

Before the investigator could answer, Coolstone had started for operations. In two steps, he had slipped, done an uncoordinated vertical half-roll, then landed very solidly on the ice-covered ramp.

As the major helped him up, the Rock said, "Maybe we had better wait a little while. It's a bit more slippery than I thought.

Coolstone Tries a Six Pack

It had been a long time since the Cold Rock had been in a real, all-out hassle, and then it wasn't legal. But now he was about to become a one-ride ACM expert at the tender mercy of IWS at Tyndall.

To start with, he wasn't even sure what ACM stood for, dog fight, tail chase, swapping…... He had heard of those and knew what they were, but air combat maneuvering was a much more respectable term, certainly, even if it did not connote his experience in F-51s on up entirely.

At the briefing, the Rock knew he was in trouble. There was going to be nothing sneaky about it. They even told one another what altitude they would be at, where they would be, and how they would engage. None of the old "meet you at 20,000 over the low cone, with everybody just as high as they could possibly get."

Prior to the briefing, the Rock figured once they were in the air, he would whip them individually or by flights, but with these new rules where everybody knew what everyone else was doing, he was beginning to worry a bit.

He knew he was in even more trouble when the briefing officer stated that there would be four F-106Bs and they would practice six-pack tactics. Just what six-pack tactics were was never clearly explained. Four airplanes and a six-pack just didn't figure. Everyone else in the room nodded sagely, so the Rock didn't dare ask the obvious question.

After the briefing, Coolstone's IP suggested they go over to the PE shop so they could start strapping things on him. The G suit came first; he was laced into it very tightly. Then came the vest and parachute, helmet and mask, and some other odds and ends that the Rock accepted without question. It was only after he had drawn all of his equipment that he discovered the IP was also an athlete. "We will walk to the bird," he was told, "it's good exercise, and the line busses are usually not there when you want them, anyhow."

Now where Coolstone came from, if the humidity was over 20%, it was a weather catastrophe. At Tyndall, 80% plus was the normal. It wasn't really hot, but for the Rock, whose idea of exercise was strolling leisurely to his car in the parking lot, the stroll along the Tyndall line with chute, G suit, helmet, etc., was a bit tedious. As a matter of fact, he had sweat through everything he had on by the time he got to the bird, which apparently had been parked in downtown Panama City on static display.

"Climb on up," said the IP, "but don't touch anything. I'll hook you up. "With the assistance of two crew chiefs and the IP, Coolstone was elevated to the cockpit.

He was plugged, hooked, and snapped in.

"Hey," said the IP, "How about that! The push-to-test button on the G suit is stuck. You'll probably have full pressure all the time, so you really won't be able to use the G suit. Pretty funny, huh?"

Coolstone immediately directed his entire attention to this very, very serious problem. He tried to dislodge the button with his pencil, never happen.

Through great effort, one which produced even heavier perspiration, he located his nail clipper and removed it from an inside pocket. Now he really had a tool. Carefully, he inserted the file point along the side of the button and gently pried it forward. It came; no, it didn't. What gave was the file point. He straightened it and tried again. Even with his highly specialized tool, the button just was not going to be dislodged. His efforts were finally reduced to glancing longingly at the stuck button every 15 to 20 seconds.

"We're cranking up," said the IP.

As the engine RPM began to increase, the G suit began to inflate. Before the Rock could get it disconnected, his eyeballs were lying on his cheek; so much for the G suit.

One thing that Coolstone noticed right away was that there was excellent visibility from the rear cockpit. He sat up a little above the pilot, and both forward and lateral visibility were just great.

"Canopy coming closed," said the pilot, and when it did, the radar scope took care of all forward visibility.

When Coolstone tried to look out of either side, he found that his helmet hit the side panels before he could really see aft to any degree at all, so much for visibility.

The flight taxied out to the runway, lined up, and with a great deal of arm waving and head nodding, leaped into the air in elements of two.

Coolstone tried to familiarize himself with the instrument panel. He located those critical instruments such as G meter, mach meter, and airspeed indicator. It was a round gauge bird, so he didn't have to figure out how to read them, at least. His attention was constantly distracted from his study, however, by a wingtip waving at him in the general vicinity of the cockpit.

They leveled at about 25, and the leader advised the flight that they would practice combat formation tactics until the drops went dry. The element moved out to a position high and down sun. The element was quite a ways out. In fact, they were out to the point that, with the dandy canopy arrangement, Coolstone was hard-pressed to keep track of them. But, suddenly, he had a local problem.

"You've got it," said the IP. "Just keep on this heading and altitude until I tell you to turn."

The bird, which had seemed reasonably stable while the IP was flying it, now was out of trim on all axes. It was extremely sensitive in pitch and bank and prone to roll in whatever direction Coolstone looked.

It had been five minutes since the Rock had seen the element or his wingman when the IP said, "Okay, make a 180 to your left, standard rate turn."

They came around, and Coolstone got just a glimpse of the wingman as he crossed over, and no indication that the element was even in this part of the world. The turns were practiced several more times, and Coolstone had gone to the full overheat position. Sweat was running into his eyes, but he had solved the stability problem and could now keep the six within five to seven hundred feet of the altitude and five to ten degrees of the heading. But it was hard work, and it took his entire attention.

Coolstone Takes Flight

"Okay," said the IP to the flight, "we will now start our engagements. The element will be the attackers on the first go, and we will be the defenders."

He advised the controllers to set them up. Coolstone quickly and gratefully released control of the aircraft to the IP and then told himself to remember why he was on the flight. He was to coolly and calmly evaluate the tactics and the aircraft's performance.

Tallyhos were called, and the fight was on. The Rock saw 5 Gs through a very narrow vision band, but he never saw the attackers. The aircraft was maneuvering all right; it was also a performing fool, but the Rock did not accomplish much cool, calm analyzing.

"Okay, break it off, and let's set it up again. This time the element will be the defenders," the IP advised the flight. Strangely enough, he seemed to keep track of everyone throughout the melee and began a short critique over the air while they were being repositioned by the controller.

He finished his critique and then said to Coolstone," What did you think of that?"

"Very impressive," said the Rock, "very impressive." To himself, he said, "If I ever get on the ground again, I think that's where I intend to stay."

"Okay," said the IP, "I'll make the attack on this one, and then you can make the next one. I'll keep you advised of what we are doing."

The position of the element was called off by the ground, and the IP advised them that he had them on radar. The Rock watched the scope intensely but could not really see much because of the scope intensity.

"Here we go," said the IP. "Burners now; got them at 11 o'clock high tallyho."

Coolstone saw them. Then he didn't, as a black haze developed that was purely a local problem. "I'm taking the low one; the wingman will get the high one, should he break first."

"Ugh," said the Rock. The Gs went down to four for a minute, and Coolstone could see that they were overshooting the defenders and were on the outside of the turn. The IP rolled up over, hung there for a moment, and then pressed the attack on home very nicely.

"Okay," he called to the flight, "Disengage, and we'll try it again. We will be the attackers once more."

"You got it," said the IP, and Coolstone bravely and reluctantly took the bird. "Now, for the first time," he thought to himself, "I'll get a chance to really know what's going on here. Get a feel for the tactics and the performance characteristics of the six at high alpha." So far, the mission had been a complete loss as far as coolly, calmly analyzing anything.

They were turned in, and the ground began calling range and azimuth. "I've got them on radar," said the IP, "20 miles, 10 degrees left, coming down fast."

In spite of himself, Coolstone felt the adrenalin beginning to flow. He strained to get a visual through the dandy canopy.

"Have you got them?" said the IP.

"Negative," said the Rock. Then he said, "Okay, now I've got them. Burners now."

The defenders, at that point, broke right into them. Coolstone yanked, banked, rolled, and saw that he had a slight advantage even though he was overshooting. He located what he assumed to be the leader and decided to press the attack on him. He was counting on his own wingman to take care of the little problem concerning the other aircraft.

He climbed sharply, pulled off the power, rolled inverted, and the enemy disappeared. He disappeared right in the middle of the canopy bar.

Desperately the Rock kicked the rudder both ways. He then picked him up again. He couldn't believe it, all he had to do was to roll back out, and he had him. This he did in the full adrenal mode, accompanied by great gasps in the interphone.

He couldn't believe his good fortune. However, he had scarcely served the purpose of the flight, i.e., to coolly and calmly analyze tactics and performance. It had been kill kill kill ever since the defender broke into them. He hadn't the slightest memory of what had transpired after that.

"Okay," said the IP. "Not bad. We'll break out by ourselves and meet the flight back at Tyndall for join up and landing. I'll demonstrate to you the capabilities of this bird."

"Rog," said the Rock, who had regained a portion of his composure by this time.

"Okay," said the IP, "first, let me show you a vertical recovery."

And, with a great flourish, Coolstone found himself pulling straight up and up and up. He locked on to the airspeed indicator. It was going down and down and down.

"Now, I'll put in some rudder," said the IP.

"Put in something," screamed Coolstone silently.

The IP added, "I'll keep the zero-G on the bird as we recover."

Fascinated, the Rock watched the airspeed work its way down to about 110 as the bird smoothly rolled through the horizon to the near vertical position. The airspeed rapidly built up again.

"I'll show you a high G high airspeed recovery - you'll notice you will get a little wing rock here."

The airspeed built up and up, and the Rock saw mach two as the recovery began. Once again, his vision band narrowed abruptly as about five and a half Gs were used for the recovery.

"You see," said his pilot, "even at high airspeeds this airplane will recover from a vertical dive with a minimum loss of altitude if you take advantage of all you can get."

"I didn't quite do what I wanted to do on that last vertical recovery," he added, "so we'll try it again."

"Rog," said the Rock weakly. "I thought you were just a little rough on that one."

"That's not what I meant," said the IP. "The airspeed didn't get quite as low as I planned." And he maneuvered the airplane so it was going straight up once again.

"Gad," thought the Rock, "do I have to go through this again? If he gets any lower, we're just flat going to turn into a pumpkin up there."

"Now," said the IP, chatting genially this time, "I'll just let it go for a while down to about 110. I'm bringing the rudder in, and I'll hold zero G. See how nice it comes around. There, we're coming through just fine. Did you get a chance to see the airspeed?"

"Boy, did I get a chance to see the airspeed!" said Coolstone. He hadn't been looking at anything else. "Eighty-five knots I saw," said the Rock.

"Not bad," said the IP, "we could get it down a little more if you really want to."

"Oh no - no, that was fine, great maneuver," said Coolstone quickly.

"Okay," said the pilot, "let's rejoin the flight and land. You've got it."

Coolstone took the bird. He was herding it with a great deal more authority than he had been during the first part of the mission. He found the flight, and while the join-up was in progress, he reluctantly turned over control of the aircraft to the IP once again.

Back in the chocks, the Rock was sitting patiently, waiting for the pilot to write up minor squawks. He had to sit there because everyone said, don't move, particularly up. It gets quite crowded, you and a slug from the parachute rattling around in one cockpit.

He thought about the flight. He was barely with the program, but he had one kill, anyhow. He had spent more time at zero G than he had in all of his previous 4,000 hours. He had seen everything from mach two to 85 knots on the gauges.

He had spent more time blacked out than he had since his 51 days, and he had thrown the bird around a bit himself, even though a cool, calm analysis had gone out the window. He found himself straightening a little bit in the cockpit.

With lots of help, he was disconnected. As he hit the ground with his 80 or 90 pounds of equipment, he turned and looked at the 6B for a moment. Later some said he snarled and looked ten years younger. He walked briskly away to catch up with his pilot.

"What do you think?" said the IP. "That's a pretty good bird, isn't it?"

"I think it will take a couple of more flights before I can really complete my analysis," said Coolstone, "but that is some airplane - that I can say for sure.

"Special Twelve"

Coolstone was ferrying an F-106 from the East Coast to Sacramento for modification. Ferry regulations being what they are, and 106s being what they are, Coolstone had been attempting to make his en route landings at F-106 bases *if* they had good weather.

His last stop had been at Minot, which had 106 facilities and good weather. It had qualified nicely. From Minot, he intended to file for Hill Field, Utah, and from there, it was just a short hop to McClellan.

At Minot Base Operations, Coolstone checked the weather closely for Hill. It was good. As a matter of fact, the only weather en route was a middle deck that ranged from broken to overcast. Hill itself was clear.

He filled out his clearance and, as legibly as possible, entered in the Remarks Section, "TACAN only. Special 12, pass to ADC radar," just as he had been carefully briefed to do at the East Coast base.

The "Special 12" jazz, while not fully understood by the Rock, seemed to be working famously so far. The radars had been giving him all sorts of help throughout his entire trip, and he hadn't even needed to ask. All he had to do was to call them. They would ask him if it was a "Special 12," and then, after an affirmative reply, they would flight-follow him, pass him automatically to the next radar without even a change in squawk, and generally give him their full attention. Coolstone had never had it so good.

He went out to his aircraft, preflighted it, and strapped in. There was a disadvantage, as he saw it, in landing at F-106 bases all the time. No one came out and oo'd and ah'd at the bird. He also liked to have interested little groups watching him for sure on takeoff because he did some of his best work with an audience. Almost unnoticed except for the tower, Coolstone became airborne.

He changed to the Center frequency and checked in. They wanted his Minot departure time, the altitude which he was climbing through, and a Dickerson estimate. He knew his departure time and his altitude, but the estimate caused him to carry ORI a bit in the cockpit. He finally was able to pass the requested info to the Center, then switched over to radar frequency and gave them a call.

"Hello, Nylon Radar, from Coolstone One. Over."

He received no answer.

"Hello, Nylon Radar, from Coolstone One. Do you read?"

Still no answer.

After he had called again and received no reply, he became a bit peeved. After all, he *was* a "Special 12," and all the previous radars had been standing by, waiting for him.

He called once again, and this time Nylon came through.

"Coolstone One from Nylon Radar. Did you call?"

"Roger, boy," said Coolstone. "I called you a couple of times. I need a parrot check and pigeons."

"Roger, Coolstone. Squawk Two."

The parrot check was completed satisfactorily, but no pigeons were forthcoming.

"Look," said Coolstone after the check was completed, "How about the pigeons?"

"Roger," said Nylon. "Pigeons to where?"

"Where?" said Coolstone. "Don't you have my flight planned route?"

"Negative," said the controller. "We don't have a thing on you, including where you took off from."

"Well," said Coolstone, quite indignantly. "I took off from Minot and am en route to Hill via Dickerson, Casper, Rock Springs, Hill. Now, give me the pigeons to Dickerson, please."

"Roger, Coolstone. The way we show you, you are now about over Dickerson and near the limits of our radar. Suggest you contact Concern Radar."

What a bunch of weenies, thought the Cold Rock. They don't understand that "Special 12" business, I bet.

He received station passage for Dickerson, switched frequencies, and gave his position report to the Center. When this was completed, he went back to the GCI frequency and called Concern.

"Hello, Concern. Hello, Concern. This is Coolstone One, Coolstone One. Over."

That ought to shake 'em up a bit, he thought, me being a "Special 12" and all. They were supposed to call me.

"Roger," a bored-sounding voice came back. "This is Concern. Go ahead."

"Look, Concern. This is Coolstone One, Coolstone One. Do you have the callsign, OK? I need pigeons and flight following, Over." A bit of the chagrin that he felt crept into his voice. They were supposed to do all of this automatically, and they knew it.

"Roger, Coolstone One from Concern. Pigeons to where, and where are you?"

"Pigeons to Casper," said Coolstone, "and I'm just southwest of Dickerson, about thirty or forty miles."

"Roger, Coolstone. Pigeons to Casper, 186°, 250 miles. Give us a call over Casper. Out."

"Thank you very much," said Coolstone, and then released the transmitter button and added, "Are you sure you can afford the info?"

Boy, he thought, this bunch over here in the remote regions are probably so far out from civilization they can't pipe the word to them. They act like they don't know what a "Special 12" is, and what kind of flight following is this? I'm supposed to give *them* a call every 200 miles or so, and tell them where I am. These guys are probably really something on an intercept.

Coolstone was tracking nicely on the Dickerson TACAN at this point. He felt very confident as he saw the mileage tick off on the DME. The undercast, which had been broken, had become almost overcast now, as the forecaster had told him, but it caused no problem, as he was undoubtedly 20,000 feet above it.

After ten minutes or so of the routine, as his eyes flicked over the instruments, he was brought up short. The TACAN was now showing off, and the DME was out. He could hear no signal from the Dickerson station. It could be that Dickerson went off the air, he thought. Anyhow I can dead-reckon myself to where I can pick up Casper, *with* Concern's help, of course.

"Hello, Concern; hello, Concern. This is Coolstone One."

Silence.

"Hello, Concern; hello, Concern. This is Coolstone One, Coolstone One. Are you there? Over."

There was simply no answer.

Coolstone held his heading carefully. He tuned in Casper TACAN but received no signal whatsoever. As he neared his arrival time for Casper, there was no doubt in his mind that his TACAN was definitely out. He tried Concern once again. Still no answer.

When his time was up for Casper, he changed back to the Center frequency, gave them a position report, very confidently delivered, then hurried back to the GCI frequency. He needed flight following badly now - some of that "Special 12" stuff, for sure.

"Hello, Concern. Hello, Concern. This is Coolstone One, Coolstone One. Over. Casper, do you read me now? Over."

There was a pause. Then he heard over the radio, "Coolstone One from Cracked Corn. Cracked Corn. Do you read?"

Coolstone didn't know who or where Cracked Corn was, but at least he had somebody.

"Cracked Corn from Coolstone. Roger, roger, boy. I read you five by. How me?"

"Coolstone from Cracked Corn. Read you five square. Do you desire assistance?"

"Roger, boy. My TACAN is out. I have been trying to raise Concern for flight following, but I can't get them. I should be about 50 miles southwest of Casper. Do you have me on your weapon?"

"Negative, Coolstone. No weapon contact. Concern advises us that he can receive you O.K., but you can't hear him. He doesn't have you on his weapon, either. He has a bird near Casper but doesn't think it's you. You are about out of our coverage, both radar and radio. Suggest you go into a port orbit to stay within our coverage, and we'll try to get radar contact with you."

"Roger, Cracked Corn, Coolstone One, entering port orbit now."

After two turns, with no further word from Cracked Corn, Coolstone called the controller again. This time Cracked Corn didn't answer. Coolstone repeated his call and very faintly heard, "Coolstone One from Cracked Corn. We have no radar contact, and you are going out of our radio coverage. We will release you now."

"Release me?" Coolstone almost shouted, "How about me squawking Mayday?"

"Tombstone from Cracked Corn. Negative on the emergency squawk, unless you wish to declare an emergency," was the rather scornful reply.

"That's Coolstone, Cracked Corn, Coolstone One, and I'm not sure where I am if you don't have me. Stand by."

Coolstone thought his situation over. He didn't really know where he was in terms of the exact location, but he did know that he couldn't be too far from Casper. But on the other hand, with the undercast showing no signs of breaking up, he couldn't be sure from here on out what was going to happen.

"Cracked Corn from Coolstone. I *am* declaring an emergency now. I'll squawk Mayday."

With that, he cranked his IFF to the emergency position and advised Cracked Corn that he was squawking Mayday.

"Coolstone from Cracked Corn. No contact. And Concern advises that the aircraft near Casper is not squawking emergency."

Coolstone digested this bit of information for a moment, then said weakly, "I guess I'm lost. Where is your station located?"

Cracked Corn advised him that they were located in the eastern portion of Montana and that he was quite a ways from them.

Panic began to seep into Coolstone's cockpit, not much and so far well controlled, but it was there. He gave in to it just a bit.

"Hello, any GCI site, any GCI site with a Mayday squawk on your scope. Give Tomb - -er Coolstone One a call."

He repeated the transmission, trying to keep his voice well-modulated, but there was a certain shrillness there that couldn't be ignored. He waited a moment and was about to give with his plaintive plea again when he heard:

"Hello, Coolstone, Coolstone One from Beyond. Do you read?"

The hair stood right up on the back of Coolstone's neck until he was able to assure himself that the ghostly quality of the voice was one of the electronics and not position.

"Hello, Beyond. Roger, boy, this is Coolstone One. Over."

"Coolstone One from Beyond. We have a Mayday squawk on our weapon. Could this be you? What is your position?"

"Roger, boy. This is Coolstone One. I am squawking Mayday, and I should be about 100 miles southwest of Casper, heading 186°, 40,000 feet. Er, ah, where are you located? And, by the way, my TACAN is out."

"Coolstone One, we are located in northwestern Montana and have a Mayday squawk 60 miles south of Great Falls, tracking about 250°. I think it's you."

"Negative, Beyond, negative. I'm holding 186°. I am sure I'm south of Casper, Wyoming. It must be another Mayday. We have wonderful radio reception, though, in spite of your being that far from me."

"Roger, Coolstone, understand, but just for laughs, turn your parrot to standby for 30 seconds, then back to Mayday."

Coolstone Takes Flight

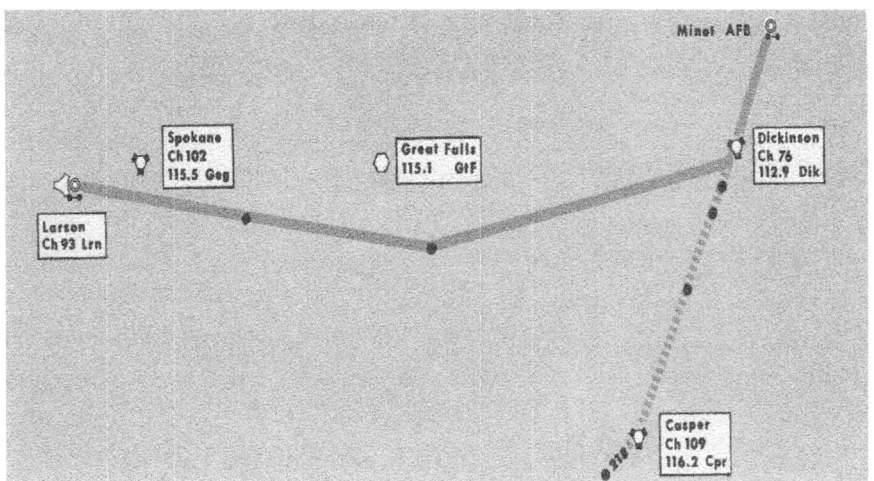

Coolstone did as directed and waited.

"Tombstone One from Beyond. There is no doubt about it. Your position is now 65 miles southwest of Great Falls. What are your desires?"

"That's Coolstone One, Beyond, not Tombstone. That can't be me. I'm holding 186° and must be 150 miles south of Casper now. And, by the way, I'm a "Special 12," for your information. I've talked to about five radar sites, and they don't know what to do about a Special 12 over in this country, I guess. You're supposed to flight-follow me all the way to Hill Field."

"Roger, Coolstone. Let me check with Cracked Corn, Concern, and Nylon and see what they have on you. Stand by."

About 30 seconds later, Beyond controller came in again.

"Tombstone, er, Coolstone from Beyond. No Special 12 info was passed to any of the radars, and besides that, you didn't tell them you were Special 12, as you were supposed to. I have another site also that confirms your position to be 75 miles southwest of Great Falls now. What are your desires?"

Coolstone had to face up to it now. They knew where he was, but he didn't. Weakly he said, "Beyond from Coolstone. I'll land at Malmstrom, I guess. Give a steer, please."

"Negative on Malmstrom," said Beyond. "The field is carrying an obscuration and snow. Suggest Geiger. I'll get the weather for you there. How's your fuel?"

"No sweat on fuel yet, Beyond. What heading do you have me tracking on?"

"We have you making 250°. Pigeons to Geiger is 175 nautical, 250°."

"Roger, Beyond," said Coolstone. "That makes my gyro off about 60°. Would you get me clearance to Geiger, please?"

"Negative on Geiger now, Coolstone. They are down in fog. Can you make it to Larson? Larson is about 275 miles, at 260°, and is carrying a broken deck at 3500 feet."

"Roger, boy. I can make it. Is that Larson AFB in Washington or where?"

"Roger, boy, it's in the central part of Washington."

"Roger, then, give me a steer."

With Beyond's help, and then when passed to Affront radar, which served Larson, who also guarded him carefully, he was able to make a gyro-out GCI-GCA into Larson. He got on the ground at Larson with about 2,000 pounds of fuel.

Coolstone Takes Flight

Coolstone taxied the aircraft in front of Base Operations, as directed. He had the interested little group out to meet him this time, but Coolstone suspected that their interest did not totally confine itself to the airplane. He parked and got out.

The AO met him with, "We don't have a flight plan for you. Did you file for here?"

"Well, no," said Coolstone. "Not exactly."

The pair started out towards Base Operations.

"As a matter of fact," Coolstone added. "I was trying to get to Salt Lake City, but ..."

Then, as he saw the AO's expression, he trailed off, "It's a long story. I don't think you'd be interested."

As they entered Base Ops, Coolstone saw that the dispatcher was trying to answer three phones at the same time. The AO took one of them, said, "Yes, sir, yes, sir, he's here," then took another and said, "Yes, sir, yes, sir. He's here right now."

The AO turned to Coolstone. "Maybe I wouldn't be interested, but there are three phones full of rank here that would be. The calls are for you."

Dejectedly, Coolstone went behind the counter and took the first phone, but before he started talking into it, almost inaudibly, he said, "And me a Special 12, too!"

Coolstone and the Weatherman

Coolstone One and Two had been terrorizing the Spokane Guard Squadron for several days on a "We're here to help you" visit. Finally, much to the relief of the Guard Commander, they had expended the majority of their vast "we are here to help you" expertise, and it was now time for them to go home.

They stumbled out to their old, weary, but hopefully trustworthy Third. As they neared, they checked it carefully for any major puddling of fluids underneath or substantial trickles that *might* indicate a problem, which would keep them beyond their last clean shorts time. They were both ready to go home but not near as prepared as their hosts were to have them go. In fact, not only was the Group Commander with them, but even the Chief of Maintenance, an unheard-of honor. He had really come along so as to closely supervise any quick-fix activities that might become necessary at the slightest hint of an abort. He had two chiefs present for the starting chores who could rebuild a T-bird (and had) in a very short while, should it become necessary.

With the preflight completed and only those few hip pocket write-ups against the bird, it was evident that the T-bird was capable of flight to Colorado Springs. The first major decision that One and Two had was whether they would be able to go direct or would be required to land at some intermediate base. They solved that problem when they found that the weather at the Springs was 4,000 broken, and the effective tailwind at altitude was 50 knots. There was no forecasted change expected either for the winds or the Colorado Springs weather.

The first meaningful dialogue Coolstone One and Two had concerning the proposed flight was about who would fly the front seat. As Two started up the ladder for the front seat position

One said: "Now, wait just a minute. You flew it out. I fly it back. OK?"

"Well," said Two with an innocently injured tone sneaking into his voice, "the chutes and stuff are already in, and I didn't think, in deference to your age, you would care to go through the exercise of changing them."

"Look," said One, "in deference to my rank, which is considerably higher than yours, and which should really not be necessary for me to point out, and in deference to my age, which is certainly not debatable, you switch the equipment, and I will fly the front seat. I remind you of the fact that you conned me into the back coming out, knowing full well that you would get two sorties, and I probably would only get one going back."

"Yes, Sir," said Rock Two, and quickly set about transferring the equipment.

They started up, got the clearance, and taxied out, failing to note the exalted expressions on the faces of their hosts.

"Not a bad outfit," said One to Two.

"Rog," said Two, "but not as professional as they could be. I sure wrote them up for not having five guys towing that aircraft. Can you imagine? Only three."

"That was pretty bad," said One, "and I got them cold turkey on those jacks underneath the 101. *Not even stenciled this year.* I will be interested to see their explanation. I didn't write them up for the light bulb burned out in the latrine. However, I just discussed it with the Commander. He assured me that it would be changed. The undated, cracked, hard-boiled eggs are going into the report. I didn't compromise on that."

The discussion was cut short as they neared the runway. They went through Last Chance, made their pre-takeoff checks, and were released by the tower to have at it. After takeoff, the T-33 wearily began its climb to 330.

This spectacular climb performance caused Two to remark, "Those climb figures are something else. If they ever were right, they must have represented a T-33 years ago that would have been a pure joy to fly."

After finally leveling off and with cruise set up (96%), the first ground speed check indicated that they were clipping along at a brisk 420. They would arrive at the Springs, all things equal, with almost 160 gallons of fuel.

Shortly after they had passed Malad City, Coolstone One called Hill Metro for Colorado Springs weather. Metro advised that the field was 4,000 broken, 50 miles visibility plus, and was forecasted to remain that way for the next several hours. This was pretty much the same weather as had been given to the pilots at Spokane. The thought did occur to One that the weather Hill gave them did sound identical to the one they initially received. One tried but couldn't remember whether the sequences came in 15 after the hour before the hour or was it on the half-hour. But no sweat, no problem. With their ground speed, they would be at the Springs in less than an hour.

It was starting to get dark from the ground up, as it does when you're flying at altitude. And up ahead now, the pilots could see a lower deck was beginning to develop. When they were almost a hundred miles out, Denver Center called "Coolstone One from Denver Center. You are cleared for descent to Flight Level 240 pilot's discretion. And what type of an approach are you requesting for the Springs?"

Now Pete Field's instrument runway was closed for construction and had been for quite a while. The only instrument recovery that could be made was an ILS to Runway 35, then circling to anything handy, or a surveillance approach to 30, which had become the primary runway during the construction period.

"Denver from Coolstone One. Request an en route with surveillance to 30. And say Colorado Springs weather, please."

"Roger, Coolstone, stand by," answered Denver.

One pulled back the power slightly and began a gradual descent. Denver came back with the weather. "4,000 broken, 50 miles vis, winds northwest at 12," he said.

"Can't hardly beat that," One told Two. "Even the winds are right down the old slot." As an afterthought, and mostly to impress Two on his thoroughness, One asked Denver what Buckley was carrying.

"Roger," said Denver, "Buckley has 100 obscured with a half mile in blowing snow."

"Roger," said the Rock. "How about Pueblo?"

"Pueblo," said the Center, "was carrying 200 overcast, one mile in snow showers on their last sequence."

"Man," said One to Two, "good thing the Springs is open. There is a lot of rotten weather around."

Two agreed.

They were cleared on down to 12 from 24, and at about 18 the little group entered the tops of the overcast. As they descended, Two commented that it was getting damned seldom between those breaks. It was solid . . . not break one.

At 12,000, they were turned over to Springs approach control radar, placed on a downwind for 30, and descended to 8,000. It was here that One found that the speed brakes would not open, and Two discovered that neither the oil pressure nor the fuel pressure instruments were working. They announced their discoveries at the same time. This caused a minute or two to be necessary so that cockpit communications could be re-established at an understandable level.

"Peanut inverter," said Two. "No sweat,"

"Unless you have your speed brakes in neutral," said One, "we just don't have any."

Fuel was about 150, which was no problem, but there were still no breaks in the cloud deck, which was beginning to really concern both pilots, even though they did not discuss it.

One had a local problem. He was trying to get down to gear lowering speed, lose another 1,000 feet, and, at the same time, radar turned them to a base and called for an even lower altitude.

With the throttle at idle and the horn blowing, One decided to level for a moment, get the speed down, lower the gear, and then get down to where he was supposed to be.

Radar called, "Tombstone One . . . er . . . Coolstone One, that is, I have a special weather observation for you. The field is now 200 obscured, one-half mile in snow, and the winds are from the north 15 gusting to 25."

"What are minimums?" One yelled to Two.

"Four hundred and one," Two answered.

"Tombstone One, from Radar. Did you copy that weather?"

"Roger, Radar. And that's Coolstone One . . . not Tombstone."

"Tombstone ... er ... Coolstone One, I believe that is below your minimums, Sir, and turn now to 320 for your final approach."

At this point, One and Two had a highly technical discussion.

"Buckley is down," said One.

"Pueblo is down," said Two.

"We have 148 gallons of fuel left," said One.

"Looks like it's here or no place," said Two.

"Roger, Radar," said One.

"Tombstone One from Radar. Visibility is now reported to be lowering on the approach end of 30 to less than a half mile." Radar didn't want to tell them how much less for fear of breaking their spirit altogether. "What are your intentions, Sir?"

"Radar, from Tombstone One. I intend to land."

The Controller's voice went up at least a half octave as he settled down to running as tight a final as he knew how.

"OK, Two," said One, "here's what we will do. I'll fly the final right on down to minimums, and you see if you can pick up the ground visually. You will be able to see through the snow from the back better than I can from the front."

"Rog," said Two, not convinced, and instinctively he tightened his lap belt and harnesses. Then he involuntarily passed his hand along the right side of the armrest, feeling for a pin that wasn't there.

It was obvious that they had a strong crosswind. The Controller had them almost 25 degrees into it, but he had killed the wind quickly as soon as he became convinced that Tombstone flight was going to run the approach.

One finally got somewhere near final approach airspeed and let the aircraft right on down. "Minimums," said One. "Do you see anything?"

"Negative," said Two. "Let it down another couple of hundred feet."

The descent continued.

"Two hundred feet," said One.

Two had his eyeballs lying flat on the canopy, but a one-dimensional blackboard with lots of snowflakes on it was all he could see, and the esthetic qualities of the view did not impress him one bit.

"You are going to have to let it down more," said Two. "I can't see a thing."

Very carefully, One eased it down. He had flown out of Pete for several years and was aware that the terrain was lower on the approach for 30 than at the runway, but he didn't have all that much faith in his altimeter.

"Two miles out," Radar was saying, and the heading was steady, which gave One some confidence that, if they ever did break out, this Cat had them lined up so they could land.

"Do you see the ground yet?" he asked Two. "I'm reading 6,100 feet, and you know what that means."

"Not a thing," said Two. Then he remembered something from his early T-bird days. Something he had never used, nor had he ever needed to use it. He remembered that the altimeter read 50 or 60 feet low with gear flaps down on final. He couldn't remember exactly how much, but he knew it read low.

"Let it on down," said Two. "Just ease it down." (Not able to explain to One why.)

Very, very reluctantly, One pulled the power back again, and very, very slowly, he started down.

Two saw the ground, but it raised the hair right up on the back of his head because it looked like he could reach out and touch it. At the same time, One saw an even 6,000 feet on his altimeter. His adrenalin level, which was already critical, went clear out of sight.

"I've got the ground," said Two. "And what's that out there to the left?" two big red balls of light had shown up about 20 degrees left of their nose.

"It's the runway!" shouted One triumphantly. "No sweat."

For the first time, Two became aware of the God-awful noises on the interphone. He held his breath momentarily. The noise level reduced considerably, but it was still high.

One set it down nicely on the snow-covered runway and, after only a brief struggle for directional control, which was really anticlimactic now, completed the landing roll.

They pulled into the parking area, shut down, and then just sat there for a minute, attempting to get pulse and respiration rates somewhere near normal.

Simultaneously, as they sat, without collusion of any kind, they both began a slow burn. By the time One and Two had arrived at Base Operations, it was a fully qualified conflagration, and it was presented promptly to the weather office.

"Tell me," said One to the forecaster.

"Yeah! Yeah!" said Two. "Tell him."

"Tell me," One continued, "I just landed out there on that runway. How do you go from 4,000 broken, 50 miles, to whatever it is now, certainly less than 200 and a half, without an intermediate observation?"

"Yeah! Yeah!" said Two. "Tell him."

"I don't really know," said the forecaster. "We don't take the observations after 1800. It's the responsibility of the civilians, then. But as far as I know, our radio is still working. Did you call?"

Having played this game for a good many years, One and Two knew they had been had. With the fire level considerably down, they left the weather office, and One found a phone. He dialed and, after a moment, said, "Let me talk to the on-duty controller."

There was a moment's delay. Then he said, "This is Tombstone . . . er . . . Coolstone One, and that was one hell of a fine approach you ran out there. Thanks a lot."

The Controller was stunned. He had received many calls from pilots, but few like this one.

The Fox and the Falcon

Coolstone considered himself reasonably affable - within limits, of course, because he was a flight leader, and, after all, he had to maintain a certain dignity. He worked at this, and his flight was a good one. The members, perhaps, didn't share Coolstone's self-appraisal as to his affability. In fact, their impressions were somewhat to the contrary, but they did respect his abilities and experience. They had to admit that while he held himself somewhat aloof, all in all, he was a good flight leader.

At times Coolstone would relax slightly - usually at the club - and talk to his flight about his Korean experiences during that conflict. But his ideas of leadership were fundamentally based on the premise that familiarity with the troops - off duty and on - broke down the lines of discipline and caused a loose operation. With the newer pilots, therefore, he was always all business. He did not encourage a first-name relationship, and at social activities, he confined his circle of friends, with whom he greatly relaxed, to his contemporaries.

The newest member of Coolstone's flight was an Air Academy graduate, just four months out of Perrin. Coolstone's background was a reflection of the hard way, and it was very difficult for him to understand why four years of Academy training was necessary for a fighter pilot.

With the limited information the Rock had been exposed to about the Air Academy, he had concluded, quite objectively, of course, that their course outline would probably give birth to some educated fools with no practical experience but with glamour status which would constantly discount any mediocrity in flying ability. The old fire, desire, and fun of flying would probably be secondary with the Academy graduates because they would be so busy analyzing the physical laws at play while racked into a tight turn or rolling in trail ... They would be all right in orbit, perhaps, just sitting there pushing buttons, engineers - but the lusty traditions of the fighter pilot would fade into the limbo of history with this generation of flyers, Coolstone sadly concluded.

However, the Academy graduate came to him with all systems in the full-go configuration, both off-duty and on. The lieutenant's enthusiasm, in fact, for even the most menial of tasks was rubbing off on the rest of the flight for the good, with the exception of those damned exercises. Coolstone was a great believer that there was only one time a sweat should be worked up, and it had nothing to do with Five BX.

In this conjunction, the Rock had obtained a T-33 for a weekend cross-country. He had pressing business at Ogden. In fact, about once a month, he had pressing business at Ogden.

Lately, he was having difficulty finding a pilot to fly with him. He had taken so many so often. It was already Thursday, and he still hadn't been able to pin down a copilot. The Rock was becoming slightly desperate.

He considered the lieutenant as a companion. He was also single and had not been away from the reservation on a cross-country since his assignment to the squadron. Good idea, thought Coolstone, and he needs the experience, too.

Coolstone found the lieutenant in the lounge. "Look," he said. "I have a T-bird scheduled for the weekend, and I thought perhaps you would like to accompany me. How about it?"

"Where are we going, Sir?" asked the lieutenant.

"Well, I'm set up for a special appointment at Ogden Saturday, but Sunday, we could go almost any place you like, within reason. Where's your home?" "It's South Dakota, Sir," said the lieutenant, "and I would like very much to visit my folks."

Now, this wasn't exactly the truth, but it wasn't a lie either. The lieutenant had a great desire to attend the football game between the Air Academy and Nebraska, which was to take place on the forthcoming Saturday. He had approached several pilots with the proposition that he could get tickets if they could get an aircraft and would go to Ellsworth, where his family would meet him. He had been completely unsuccessful.

He mulled over the possibility of getting Coolstone to amend his flight plan so that they would go to Ellsworth on Saturday morning, attend the game, and then proceed to Hill on Sunday.

"Sir," he said. "Would it be at all possible to work it so we can go to Ellsworth Saturday, then Ogden on Sunday? I can get tickets for the football game between Nebraska and the Air Force Academy."

Coolstone frowned, then said crisply, "No, no possibility at all. In the first place, the Air Force doesn't like us to make special trips for football games and that sort of thing, and in the second place, I have a firm commitment for Ogden on Saturday night, and that's the way it will have to be. We can get to Ellsworth Sunday and back here Sunday night, however. If you don't want to go, I can get somebody else."

"Oh, that's OK, Sir," said the lieutenant quickly. "I want to go. I'll be real pleased to go."

"All right," said the Rock. "You get the flight plan figured, fill out the 21A's, and take care of the 175. You need the experience."

On the morning they were to leave, the Rock came down to the squadron early and found the lieutenant had already completed the necessary paperwork.

Coolstone checked the clearance carefully, reviewed the 21A's, then signed the clearance, checked the weather, and went out to the bird.

Coolstone Takes Flight

The local weather was about 500 overcast, with five miles viz. Ogden was clear.

They preflighted the airplane together. Coolstone climbed in the back seat and strapped himself in while the lieutenant climbed in front. When the interphone came on, he advised the lieutenant to handle all the radio calls, including the clearance.

The lieutenant checked in with the tower, then called for their ATC clearance. After a short delay …. "Hello, Coolstone One, Paine Tower. Have your clearance. Are you ready to copy?"

Before the lieutenant answered, he said, "Sir, there is an unusual amount of static in the interphone. I believe it is coming from your microphone. Perhaps you should unplug, and I'll get the clearance."

"I am reading them five square," said the Rock, "but go ahead," and he unplugged. In a short while, the lieutenant indicated that Coolstone should hook up again. Coolstone did so and asked how the clearance read.

"Just as filed," said the lieutenant and started the bird.

They made the standard departure. However, once at altitude, they seemed to be held on 080 much longer than normal.

"Hello, Seattle Center; this is Coolstone One. Why are you still holding us on 080? Over."

"Sir," said the lieutenant. "Let me ask them that. You cause so much static when you transmit. I'm sure they couldn't receive you. Would you please unplug?"

"OK," said the Rock disgustedly. "But tell them to start us south. We are going in the wrong direction," and he unplugged.

After a short delay, the lieutenant signaled him to come back on the radio. "Sir," he said, "they have routed us through Spokane, then south. With the winds astern, there is no problem with fuel."

"What in the world did they do that for?" asked the Rock.

"They said something about a bomber stream," was the lieutenant's reply. "They couldn't get us an altitude below 45,000 feet."

"That's SAC for you," grumbled the Rock. "They run the Air Force."

As they reached Spokane, the lieutenant once again asked the Rock to unplug, as the static was still bad. Coolstone did so. When he came back on again, the lieutenant told him, "They want us to go east just a little further before we head south."

"For Pete's sake," said the Rock. "Tell them negative, negative. We will never make it to Ogden. The first thing you know, we'll have to land at Mountain Home and refuel if this keeps up. I have refigured the flight plan, and it is close right now. If the winds don't hold up, we haven't a prayer."

"I'll give them a call," said the lieutenant, "if you'll un..."

"Yes, I know," said the Rock, "I'll unplug."

They were over an overcast, but they were grinding off miles at about seven per minute, and even though Coolstone didn't know their exact position, he knew it would be but a brief time before it would be too late to make Ogden. He waited and waited for the lieutenant to signal him to hook up. Finally, just the glimmer of an ugly suspicion took shape in the back of his mind. As it developed, he became certain that it was an accurate one. He plugged back in. The radio was quiet.

"Lieutenant," he said. "What Center control are we under now?"

"Great Falls, Sir," was the weak reply.

"Great Falls Center, this is Coolstone One. Over."

"Roger, Coolstone. This is Great Falls. Go ahead." "Great Falls from Coolstone. What is my destination?"

"Would you say that again, please?" the Center asked incredulously.

"Better let me check, Sir," said the lieutenant quickly, "And unplug. The static is …"

"Never mind," said Coolstone. "Center, I said, 'What is my destination?"

"Stand by one," said the Center. Into the interphone, Coolstone said very quietly to the lieutenant, "If I find out what I think I am going to find out, you are going to be a very sad young first lieutenant."

"Roger, Sir," said the lieutenant.

"Tombstone One from Great Falls Center. Your destination is Ellsworth Air Force Base. Is there some problem?"

"That's Coolstone One, not Tombstone One, and stand by one."

"Roger, Tomb …. er Coolstone. Center standing by."

Quickly the Rock checked his chart to see if it would be possible to change destinations, but it was clear from his present position there was not now even enough fuel remaining to go to Mountain Home.

"Lieutenant," said Coolstone. "Of my three alternatives, court-martial FEB and murder, I favor the latter. But since I am unable to get close enough to you right now, I'll wait until we land at Ellsworth to make my final decision."

"Sir, please, please let me explain," said the lieutenant desperately.

"Don't even talk to me right now. Keep extremely quiet for the rest of the flight. I suggest that you unplug."

After landing at Ellsworth, the quiet pair entered Base Operations, with the lieutenant maintaining a respectful interval two paces to the rear and one to the left. An elderly couple approached them and greeted the lieutenant with much warmth. They were obviously his parents.

"We were so glad to get your phone call Thursday night telling us that you would be here. Now let's hurry, so we can get down to the game," said the elderly gentleman.

"Yes, Sir, Dad," said the lieutenant. "And I want to introduce to you one of the Air Force's top flight leaders. This is Coolstone One," he said proudly, "my flight leader and a pilot among pilots."

"Yes," said the lieutenant's mother, "It is a real pleasure to meet you. How fortunate for him to be assigned to your flight. We don't even worry about our son when we know he is in such fine hands. 'Professional,' I believe was the term he used to describe you, and we were so pleased when he called and told us that it was your idea to bring him here to see us and the ballgame."

Coolstone became unplugged once again.

On the way back home, Coolstone advised the lieutenant to maintain a close silence, under a minimum penalty of death, about where they'd been and how they had gotten there. However, as the Rock came to work Monday morning, he was greeted by some rather suspicious smirks on the part of other members of the squadron.

"How was the trip to Ogden?" he was asked over and over, amid much laughter. "Fine," was his brief, terse reply.

Coolstone cornered the Ops Officer. "Look," he said. "I have a question to ask you, and I'd appreciate it if you'd keep this discussion strictly confidential."

"Sure," said the Ops Officer. "What's on your mind?" And he, too obviously, was experiencing difficulty controlling a smile.

"Did you have anything to do with that cross-country of mine?" asked the Rock.

"Well," said the Ops Officer. "I did sign a clearance to Ellsworth for some member of your flight."

"Did you know that I wanted to go to Ogden, as usual?"

"Well, maybe," said the Ops Officer, "I told the lieutenant that if he could get that clearance by you, more power to him, but it wasn't my idea. We've been waiting to see where you ended up. All the squadron is interested."

As he turned away, almost to himself, the Rock mumbled, some of the material taught at that Academy obviously isn't described in their course outline."

Weekend Cross Country

Coolstone was in the coffee lounge sipping the black brew and telling war stories born of his six months of rated service. He was waving his arms with such vigor that, had he possessed just one feather, he would have been airborne.

In the middle of his highly animated story, he caught the entrance of his flight leader. This could be good, or it could be bad. As his flight leader caught his eye, he suspected the latter. Coolstone's voice faded perceptibly and finally trailed off into silence, much to the disappointment of his audience.

The captain came up to him and said, "Coolstone, come on over to the coffee bar a moment. I want to talk to you."

The Cold Rock did so reluctantly.

"How would you like to go on a cross-country this weekend?" asked his flight leader. "We can leave tomorrow afternoon and slip down to Tyndall, say, and then play it by ear-Maybe Chanute, the east coast, and then back again. We could get formation and nighttime in and come back on Sunday."

"It sounds real good, sir," the Cold Rock answered, much relieved. He'd heard about these cross-country flights in flying school. Wow! "Yes, sir, I'm your boy."

I'm all ready for that cross-country, Sir!

"OK," said the captain. "We have the planes, and this is a good chance for you to get a lot of flying time in. Come on with me, and we'll do some flight planning."

The next morning Coolstone reported early for duty with his B-4 bag. In it were his best *hunting* clothes, and he was ready. He checked with Ops. Sure enough, two F-106's were still earmarked for him and his flight commander. Man, the stories he'd have to tell when he got back from this one!

After the morning briefing, he met his flight commander, and it was sad. The captain had a sick child or something. He couldn't go. But he did tell Coolstone that if he could find someone to go with him, the flight could still be made.

The Cold Rock, with hopes somewhat raised, went looking. He found another second lieutenant, one that he knew would be a good cross-country companion, and asked him if he would be interested. Would he? You bet.

Coolstone Takes Flight

The two of them kept their plans very secretive, as, even with their limited experience in the Air Force, they had found that good deals often, for reasons not readily identifiable, seemed to gravitate towards the rank.

At noon they shirt-tailed it over to Operations and filed their clearance. There wasn't a lot to do other than just fill out the 175 because the captain and Coolstone had done the flight planning for the first leg very thoroughly the evening before. But there was considerable discussion as to who would lead and who would be identified as flight commander. They compared everything – dates of rank, serial numbers, even their weight - but finally, Coolstone pointed out that, after all, if it had not been for him, his buddy would not even be going. Coolstone won, and the flight would be called Coolstone One and Two.

After completing their clearance, they went out to the line. At the airplane, Coolstone One was deeply touched to see that he had Colonel Queen's plane. It shone. It was pretty, and it had four great big beautiful stripes around the fuselage. It also had Colonel Queen's name in big letters on the side. A ship worthy of the best, thought Coolstone to himself.

The flight for Tyndall departed on schedule and was conducted in a very uneventful professional manner.

While they were being reserviced, the two of them went up to the snack bar and had an early supper. It was beginning to get dark, but this caused them not too much concern.

They went back down to Base Ops to file. While their flight leader had not completed the planning on the leg to Chanute, other than indicating that Chanute might be a good second leg, the two did a minimum of flight planning on their own since it was only 600 nautical and it was getting dark. They didn't pay too much attention to ground speeds or fuel requirements.

When they were actually filing the clearance, Coolstone Two once again asked for a turn at the lead, but One was adamant. He would be the flight leader.

Preflight and engine start was normal. However, by the time they arrived at the end of the runway, it was definitely dark. Coolstone One called for and received runway clearance. He and Two lined up. Coolstone One made a great show of giving all the proper hand signals, but the night was black, and Two was yellow, so they became separated on the formation takeoff.

Coolstone One looked around quickly once he had started the turn after takeoff. "Where are you, Two?" he asked.

"I'm coming up on your right-wing, One. Whoops, I overshot."

"Boy, did you!" said Coolstone, bringing his head up from well inside the cockpit, where he had ducked involuntarily as Two's wing lights had flashed over the top of his cockpit. "Try it again. You have me in sight?"

"Roger, I got you. Here I come again,"

Coolstone One felt the jet wash this time as Coolstone Two overshot him with an overtake speed of at least 75 knots.

After several such maneuvers, all conducted at low altitude, Two finally got on One's wing, and they climbed out, more or less on course. Leveled at 40,000, with the flight reasonably intact, Coolstone gave his attention to his navigation.

Montgomery was the first checkpoint. As they passed over it, Coolstone One gave his position report.

He made a routine fuel check and ground speed and became somewhat uneasy. Since the planning for this part of the flight was a little loose, he didn't know what fuel he was supposed to have, but he had a strong hunch he didn't have it. The more he looked at it, the more he just flat didn't like it.

"Coolstone Two from One," he called.

"Go ahead, One. This is Two."

"Two from One. How would you like to take the lead for a little while, just to get some practice?"

How would he like it? Coolstone Two had been dreaming about leading a fighter flight ever since he had been old enough to know what fighters were. He felt greatly honored and not just a little humble to have such glories his.

"Roger, buddy," he answered. "I'm coming up on the right side."

"Got you, boy," said Coolstone One. "You're the leader."

Coolstone Two immediately busied himself getting out the charts and his computer, and very businesslike (or professionally, if you wish), he took on the navigational chores.

Birmingham was the second checkpoint, just minutes away. He tuned it on his omni and felt just great. As he got station passage on Birmingham, he began to have some doubts. The fuel situation didn't look too good. Even with the loose flight planning, he began to wonder if all was as it should be. He checked out the ground speed. While they should have been getting almost 500, it checked in at about 410.

"Two from One. How about holding it a little steadier? You're wobbling all over the sky."

"Roger, One," said Two and went on with his figuring concerning the navigation.

After several more complaints from One about holding it steady, Two could see that there was a little over 400 miles remaining. He was burning about 2800 pounds an hour, and all he had remaining was about 3400 pounds. A suspicion crossed his mind. "I've been had." He went on for about 10 minutes more, then, "Coolstone One from Two. Say, I'm having a little omni trouble. Maybe you'd better take the lead now."

"Two from One. No, you go ahead. I'm keeping track."

"One from Two. It's fluctuating pretty badly. I'm dropping back."

Reluctantly One said, "OK, I'll take it."

Coolstone One picked up the thread of the navigation once again and was just as unhappy as he had been originally to find that nothing had changed. On the other side of Nashville now, even he could see that they would arrive at Chanute with not much over 500 pounds. This was playing it too close.

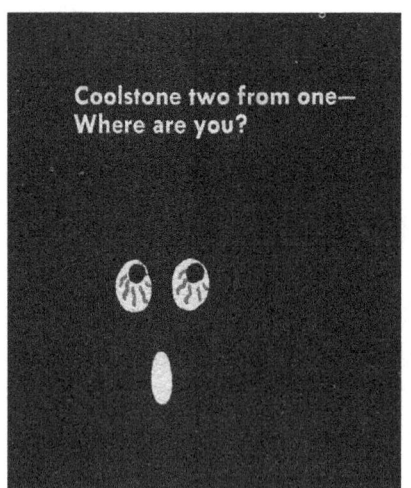

"Two from One. I think I've had a complete omni failure. You'd better take over the lead."

"Mine's fluctuating quite badly," said Two, mentally cursing himself for not going whole hog the first time and not just calling his omni completely out when he had the chance.

"Go ahead," One said. I'll drop back on your wing."

Very reluctantly, now Two said, "Well, OK, but just for a while."

By the time the exchange was completed and the flight had settled down again, they were at Evansville with 140 nautical miles to go.

"Boy," thought Two. "It's going to be close, close, close." He tuned in the Rantoul omni and headed straight for it.

He strained his eyes into the blackness ahead. There were lots of lights on the ground, but nothing that looked like a runway. Then, out of the corner of his eye, he saw One easing up. He knew One had seen something. Looking ahead again, he could see a green beacon and even a few runway lights now.

"Let's start down," said Two.

"I'll take the lead," said One.

"I've got it," said Two.

"I'll take it," said One.

"I have the runway in sight," said Two.

"So have I," said One, "And I will remind you that I am the flight leader on the clearance."

Two gave it to him.

"Hello, Chanute Tower. This is Coolstone One with a flight of two."

"Roger, Coolstone. This is Chanute. Go ahead."

"Chanute from Coolstone One. Cancel my IFR. I have the runway in sight. What is your traffic?

"Roger, Coolstone. Traffic is on runway 27. Wind's from the west at 7, altimeter setting 3003. Give us a call on initial."

"Roger, roger, boy."

One and Two were almost abreast as they raced to the initial. Coolstone One managed to maintain just a slight lead, and Two gave in again as they jockeyed for the initial.

"Chanute from Coolstone Flight," said One, with considerable confidence returning to his voice, "turning on initial for 27." Coolstone noted that Chanute's runway certainly looked short at night.

There was a silence, then, when the flight was just about to break, "Tombstone One and Two, from Chanute Tower. If you are on initial for an airport, it's not this one. Suggest you pull up and rehome Rantoul."

"You got the lead," said One.

"You keep it," said Two.

"My omni is out," said One.

"You're the scheduled flight leader," said Two.

Coolstone Takes Flight

Photofinish to the 'Initial'

One gave in. He pulled the flight up and, turning very steeply near the airport they were over, he looked for Chanute. Try as he might, he couldn't find it.

Personnel at the field over which they were flying, of course, heard this commotion and, not taking any chances, turned on all the field's lights. This was enough for Coolstone. A bird in the hand is worth two pranged in the bush. He reversed his turn violently and hit the initial again. Even Eddie Rickenbacker couldn't have stayed on his wing. He lost Two.

Now two runways were showing lights. Coolstone One landed on one; Coolstone Two landed on the other. They merged at the intersection with tenths of seconds between their passage. On the ramp, they flamed out.

After they had strength enough, they got out of their birds and found they were at a small civilian airfield 20 miles south of Chanute. The runways they had landed on were each 5300 feet. Good drag chutes had saved the day.

Now they had a real problem. How were they going to get out of this mess with their skins? They had to have fuel and starting equipment.

They would have to scrounge it somehow or else just throw themselves on the mercy of the court. When the old man got wind of this, and their flight leader and Flight Service - wow! They were in trouble.

Then Coolstone One received a visitation from that touch of near genius that often was near him. He strode manfully over to the radio shack at the field, picked up the phone, and called Chanute long distance.

"What are you going to do?" asked Two.

Coolstone One just smiled. Coolstone Two maneuvered himself into position so that he could listen to the receiver.

"Hello, Chanute Operator. Please connect me with the Transient Service Section."

There was a slight delay, then, "Transient Service. Sergeant Blake speaking, sir."

"Hello, Sergeant. I'm over at the University Airport with two 106's. Please send fuel and starting equipment over to Colonel Queen's airplane."

"Yes, sir, colonel," said the sergeant. "It'll be right over."

"Thank you, sergeant, and, by the way, who is your commander? I'll be glad to put in a good word for you."

"No need to, sir, no need at all. I'm glad to do it."

Coolstone Two's mouth dropped open, and his eyes shone with sheer worship.

Coolstone Takes Flight

Monday, back at the home patch, all of the coffee shop was waiting breathlessly for Coolstone's discussion of the weekend's events. But they were to be badly disappointed.

At about five minutes to eight, Coolstone One and Two came in and went quietly over to a corner by themselves. It was reported later by some who normally are of unquestionable veracity that a knife came into view. Both cut their right hands slightly until blood was seen to flow. Then they shook hands solemnly, reminiscent of the Indian blood brother's ritual.

Try as they might, those in the coffee shop crowd have never found out to this day what happened on that weekend cross-country flight.

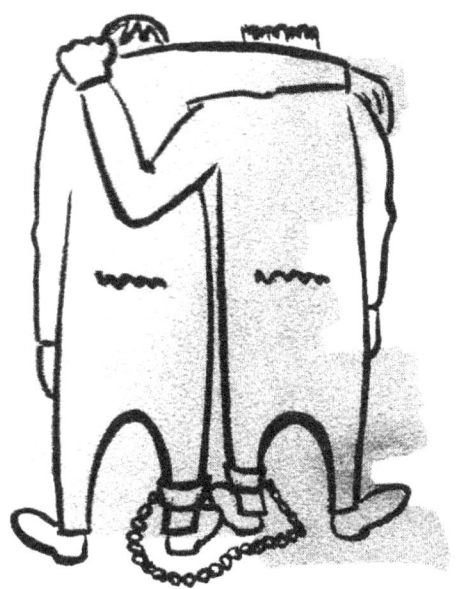

Rumors, Rumors, Rumors

The first jet airplane that Coolstone ever flew didn't have an ejection seat. This didn't bother him in the slightest because he had never flown an airplane with an ejection seat. They told him for the 84B, "If you get into trouble, just dive for the wing tip like you would in a P-51. Or, if you have time, roll it inverted, put in full forward trim, get rid of the canopy, undo the lap belt, and the rest will take care of itself."

Now they had decided to put ejection seats in the F-94As. The first thing the pilots noticed after the modification was that the fuselage tank, which had held over 100 gallons without an ejection seat, now only held 55. This irritated everybody because sweating fuel was the name of the game, even with the large fuselage tank.

Another problem, Coolstone was pretty nervous about sitting on the thing in the first place. It wouldn't have surprised him a bit to be flung to the wind every time he raised or lowered it. The installation of the ejection equipment was not at all to most of the pilots' liking.

When Coolstone's squadron came up on alert in 1951, scrambles were plentiful. And, at McChord, when the weather really got down, not the normal weather which, in itself, would have gagged a buzzard, but the kind where you need a seeing eye dog just to get to the taxiway, the folks at the blockhouse really had themselves a ball. They scrambled on everything from a flock of geese to the scheduled airliners, which always came in from the same place at the same time. So, when driving to the squadron one evening to go on alert in the most miserable weather that The Rock could imagine, he knew it was going to be a tough 24 hours.

Alert was pulled in the crew lounge, and the two aircraft on five were hangared in a corrugated tin lean-to out by the main taxiway. When you scrambled, you had to run down a flight of steep, narrow stairs, out the hangar door, down a sidewalk along the side of the hangar, across the ramp, then to the lean-to where the airplanes were. The taxiway took you to the end of a 5,000-foot runway, where you took off to the north over Tacoma. The citizens of South Tacoma knew this only too well.

Another thing about the alert operation, there were all sorts of false alarms. "Red One to Standby" rang out through the squadron area constantly day and night. It was about five to one; you wouldn't scramble from standby, but that one was enough to keep you honest. So, when on alert, you did your thing and ran your mile with great enthusiasm every time it was "Red One to Standby."

Coolstone arrived at the Squadron area and met his RO, who had been in Beaufighters in War II and who said he had never panicked since he had no adrenalin left whatsoever. They set up on five out in the lean-to, went back to the lounge, got some coffee, and waited for the other crew to finish setting up their aircraft,

"I guess I'll check the weather," said Rock One to his faithful RO, Rock Two.

Two watched One carefully as he talked to the weatherman because Two had learned from past experience that he could tell what the weather was going to be by the amount of white showing in One's eyes. One hung up.

"Bad, huh?" said Two.

"Bad, bad, bad," said One and added, "What's more, it's going to get worse, if that's possible. Storms are going to be going through here all night, keeping ceilings and vis at minimums and below. There'll even be some thunderstorms."

Two's eyes began to show a little white also in spite of himself." What have we got for an alternate?" he asked.

"Larson," said One. "The weatherman says it will stay above 2,000 feet, with rain all night."

The second alert crew came back, got their coffee, and now the negotiations began. The two crews on five rotated the number one position every four hours. The trick was to second-guess when all the action would come and compare it to the forecast. The crew, who had done this the best, would trade the early morning shift for a much more desirable midnight shift as a magnanimous gesture if it looked like the weather was going to be bad during the high action period. This time there was no quarrel. They matched for it, and Coolstone's crew was number one first.

"Have you flown that new ejection seat yet?" the second pilot asked The Rock.

"Yeah. How about it?" said Coolstone. "It cost us 50 gallons of fuel, and we will probably end up blowing somebody right over the top of the main hangar."

"That's not all," said the second pilot. "You know what I heard?" And without waiting for an answer, he added, "A guy tried it last week. Lost both his feet."

"No!" said Coolstone, properly horrified.

"Yep," said the second pilot. "Both feet came off clean. Hit the bow of the windscreen."

"It doesn't surprise me," said The Rock. "But you'd think that someone would have figured that out before they put that seat in."

"Are you kidding?" said the second pilot. "I heard that even the tests were run from a mockup without a windshield on it. And what's more, when they fired the seat, the whole mockup came unglued, so they only had one firing. You get about 80 Gs, they say, just from the seat firing. Bad news."

"Bad news is right," said The Rock. "I didn't trust that thing from the beginning."

At about 2130, The Rock casually strolled over to the window and checked the weather. It was bad. In fact, it was raining so hard he couldn't even see the lean-to where the aircraft were. He sat back down, picked up a much-thumbed magazine, and, at this point, "Red One to Standby" roared out of the intercom. One and Two did their thing. Down the stairs, out the door, down the side of the hangar, across the ramp, and, drenched, they arrived at the lean-to.

Two beat One slightly and, therefore, started up the ladder first. This irritated One. It wasn't the first time that Two had done this to him. "I'm going to talk to him about it when we get down," he thought to himself. "The Captain should be the first one on board and the last one out. Any other way looks bad." He got himself in and put his helmet on his wet head just in time to hear somebody give someone scramble instructions.

"They've got to be kidding," thought One.

"Doo Dad from Coolstone One, on standby."

"Roger, Coolstone. This is Doo Dad. Scramble. Gate climb, heading 260, Angels twenty."

"Roger," said Coolstone. "Cranking up now."

"How do you hear?" he asked Two.

"Loud and clear," said Two, "but I don't think I am going to like it."

"Looks like we will stay at Larson tonight," said the Rock. "We'll never get back in here."

At the end of the runway, he received tower clearance, lined up, advanced the power, checked the instruments, and plugged in the burner. He checked his eyelids, felt the thrust, and released the brakes. As he began the roll, the rain on the windscreen blurred the runway lights just enough so that the Rock had his entire attention concentrated on them. He glanced in the cockpit, saw the airspeed moving through 110, and began to raise the nose. Out of the corner of his eye, he saw an amber light flicker just momentarily. It was the overheat light, he was sure. He stared directly at it for a moment, but it was out. "Abort" flashed through his mind, followed directly by three other flashes. One, the General gets tight-jawed when you abort; Two, no barriers; Three, less than 2,000 feet left. He pressed on. In the air, he pulled up his gear, milked up the flaps, picked up his climb speed and heading, and called radar.

"Doo Dad Control from Coolstone One. Heading 260, climbing to Angels 20."

"Roger," said Doo Dad. "Our weapon's bent. You will be controlled by Tarnish. Check in with them when you are level."

"Boy," said One to Two, "now I know we aren't going to get back into McChord. Ain't no way with that ADF. That needle's flopping around from side to side. Precip static is wipin' it out."

They continued with their climb, and Coolstone held his heading even though the turbulence had increased to the point that he was really having to work at it. Occasionally, lightning lit the clouds up around him to a bright purple. He promptly turned up all the cockpit lights to full on.

At just about 18,000 feet, Coolstone's way of life was adjusted dramatically. The engine groaned, lost RPM, the EGT climbed rapidly, and the overheat light came on steady.

"We've had it," said One.

"What's wrong?" said Two.

"The engine's comin' unglued," said One. "Looks like we may have to get out of this thing."

"Roger," said Two slowly. "Ready anytime you are."

The noise quit, and the EGT came back down slowly. The RPM was about 60 percent since The Rock had smartly snatched the throttle at the onset.

"We'll start back down," he said to Two, "and see how close we can get anyhow."

"Doo Dad from Coolstone One declaring an emergency. Please get a clearance from McChord and tell them to crank up their GCA. We may have to eject."

Then to himself, he thought, "Eject? Lose my feet? Eighty Gs? It's going to have to get a lot worse than it is right now for that to happen."

He completed a 180, tried to tune the ADF better, then tried to null the station, but he could get nothing. "We can't get back in there," he said to Two. "I don't even know where we are except west."

"Doo Dad from Coolstone One. I can't get TCM, so I'm heading for Larson. Tell them I'm coming and have GCI ready when I get across the mountains."

He pushed up the power and, at about 95 percent, the engine did it again ... groaned, growled, grumbled, with the RPM starting down and the EGT going up. The overheat light was always on.

Coolstone once again pulled the throttle smartly aft. He was at 16,000, but Rainier was just over 15,000, so he decided, rather than try for more power than the engine liked (obviously), he would put his throttle at about 85 percent and try to hold his altitude.

The aircraft just wouldn't fly with 85 percent.

"Bad, bad, bad," he said to Two. "Something is really wrong with this engine."

"I was beginning to get that idea," said Two. "Where do you want to get out at?"

"Look," said One, "I'm not getting out until this thing absolutely quits, blows up, or comes apart. You lose your feet if you eject from this front seat."

"How about the back seat?" asked Two, genuinely alarmed.

"No sweat," said One. "You haven't got a canopy bow on a windscreen."

"Roger," said Two, relieved slightly. "I'll go anytime you are ready."

The Rock slowly eased up the power. He stopped at 90%. It still wasn't enough to hold altitude. He eased it up to 95. Yep. That definitely was too much. The grinding began again, with some rather distinct thumps. The Rock was ready for it this time. He pulled the power immediately back to 92 and waited. The engine settled back down again.

By now, Coolstone could look away from the gleaming yellow overheat light for maybe a second or two at a time. And, at 200 knots, he was holding his altitude. He pressed on. Why couldn't he have been a lawyer, he thought, like his mother always wanted? He held his heading and altitude and drove east.

Finally, he heard on the radio, "Coolstone One, this is Bright Light Control. I have an emergency squawk on an Easterly heading just east of the mountains. Is that you?"

"Bright Light from Coolstone One. I hope so. I'm heading 085 at 16. Need pigeons to Larson, a GCI/GCA, and, what's Larson's weather,"

"Roger, Coolstone, I've got you. Turn one zero five for Larson, and you're about 110 miles out at the present time. Larson's last observation was 1500 overcast 5 miles in rain."

"Roger, roger, boy," said Coolstone. "I'll start down about 40 out."

One and Two collectively sighed, relaxed from rigid to tense, and the interphone breathing rate was halved almost immediately.

"Can't figure out what's wrong with this thing," said Coolstone One. "Something serious has happened to that engine. We're just limping along here with 92 percent. We should be doing over 300 instead of 200. And that overheat light hasn't gone out yet. The EGT is a little high -- that's about all I can see wrong but ... it looks like we are going to make it now."

"Rog," said Two. "I had no desire to eject back there over those mountains, or water, or whatever we were over. I think my survival training would have been overtaxed quite a bit."

"You and me, Babe," said Rock One. "I could see myself floating down with no feet and about a foot tall after pulling those 80 Gs on ejection."

"Eighty Gs!" said Two. "You never told me about that."

"Didn't have time," said One.

"Coolstone One from Bright Light. You are about 40 miles out now. Suggest you start a rate of descent, and GCA is standing by."

"Roger, roger," said the Rock and pulled the power off to about 80 percent, holding 200 knots. The bird descended nicely. It wasn't long before he had checked in with the GCA controller and was vectored to the final. He was then handed off to the final approach controller. He checked in.

"GCA from Coolstone One. I am going to hold my gear until I start down because I have an engine problem. If I have to use too much power, I am afraid the engine will quit."

"Roger, Tombstone One. I understand you will be at your rate of descent in about 30 seconds."

"That's Coolstone One, not Tombstone," said the Rock, "and I'm putting out the gear now."

He watched as the nose gear showed safe, the right main gear safe, but the left main said: "up, up, up."

"Radar from Tombstone, er Coolstone One. I have an unsafe gear, and I'm going to have to take it around."

"Roger, Tombstone, er... Coolstone One. I understand your gear is unsafe."

"Roger," said The Rock, and he advanced the throttle slowly as he cycled the gear. At about 90 percent, the engine gave a tremendous thump - worse than any before, then it vibrated threateningly, regardless of the power setting.

"Keep talking," said The Rock to GCA. "I am going to have to land, after all."

"Roger, Tombstone. You are high on the glide path. Descend immediately. Get it down. Get it down."

The Rock pulled off the power and dropped the gear again. The left gear still was "unsafe." He used the emergency gear extension. It was still "unsafe." He advised Two, "Here's what I am going to do. I will touch it down on the right gear, then the nose gear, and I won't let it down on the left gear until I absolutely have to. If the gear is not actually down, we should be going slowly enough by then so we won't ding anything too badly."

"Roger," said Two without a lot of enthusiasm.

The GCA final controller kept talking, and, at about three miles, Coolstone saw the field. He was holding 80 percent to keep the bird flying, and the engine vibrations were horrendous. He got to the threshold and started his flare. He let it down very gently.

Now, Larson is 500 feet wide. McChord is 175 feet wide ... so as the Rock dropped down into the black hole, he tried to land the bird about 10 feet in the air. It didn't land. He held it off. It stalled.

He made one of the hardest landings that he had ever made in his entire life, and ... it was on all three gears.

"The gear is down all right," said Two to One.

"GCA from Tombstone One. The gear was down. Thanks."

When they finally got to the parking area, followed by an impressive array of fire equipment, The Rock shut it down and wasn't worried about who got out of the bird first. The weakness in his legs caused his ladder operation to be very, very nervous. As he hit the ground, the crew chief said, "Come here a minute. I want to show you something. Look." He pointed.

Coolstone looked and saw from the plenum chamber back every raindrop was turning to steam as it hit the fuselage.

"Pretty hot," the crew chief said.

"Roger," said Coolstone weakly. "Pretty hot."

He then heard another of the crew chiefs yell. "Look back here, Lieutenant!" He was shining a light up the tailpipe. "Look," he said. "There's not enough of those turbine blades left to do anything with. I don't see how it could fly."

Roger G. Crewse

It was two days before Rock One and Two got back to their Squadron. "The Old Man wants to see both of you," they were advised. They went to his office, knocked, were invited in, and saluted.

"Good to see you fellows," said the Commander and shook both their hands. "Boy, I am sure glad you made it. That just shows you how much more reliability we have in jet engines than we do in conventional ones. I've always said that, and I was just real pleased with your operation. You could have bailed out just anytime. We will tell the whole squadron about it, and maybe even the General will give you a medal. Real proud of you boys ... the way you handled that emergency. They told me on the phone from Larson that the nozzle diaphragm was up against the turbine, the turbine blades had hit the eyelids when they came off, causing the eyelids to stay partially open, and the aft bearing was completely shot. They couldn't even rotate that engine by hand after you shut it off. You could have bailed out anytime you wanted to, and nobody would have said a word to you, but I am sure pleased you brought it in. How did you manage to do that."

"Well, it was this way," The Rock said weakly. "I heard this rumor about losing your feet if you eject. You hit them right on the bow of the windshield. When I got in the airplane that night, I looked, and sure enough, that bow is going to get your feet every time."

The Old Man jumped out of his chair and looked at them. "Lose your feet! Like hell you will!" he shouted. "That seat doesn't come straight up. It slants back. Your feet aren't going to be anywhere near that canopy bow. How stupid can you get?" His question went unanswered as he stared at the pair. Then he added: "We are going to brief the squadron all right, but the subject will be a little different than I had originally planned."

Decisions, Decisions

As an IP in the T-33, Coolstone had been tapped to take his Base Commander to Wright-Patterson. Now, the colonel had an instrument card coming up, and he had elected, much to Coolstone's surprise, to get some hood time in the back seat. The colonel had even run the approach into Wright-Pat, complete with the GCA, working very hard and doing a pretty good job for an old man, Coolstone conceded.

When they entered Operations, the colonel said, "Coolstone, why don't you take the bird and get some flying time on it? Go anywhere you like, but be back in time for an eight o'clock takeoff tomorrow. I've got a conference at home that's very important, and it's to start at 1400 hours."

"Roger, roger, sir," said Coolstone with much joy. "I believe I'll go on up to Wurtsmith if you don't mind. I have a buddy up there I haven't seen for years."

"OK," said the colonel, "but be back here in time for an eight o'clock takeoff in the morning."

"No sweat, sir," said the Cold Rock. "I'll be here."

Coolstone said goodbye to the colonel and checked the weather for Wurtsmith. It was loud and clear. He filed his clearance IFR, just to keep out of trouble. As near as Coolstone could tell, it took a Philadelphia lawyer these days to know how to go VFR anyhow.

The flight was just over 300 nautical, but Coolstone took full tips anyhow. After a very short delay for ATC clearance, Coolstone was airborne. He climbed to 22,500, pulled the power back to 600°, which gave him a right brisk airspeed, and settled down to enjoy himself.

East of his course, there was some cloud cover, but with the exception of a small overcast area, as he passed Detroit, the route itself was VFR. Forty-five minutes later, he had Wurtsmith in sight. He canceled his IFR with the Center and descended. He switched to tower frequency and gave them a call.

"Hello, Wurtsmith Tower. This is Coolstone One, about five minutes out, requesting landing instructions for a T-33."

"Roger, Coolstone. This is Wurtsmith. We are recovering two flights of 102's and three flights of 89's. Because of our construction, it is necessary to taxi these aircraft back down the active. Is your fuel situation such that you can hold out of traffic for about 20 minutes?"

"Roger, roger, boy," said Coolstone. "I'm long on fuel, anyhow. Give me a call when I'm cleared to come in."

Coolstone Takes Flight

Coolstone was level at 3,000 and decided to take a tour of the area. He started up the coast of Lake Huron, admiring the lakes and streams inland. He wagered that the water fairly teemed with fish. "Some guys have all the luck," he thought. "Imagine getting an assignment to a beautiful spot like this! How fat can you get?" (There are some who would quarrel rather vigorously with Coolstone's opinion here.)

He spent about ten minutes on course up the coast, then turned around and started back down again. He automatically maneuvered out over the water so he could enter the initial for the active. Then he realized what he was doing and came right back over land. This flying over water didn't show him a thing.

As he neared the field, he veered sharply out over the lake, then cut back in just as sharply to a very, very short initial.

"Hello, Wurtsmith Tower; this is Coolstone One, turning a short initial for Runway 24."

"Roger," said the tower. "Hold out of traffic another three or four minutes. There are two aircraft remaining to taxi back."

"Roger, roger, boy," said Coolstone.

He cruised over the base and looking down, and he could see that they were really tearing the place up. Men and equipment were all over.

A slight doubt gnawed at his mind. Maybe he should have checked NOTAMs. But his old buddy buddy would keep him out of trouble, even if the base was on Official Business.

"Hello, Coolstone, from Wurtsmith Tower. You are cleared to enter the initial for 24 now. However, Base Operations advises if you land here, you will not be able to take off until tomorrow afternoon. This field will be closed due to construction. What are your intentions?"

"Stand by one," said Coolstone.

He checked his fuel quickly-290 gallons remained. He dug frantically for a map, saw that Selfridge was reasonably close by, eyeballed the distance, and saw it to be about 120 nautical.

"How's the weather at Selfridge?" he asked the tower.

Coolstone Takes Flight

"Stand by one," they replied.

Standing by, Coolstone calculated his fuel. If he left for Selfridge right now, he could arrive there easily with 100 gallons. That was plenty good enough, better than facing the colonel (bird) some six hours after he was supposed to be back at Wright-Pat. He figured that if he climbed to 20, he'd have plenty of fuel remaining.

"Coolstone from Wurtsmith Tower. Selfridge is reporting 8,000 broken to overcast, 15 miles visibility, with rain showers to the west. Weather says they're not forecast to go below minimums necessary for an alternate."

"Roger, boy. Thanks a lot," said Coolstone. "I will go to Approach Control frequency and file a clearance with them." He switched channels and "Wurtsmith Approach Control from Coolstone One."

"Roger, Coolstone, go ahead."

"Wurtsmith Approach Control, Coolstone One, a T-33. I want to change my destination from Wurtsmith direct to Selfridge, 20,000, estimating 20 minutes in route. Have approximately one hour of fuel remaining." (There was a bit of fuel stretching here, but he knew he'd have enough fuel anyhow.)

"Roger, Coolstone; will forward your clearance to the Center for their approval."

"Roger, roger, boy," said Coolstone. "Call this in as soon as you can, so if the Center doesn't approve, I can come back to Wurtsmith and land if I have to or find a different destination."

Coolstone started his climb-out and leveled at 20,000 with about 210 gallons of fuel remaining. He was in the clear, but ahead he could see there would be build-ups. After about ten more minutes, it was necessary for him to circumnavigate some of the higher clouds, but the deck was actually still broken, and he knew he could duck down underneath any time he wished.

"Hello, Coolstone One. This is Detroit Center. Come in, please."

"Hello, Detroit Center. This is Coolstone One. Go ahead."

"Roger, Coolstone. Detroit ATC clears you to the Selfridge airport from your present position via direct Selfridge TVOR. Cleared to maintain 20,000 feet. Contact Selfridge Approach Control when you're five minutes out."

"Roger, roger, boy," said Coolstone with a sigh of relief. At least he was legal now.

He decided to call Approach Control a little early, just to see if that weather was holding up. It didn't look too good. He could see that there was almost a solid line of higher clouds ahead of him now.

"Hello, Selfridge Approach Control. This is Coolstone One. Come in, please."

"Roger, Coolstone One. This is Selfridge. Go ahead."

"Selfridge, from Coolstone One. About 12 to 15 minutes out. What is your latest weather?"

"Coolstone from Selfridge. We are reporting 8,000 broken, about 15 miles vis, and there are rain showers of unknown intensity to the west."

"Roger," said Coolstone. "Thank you."

Coolstone Takes Flight

Coolstone waited another two or three minutes, right up to the point where he'd have to enter the clouds - and decided to slip down underneath, just to check. If it was OK, he'd cancel out his IFR and go in VFR. He was sure that it would be OK. Down he went, with a great flourish, speed boards and all.

At 7,000, he was underneath. He leveled and stared into a curtain of heavy rain. He couldn't see a thing. A momentary haze of confusion settled over the cockpit. Now he was down to two choices, neither of them particularly desirable. He could either press on through the rain, trying to get VFR underneath while actually IFR, and hope to pick up a visual on Selfridge, or he could climb up to 20,000, waste precious fuel, and make an IFR let-down.

He held 7,000 feet for another 30 seconds or so, and then, not even able to see the ground, up he went. He passed through 15, then 18, and leveled at 20. He was flat on instruments now, no holes. He knew he was getting close to Selfridge TVOR and began looking wildly for the Northeast Let-down Book. He had the Southwest, the Southeast, and the Northwest, but no Northeast. Oh, no, the colonel had used it to get in Wright-Pat. The book was in the back seat.

Just as this shattering discovery presented itself, Coolstone got TVOR passage, and, at the same time: "Hello, Coolstone One. This is Selfridge. Our weather is now 6,000 overcast, ten miles, and light rain. What is your position?"

"Selfridge from Coolstone One. I am passing the VOR right now, and I need let-down instructions."

"Roger, Coolstone. You're cleared for a standard jet approach off the TVOR. Give us a call when starting penetration."

"Selfridge Approach Control from Coolstone One. I don't have the let-down plate for the TVOR penetration."

"Roger, Coolstone," said Selfridge. "You're cleared for the approach off the omni or the radio range. Give Approach Control a call when starting penetration. What penetration do you intend to use?"

"Er - ah - uh - er, Approach Control, I don't have any let-down plates. Give me the headings and altitudes, will you?" It pained Coolstone deeply to admit this, but he couldn't bluff it out if he wanted to. He was down to 90 gallons of fuel now, and he had to get down.

"Tombstone One from Selfridge. The heading for the TVOR letdown is 035° outbound, left penetration turn at half your penetration altitude, track inbound at 187° to Selfridge radio, arrive at Selfridge radio at 1500 feet."

"Tower, that's Coolstone, Coolstone One, not Tombstone. I'll be departing the TVOR in about one minute."

"Roger, Tomb ... er, Coolstone. Give us a call on penetration turn."

Coolstone gyrated around in a very unusual type of procedure turn, found himself once again at the TVOR, took up the heading the tower had given him, dumped the speed boards, and pulled his power back for the penetration.

Now he had one more problem, just a slight one, admittedly, but since he didn't have a let-down plate, he didn't even know where Selfridge Field was from the range station, and he wasn't about to ask. He figured he'd just keep going towards the TVOR after he'd passed the range station and hoped that he could pick up the field visually.

Coolstone Takes Flight

As he came out of his penetration turn, he broke out of the first layer of clouds and could see the ground by looking straight down. The rain was pretty heavy. He was on top of another broken layer, and as he passed 5,000 feet, he found himself going through it. At 3,000 feet, he was out once again and could maintain VFR. However, he didn't have the field in sight.

"Hello, Selfridge Approach Control. This is Coolstone One. I'm VFR now. Give me landing instructions, please."

"Roger, Tomb-, er, Coolstone. Go to Tower frequency for your landing instructions."

Coolstone changed the frequency, then, "Hello, Selfridge Tower. This is Coolstone One in T-33 for landing instructions. Over."

"Roger, Coolstone. You're cleared to land on Runway 18. Call entering the initial for 18. Wind is five knots from the south."

"Roger," Coolstone answered. "I understand Runway 8."

The Cold Rock was now really painting the canopy with his eyeballs. The rain was just bad enough to ruin his visibility. He kept out to the right of the TVOR track, trying to pick up the runway to his left. At the last moment, he saw it through the rain very blurred, and he turned to the 080-runway heading.

He found that there was a runway near that heading and was about to call the tower that he was on initial when: "Coolstone One from Selfridge Tower. We have you in sight, and you're cleared to land out of that base leg if you wish. Over."

This shook up Coolstone badly. He wasn't on a base leg. He was turning on a short initial to Runway 080.

"Look, Tower; I'm on initial to Runway 080. Am I cleared to land?"

"*Tombstone* One from Selfridge. We don't have a runway 080, but you're cleared to land on anything we do have, except the east-west taxiway. There's a 102 on it."

"Roger," then very weakly. "Tombstone One out."

Snowbunny Go Home

They were going to fire down at Tyndall. Yes, sir, they were leaving the frozen north right in the middle of the freeze and going due south - just a weekend to be sure, but two or three days in the sun were better than none.

Coolstone had arranged with his boss to get the weekend off beginning on Wednesday. The old clothing store would just have to get along without him for three or four days. Now all he had to do was convince his squadron CO that, since he was low on flying time, he should logically be allowed to take one of the firing birds on a cross-country which would bring him into Tyndall in time for the firing.

He found the CO. "Look, Maj," he said, "I think if I work real hard, I could get a couple of days off from the job if I played my cards just exactly right. Then I could get eight or ten flying hours in and arrive at Tyndall Friday night all ready for action Saturday morning."

"I don't know," said his commander. "You *could* use the time, but I don't know. We're all behind, and we're only taking eight birds down there. If something happens to yours, we'd be a little tight. I'm a bit worried about sending one off in the toolies."

"Look," said the Rock. "I could play it so that I would be real close Friday and have just a little hop left. That way, if something did go wrong, I could get it fixed and still get it over there."

"I'll tell you what," said the Old Man. "If you can get off Wednesday from your job and get the bird to Tyndall by Friday afternoon, in flying shape, OK, but do you think you can get away from your job?"

"Oh . . . I think so," said the Rock. "I might be able to arrange it. Maybe you'll have to call him or something. Let me try it first. They have a terrible time getting along without me. But consider it done unless I let you know."

"OK," said the Major, "but you'd better damned well be at Tyndall in time for that first mission Saturday morning. Now, if you have any trouble at all, call me . . . OK, OK, collect," as he saw the question starting to form in Coolstone's eyes. "Call me collect, and we'll get the Goon over after you if you get within a day of Tyndall. We'll be at Tyndall Friday afternoon, so call us there if it's after noon Friday and anything happens. But if something happens on Wednesday or Thursday, call me here. Now don't take any chances. If it just doesn't look good, give me a ring."

"Yes, sir, yes, sir. You can count on me."

"That's what I'm afraid of," mumbled the Major as he turned away.

The Rock chose not to hear.

Coolstone Takes Flight

It was eight o'clock and ten below on Wednesday morning when the Rock began the preflight of his F-100A. By the time he had finished it, his local temperature was about thirty below. He went back into Ops and filed due south; no dog legs, no side trips, just due south. He decided if he could find any base above 32°, he would stay there and fly local until Friday.

He climbed into the 100 and started it up. The Guard maintenance troops working on the line envied him greatly because they knew that Coolstone's cross-country flight was more than an accumulation of ten to twelve hours of flying time. In fact, some of the things he had accumulated on past cross-countries were very impressive indeed. How he had accumulated them was also worthy of consideration.

Coolstone literally split the subzero air as he engaged the afterburner and, with just a little less than his normal restraint, hauled the bird into the air well before any normal pilot would, he told himself, for he knew the troops were watching and would expect at least this much from him. He turned south, and that was the heading he firmly held.

Friday morning, after having spent about 12 hours patrolling the Mexican border and the Gulf of Mexico Wednesday and Thursday, and after having had an extremely good time Thursday night, boy, was he thawed out! If he had been thawed anymore, he wouldn't have been able to get up. As it was, he decided to have a leisurely breakfast, go down to the line and check the bird over, file early, and take off at about 1300 hours for Tyndall. The flight would be less than two hours, and he would probably get to Tyndall before, or at least by the same time as the rest of the 100's and the Goon, he told himself.

He stuck to his schedule, and at about five to one, he lined up, released the brakes, engaged the A/B, and had at it.

It felt good to get out and just do nothing but fly an airplane, he told himself.

The bird came into the air gently. The Rock picked up the gear; then he lowered the nose slightly to establish his climb speed. Yes, sir, the gravel agitators didn't know what they were missing - nothing like it, prestige both on base and in town. The thrill of the open sky – the knowledge that you were doing a darned good job, an important one - and finally that you were having fun doing it.

Faintly in the background, just above the reassuring roar of the J-57, he was sure he could hear the high notes, at least, of the Star-Spangled Banner. To a more objective observer, the noise would have probably been more closely associated with Taps. And, as the last faint notes faded out, a sudden and rather violent vibration replaced them. Coolstone felt the aircraft surge several times, and then it settled down with a more or less constant shudder.

When the Rock finally got his eyeballs caged so their rotation set up by the adrenalin surge was stopped, he could find absolutely nothing wrong indicated by the engine instruments. But something *was* wrong, and it wasn't getting any better.

"Hello, Riley Tower, Riley Tower. This is Coolstone One, over," he said hurriedly.

"Roger, Coolstone One from Riley. Over."

"Riley from Coolstone. I have a problem - a heavy vibration and surges, and I'm coming back in."

"Roger, Tombstone. Do you wish to declare an emergency?"

"Riley Tower, that's Coolstone One, not Tombstone; and yes, I want to declare an emergency. Do you have me in sight?"

"Roger, Tomb, er, Coolstone. Crash crews will be standing by, and you are cleared to land. I have you in sight."

The Rock entered a long base, and as he turned final, he dropped the gear. He was hot because he was heavy, but no sweat if the chute came out. He touched down lightly, pulled the chute, and nothing happened.

"You've got a streamer," said the tower. "In fact, it was streaming throughout your pattern in the air."

"Roger," said the Rock, and his braking actions were just full of technique. He barely got stopped; the brakes were mighty hot.

When he pulled off the runway onto a taxiway, one of the crash crewmen signaled him wildly to shut down. This he did promptly.

Coolstone got out of the bird as gracefully as possible since he had retained his helmet and chute.

One of the firemen ran up to him. "Better get away, sir," he said. "There's raw fuel running out over the wings, and the brakes are smoking. They must be awfully hot."

The Rock quickly put a respectable distance between him and the bird. But even then, he could see that there was indeed a fuel leak of impressive magnitude. The right wing seemed to be literally seeping fuel. It was completely saturated.

In time the brakes cooled, and the crash crews released the bird to be towed back to the parking lot. Coolstone placed his chute and helmet on the wing and told an alert crewman, "Just put them in the cockpit." He was then taken to Base Ops by the AO.

Coolstone called the transient maintenance people and requested that the fuel leak be worked on right away. "Look," he said, "I'd appreciate it if you'd expedite this fuel system business. I've got to get to Tyndall tonight so that I can fly because we're having a gunnery exercise starting the first thing in the morning. By the way, my drag chute deployed and streamed in the air just after takeoff. It almost caused me an accident. You people installed it. This time I'll take care of it myself." Perhaps he shouldn't have added the bit about the chute.

"We'll get right on it, sir," he was told. No comments were made on the chute malfunction.

About eight hours later, he was still being told, "We expect to have it fixed momentarily, sir," and he decided he'd better let the Old Man know what happened - why he wasn't at Tyndall. He found a phone and placed the call. "Collect," he emphasized.

He heard the Major's voice. "OK, OK," he said, "I know where you are. Now, tell me, why are you there?"

Not even a "hello," Coolstone noted. Just as well if I don't tell him the whole story at once, he calculated rapidly.

"Look, sir," said the Rock. (It had been a day or two since so much conviction had been in a "sir.") "I developed a fuel leak. They're working on it, but so far, no luck. I should be there first thing in the morning. In fact, as soon as they get it fixed, I'll head for Tyndall. No sweat, I'll be there."

"OK, OK," said the CO, "But get here. Understand? Keep me posted if anything goes wrong. Yeah, yeah, collect."

The Rock hung up the phone, then called transient maintenance again.

"Momentarily, momentarily," he was told, "they would have the bird fixed.

Coolstone Takes Flight

It was almost midnight, so he decided to sack out in Base Ops after he had told the maintenance troops to wake him up as soon as they had finished with the job.

The next morning at six, he awoke, bent and aching but conscious. He stumbled over to the dispatch counter and dialed transient maintenance.

"How's it going on the 100?" he asked.

"What 100?" was the answer.

"That 100A with the fuel leak," he stated with a noticeable increase in volume.

"Oh, that 100," said the voice on the other end. "Maintenance Control refused your work order last night. We'll be able to get to that bird about 0900 Monday morning."

"What?" said Coolstone. "What did you say? Not until Monday? Let me speak to your leader."

"Look, sir," said the voice. "I am as close to a leader as you'll get to today. This is Saturday."

The Rock went into shock. He hung up the phone. Then he called his own leader, collect, of course. He explained the situation. The CO told him to stand by for a moment.

Soon the Rock was pleased to hear the voice of one of his own line chiefs on the phone. "Tell me about this fuel leak," the sergeant said.

Coolstone explained, without including the chute incident, of course.

The sergeant thought for a moment, and then he said, "Short of someone hitting the wing with buckshot, it sounds as if your problem is caused by the safety chain under the cap seal. Check that out first."

The Rock thanked him profusely, then he heard the Old Man on the phone again, "Call me back if you can't get it fixed; then we'll try something else. What's the matter with transient service there? This troubleshooting by telephone is not only expensive but rather hit or miss. If you have any more trouble with that transient outfit, start calling the bosses. Now listen – you get here just as soon as you can; you can still make it in time for the afternoon missions if you hurry."

"Yes, sir; yes, sir," said the Rock. He hung up and immediately headed for the bird. As he passed the transient alert lounge, one of the crewmen put down his magazine and followed him out. Sure enough, the chain *was* under the cap seal, but the crewman who had come along with him also spotted some hydraulic fluid around the wheel.

On close examination, it was obvious that the brake seals were ruined from the heat generated in the landing the day before. "Have to be changed," said the crewman, "and we won't even be able to get a new brake until Monday, let alone a jack and the wrenches. We just don't cotton to transients around here. 'Snowbunnies,' the bosses call 'em. They load us up just to get away from the cold, and we knew that you were one right away when we saw that 'Connecticut Air National Guard' on your bird."

The Rock didn't answer. He sprinted back to Base Ops, where he started thumbing through the Base directory. He started with the colonels and worked down. He finally located the Maintenance Squadron commander. He explained his situation, what he needed, and why he couldn't wait until Monday. "Look, sir," he said, "this whole thing wouldn't even have happened if the chute was installed right in the first place by your people." He probably shouldn't have said that.

Coolstone Takes Flight

The most he got out of the Maintenance Squadron commander was the promise of a jack.

Coolstone hung up, then called his Squadron Commander again, collect. He dreaded telling him the brake story. "Sir," he said, very, very respectfully, "I forgot to mention before that I almost made it over there once, heh, heh," he laughed weakly. "But they didn't install the drag chute here at Riley, right, so it came out on takeoff. I didn't know what it was, had to declare an emergency, and land heavy. I burned out the brake." The Rock held the phone well away from his ear and waited a respectable interval before he attempted to talk again. "I don't know when it will get fixed. Ah . . . they don't like transients here very well - call us "snowbunnies." They won't work on the bird this weekend - won't get the parts - won't get the men who know how to change a brake. But I did get a jack lined up," he added almost hopefully.

"OK, OK," said the Old Man. "I'll send the Goon and a brake. See if you can get over here in time to fly home with us tomorrow afternoon, at least. Let's see; it's 1100 here now. The Goon should get there around five. Firing will be over here for the day, so you can either take off tonight or early in the morning. We can at least use the bird on tomorrow's missions. *Please* try to get it here . . . try hard. Isn't there a general or something on that base that you can call?"

"I've tried every one I could get to. They just don't like transients here, sir. Really, you can't believe how they don't like transients here."

The Goon arrived at about 1900, and the brake was changed at about 2000, but there was no one to sign off the job. "Can't do it until Monday," said the transient crewmen. "We don't just call people out on the weekends, you know."

"I'm beginning to believe that you're right," said the Rock. "You just forget about signing anything off. I'll take care of it myself." With a great flourish which indicated much more confidence than he really possessed, he signed off the form himself.

Coolstone figured that now he might just as well wait until morning because it would be almost midnight before he got to Tyndall now. He returned to his bench in Base Ops.

The next morning (Sunday) early, very early, the Rock filed his clearance, went out to the bird, and made the walkaround. He climbed up to the cockpit and started to get in. His chute was in place, but his helmet was not. He could see the helmet, though. It was clearly visible. There, above and behind the ejection seat, was the helmet, now with a slight mod. It had been crushed when the canopy was closed the day before-or was it two days before?

Coolstone, thoroughly defeated, walked slowly back to Operations. "I don't suppose I could get a helmet before Monday, could I?" he asked the AO. "One of your men closed the canopy on mine, and it's crushed."

"Not likely," he was told. "We don't particularly care for transients here too well. They flock in on us on the weekend from the north, and this place is really closed down on the weekend. We can't be calling people out all the time."

Coolstone didn't answer him but picked up the phone and dialed the operator. "Tyndall," he told her, "Collect. Tell them it's Tombstone One calling."

Coolstone Meets the Mustang

Coolstone was raised on a diet of airplanes. His father was a pilot, and as long as the Rock could remember, he too, had wanted to become an Air Force pilot.

His dad, a colonel now and considerably older and wiser, still constantly spoke of the old P-51 (not the F) that he flew in World War II. It was the ultimate in fighter aircraft. He had often told his son the last true tactical aircraft built. (It was also the last true fighter aircraft the colonel had flown.)

When he had become old enough, Coolstone found that he was not physically qualified to enter the flying cadet program. Consequently, much to his disappointment, he found himself in the Air Force all right; but as an airman second, working on aircraft instead of flying. His great desire to fly was not abated, however, by such a minor handicap, and therefore he committed most of his monthly income to private flying lessons. He joined the Aero Club, and as time progressed and after about 100 hours in the air, the Cold Rock qualified as a commercial pilot, single-engine type.

Now Coolstone had a friend. He was a very good friend in several ways, not the least of which was the fact that his friend was extremely wealthy in his own right and was backed up by an extremely wealthy and indulgent family. His friend, too, was an airman second, interested in flying.

They roomed together, Coolstone and his friend, and in the course of many discussions concerning flying, the Rock often referred to the P-51 as described by his father. It was the smoothest, most stable aircraft, the Rock told his friend, and it was a real fighter.

"My dad shot down seven enemy aircraft with the 51," he added, "and he said there was no other plane in the sky during its time that could keep up with the 51."

On other evenings and during other discussions, Coolstone told and retold the 51 stories; about his dad's flying experience, which even the old man would have scarcely recognized.

One evening, as they were discussing their favorite subject over several bottles of BX beer, Coolstone's friend, obviously oversold, said, "Why don't we buy a P-51 for ourselves? They're easy to fly. We can keep it at the civilian airport and just think what the guys in the Aero Club will say when they see us fly by in our P-51!"

Coolstone's eyeballs exposed themselves so that their full rosy red configuration was revealed. "That's a real idea!" said the Rock. "It would really be something, but it would cost too much. But if we did have one, I'd fly over to McClellan and see the old man. I might even let him fly it if he played his cards right."

Coolstone Takes Flight

The two, in the glow of the evening, examined this new possibility in some detail. This was done wistfully by the Rock but seriously by his friend.

When it finally became apparent to Coolstone that Friendo was dead serious and could and would buy a P-51, the effects of about one full six-pack were neutralized.

"You really mean it?" gasped Coolstone to Friendo.

"Of course I do," said his friend. "Let's look at the papers and see if we can find one advertised. If they don't want too much for it, we can get it, or at least we can go out and look one over. I've never even seen a P-51 close-up."

Except for World War II pictures which featured his father more prominently than the P-51, neither had Coolstone seen a Mustang close up.

During the ensuing week, the pair searched newspapers and trade magazines for advertised P-51s. Eventually, they found one quite nearby that sounded good.

"F-51D," the ad read, "for sale. No reasonable offer refused. Excellent condition; certified; engine recently overhauled; equipped with a passenger seat."

"How about that!" Friendo said. "I could even ride with you as a passenger while I'm learning to fly. Let's call that one right now before someone else buys it. It may even be sold already. It sounds too good to be true."

Hurriedly, Coolstone called the number listed. He talked to the owner.

"While there have been many inquiries," the owner said, "and there will be many people out to see the bird tomorrow, as yet, it hasn't been sold."

"We'll be out first thing in the morning," said Coolstone. "Don't let anyone buy it before we see it. OK?"

Very reluctantly, the owner agreed to hold the aircraft overnight just for them, but not one minute longer.

That evening, during the excited discussion and with the anticipation of ownership of a real live 51 in their immediate future, Coolstone brought out a new story of his father and the Mustang, which he'd been saving for just such a special occasion.

"They used to land it from a loop," said the Rock. "Dad said they would come right in on the deck, 350 maybe, and after they did their victory rolls, of course, they'd pitch up" (101 pilots, please excuse the term); "go in trail, drop their gear and flaps at the top of the loop, and have all four birds touch down at the same time on the runway as they completed the loop. Dad said that once you got it pointed, the 51 would land itself."

His friend was impressed. So would have been Coolstone's father had he heard the story.

"I've got an idea," said his friend, now completely carried away with the spirit of the evening. "Let's fly the bird over to McClellan, find a civilian strip that's close, and surprise your dad."

"How about that!" said Coolstone delightedly. "How about that! Boy, will Dad be pleased!"

With little sleep behind them, the next morning, the Rock and Friendo appeared at the airport. With their anticipated new status as 51 owners, they used a cab.

The owner arrived at the same time. Quite understandably, he was also eager. When he sighted the pair, he called to them. "Over here," he said. "The 51 is over here behind the hangar."

Coolstone and his friend, their self-control thrown to the winds, ran briskly toward the hangar, sprinted around it, and pulled up as they saw it, a P-51, gasping at its beauty. At least Friendo did.

Coolstone gasped, but his motivation was slightly different. It looked like rather more of a handful than he had gathered from his father's description of the machine. In fact, if he held his head just right, it looked downright mean.

"What a beauty!" his friend said. "Isn't it a beauty?" he asked.

"Oh, yes," gulped the Rock. "It's pretty. . . ." he trailed off.

He's all choked up with emotion, thought his friend.

Coolstone was choked up a bit, and with emotion too, but there are lots of emotions, and the one Coolstone was experiencing was not generated by beauty. He sidled up to the owner and said, "Say, how does that thing . . . . er, 51, fly?"

"Like a dream, son, like a dream. All you have to do is read the dash one, and there's nothing to it. It practically lands itself. All you have to do is get it pointed."

Since this supported pretty much what his dad had always said, it went far toward quieting Coolstone's doubts. "If you boys want this bird," said the owner, "I'll tell you what I'm going to do. Just so there is absolutely no problem, I'll let you shoot a few landings from the back seat of a T-6, so you'll kind of get the feel of things. Then I'll take you around the pattern in the 51 in the back seat. You can see the gauges and kind of get the idea of how easy it is to fly. Then we'll both know that you'll be able to fly it just fine."

"How about that!" said Friendo, getting out his checkbook.

"Yeah, how about that!" said Coolstone. He was feeling much better now. With a couple of landings in the T-6, he was sure he could fly the Mustang, he told himself.

"We'll take it," said his friend. "How much?"

"Well," said the owner. "Would you go five thousand?"

"Sold," said Friendo.

"That's a lot of money," said Coolstone, but Friendo didn't hear him, and the owner wouldn't.

Coolstone's back-seat landings in the T-6 were quite shaky. In fact, he required considerable guidance on each. At the end of the fifth, during which he had only required assistance on the rudders, the owner declared him proficient. He told Coolstone, "This T-6 is about one hundred times harder to land than the 51. You're doing so well now that you'll have no problem at all with the Mustang, especially after a piggyback ride. And besides, a landing is a landing in any plane. You know that with all your flying time."

At the end of the piggyback ride, where about all Coolstone had been able to observe was a strategically located mole on the crown of the owner's head, he was declared combat-ready. Now he was given the dash-one. He read about things he had never heard of before. In fact, he read about things even his dad had never heard of before.

"What's this cooling door switch business?" he asked.

"Don't worry about it," said the owner. "Just leave all the switches in automatic, and everything will take care of itself. All you really need to know is the stall speed and the pattern speeds. Keep the fuel selector on the full tanks and lead it with a little rudder when you give it power, of course. There is a little torque, very little, that develops at about 50 inches. If I were you, I'd write the RPM and power settings down on a card. That's what I did, and I didn't have any trouble. That's about all there is to it. This plane is stable and easy to fly."

With another 15 minutes spent on the dash-one (a total of 45 thus expended), Coolstone considered himself ready.

"I'll help you start it, just so you'll see how it's done" said the owner as the trio walked out to the bird.

"I need a map," said the Rock.

"A map?" said the owner. "What for?"

"We're going to Sacramento," said the Rock.

"Sacramento!' said the owner, in a voice that broke while he was mentally calculating if he could get the check to the bank before they got to Sacramento. "What in the world for?"

"I want to show the 51 to my dad," said Coolstone proudly. "He flew it in World War II, you know."

"Is that right!" said the owner desperately. "Are you sure you shouldn't shoot at least one landing here before you take it to Sacramento?"

"A landing is a landing," said the Rock bravely, "here or Sacramento."

"Yeah, that's right," said Friendo, and it was obvious that he didn't understand the problem.

"Are you both going?" said the owner incredulously.

"But of course," said Friendo. "It's my airplane."

The issue was thereby settled.

The owner had a sinking spell.

He dug into his overall pockets and finally located a grease-smudged chart and wordlessly handed it to Coolstone. The Rock stuffed it into his pocket without looking at it, figuring that he'd have plenty of time on his way to Sacramento.

Coolstone Takes Flight

They started the bird and closed the canopy. The taxiing began. It wasn't as bad as the T-6 to taxi, thought the Rock, for he'd had considerable trouble herding the 6 out to the runway. He lined up the 51, released the brakes, and gingerly advanced the power. When he had as much as 40 inches on and found the torque was indeed mild, as described by the owner, he gained confidence and briskly advanced the throttle to the stop, a full 60 inches.

That was the last clear recollection he had until becoming airborne. He used all of several runways in every direction before he had gotten the 51 in the air.

"Terrific," chortled his friend in his ear. "What power! What a pilot!"

From the viewpoint of a casual observer on the ground, the owner had assumed a rather unusual position. He was holding his head with both hands, while bending forward from the waist. He was moving his head rhythmically from left to right, carefully timed to "Oh, noes," which were repeated over and over again. Back in the air now, Coolstone, Friendo, and Mustang were pursuing a somewhat erratic but determined course for Sacramento. Friendo was ecstatic. Coolstone was operating at a level somewhat back from that position.

A small civilian airport with a 4,000-foot dirt strip was located on the map quite close to McClellan. It was there that they intended to land.

With somewhat more respect for the throttle than he had demonstrated before takeoff, the Rock felt out the 51, and other than occasionally using the aileron trim tab instead of the rudder, he was able to control it quite to his satisfaction. For the first time, he really began to understand that thrill of flying that only 51 pilots ever experienced, according to his dad.

Up ahead now, he could see Sacramento. With a grease-smudged map, Coolstone attempted to orient himself. Finally, he found the strip. Four thousand feet looked mighty short from the air. He decided with no debate whatsoever not to loop. He spotted the wind sock and saw that it indicated a crosswind.

The ease of landing the 51 described by both his father and the former owner came to mind, and he forgot the crosswind. He entered the downwind, dropped gear flaps, and *carefully* advanced the throttle.

"Beautiful! Beautiful!" said Friendo.

As he turned final, he found that he was drifting quite briskly to his left. In fact, that crosswind was of quite startling proportions.

"A landing is a landing," Coolstone grimly told himself. He used a crab. It wasn't enough. He used more crab. It still wasn't enough. He finally dropped a wing into the wind. It held. At the point of touchdown, with crab and wing low, and as he told himself once again, "A landing is a landing," he hit on the right gear, then on the left gear, then ballooned, then dumped the stick, then caught the prop. Then a skid developed to the left.

It was at this point that Coolstone had his loop on landing, but not quite as his father had described. Onlookers, impressed by this exhibition, rushed to the 51 and extricated the shaken but uninjured pair from the Mustang, which really, all things considered, wasn't damaged badly at all.

As he recovered from the shock of the landing, which *was* a landing indeed, Coolstone went over to one of the hangars, found a phone, and placed a call to his father.

"Hello, Dad," he said. "Guess where I am. Over at the local airport."

Coolstone Takes Flight

"What did you come in on?" asked the colonel.

"In my own 51," said Coolstone proudly. "My friend and I bought it."

"51?" said his father. "Cessna? Piper? I don't think I ever heard of it."

"A 51D, Dad, P-51D," said Coolstone. "The old Mustang. We bought it, and I brought it over here for you to see. But, say, we had a little trouble with the landing. There are a few things you didn't tell me about that airplane."

The phone went dead- absolutely dead. There was no sound from the other end.

Experience Wills Out

"Hello, Gage Radio; this is Coolstone One. Over."

"Roger, Coolstone One. This is Gage. Go ahead."

"Gage Radio, from Coolstone One. About 17 miles east of your station, 18,000 flight level, request altitude change from 18 to VFR on top."

"Roger, Coolstone. Stand by for ATC clearance. "

Coolstone was taking a rated passenger from R. G. to Albuquerque for a meeting on missile safety. A fact staggering to Coolstone's way of thinking was that his passenger was a pilot who had never flown a jet. He didn't even have an altitude card! Coolstone had been forced to fly at 18,000, therefore, but he didn't like the looks of the fuel situation, which had been worrying him ever since he had rolled up on Gage with a little under 400 gallons, with almost 400 nautical miles yet to go.

He had debated the question rather thoroughly in his own mind after eliminating the several courses of action open to him, such as landing at an intermediate base or just flat turning around and going back to R. G. He decided to climb to about 35,000. You can always make money climbing, and this guy was a pilot, altitude card or not.

"Hello, Coolstone One; this is Gage Radio. ATC clears you to climb in VFR conditions to VFR on top from your present position. Over."

"Roger, roger, boy. I understand I am cleared to VFR on top. Over."

Coolstone passed over Dalhart while still climbing, and this didn't give him much to go on. When he leveled, he had 250 gallons of fuel and now about 250 miles to go. He did some perfectly marvelous mental gyrations, using four gallons a minute fuel consumption and six miles per minute ground speed. He concluded that he would arrive at Kirtland with about 80 gallons of fuel, or enough for 20 more minutes. He was legal.

The weather was perfectly clear and beautiful. The Cold Rock relaxed and began to enjoy the flight once again.

"Fine day, isn't it?" he asked his passenger.

"Yeah," came the uninspired reply.

"You really get a view up here," said Coolstone, trying once again.

"Yeah," replied the passenger, giving every indication of complete boredom.

The Cold Rock's hackles rose just a bit. "This guy has never even been up in a jet before, and all I get out of him is 'Yeah.' I'll try this on him."

"You ought to see it at 55,000 feet," he said, jacking his own maximum altitude up about six thousand feet. "There's nothing like it. This is the only kind of flying there is, *jet,* I mean. But I forgot, you don't fly them, do you?"

"Mmmmmm. Never had any need to," said the passenger.

Boy, thought Coolstone. This guy ought to be buried; he's dead. Then he said with what he thought was a coup de grace, "Yeah, I've been flying jets since, oh, let's see, '48, I guess." (It was actually closer to '50.) "All kinds-84Bs, Cs, and Gs, 94As through Cs, and 89Hs, and, of course, now the 102. I haven't been current in conventional aircraft since '51," he said somewhat smugly and waited for an appropriate reaction from his passenger.

"Mmmm," was all he got.

This minimal reaction goaded Coolstone to even further conversation. "Since I've flown jets for so long, I know that at 35,000, the Third burns about four gallons a minute. Our ground speed would be about six miles a minute, and with 250 or so miles to go and 250 gallons to do it in, we'll have about 80 gallons when we get to Kirtland. That's why I climbed. I've got it right here in the ole head, experience, don't need to look at anything."

"Mmmm," came the reaction from the back seat.

"Forget it," Coolstone told himself. "This guy's idea of a thrill is probably steep turns in the L-20."

Coolstone got his map out, and according to his ETA, he was about five miles out of Anton. Even with all his broad jet experience, he had never been able to pinpoint himself exactly at 35,000 feet. It all looked the same down there. Just a bit nervous now, Coolstone saw he was down to 170 on the counter, and even though he knew there was no sweat, he sweat.

The time dragged on. Coolstone's inclination to sparkling conversation had completely faded. Five minutes more, 130 gallons of fuel, and Coolstone was sitting erect in the cockpit with his eyes riveted to the RMI. Even with such wondrous powers of concentration focused directly upon it, however, the needle showed no inclination to move.

"Winds," he thought. What were the winds? With all his broad experience, he had allowed (rule of thumb) for about 50 knots headwind, going west, but what were they actually? His weather briefing only covered 18,000.

Coolstone scanned the map for (not clear) any kind of field. Kirtland was the only one now within his meager range. He spotted nothing on the ground that looked like a field. Five minutes more, 110 gallons. He still hadn't passed Anton. He couldn't believe that the winds could do this to him. In his broad experience, never, never, never had he lost money by climbing. If he got a station passage right now, he was astonished to see his ground speed would have been about 260 knots. At 35,000 feet, how could that be?

Then on the radio, "Hello, Coolstone One, Coolstone One. Albuquerque Center. Give me a call, please."

"Roger, Albuquerque Center, this is Coolstone. Go ahead."

"Coolstone from Albuquerque. What is your position? Have you passed Anton yet?"

"Negative, negative. In fact, I ran into some *terrible* high winds here at 35,000, and I don't know whether I'll even make Kirtland or not."

"Roger, Coolstone, what are your intentions?"

"Stand by for a moment," said Coolstone.

Coolstone Takes Flight

In all of Coolstone's jet experience, he also had never known of a time when, if he descended, he'd make money, and, as far as a change of destination was concerned, there just wasn't any place he could change to.

While he was cogitating, Anton station passage was indicated on his RMI. His leading-edge tanks were dry, and now his fuselage tank was showing about 95 gallons. He had 100 miles to go! A quick check of his ground speed showed that it would take him about 21 minutes to reach Kirtland with 18 minutes worth of fuel.

There was only one decision to make, experienced or not.

"Hello, Albuquerque Center. This is Coolstone. Cancel my IFR and alert Kirtland Tower to a low-fuel emergency. Tell them I'm not sure I'll make it.".

"Roger, Coolstone," said the Center.

The Cold Rock figured he'd hold his altitude for about 10 minutes, then start an idle descent when he had about 50 gallons on the clock.

"Low on fuel?" the passenger in the back seat asked him innocently.

"Low on fuel?" snorted Coolstone. "Yes, we're low on fuel. The winds are twice as high as I expected, maybe three times. I don't know. I'm going to hold at 35,000 for another few minutes, then start an idle letdown."

"That's fine," said the pilot in the back seat.

"We may not make it," said Coolstone, letting just a hint of the panic he was beginning to feel creep into his voice. "The engine may flame out."

"Mumm," came the reply from the back seat.

Here I am with sweat running out my ears, thought Coolstone, and all this guy can say is "Mumm."

Being a firm believer that if you can keep your head when all about you are losing theirs, you just don't understand the situation. Coolstone proceeded to explain the situation in great detail to his passenger, ending with, "Now, let's run through our bailout procedures."

"Roger," said the pilot in the back seat.

No gasps, shouts, or moans. This guy says just plain "Roger." He doesn't understand, thought Coolstone incredulously.

Coolstone went through the ejection procedures with his passenger in great detail. No matter what it did to the pilot in the back seat, it helped Coolstone pass the longest ten minutes of the year. Then, with 50 gallons and with Kirtland in sight way ahead, Coolstone started his let-down from 35,000.

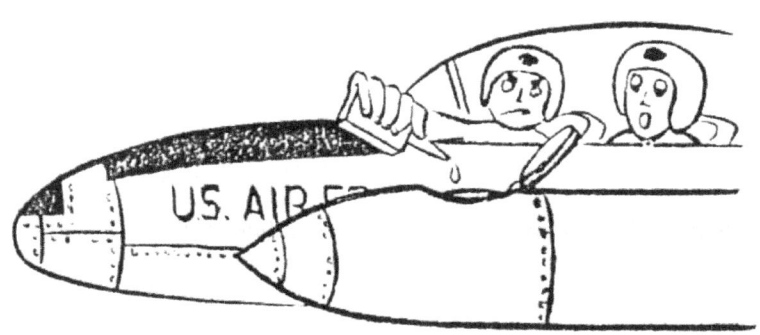

The Lighter Fluid is all gone – now what'll we use for Fuel ?

Coolstone Takes Flight

On the radio now, guard channel, " Hello, Tombstone One, Tombstone One. This is Kirtland Tower. Do you read me?"

"Kirtland, that's Coolstone, not Tombstone, Coolstone One, and I read you loud and clear."

"Roger, Tomb-, er, Coolstone One. What is your position? ATC advises you have a low-fuel emergency. Do you want the fire truck standing by?"

"Negative, Kirtland. If I get that close, I won't need them. I'm about 40 out now, and I'll level at 10,000. I'm planning on entering the base leg for your north-south runway if I don't flame out first."

"Roger, Tombstone, er, Coolstone. Traffic is held out. Take any runway you want. For your information, the winds are from the south at 15."

The fuselage tank was showing 20 gallons now. Somewhere in Coolstone's vast experience, he remembered someone saying, "Don't ever trust the liquidometer when it's indicating under 50 gallons. You might flame out at any time."

"Are we going to make it?" the passenger asked quietly.

"How do I know?" shouted Coolstone.

He angled for a base leg to the south runway.

He held his gear as he entered the runway. Ten gallons now in the fuselage tank, and he wasn't even sure that he was right. As he neared the turn on final, he saw he was high, even for the long runway. He dropped his gear, flaps, and speed brakes, turned onto final, and found he was low now. He added power, almost full throttle. It hurt him deeply to do so. Then he had it made, on the ground in a minimum number of pieces and the cockpit full of sweat.

Coolstone stopped the aircraft on the runway near a taxiway turnoff. He didn't trust himself to attempt a maneuver as complicated as a turn in his present unlaced condition. The engine quit.

"Hello, Kirtland Tower, this is Tombstone One, er, Coolstone One: I need a tug." There was a quiver in Coolstone's voice.

"Roger, Tombstone," said the Tower. "What's the matter? Did you flame out?"

There was silence in the cockpit for a moment. Then, before Coolstone was able to answer, the non-jet pilot passenger in the back seat transmitted, "Kirtland Tower, in a classic application of his *broad* jet experience, Coolstone One's fuel came out even."

Ferry Flights are Not Easy, Either

A T-33 was sitting innocently on the line, and directly in front of it was a master sergeant, his hands in his pockets, shaking his head sadly.

One of the T-bird crewmen came up to him. "Got troubles with 566 again, Sarge?" he asked.

"Have I got troubles? This bird is a real lemon. Now, for Pete's sake, we can't get it started about every fifth or sixth time. I've got everything changed I can think of, but nevertheless, no ignition about once in five attempts. I don't know what to do about it."

"Say, isn't this the same one where the gear won't come up every once in a while?"

"Yeah, that's just one of the minor items. The pilots claim it flies slaunchwise, whatever that means, ever since we changed the rudder after that unreportable accident - you know, the one where the tug driver hit the tail. He claimed the bird backed into him."

"Do I know? I worked all night on that thing. The CO said he wanted to see it rolled out of the hangar at 0730 the next morning in flying condition."

"Well," said the sergeant. "We've trimmed and retrimmed, but the bird still doesn't fly right. And, of course, that fuselage pump, every so often, the circuit breaker pops, and then it won't pop for maybe eight or nine hours, then out again it comes. We've changed two pumps, and it doesn't make any difference."

"Yeah, I know what you mean," said the airman. "The first time that happened was right after Ole's lunch turned up missing when we were doing that mod to the fuselage cap. You don't suppose, no, it couldn't be ..."

" And," added the sergeant, "spongy brakes. We've had spongy brakes written up so many times on this bird that I've even sworn off seafood, and the system's been bled so many times that we've run Supply out of brake fluid. Then there's radios-intermittent, everything intermittent. Tailpipe temperature too low, then too high. You get 101%, then only 98%. A real dog, if I've ever seen one. I've checked, and we've spent more man hours on this bird in the past month than on any three fighters we own. The thing's got me beat; every flight's a test flight. If I could just get one OK flight on 566, I might even re-up."

"How about those inverters, Sarge; I know you were having some troubles with them. The electricians were complaining bitterly."

"Well, it's real simple. Either both won't work, or they both work. It always happens in the air and never on the ground. We've changed everything we can think of. The pilot will be flying along, and the inverter light comes on, and he tries to change over, and neither one works. Then pretty soon, the light goes off, and the inverters are both working again. They can't figure it out."

While the two were talking, they had strolled over to the T-bird hangar. As they were entering, a very excited airman came running toward them.

"Sergeant," he called, waving a yellow paper in his hand. "We've done it, we've done it." The airman was practically out of breath.

"Slow down, boy," said the sergeant. "What have we done?"

"We have orders to transfer T-33 566. A ferry pilot will be here in three days. Can you imagine? We're going to get rid of old 566!"

The sergeant was overwhelmed. He was speechless. "A miracle," he murmured.

Quite a group of the T-bird people had gathered around due to the excitement exhibited by the messenger. When they heard what had happened, cheers went up. They slapped each other on the back. Congratulations flowed unchecked. There was talk of a party.

Then the sergeant brought them back to reality. "We've got to get the damned thing running just long enough to get it out of range of the field, anyway. Let's go."

Sitting at his desk in a Base Ops far away, the Operations Officer was talking to his assistant. "We've got to find a pilot to go after that T-bird we're getting from Duluth. How about you? Are you interested?"

"Never hoppen," said the assistant. "Those ferry flights are poison. You get the honor and the privilege of flying the squadron's dog every time. You say the bird's at Duluth?"

"Yes, that's right.".

"I don't remember losing a thing up there. Count me out."

"Well, I'm going to have to find somebody. Give me the T-bird pilot roster, and I'll see if I can find someone who will go up there."

An hour later, after the Ops Officer had contacted almost everyone on the list who was qualified for a ferry flight, he still hadn't been able to tie any pilot down. He had heard a variety of excuses, ranging from sick kids to; I'm working on a paper for the colonel. The real trouble, of course, was that at one time or another, all the pilots contacted had ferried aircraft between squadrons and knew what they would be up against.

The Ops Officer called in his assistant again and said, "These guys all know the score. I'm afraid it's going to take an act of Congress to get that bird down here."

"Well, let's see," said the assistant. "I might know one guy, but you'd have to handle it just right."

"Who?"

"Coolstone. But he's got to think it's a deal. Do you want to try it?'"

"Why not?" said the Ops Officer.

A call was put in for the Cold Rock, and soon he was on the line.

"Say, Coolstone," said the Ops Officer, "but first, is there anyone around who can overhear you?"

"No," said Coolstone. "There's no one near. What's this all about?"

"Well," said the Ops Officer. "I've got a deal for you. But first, you must promise not to let it get out if you don't want it. I'll be mobbed if you do."

"OK, OK," said Coolstone enthusiastically. "What is it?"

"Well," said the Ops Officer, dropping his voice confidentially. "Now, you won't say anything, sure?"

"No," said Coolstone, "I won't breathe a word."

The Cold Rock had heard of the way these good deals got passed around. Before, he had been bitter. Now it was his turn, and he felt a little thrill.

"Well," said the Ops Officer, whispering now. "We have a T-33 to pick up at Duluth and ferry back down here to us."

"What's so hot about that?" said Coolstone in a rather hoarse whisper, then in an almost normal tone, "I've ferried aircraft before. It ain't good."

"But Duluth," continued the Ops Officer. "This is different. Have you ever been there?" he added, holding his breath for Coolstone's answer.

"Well, no," said the Rock, "but I've ferried aircraft before, and I don't want any part of it, unless" – his voice dwindled off, then he continued, "but I have never heard much about Duluth being a real good deal."

"You haven't?" said the Ops Officer, letting a tone of utter amazement enter his voice. "You have never heard of," and his voice dropped once again, "the Highlands?"

"The Highlands?" said Coolstone. "No, I don't think so."

"Boy," said the Ops Officer. "You've been nowhere, absolutely nowhere. Here, let me tell you about it." And now his voice dwindled down to just the faintest of whispers.

"No," said Coolstone, listening. "You don't say! Is that right?" he said incredulously. " Boy, golly, count me in. When do I leave?"

"We'll fly you up tomorrow night, and then the next morning, you can bring the bird back here. OK?"

"It's a deal," said Coolstone. "And thanks, thanks a lot."

The Ops Officer put down the phone and looked at the Assistant Ops Officer. He gave him a big wink. They silently shook hands.

At Duluth, with the zero hour drawing near, the activity around 566 was wondrous to see. The T-bird flight was out en masse. They had done everything to the bird but start it. This they were deferring since it had been started three times, OK, and they didn't want to press their luck with a fourth. They even had a man straddling the canopy, polishing for all he was worth. It was as clear as a canopy ever had been.

Then, "Here he comes," said someone.

Sure enough, Coolstone was being led by the T-33 flight chief down the line. As they neared T-33 566, on a signal from the flight chief, the men formed a flight at the strictest attention. As he and Coolstone arrived, he popped his finest salute and said, "Sir, your aircraft is ready for flight."

Coolstone was overwhelmed. Never had he been treated in such a manner.

"Fetch his bag," the flight chief directed, and then he added, "Sir, you just go right on down to Base Ops and file out. We'll preflight the bird for you and start it up. All you will have to do is climb in and go.

"Now you just go right on down and file that clearance. We have a staff car for you," he said, gesturing, and not only one but two staff cars rolled up. The drivers leaped out, opened the rear doors, and stood at attention. "What's your choice, sir, a Ford or a Chevrolet?" asked the flight chief.

"What's going on here?" said Coolstone, dumbfounded. "What's with you guys, anyhow?"

"Nothing, sir, this is completely normal at this base—only the best of service provided transient crews. Your choice," he said, bringing the staff cars once again to Coolstone's attention.

Well, thought Coolstone. My reputation has undoubtedly preceded me and makes up for last night. Highlands, indeed! I might as well soak up some of this VIP treatment. He climbed into one of the staff cars, and the driver of the other made a great show of being extremely disappointed.

As soon as Coolstone and the car were out of sight, a great flurry of action took place.

"OK, OK, you guys," said the Sgt. "Let's see if we can get this monstrosity cranked up."

Thirty minutes later, Coolstone returned, and once again, the T-bird flight was called to attention, and the flight chief popped a snappy salute as Coolstone climbed up into the cockpit. The engine was running. All Coolstone had to do was strap in and get his clearance. This he did. Once again, he was amazed and pleased with the service.

As he started out from the line, a left turn was necessary. The left brake pedal went clear to the stop. He pumped wildly on the peddle, and the brake came back in. He just barely cleared an F-102 parked ahead of him. He looked back to where the T-bird people were standing. They had been so good to him that it seemed a shame to bring the bird back.

Then, as he looked closer, he thought to himself, if I didn't know better, it would appear that they are praying – on their knees yet! He pumped the brake again, and it felt OK, so he kept going. As he continued out on the taxiway, even over the sound of the engine, he heard something that could be considered cheering. He looked back, and to his surprise, he saw the T-bird crew now dancing, wilding, slapping one another on the back, and, yes, cheering. They're nuts, he thought, clear out of their minds.

He got out to the end of the runway and lined up for the roll. He held the brakes and advanced the throttle to 100%. The tailpipe temperature was a little high, and the RPM was 101%. He got it back to 100%, and the TPT came back into the cage. He released the brakes and was on his way. Acceleration speed was eight knots low, which was nothing, of course, and the takeoff roll seemed to be about 1,000 feet over that which he had calculated, but so what? He got the bird in the air, but try as he might, the gear would not come up.

Then, when he tried to report his predicament to the tower, the radio was out. He could hear the tower, and the tower could hear about two words of what he said, but the radio was intermittent. Then, much to his surprise, he noted that the inverter light had come on. He changed inverters, and the light remained on.

He checked for circuit breakers, and he found one out, but it wasn't for the inverter; it was for the fuselage tank. He pushed it back in, and it came out again.

He attempted to call the tower again, but it was no use. The radio was still intermittent.

He decided to fly around in the local area and burn some of the fuel down before he came in to land. After the tips emptied, he tried the gear one more time, and up they came, perfectly normal. He tried calling the tower. Sure enough, the radio worked fine, and as he was calling the tower, the inverter light went out, and the gyros erected.

Well, he thought, I might just as well try the fuselage tank circuit breaker again, and, sure enough, it stayed in. He entered the initial and landed, and after he had lowered the nose, he went for the brakes. Both of them hit the stops. He pumped frantically, and they came back in. The roll was normal.

At least, he thought, the TPT and the RPM would still be high, so he held the brakes and ran the engine up to full throttle after he had pulled off the runway. This time he had 98% and 620° on the tailpipe temperature.

He taxied back into the line and was amazed to see tears running down the face of the man parking him. Just behind the airman parking him, he saw the sergeant beating his head on the concrete.

The ladder was placed alongside the aircraft, and one of the airmen sadly climbed it. "What's wrong, sir?" he asked.

"Well," said Coolstone. "It's the strangest thing. Right now, nothing, but when I took off, everything went to pieces. It's the darndest thing I ever saw. I believe this bird needs a test hop. Would you get my staff car back?"

"Car? Car?" said the crew chief. "They don't provide cars for transient officers at this base."

Coolstone Plans? A Flight

Coolstone always tried to visit each of the Interceptor bases under his command at least once a month. Usually, he and one of his Sector Commanders would go together and, if at all possible, drop into one of their bases with little or no notice. While this shook the troops up a bit, it did give Coolstone a good idea of how the actual operation was conducted.

Therefore, early one spring morning, Coolstone and his Aide were airborne in a T-33 en route to Portland. Here they would pick up the Sector Commander and continue on to Kingsley.

Coolstone had long ago given up any attempt at keeping current on the myriad of small changing details involving flight rules while also running a Division at the same time. The Rock left the flight planning to his Aide, as he did the actual airborne compliance with the numerous flight requirements. Whether he knew it or not, on more than one occasion, a violation had been narrowly averted only because his Aide had, very diplomatically, of course, exerted just enough pressure to keep them legal. The Aide was well aware that, had he not played his cards just right on several flights, there would have been voice reports from the Venus probe instead of "Heavenly Music."

The weather was good, just a middle-broken deck with bases at about eight and tops at eleven. Coolstone's Aide had filed an on-top clearance, and they were flying at 24.5 angels. With only 100 in the tips at takeoff, they were well below landing weight when they arrived at the Portland Omni. Coolstone was all for a VFR letdown, but his Aide, who was handling the radios, set up a penetration. Coolstone went along with the clearance; however, he did make a rather abbreviated penetration, canceling IFR as soon as they were under the deck.

On the ground, Coolstone was met by the Sector Commander, and the two discussed some highly technical matters over a cup of coffee while their Aides waited for them in Ops.

"Look," said Coolstone. "It's a beautiful day. The weather is good. Let's just be pilots for a change, you know, like we used to. Why don't we file as a flight down to Kingsley and do it all ourselves, just let the boys sit there in the back seat and watch for red lights? I'm fed up with this never flying except on business, then being rushed so much that the bird might as well be a taxicab. Let's tell them to just take care of the preflight, and we'll do everything else. How about it?"

"Well," said the Sector Commander, moving into the spirit of the thing, "It sounds fine, a welcome change. I feel exactly the same way." Then he added, a bit reluctantly, "My formation work may be a little rusty, but let's do it."

Coolstone called the Aides over. "We've got an idea," he told them. "You two go on out and preflight the birds. We'll take care of everything else for a change. It will do us good. We'll file as a flight, and all you two will do is watch for red lights. Come on," he said to the Sector Commander. "Let's show these two how fighter pilots operate."

"Sir," said Coolstone's Aide. "Ah-er-don't you think we should help-ah-er-do some of the paperwork," he added hastily, knowing full well how much the Old Man hated the piles and piles of paper he was faced with each day.

"Forget it," said Coolstone. "Get the birds ready and just hang on. Besides, you already have the flight card filled out for the trip." With a noticeable spring to their steps and smiles on their faces, the two generals headed for Fighter Ops.

They stood before the wall map for a moment, sighting their course. As they did so, Coolstone spoke to the Sector Commander. "Do you want to – ah, lead?" he asked.

The Sector Commander involuntarily glanced at Coolstone's collar. There was one more star than on his, "Oh, no, no," he said. "You go ahead. I'll fly the wing."

"Roger, roger," said the Rock as he walked over to the Dispatcher's desk. He filed a rather abbreviated 175. "We'll call the flight Coolstone One and Two," he told the sergeant. "Just file direct Eugene, direct Kingsley. On top. Where do I sign?"

"Sir," the Dispatcher started to protest. "There's a little more to it.." He trailed off weakly.

"Oh, just fill in the details from the clearance my Aide turned in. Do I sign here?" and without waiting for an answer, he signed his name quickly.

Coolstone One and Two entered the waiting staff car and went on out to the aircraft. The T-33s were ready. With a jaunty wave, each boarded his own bird.

When the intercom came on, Coolstone told his Aide: "I'll handle the whole works radio and all. You just sit back and enjoy the trip."

"Roger, sir," said the Aide.

Soon after the birds were started, Coolstone Two checked in.

"Roger, roger," said One. "Five square. How me?" Then he added, "Are you ready to taxi?"

"Read you five by, and we're ready to taxi," answered Two.

Coolstone called the tower and received taxi instructions. The flight headed for the active.

No clearance, thought the Aide. The Old Man must have filed VFR. He was tempted to make a remark to that effect, but he remembered his instructions, namely, to sit back and enjoy the trip.

The flight received runway clearance, taxied into position, and, as One was advancing power, Two called.

"Maybe it would be better if we took off individually," he said rather hesitantly. "I'll join up as you turn out. Okay?"

"Roger," said One. "Follow me in 30 seconds." At the same time, he released the brakes.

After the flight was airborne, while there were some undue throttle manipulations on Two's part, the join-up wasn't bad. After he had settled down, Two was actually holding a pretty good position on One's right wing.

They climbed out on course, carefully avoiding all clouds as they did so. The broken deck was still the same as when they landed, about six-tenths, with gigantic holes. One, using the flight card his Aide had prepared, dialed in the frequency and course for Eugene Omni. He centered the course needle and felt just fine.

There was nothing like it, he thought. No matter how far down the road you were, leading a flight stirred up the wild blue yonder in you. He was also greatly pleased to see that Two was flying an excellent formation.

As he glanced admiringly at Two's formation position, he noticed that Two's Aide was staring rather fixedly at him. Although the Aide's face was not clearly visible, it appeared to Coolstone that the eyes alone connoted a rather pleading expression. Must be imagination, he thought, as he discounted his impression. More likely, it is admiration I'm seeing.

He changed to the tactical and checked in with radar. Then he called Two. "How are you doing?" he asked.

"Fine," said Two, and he was looking like a pro.

Well, he should, thought the Rock. Between the two of us, probably about ten thousand hours of fighter time are represented.

As the flight was approaching Eugene, Coolstone received a call over the radio, "Coolstone One, Short Stuff leader. Do you read?"

"Roger, Short Stuff, this is Coolstone. Five square, how me?"

"Five square," said Short Stuff. "Would you like an escort to Kingsley?"

"Sounds good," said Coolstone. "How many in your flight?"

"I have a flight of two F-101s," said Short Stuff.

"What's your position? Join up on my left wing. We are a flight of two T-33's," he added with pardonable pride.

During this exchange, the Omni swung, and Coolstone quickly tuned in Klamath Falls. He just homed on it.

Short Stuff leader told Coolstone radar was bringing them in, and soon the flight became visible.

The 101's approached Coolstone from his ten o'clock position and made a large circle to the left, neatly coming up on the Rock's left wing.

Because Coolstone was indicating only about 260, the 101's (with flaps, speed boards, and RO's out) were experiencing some difficulty staying in the air.

"Coolstone from Short Stuff. Can you increase your speed, please? About 300 would be fine. This is a little slow for us."

"Roger," answered Coolstone and increased his power to 100%.

Through the holes in the broken deck, Coolstone could make out Kingsley up ahead. He could see they would have to start a letdown pretty soon. He looked out at the formation. The 101's were really tucked in now, and Two, not to be outdone, was waving a tip tank in the general vicinity of Coolstone's cockpit.

He changed pitch just slightly and started the descent. He was very careful so that none of his movements were sudden. He glanced down at the airspeed indicator and noted that his speed was increasing rapidly. The cockpit temperature seemed to be rising somewhat also. He pulled off power, then put it back on again as the flight started to overrun. He felt a slight burble and glanced at the airspeed indicator once again. They were on the mach.

The cockpit temperature increased a bit more. Got to slow down some, thought Coolstone. Smoothly now, he told himself smoothly. Therefore, very smoothly, he activated the speed brakes.

The bird immediately flew clear out of the formation. In fact, Two and the F-101's were caught flatfooted to the point where everything they did was wrong. They fought to regain their leader, who was wildly trimming nose down.

As he passed through his position of lead ship, going down this time, wing tip clearance was quite limited. With the assistance of some skillful elevator activity, he settled the bird down, and the flight quickly rejoined.

It was downright hot now in the cockpit. He fumbled with the rheostat.

He decided he had better call the tower. "Hello, Kingsley tower. This is Coolstone One with a flight of four for landing instructions. Over."

"Roger, Coolstone, this is Kingsley. Landing to the north, Runway 32, winds from the north at seven, and altimeter is 3001. You are cleared to make a flyby with your formation if you so desire. Over."

Coolstone had had about all of the formation flying he needed for the year if the truth were known. But under these conditions, it was a matter of honor now. "Roger," he told the tower. "We'll make a flyby."

"Give us a call turning initial," answered Kingsley.

Coolstone was letting down almost parallel to the runway now. He leveled at 5,500 and, this time, called the flight as he brought in the boards. The bases of the clouds were about a thousand feet above them, but the air was quite turbulent. The flight was very tight, the speed about 300. They were south of the field now, and Coolstone turned the flight onto a wide base leg.

The element was still on the left. As they approached the turn for initial, Coolstone's Aide spoke for the first time. There had been heavy breathing a time or two up until now, but no words. "Er – sir," he said, "You probably should either change the element over to the right wing or make a 270 to the right so they will have a little less trouble in the turn."

They had progressed to the point where, if a left turn on the initial were to be made, it would have to be done immediately.

Coolstone hesitated for only a moment, then made a command decision. "What the hell," he told his Aide. "They're fighter pilots, aren't they?"

He wrapped the bird up into a 45° bank to the left and fed in the necessary back pressure to keep the nose up. He glanced into the rear-view mirror as a movement there caught his attention. Briefly, he saw that the Aide had placed both hands on top of his helmet. What in the world, he thought. But he didn't have time to analyze the action, for, as he glanced down at the 101's, whose pilots were game, you had to admit that he saw the birds quiver, then shake, then quickly disappear. What's the matter with them? Thought the Cold Rock. I'm giving them 300 knots.

He looked over to where Two should have been and couldn't find him. Looking forward, he saw that the turn was a little more than complete, and he snapped the wings level. Shortly after he did so, Two was the leader – a way-out leader.

Coolstone Takes Flight

Coolstone advised the tower his flight was on the initial for his flyby and was given clearance.

The 101's were doing their very best to get back into formation, and Two was working feverishly to dampen out his power changes, but still, there was very little you could actually call a flight as they crossed the field boundary. Coolstone was quite put out.

What was it with those guys? They just didn't make fighter pilots anymore. That was all there was to it.

At this point, Short Stuff Mobile felt it necessary to comment. "Coolstone flight from Mobile," he said. "You looked like a bunch of crows out there."

Coolstone chose not to receive the transmission.

One of the other pilots in the air (there was no identifier used) answered for him. "Mobile," he sang our cheerily. "You don't know who's leading that flight, but I'll bet you find out."

The flight landed individually.

Coolstone was met by the Base Commander when they parked. No comment was made on the formation. Coolstone was a wreck. The sweat had completely soaked the back of his flying suit jacket. He was tired all over. Two came over to the group with his Aide. Even though a brisk cool breeze was blowing, perspiration was still in evidence on his face. His steps were slow. He also had no comments to make on the formation.

The group went into Operations.

As they entered, the Airdrome Officer approached them. "Sir, were you Tombstone flight leader?" he asked. "FAA is on the line, and they would like to talk to Tombstone. Something about a clearance you didn't get and some position reports they didn't get. Would you like to talk with them?" Coolstone looked for his Aide, who was just out of earshot. He called him over.

"Look," he said, "there seems to be a little trouble with FAA, something about a clearance. Why don't you go ahead and talk to them? By the way, we'll be leaving at about 1500. Take care of the clearance and so on. We'll go back individually." Then he dropped his voice so that no one else could hear. "See if you can explain to FAA what happened. Tell them I'll write them a letter, you know, keep it informal if you can."

"Roger, sir," his Aide answered with more conviction than he felt. "I'll think of something."

Coolstone Beats the System……..

Coolstone was TDY to Hamilton from McChord. It was supposed to have been a one-day deal; go down in the morning, drop off a passenger, and back again that afternoon.

"A quick deal," his Ops Officer had said. "The weather's fine, and you'll get lots of flying time."

Well, now it was three days later, three days in the beautiful San Francisco Bay area, in a moldy flying suit, living on snack-bar food, pocketbooks, and a deodorant stick. Three days because of lousy weather in the McChord area.

Even with the deodorant stick liberally applied, Coolstone noticed that he always had plenty of room in an otherwise crowded snack bar. He had bought shorts, socks, and shaving equipment, and, while holding out to the very last moment, as late as the day before, he finally had to break down and buy a toothbrush and toothpaste. This made a grand total of four toothbrushes, five razors, and numerous partially used tubes of toothpaste now held by Coolstone, for this was not the first time he had been caught out.

He had about concluded that the reason hazard's flying pay was established the first time a far-sighted aviation pioneer with political pull had been weathered in unexpectedly.

Without hope, Coolstone entered the Base Weather Station for the umpteenth time. If there is such a thing as destination fixation, Coolstone had an acute case. He was ready to go, go, go.

He was greeted cordially by the forecaster, who had come to know him very well. "Good morning, good morning, Coolstone. I have good news for you. A strange thing has happened. McChord is now reporting 500 scattered and 15 miles on their last sequence. The surrounding bases of Paine, Portland, and Boeing are still down below minimums, but it looks like they will break out soon since good old McFog is almost clear. Let's sweat out another sequence."

But he was talking to himself, for Coolstone had taken off to the BOQ at the "500 scattered" point.

In less than 30 minutes, Coolstone arrived back at Base Operations, slightly out of breath and carrying a brown bag that held his scanties and toilet equipment. He grabbed a well-worn 175 that had been filled out for three days, changed the date, and trotted into the weather station once again. He shoved the clearance toward the forecaster and said, "Here, Wag, put the weather on this thing quick before something happens."

"Coolstone," said the forecaster, "You had better wait out one more sequence here and be sure that McChord is really going to stay up. I don't know that I can give you a forecast that wouldn't require an alternate, and there just isn't any alternate close enough for your purposes."

"Oh, come off of it, Wag," said Coolstone. "Kingsley is wide open. When I get to Medford, I'll call for weather at McChord. If it's bad, I'll go back into Kingsley. No sweat."

"Well, yes," said the forecaster, "Kingsley will stay up, but can you use it for an alternate as far as the 175 goes?"

"Not quite," said Coolstone, "but McChord is practically clear. I don't need an alternate. I'll just keep Kingsley as my ace in the hole and check the weather for McChord along the way."

"Well, OK," said the forecaster, somewhat doubtfully, "but I wish you'd wait about an hour. I'd feel much better if one of those other stations near McChord breaks out also."

"You worry too much. All weather prophets are pessimists."

The forecaster reluctantly gave Coolstone a McChord forecast for clearing conditions which required no alternate, and the Cold Rock filed his clearance and headed for his T-33. At the bird, he found two alert crewmen all ready and waiting.

"Taking your lunch with you, sir?" asked one, pointing at Coolstone's brown bag.

"Ah, er, negative," said the Rock. "Got some parts in here. How about putting the bag in the nose?"

"Sure enough, sir, said the crewman, taking the bag. He looked somewhat dubiously at it but shrugged and raised the left gun bay door with one hand, intending to place the bag in the front part of the bay with the other.

Now, the wind was fairly brisk out on the ramp, and the alert crewman was just a bit clumsy, so the bag got away from him. Two pairs of shorts and three pairs of socks were picked up by the wind and distributed in an interesting pattern along the ramp, gaining speed as they went. The startled crewman stood with mouth agape, not only at seeing the contents of the bag but also at Coolstone's brilliant display of broken-field running.

When Coolstone returned clutching his unmentionables in his hand, he quickly mounted the bird and got out of there. Try as he might, he couldn't completely ignore the sly looks of the alert crewmen.

By the time Coolstone arrived over Red Bluff, he had regained some of his composure and settled down for a routine flight. He made his position report and headed for Medford.

He could see that the Klamath Falls area was clear, and there was no doubt that it would stay that way.

Coolstone Takes Flight

He settled back in his seat and considered the last three days. "How about that?" he thought. "Three days in San Francisco in a lousy flying suit! The next time I get talked into one of these quick trips, I'll have my head examined."

Coolstone had taken this oath on several different occasions. His stomach was protesting slightly from the three days' steady diet of short orders, and the 29,000-foot altitude at which he was flying did nothing for it. He burped gently.

After station passage over Medford, he called the center.

"Seattle Center, Seattle Center. This is Coolstone One, Coolstone One, Medford, over."

"Roger, Coolstone One, this is Seattle Center. Go ahead."

"Seattle Center, this is Coolstone One, over Medford at 36, flight level 290, estimating McChord at 10. What is the latest weather you have for McChord? Over."

"Roger, on your position, Coolstone. Stand by for the weather."

"Roger," said Coolstone. Up ahead, he could see the low stuff starting. It looked fairly solid and plenty low. But this didn't surprise him because the sequences he had read at Hamilton had led him to expect it.

Then, over the radio, "Coolstone from Seattle Center. Our latest weather for McChord is 500 scattered and 15 miles."

"Roger, boy," said Coolstone. "How about Paine, Portland, and Boeing?"

"All of the bases in the area but McChord are fogged in," said the Center. "Boeing is 100, obscured, and ¼ mile, Portland is 100, obscured and 1/16th, and Paine is 200, obscured and ¼ mile, all in fog."

"Roger, roger, boy," said Coolstone. "Thanks a lot."

Coolstone was pretty sure that the weather he had just received from the Center was from the identical sequences he had read at Hamilton Weather Station. Because of some other distasteful experiences concerning the weather, he did wonder why McChord had held up with the other bases down. He wondered considerably more about this than before he had taken off in the throes of destination fixation.

Now was the time to use the old head, thought the Rock. None of this business of reading the last sequence to him. He'd get it from the horse's mouth. He'd outsmart the system for a change.

He advised the Center that he'd be off their frequency for a while and changed to channel 10 for GCI.

"Hello, Big Eye, hello, Big Eye. This is Coolstone One, over."

"Roger, Coolstone One. This is Big Eye. Go ahead."

"Big Eye from Coolstone One. Can you get me a phone patch through Big Flap to Shirttail Ops? Over."

"Roger, Coolstone," said Big Eye. "We'll try. I'll get the division first, and then you tell them who you want to talk to."

There was a slight delay. Then Big Eye told Coolstone to go ahead. The division was on.

"Hello, Big Flap, this is Coolstone. Do you read me?"

Coolstone Takes Flight

"Roger, Coolstone. This is Big Flap. Read you three by three. What can we do for you?"

"Big Flap from Coolstone. Read you about three by three, too. Would you please patch me through to Shirttail Ops? I want to talk to a pilot at the alert hangar."

"Roger, boy, stand by. We'll get the patch."

Then Coolstone could hear very weakly a voice saying that it was Shirttail Ops, to go ahead. Coolstone attempted to get patched through to the alert hangar from Shirttail Ops, but he just couldn't make himself understood by the squadron alert center. He finally called back to Big Eye again. "Look, Big Eye," he said, "How about relaying my transmissions to Shirttail Ops? Tell them to get one of the alert pilots on the horn so I can find out what the exact McChord weather is. Tell him it's me, Coolstone."

"Roger," said Big Eye. "Stand by."

At this time, Coolstone was approaching Portland. He had to make a decision soon. He couldn't go all the way to McChord and get back to Kingsley gracefully. He was extremely anxious to hear from the alert pilot. He knew he'd get the exact weather that existed right now. This would make up his mind for him.

Finally, Big Eye called. "The pilot at the alert hangar said it's 500 scattered with 15 miles, over."

Much relieved, Coolstone thanked Big Eye and returned to the FAA frequency. That's better, thought Coolstone. That beats the old system - none of this sequence reading. I've got the straight weather. It's the first break I've had in three days.

He made his report at Portland to Seattle Center, was cleared to descend to 20,000 feet, and was advised to contact McChord Approach Control five minutes out.

Up ahead now, Coolstone could see some large breaks in the overcast. They weren't overabundant, and what there was seemed to be east of McChord. They *were* holes in any case.

Five minutes out, he contacted Approach Control and received a clearance for the TVOR penetration.

"What's your present, McChord weather?" he asked, really not caring because he knew.

"Roger," said Approach Control. "Present McChord weather is 300 obscured, ¾ mile, light fog, and drizzle, over."

"300 obscured, and ¾," croaked Coolstone. "What happened to all that 500 scattered jazz you had about 20 minutes ago?"

"Coolstone, from Approach Control. We did break out a couple of hours ago, but the low stuff formed again, and it's been in here, I'd say, about 45 minutes."

What's with the alert pilot? Thought Coolstone. Now he had really had it. He couldn't possibly go back to Kingsley. For one thing, he hadn't used very good cruise control on the whole flight because he had been in such a rush to get home. He could hack 300 and ¾ on his back. It was just that he had lost his hole card in the form of Kingsley. He didn't like the idea of doing this at all.

He received TVOR passage, called Approach Control, and started his penetration. GCI picked him up in the penetration turn and took control. Coolstone wasn't worried about this GCA. He had made it many times.

Coolstone Takes Flight

You couldn't be stationed at McChord for very long without making some type of weather approach, and he had made plenty of them.

GCI established him on final, and Coolstone hit the top of the clouds at about 1,000 feet. He rode the glide path down very well. While on glide slope and center line GCA called minimums and told him to take over the land visually. There was just one problem – Coolstone couldn't see a thing except for trees directly below him. It couldn't be, he thought, but it was. He poured the power on for a missed approach. There was nothing else to do.

He got himself and the bird under control again. Then he called GCA, his voice betraying that he was somewhat shaken. "I couldn't see a thing. I'm going around. Missed approach. How about landing to the south this time? Is the weather any better at that end of the runway?"

"Tombstone one from GCA. Weather is now reporting 200 obscured, ¼ mile visibility with fog. What are your intentions?"

"It's Coolstone One, GCA, not Tombstone. Give me a south approach this time."

"Roger, Tomb--er, Coolstone. Turn right to heading of 340."

"Roger, GCA," Coolstone said. GCA positioned Coolstone on the final for runway 16, and the Cold Rock pasted himself on the glide path. He had minimums again, and this time he let the bird on down, practically standing up in the cockpit trying to see the runway. He was just about to start the go-around once again when he finally picked up the approach lights, saw the threshold, then the runway, and was able to land.

When he could talk again, he called GCA. "This is Tombstone One, GCA. I made it (gasp, puff). Thanks a lot."

Coolstone taxied to the squadron area, left his equipment in the bird, got a car, and headed for the alert hangar. He had a man to see. While driving over, he worked himself up into quite a frenzy. How could that alert pilot be so wrong? All he had to do was look out the window and tell him what he saw.

Where's the Alert Pilot?

He got to the hangar, stomped up the stairs, fighting mad, burst into the lounge, and demanded furiously in evenly spaced words, "Who was on that phone patch that gave me the weather?"

There was a momentary silence, then one of the alert pilots looked up from a well-worn paper-backed novel with no title visible. "It was me," said the pilot. "I was glad to help you out."

"Help me out?" roared Coolstone. "You said it was 500 scattered and 15. I just cracked 100 and ¼ if it was a foot. GCA said it's been like this for an hour. Come here and look out the window."

"I couldn't see anything out of the window," said the alert pilot. "So I just read you the last sequence."

You've Got It Coolstone

Because of his broad and varied experience in all phases of the Aerospace Defense Command's operations, Coolstone One had been selected as a member of that most elite group of all, the ADCOM ORI Team. Coolstone just felt so proud and so pleased with his good fortune he could hardly contain himself. He could scarcely believe that such an honor could be his. There were quite a few others that could scarcely believe it, either. There was, however, a small inner group of headquarters' experienced troops, wise to the ways of the system, that felt that a type such as Coolstone would serve the command well. This conclusion was based on the theory that it took one to know one, and this was really why he was selected.

The secret plans had been drawn. The date had been set. The roving street fighters were about to be unleashed upon the command once again. The target of their attention the 25th Air Division. Because this was the first

ORI since Coolstone was assigned, he was sent to Paine AFB to observe – they said.

What it really did was to keep him out of the way as much as possible. T-bird targets were to be launched from Paine at the secret time that Coolstone knew. He, therefore, awakened at his BOQ room around 0100. He shaved, shined, and otherwise readied himself for his first assault upon the unwary.

His bright new orange flying suit was not resplendent with the appropriate patches, badges, and personal alterations, much to his chagrin. He had managed to scrounge it just before the classified departure time from Peterson Field and had not been able to procure the proper embellishments. He did, however, have a snappy scarf, and his major's leaves shone and were carefully positioned. As he arrived in the squadron ops, it was clear to see that there had been an intelligence leak. Many of the fighter squadron pilots were there and ready. The target pilots were also there, nervously going over their routes. The activity was stimulating to an old war horse such as he, and he found himself wishing to be a direct part of the action. The many times he had been a direct part of the action, he had spent most of the time wishing quite the opposite.

While he wasn't particularly avoided, on the other hand, he was not receiving the attention he figured a representative of the head shed should. For several minutes he observed as he was supposed to do, clearly outside the action, and then, no longer able to contain himself, he sidled up to the ops officer and 'lowed as how he'd noticed they were pretty busy and could he help in any way?

"Well," said the ops type, "we're looking for a body to fly with the colonel on one of the T-bird target missions. Would you be interested?"

Coolstone quickly mentally reviewed his instructions. He could remember no remarks to the effect that he shouldn't observe from a target bird.

Coolstone Takes Flight

"Sounds fine," he said, "I would be glad to fill the hole."

The ops type introduced him to a graying colonel and gave him a target folder, bird number, takeoff times, and the other many details that the target pilot must have to sneak around in the middle of the night effectively. The Rock looked over the target route altitude and saw that they were going out to the west, well out, over the Pacific. He immediately had some second thoughts about being part of the action. At least they were not going to thrash around at low altitude. That was some consolation. He wandered over to the P.E. shop very casually and drew everything that they had for water survival.

The formal briefing was very well conducted, thought Coolstone, and he made a note to that effect. After it was over, he and the colonel went out to the bird.

He helped the colonel with the preflight. He held the flashlight mainly and pointed it at the appropriate places called out to him by the colonel from the checklist. It was a slow but very thorough preflight. Coolstone noticed that the colonel was either somewhat uncertain about his procedures or was, for Coolstone's benefit, touching bases that Coolstone hadn't seen touched for five years.

They strapped in, the colonel in front, of course, got the power, and on the interphone, the colonel, once again, called off each prestart check from the checklist. The colonel then began to start the engine, and he also called off to Coolstone each procedure as he accomplished the action. At exactly the right time, they arrived at the end of the runway.

"How do you want to work this?" asked the colonel. "Do you want me to take care of the flying, and you handle the radios?"

"Sounds fine," said the Rock. "I'll handle the radios and the navigation for you if you like."

"OK," said the colonel, "you take the radios."

"Rog," said Coolstone, and he checked in with the tower for their IFR clearance which had not yet been received as they were taxiing out. He got the clearance and fumbled it only slightly on readback, which, in itself, was a minor miracle. There was a ceiling at about 4,000 and tops were estimated at 12,000. Out to sea, the weather was even better - strictly a no-sweat flight.

The tower released them for takeoff, and once again, the colonel carefully called all pre-takeoff checks. Then they had at it. The takeoff was normal.

They checked in with departure control, established their climb heading and airspeed, but just before they entered the cloud deck, the colonel said, "You've got it."

Coolstone wasn't ready and really didn't want it, but he took it and shook the stick, indicating he had it. The Rock glued his eyes to the instruments and attempted to maintain some semblance of a climb attitude that would get them through to the tops. He began to experience a slight case of vertigo. He had a death grip on the stick. He could see that if they didn't get on top pretty soon, they wouldn't. He had about arrived at the point where he felt that he would have to give it back to the colonel before he fell out of the airplane when he noted they had finally broken out.

"I've got it," said the colonel.

"Rog," said the Rock, between gasps.

The target mission was uneventful. They were intercepted on schedule, and Coolstone mentally noted to include on his observation report that the 25th's systems were all go and procedures and effectiveness were good. "Tips dry, leading-edge checked, wing tanks on," said the colonel.

Coolstone Takes Flight

One thing about this cat thought the Rock, he keeps you informed. They headed back for Paine, were handed off to Approach Control, and started their descent. Coolstone was tidying up the cockpit a bit, stowing charts and cards.

He hadn't flown with many colonels. But unless this one was from SAC, he certainly operated strangely, much differently than the fighter squadron pilots. Everything he did, he did very deliberately and always advised Coolstone before he did it.

Coolstone could see that they were nearing the cloud deck again, and just before they entered, the colonel said, "You've got it."

Once again, the Rock wasn't ready and didn't want it. "I've got it," he said weakly and wondered to himself what was wrong with this guy. Every time they got near a cloud, it was "You've got it."

Coolstone was really spring-loaded to the vertigo position this time, but he hung on as best he could to the attitude that the colonel had established during the descent. They kind of fell out of the bottom of the clouds, and Coolstone didn't wait. He quickly said, "You've got it."

"Roger," said the colonel, and added, "Do you want to cancel IFR and go on in and pitch, or shall we make it an ILS?"

"Suit yourself, sir," replied the Rock, "And do you have the field in sight?"

"Roger," said the colonel. "I've got it dead ahead."

"Paine tower from Coolstone One. Have field in sight. Please cancel IFR. And we need landing instructions, please."

"Roger, Coolstone," said the tower, "IFR canceled. Landing is to the north, runway 34, report five miles on initial."

The colonel quickly and smoothly set them up on an initial approach.

Coolstone rested his elbows on the canopy rails and relaxed for the routine pattern and landing. The colonel pitched, "You've got it," he said.

Coolstone scrambled for the stick, pumped it a time or two, leveled the wings for the downwind, and said, "You've got it."

The colonel called gear and flaps, started the turn for the base, and said, "You've got it."

"What's with this cat, thought the Rock as he herded the bird generally towards the final, and then he said, desperately, "Colonel, you've got it."

"Look," said the colonel, you're the IP. I've never flown this machine before, and with the night landing and everything, I think you'd better take it. I probably should have been in the rear seat, anyhow."

A great burst of adrenalin caused Coolstone to stand up in the cockpit as he jammed the throttle to the full position. "Colonel," he said desperately, "I'm not an IP; I'm an RO. I can't land this thing. You've got it, and I never want it again!"

The colonel took it. "This is rather awkward," he said, "I sure hate to get everybody on the ground upset."

Coolstone, now working on a level slightly below full panic, put his broad experience to good use at last. "Look," he said, "why not declare just a minor emergency? You know, just enough to get the fire trucks out but not enough to bring out the whole base. I would just as soon not have any more publicity than necessary myself. How about an unsafe gear? That ought to work."

Coolstone Takes Flight

"Great idea," answered the colonel. "Go ahead and give them a call. And look," added the colonel, "I appreciate your help. Don't sweat it too much. I think I can get this thing down in the correct number of pieces."

Coolstone relaxed to rigid, then said with a great deal of bravado, which took extreme self-control, "My end goes where your end goes, colonel; I'm with you."

He then called the tower "Paine tower from Coolstone One. We have an unsafe gear indication and are going around. Please get the fire trucks out." The note of desperation in his voice belied the minor nature of the declared emergency.

"Roger, Coolstone," replied the tower. "We saw you as you went over. They look like they are down to us. Emergency vehicles are alerted."

"Roger, tower, we will make a large box pattern and land."

"Coolstone One from mobile control. Do you need any help? I'll read the checklist for you if you like."

"Negative; I don't believe there's anything you can do," said Coolstone. "Particularly from down there."

The colonel made a big box pattern - big - big - big.

"Roger, Coolstone," said the tower, "we don't have you in sight. I think you went over the horizon. How far out are you?"

"We're a ways out, all right," replied Coolstone, "BUT WE'RE WORKING ON THIS GEAR."

"Roger," said the tower, "call us when you're turning final."

Three other aircraft came in and pitched and landed ahead of them without disturbing their pattern in the slightest.

"Tombstone One from Paine. Are you still going to land here? And is your gear still unsafe?"

"That's Coolstone One," said the Rock, "Coolstone One, and yes, we're still coming in, and yes, we still have the emergency."

"Roger, Tomb - er - Coolstone. Do you have the field in sight yet?"

"Roger, roger," said the Rock, "I can see it up ahead. We're on final now."

"Roger," said the tower, and added dryly, "you're cleared to land whenever you get here."

Coolstone Takes Flight

The moment of truth had finally arrived, accompanied by numerous power changes, but either because of his several thousand hours or a lot of luck, the colonel greased it in but was about halfway down the runway.

"Tombstone One from mobile control. You'd better take it around; you're down too far. Tombstone One, take it around, take it around, you're too far down, too hot."

"Negative," said the Rock weakly. "We'll keep what we've got."

The radio was silent for several moments.

Then, "Tower, this is Tombstone One; please send a truck out to the barrier. We seem to be somewhat entangled."

Coolstone Ends an Era

Coolstone had noticed the P-51s flying around quite often. He would see flights of two or four almost daily. At first, he thought they were transient, but their frequency was such that it didn't seem possible that they were not coming from a local air base. He worked his way down to the old airport by the river, and sure enough, he could see the 51s parked at one end. He drove to the fighter area and found that the ramp, hangars, and admin building for something called a Guard Squadron were fenced off from the rest of the airport. He stopped for a minute just to admire the fighters. He also saw considerable action on the ramp. People were actually making motions like they might be working on airplanes. He saw a pilot strolling out to one. He saw the pilot get in one. He saw the pilot start one, taxi out, and take off. That did it. He drove into the admin area, parked, and went into the building that advertised itself as Fighter Squadron Headquarters. A sergeant was at a desk typing.

"What can I do for you?" he asked.

"I am, or I was a pilot," answered Coolstone, "and I would like to see how I go about getting into this outfit. Are you taking any pilots?"

"Well, we might be," said the sergeant, "but you'd better talk to the Old Man before you do anything else. He's right in there," the sergeant said, pointing to an open office door. "I'll see if he's busy."

The sergeant went in and was back out in less than 5 seconds. "Go on in," he said to Coolstone.

The Rock wished he had a haircut or at least had shined his shoes a bit. First impressions were important, he knew, but he was like he was now, so in he went. He saw a short, medium-fat, dark-haired man in a faded green flying suit who greeted him with an inch-and-a-half cigar butt clenched between his teeth. "Sit down," the Major said after the introductions were over. "What's on your mind?"

"I'd kinda like to see about... er, maybe getting into your outfit," trailed off the Rock, knowing full well he had blown it.

Coolstone Takes Flight

"Hm-m-m-m," said the major. "How many flying hours do you have?"

"About 1800," answered Coolstone (he actually had 1710). "I haven't flown much since the war was over. I have been in that Reserve outfit out at the base, but they don't fly much."

"What did you fly in War II?" asked the major. Coolstone had been afraid of this question from the onset. "B-25s." said the Rock. (He had two flights overseas with a friend of his.) "And," he added weakly, "a little C-47 time."

"How much C-47 time?" asked the Old Man.

"About 1400 hours," said Coolstone very reluctantly.

"Gooney Birds," snorted the commander. "You flew Gooney Birds 1400 hours, and now you want me to take you into this outfit when I've got fighter pilots queued up for blocks waiting to get in. No way." said the major. "No way at all. This is a fighter outfit, and I want fighter pilots only. Sorry, but you're wasting your time here."

He stood up, obviously ending the conversation. The cigar was still clenched in his teeth, had never been removed, and was completely dead as far as the Rock could see.

"Look," Coolstone said to him. "I was a pretty good pilot. I think I could hack it." But the Old Man had quit listening to him at the C-47 point.

Reluctantly Coolstone made his exit. Well, that was that. And, for the next two or three months, Coolstone's relationship with aviation was limited to weekly pilgrimages to the Guard Base, hanging over the fence, watching the '51s taking off and landing, and, occasionally, talking to the chosen few who flew them. He ate lunch with them and generally ingratiated himself into their midst. They always talked flying, particularly just after they landed. He was amazed to find that some were teachers, one was a lawyer, and another was a doctor. There was a dentist, a policeman, a stockbroker, and several were airline pilots, but all of them, everyone, were fighter pilots first.

On three more occasions, Coolstone approached the Old Man. The last time he was invited out before he got in. The sergeant had stopped him as soon as he came through the door.

One Sunday afternoon, as he was about to leave his own personal Mobile Control position, a major, whom the Rock recognized as the Guard Advisor, came up to him. Coolstone had met him before, but he had an Italian name that the Rock could not remember.

"Look," said the advisor, "Do you really want to get in this outfit? I mean, no fooling? Without any fighter time, it will be rough. Three or four of these guys are aces, and there are probably 30 to 40 more victories if you total the kills of everyone now assigned to the squadron. And, they don't give much quarter to a new boy."

"I don't care what they do." said the Rock. "More than ever, I want to get in that outfit. I want to fly that machine so bad I can taste it. But the commander has told me three times, not only 'No' but 'Hell No.' I try to stay out of his sight as much as possible now. I've bugged him a lot."

"Well," said the advisor, "I'll tell you how to get in the outfit, but first, you've got to promise me that my name will NOT be mentioned at all."

Coolstone nodded in agreement.

"Now, here's what you do. Go over to the wing. Take any job they have open, no matter what. Then immediately apply for the squadron. Whenever an opening comes for pilots in the squadron, they have to take the applications from the wing first. OK?"

Coolstone Takes Flight

Coolstone nodded.

"Now, for God's sake, don't tell ANYONE I was a part of this. Good luck." said the Advisor, and he walked away, leaving Coolstone with a full adrenalin flow and his mouth still open to thank him.

Three months after taking the advisor at his word, Coolstone had been notified by the wing that his transfer to the squadron was approved. He was also told that he should go out to the squadron and talk to the commander. He was to be assigned the following month officially. Coolstone did just that. This time, he had his pinks and greens on, his shoes shined, and his hair cut. He walked boldly into the squadron headquarters and told the sergeant, who was obviously surprised to see him, "I want to see the commander, and before you say 'No,' I want you to know I am assigned to this outfit or will be as of next month, as one of his new pilots."

Now the sergeant had seen this little drama unfold from the beginning. Secretly he had been on Coolstone's side. There weren't too many people who had the nerve enough to hit the Old Man up three times running for anything and still take "No" for an answer.

"I don't think he's going to like it," he told the Rock. "In fact, I think he might get violent and dangerous when he finds out you are going to be a new pilot here. But I'll tell him."

The sergeant disappeared into the commander's office, then returned. "Go on in," he said. Then he whispered, "I didn't tell him it was you. Just that a new pilot was reporting."

The Rock went in, saluted smartly, and said, "Sir, First Lieutenant Coolstone reporting as ordered."

The salute surprised the Old Man almost as much as seeing Coolstone, but gamely he returned the salute even though he didn't get the two-inch cigar butt out of his mouth until afterward. It was the first time Coolstone had ever seen it out at all.

"What are YOU doing here?" he asked the Rock wearily. "I've told you, it seems like a dozen times, you CAN'T get in here. Now you are wasting my time."

"Sir," said Coolstone, "I AM in. I'm your new fighter pilot. I transferred from the wing."

"Oh-h-h-h no," groaned the Old Man. "They can't DO that to me."

He reached for the phone, dialed a number, grunted a salutation, then said, "What's this guy Coolstone doing over here? He tells me you transferred him to me. He's a Gooney Bird pilot, for gosh sake. I can't use him. He knows exactly how I feel. If we put him in a 30-degree bank, he will probably declare an emergency. What am I supposed to do with him?"

There was silence as the Old Man absorbed the information given to him by the person on the other end of the line. Finally, he said, "Yes, Sir. Yes, Sir. I understand. I will take care of it." and then he hung up.

He turned to Coolstone. "OK," he said. "I don't know exactly how you did it, but you did. Now, here's what else you are going to do. Starting next month, when you are officially transferred to me, you're going to get three rides in a T-6. That's all. Have you flown one before?"

Coolstone shook his head.

"Then, you're going to solo the '51. If you live through that, you will be assigned to B Flight as a duty pilot. Then we're going to fly your butt off. You'll have to come out here at least twice a week and every weekend. If you can't hack any of this, just say so right now. You can stay at the wing, and you can save everybody a lot of trouble."

Coolstone Takes Flight

Coolstone took a deep breath. There was no problem getting away to fly, but he had never flown a T-6. In fact, with the exception of holding the stick for 30 minutes three times in the Reserve outfit, he really had not flown anything for almost a year. But he knew he could do it.

"No problem," he said confidently to the commander. "No problem at all." He saluted, stepped back, did an about-face without getting his feet tangled, and left the office.

The sergeant was impressed. He smiled and gave Coolstone the Victory sign. Coolstone smiled back, put his hat on firmly, and walked out of the building. He met the advisor coming in.

"How did it go?" the advisor asked.

"He was pretty hot," said the Rock. "Starting next month, I get three T-6 rides and then solo the '51. Then I have to fly twice a week and every weekend until I get up to speed. The only thing I am going to have a problem with, I think, is the T-6. I've never flown it before. I haven't flown anything for a year."

"Boy," said the advisor. "He really put it to you. That's the routine they give the experienced fighter pilots: You have a problem."

"Yeah, I know," said the Rock. "Is the T-6 much?"

"Well, no," said the major, "if you have flown it before, you could come up to speed pretty fast. But, three rides, cold. I don't know."

The advisor stood for a minute thinking. Then he said, "I'll tell you what. For the rest of the month, every day when the weather is OK, you meet me out here after five. Be sure it's after five, and don't let anyone see you. We'll fly the hell out of the T-6. If we don't get caught, I'll have you in Cuban Eights before you get your first ride with the squadron."

Coolstone didn't know what a Cuban Eight was, but before it was over, he found out. He found out a lot of things in the next two weeks. When he reported to the squadron on his first drill, he had almost 50 hours of T-6 time under his belt.

Well, he got the three T-6 rides, he soloed the '51 on his fourth ride in the squadron, and he flew four to five times a week until he had 50 hours in the airplane and he had some very traumatic experiences. He had fallen out of everything there was to fall out of, but he didn't declare an emergency. He wanted to a couple of times, particularly when they started rolling from wing to wing when they went from echelon to fingertip and vice versa. He might have declared an emergency, but he fell out a lot then too.

The squadron pilots were good, and they knew it. They were airplane drivers of the first water, and they could stack up with anybody. When they were converted to 84Bs, they came up to speed quickly and flew them well, even though they weren't exactly sure just how all that hot air blowing out the back made them go.

And when they were recalled for Korea, it was like an extended two-week encampment. Some of the squadron pilots went immediately to Japan, then Korea, and they didn't have to go through any CCTS. Nobody turned in their wing or tried to quit, even though there were some real hardships involved, particularly with those people who were running their own businesses.

Nor, when they received their first inspection, was it any surprise that they got nothing but shocked and respectful looks from the inspectors. Coolstone also got a shock. He and three others had qualified in gunnery and had instrument cards too. A deadly combination, Coolstone found. This made them eligible for an assignment to the All-Weather School at Tyndall. The colonel (the Old Man had been promoted) seemed genuinely sorry to see the Rock go. In the past five years, while Coolstone was in the squadron, he had given the Old Man some real grounds that would have

Coolstone Takes Flight

gotten rid of him easily. The most notable of these concerned a County Fair at the Rock's hometown.

"They want lots of flying over the Fair," the Rock told the squadron. "Hit them anytime on the way out or when coming back. They will love us down there."

You will never fly another Air force aircraft!!

Well, the first flight of four hit them at 7:30 on a Sunday morning. This got quite a few folks' attention. The next flight hit them at 11:30. This turned out the church congregation that was right next to the Fair Ground. By the time the Rock's flight got over, a horse show was on. On about his fourth pass, and, while he was performing an intricate maneuver, inverted, the Fair folks had seen far too many F-84s. The horses were panicking and stampeding, people were falling off them, and it was reliably reported that one show sow miscarried. They called the sheriff, who called the squadron, who called Coolstone out of the sky. Coolstone reported to the Old Man in his suntans. He saluted. The Old Man came right up to him, grabbed his wings, which were the bayonet-fastened type, ripped them right off his shirt, and told him he would never fly another Air Force aircraft.

Coolstone had felt tears gathering in his eyes as he stumbled out of the office. But, for the next three months, all that happened was that he was not scheduled to fly and pulled either AO, OD, or Mobile Control on every drill.

The Old Man said not one word to him.

His flight leader told him to hang tough. If the Old Man was out to get rid of him, he would have done it a week after the buzzing. Sure enough, one day, his name was on the flying schedule. His flight commander told him, "Get out there and fly - right now. Don't wait for the rest of us. It might be a mistake."

Coolstone did, and there was never another word said. He flew regularly. Coolstone also had never buzzed again. Never, never, never.

The Rock spent his 21 months of active duty in All-Weather Squadrons. He spent a year of it in the Korean F-94 Squadron. Then, with a good many of his Guard friends, after the 21 months were up, he went home and was a civilian again.

Pulling alert is always miserable. It doesn't make much difference what kind of an alert it is. You have a tendency to tense up, pump adrenalin and watch the weather reports a lot if you think there's a chance you're going to scramble. As a matter of fact, when you pull alert at night in Vietnam, just the idea of a scramble in an F-100, for real, will get anybody's attention. There were two of them on, and, with any luck at all, they would scramble in pairs should the occasion arise. But, about the only thing that would cause a night scramble was troops in contact.

The Rock had checked the weather, and, except for a line of thunderstorms well south of them, it was great. Two, his trusty wingman, had sacked out. Coolstone wasn't quite ready for sleep yet. They had come on duty at 2300, and it was now about 0100. With the briefing, preflight, and his adrenalin level, which was just now starting to reduce some, Coolstone had not yet been able to think about sleep.

Coolstone Takes Flight

They were two months in Vietnam, and it hardly seemed that long. They had been recalled about five months earlier, spent a couple of months exercising their armament systems by practicing strafing, bombing, and dropping napalm, all of the real stuff, then 25 pilots and 25 F-100S started overseas. Fourteen air refuelings later and three landings (no aborts, no delays), they were in place.

Charlie had said "Hello" that night. He said it with mortars and rockets. They all knew right then that this time it was for real.

Coolstone was a pilot, all right. Had been since he was 22. He also was a lawyer with his own practice, a practice which had been interrupted twice now by recalls. "He just might stay in this time," he thought. "Doesn't seem practical to keep fiddling with the law practice when, in fact, my primary interest is flying."

Lots of professional men in the Guard; just why, he wasn't sure. Most of them had come off active duty as he had wanted to keep their hand in regardless of what their Air Force skills were, so they joined the Guard.

He chuckled to himself. The BIG general had visited them two weeks or so after they had arrived. Two 100s were taxiing in. "When are you going to start flying combat?" the general had asked the Old Man.

The Old Man looked at him for a moment, then pointed down to the two '100s just parking. "Missions 299 and 300, sir, just taxiing in."

The BIG general was amazed.

"But, why shouldn't we be able to get right at it? The 25 pilots average 4000 hours total, each 2400 hours of fighter time, and all have more than 1000 hours in the '100. Then look at our maintenance people. So good you couldn't believe it." He laughed right out loud this time when he thought about the division commander, a one-star, asking the Old Man how they could go so long without a dud.

"Dud time," the general explained, "had never been longer than three days before the Guard outfit had gotten there. The Guard started with a week before they had a dud and had stretched it out to two weeks several times."

"Darned if I know," said the Old Man. "Let me call." He talked to the armament NCO, hung up, and then said to the general, "Doc preps them at night, and they've just got to be right before he hangs them."

"Doc," said the general, laughing a bit. "He must be some kind of an armorer."

"Well," said the Old Man, "Not really. He has a Ph.D. in history. Two of his crewmen have Ph.D.s in other things. I'm not sure just what. They're all teachers. In fact, on our arming crews, there are three Ph.D.s, a CPA, the Vice President of the First National Bank, and a silver miner from Climax, just to keep them all honest."

The general shook his head. "No wonder," he said. "Say, could we borrow one of them? Just to give a little OJT?"

"Sure," said the Old Man. "But you'd better talk to Doc first. He's pretty fussy about what his people do."

"How do you keep those people hanging bombs on a part-time basis at home?" asked the general.

"Oh," the Old Man had answered, "I guess they just like to do it. I couldn't keep them from it if I wanted to, and I certainly don't."

Coolstone Takes Flight

With a little smile on his face and completely relaxed now, the Rock dozed a little bit. He was prideful in his organization. They WERE good.

The alert phone rang. It rang with its miserably insistent, not-to-be-denied, characteristic, obscene tone. The Rock grabbed it. "Troops in contact," said the urgent voice on the other end. "Scramble." He gave Coolstone a TACAN fix off of Bien Hoa and told him the FAC's call sign.

"Let's go," Coolstone shouted to Two, raced out to the revetments where their birds were, and arrived just as the crew chiefs started the APUs. They cranked up and scrambled individually. It was a black, black night. No moon, but - no weather. He could see Two bobbing around on the right-hand side in a spread formation. He leveled at 16.5 and headed south. He checked in and was told to "Expedite! Expedite! It's urgent."

"Burner in," said Coolstone as they were about 120 nautical miles from the target. Up ahead, the Rock could see lightning. The lightning revealed large buildups. Near the TACAN fix he had been given, he was well embedded in a thunderstorm. He called the FAC, reported in, and told him they had two napalms, two high drags, and 800 rounds of 20 MM each.

"Rog," said the FAC. "You're going to have to get right down very low. The ceiling's not much, and it's raining. It's a fire support base, and the Commies are on and through the fence. The commander wants napalm right on the fence, and he says to hurry. They are really hurting."

Coolstone dropped the boards and pushed on over, down through the thunderstorm. He lost Two. The Rock broke out at 1500.

"Where are you?" he asked the FAC. "I see lots of tracers and fires, but which is the target?"

"I don't have a visual on you," said the FAC, "but the target is about 100 meters square. There's a red light on each corner. It's right in the middle of where you see the tracers and the fire."

But now Coolstone wasn't seeing a thing. He was in the middle of a rain storm, indicating about 450. "I can't see you," said the FAC. "Where are you now?" "I'm north of the fire," said the Rock. He could see again.

"I'm coming up in trail," said Two, who also had a real good head of steam up.

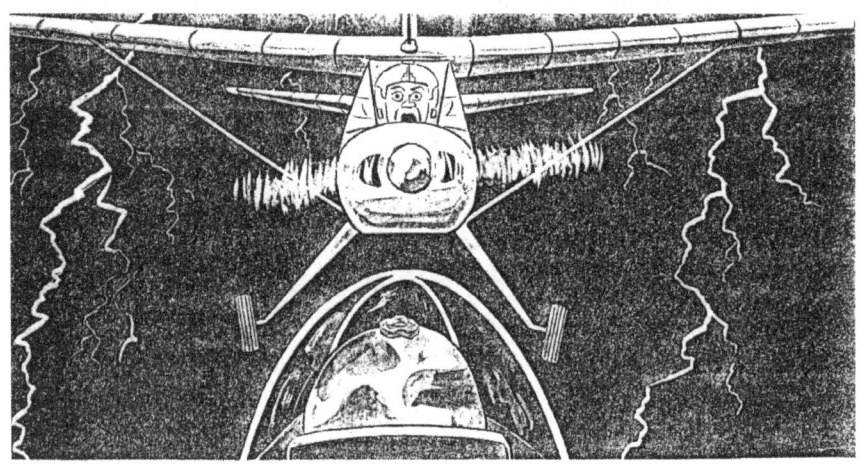

I SEE YOU TOO!

"I see you," said the FAC as One flashed by him head-on." I see you too," said the Rock, who had had a windscreen full of him for a while.

"I'm in the clouds," said Two. "I had to pull up to miss the FAC." "You have the target dead ahead now," said FAC. "Please expedite."

"Burner in," said Coolstone. "Burner out," he added immediately as almost every gun within twenty miles zeroed in on him.

"I got the message," said Two. "I'm back in the clouds again."

Coolstone Takes Flight

Coolstone saw a tiny, tiny target with dim, very dim, red lights. He had never seen such a small target in his life. "I think I've got it," he told the FAC.

"Lay it on the fence," the FAC said again. "Lay it right on. The commander says he's got to have it."

"Lay it on the fence," thought Coolstone. "I'll never make it."

"Put it on the compound side of the fence," said the FAC, "or they've had it."

The Rock was down to 100 feet and 500 knots. "Just a little fast," he said to himself. He suddenly saw that he was off to the right as he neared the target. He saw that if he kept going as he was, he'd drop his napalm dead center in the compound. He quickly banked left, then right, saw the fence, and punched the napalm.

The whole sky lit up behind him. To complicate matters, a flare came down through the clouds ahead of him from a flare ship that was above. It looked like he was flying into a wall. But what really bothered him - he was sure that he had dropped it on the good guys. He was just a little sick. Nobody said anything. He broke back around to set up another run. The FAC came on.

"It was perfect, Coolstone! Perfect! Right on the wire! They are on the run. Drop the next one 100 meters off the wire. They're bailing out!"

Coolstone relaxed. Then he immediately tensed. He met Two, head-on, level.

Two pulled up. "I'm in the weather again," he said to One. "Was that you?"

"For God's sake," said Coolstone. "Get down here and STAY down here."

"Roger," said Two. "I've got the target, and I'm rolling in now."

They dropped all their ordnance, then strafed a bit just because it was there, and went home. As they were walking into the alert trailer, the phone rang.

"Were you on that flight?" a voice asked Coolstone. "The one down south?"

"Roger," said the Rock, just a bit reluctant to admit it. "We weren't too organized, I'm afraid."

"I don't know about that," said the voice. "I command that brigade, and you saved our bacon. We found 54 dead VC on the wire, some more next to it. They just flat-bugged out when you dropped that first napalm. Great work!"

The next morning after they had been relieved, One and Two were called to the Old Man's office. "Heard you had a little action last night. Sounds like you did good work."

"Yeah," said Coolstone. Then he closed the office door. "Look, Boss. There's something we had better tell you about that mission, and we'd just as soon you wouldn't spread it around too much. You see, two lost me on the letdown through the thunderstorms. Then we almost hit the FAC. Then I almost hit Two again, head on, and ...."

* * *

By outlasting a good many of his friends, Coolstone was now the Guard group commander. He sat in his office with his feet up on the desk. He stared out the window that overlooked the parking area, just as busy as it had been 27 years before when he had hung over the fence for the first time and looked at it. They were on a great runway, had great facilities, he had a bunch of crews that really knew their business and their maintenance was top-notch, but he felt horrible. He had just been advised that his unit, among several others, would be completely shut down and disbanded within six months.

"Well," he thought to himself, "they've reached for us three or four times, and we've always been there. I wonder what's going to happen the next time they reach."

No Lace on Coolstone

The Cold Rock was on alert, fifteen minutes, really, and the weather was down. Mandatory was the word. With fifteen-minute status, plus the mandatory weather, he wasn't too concerned about any action for the rest of the night. Just before retiring, he and his faithful RIO went down to the Voodoo and gave it one last check.

Coolstone One and Two were a very striking combination. Coolstone One was about six two two hundred pounds, more or less, barrel-chested even though his chest was running down further than it used to. He was slow and deliberate in his actions, and only the scramble horn could really get him moving. Two, his fearless RIO, was about five six, a hundred and thirty, wirey, nervous, and quick. The pair pulled alert often together, probably because their great differences in size and personalities provided some unnamed attraction.

When they returned from checking the bird, they decided to sack out. They knew that unless an extremely critical situation developed, there would be no problems during the night.

"Look," said One to Two, "if something should come up, I'll get on the horn to Bloodshot, and you get out to the bird more skosh. If we have to go, it will take some time to get everything cranked up, and I'll want to check the weather real good again for alternates. You can get things rolling down at the bird."

"Rog," said Two, and quickly peeled off his shoes and flying suit. He placed them at the foot of his top bunk. One did the same with his clothes at the foot of the bottom bunk. Sacked out, the Rock burped gently, greased in a landing or two under very, very trying circumstances, sighed contentedly, and fell asleep.

Two had the target all the way, head on, rate of closure fifteen hundred knots, locked on, but at B time, the pilot fouled it up. He sighed, rolled over, knocked his suit off the end of the bed, and fell asleep also.

Some people count sheep. Several hours later, One was awakened by an urgent voice telling him that Bloodshot was on the line. He got up and took the call.

"This is Coolstone, Bloodshot; go ahead."

"Roger, boy, we have an emergency. May have to scramble you since you are the closest to the bogie."

"Hey, wait a minute," said the Chilled Rock, "We're nothing and nothing here. What about the Guard Squadron? Let them have it."

Coolstone Takes Flight

"The way the bogie's tracking," said Bloodshot, "they couldn't get to it. You're about the only ones that can get it. We have an alternate for you, pretty much on the way. The emergency is a B-52."

"Stand by," said Coolstone, and raced over to where Two was sleeping, woke him up quickly, and told him, "Better get going. It looks like we're going to have to scramble." Two came up blinking and scrambling for clothes.

One got back on the horn to Bloodshot and said, "What's wrong with that aluminum cloud anyhow? Are they down to seven engines?"

"Negative," said Bloodshot, "they've had an electrical fire, lost their navigation equipment, and lost their radio shortly after they declared the emergency. They are circling now, waiting for help. Wait, a second-the Division Commander has Okayed the scramble, so go! How long will it take?"

"We are on our way now," said the Rock, and visions of air medals passed before his eyes. As he raced back to the sleeping room, the horn began to sound, which provided One with more motivation than he really needed. He found his shoes and flying suit, along with the survival vest. He tried to don the suit but couldn't even get one leg in it. He tried again, desperately, but it was impossible. He looked at the suit closely and saw, to his horror, that it was Two's.

The horn was still sounding, his adrenalin was pumping, and he hesitated only momentarily, much to his credit, and then he put on his shoes and vest and scrambled in his skivvies. He raced down to the aircraft, and as he took to the ladder, the crew chief stared and then said, "Dressed a little light, aren't you, Sir?"

Coolstone just glared and mounted the bird. When he finally got strapped in and connected, he shouted at Two, "You've got my suit!"

"Thought something was funny," said Two, "I tripped all the way up the ladder. I almost fell off."

"I don't have a flying suit," said One, "I am in my skivvies."

"Rog," said Two, "I've got the vector for us, and it's gate to 40,000."

One started the engines, cleared the barn, but when the Rock saw the weather, he forgot all about his clothing problem. He cautiously lined up, checked his instruments for sure, real good, hesitated but a minute, released the brakes, lit the burners, and was IFR approximately twelve seconds later. He switched to Bloodshot's frequency and checked in.

"Roger, boy, got you five square and have you on the weapon. The fifty two is still circling. She's about two hundred nautical miles, two five zero, and last reported 35,000."

Coolstone Takes Flight

"Roger, boy," said One, "What have you got for an alternate?"

"Standby one," said Bloodshot, "We're checking on it right now."

"What d'ya mean you're checking on it?" said Coolstone, "There's no chance of getting back to home plate. It was terrible on takeoff. Where are we going to take the B-52, Bloodshot?"

"Standby one," said Bloodshot, "We're checking on it now."

One acknowledged disgustedly.

Two complained gently, "It's a little hot in here, don't you think, One?"

"Look," said One, "from where I'm sitting, it's extremely drafty. If you sweat, you sweat."

"Coolstone from Bloodshot. The B-52 just called in; he's got his fire out and radios back. They don't need you now, and I think they're heading for Bermuda or some such place. Your alternate is doing fine, and it's the municipal airport."

"Municipal!" shouted the Rock, "I'm not going into any municipal airport, and that is final. Find something else, and it's gotta be Air Force, understand, Air Force!"

"Rog," said Bloodshot, "Standby."

"Well, Two," said One. "You've really got me in a mess. Can you imagine pulling up in front of an airline terminal and me getting out of the bird, no ladder, in my skivvies?"

"We've got a great set here," said Two. "Too bad we couldn't run on something."

"Wait till we get on the ground, boy; you'll be running."

"Coolstone One from Bloodshot. Everything is below minimums within range except the municipal. The Colonel has checked with them, and they can handle you fine. They even said they would pull you up right next to the terminal, and you could have the run of the place. The airline passengers waiting will get a big kick out of seeing a fighter and will undoubtedly want to talk to the crew."

"I think I'm sick," said One, "and I'm going to kill you, Two."

"Great set," said Two.

"Bloodshot from Coolstone One. I think I have just had a radio failure. If you read, I'm heading for home plate."

"Tombstone One from Bloodshot. The Colonel says you are to land at the municipal airport. Do you understand? Home plate is lousy."

"That's Coolstone One, Bloodshot, not Tombstone. And I have had a radio failure, and that's it."

"Look," said Two, sounding a little worried for the first time, "let's go to the municipal. You stay in the cockpit, kinda like a static display, and I'll get out and lead the guided tour. When the weather gets better at home, we can go ahead and take off."

"You've gotta be kidding," said One. "We're not forecasted to get above minimums for eight hours. We're going to home plate now."

The Rock made his penetration and three practice ILSs. On the fourth, One's hair was up on the back of his neck, and Two's voice had become squeaky.

Coolstone Takes Flight

"That is it," Coolstone said to Two. "If we don't make it, we're going to have to punch."

As he hit the middle marker, he forced himself to keep the bean mixing to a minimum. He had the cross hairs dead center. The practice did help. A long, long time after passing through minimums, he got a glimmer of the strobes, then the threshold lights, and then *a* runway light. He chopped the power and landed. There was a rush of fast breathing on the intercom, which had been absolutely silent since the middle marker.

As he turned off the runway, Coolstone found that his legs were shaking to a point where control was marginal. He was forced to stop for a moment.

"Man," said Two, "you are one instrument pilot. I was kinda worried there for a minute."

"No sweat," said One, forgetting he had been planning an assassination just minutes before. Because of the visibility and the leg problem, it took Coolstone a long time to get to the pits, long enough, in fact, so that when he did finally arrive, quite an impressive-looking little group had assembled.

"Hey," said Two, "The Colonel's out there, the Squadron Commander, and the Ops Officer also."

Coolstone One did not answer. They shut down and were chocked, the ladder was up, and Two was out. One was still extremely busy in the cockpit.

He hadn't even found the time to look out, but he knew he couldn't delay the inevitable, and finally, he slowly stood up and climbed down the ladder. The reception group moved forward as a man stopped, stared, and then obviously were victims of a serious emotional disorder.

Two quickly told them that his set was good and there had been no intercepts. He was excused from the debriefing, but he hung around outside of the office, waiting. He thought it only proper. Occasionally he could hear high-pitched voices and catch a word or two. He wished he hadn't.

It had been fairly quiet in the debriefing office for about five minutes before Two heard the door open. The group came out with One in the trail position. The Squadron Commander stopped, went back to Coolstone One, walked around him very slowly, looking him over carefully, then said, "Coolstone, you're going to have to talk to your wife about the kind of bleach she is using."

Coolstone Lights a Stogie

When you were stationed at McChord in the winter, any TDY south was good news. Therefore, when the 89s were grounded - bad wings, bad engines, or both (Coolstone wasn't sure), the squadron at McChord with its 94s picked up the alert commitment at Hamilton. A real sweet deal. The crews were cycled two weeks down, then two weeks back at McChord. The bad news was that with the exception of the flight down and back, it was all alert-24 hours on and 24 hours off - not that a few of the crews didn't make it into the San Francisco area on their 24 off. In fact, considerable cultural exchanges took place during the 24 hours off from alert. More cultural exchanges than sleep, usually.

Coolstone had been down to Hamilton from McChord twice before since the 89s had been grounded. He and his fearless RO (Two) were now on their third tour. During each 24-hour alert tour, at least three or four scrambles were made by all four crews. The reason for this high-level activity was that the ADIZ was narrow and the tolerances even narrower.

Unless you were 5 minutes within your ETA and within 20 miles of your track, you were declared unknown. This immediately required a scramble. The contract cargo bird pilots coming in from FEAF just weren't too impressed by the ADIZ requirements. Thus, the many scrambles.

In January, as it now was, almost every night, the vis went down in fog. That "cat" kept creeping in and paused a lot longer than the man said, usually all night. Once on top, though at about 1000 or 2000 feet, it was almost always clear. Intercepts at night were a lot more sporting than the daylight ones. The interceptee didn't know he was being had, and the interceptor was blacked out and had to belly up real close to get aircraft type and numbers. Flying formation with a DC-4 tail at 8000 feet or so, indicating about 150, was a fairly demanding chore. In the day, not much to it. Just get the type and press on. At night, another story!

About halfway through Coolstone's first tour, it became clear that they could not support two-ship scrambles. It just flat-ran them out of aircraft and crews before the night was over. So, the CO decided that they'd use single-ship scrambles and that four scrambles per crew was max during any 24-hour period. After that, you had to be replaced. This happened fairly often, even with just one aircraft per scramble. Needless to say, the crew that was called up got all emotional about it, particularly if the weather was rotten.

Hamilton really didn't have a bona fide IFR letdown or recovery. When IFR conditions did exist, other than just fog, it was necessary for the crews to divert. They sometimes landed at Fairfield Susson or at the Navy base. That also meant another crew had to be called out.

What was really frustrating, though, was that, with the exception of the ADC system, apparently, nobody really cared about the ADIZ violations. The aircraft type and numbers were carefully logged and passed to the civilian agencies for action, but as far as anyone knew, nothing was ever done about it. Hence no decrease in the 10 to 12 scrambles each night on contract aircraft coming back from Korea. Some of these aircraft carried only freight, but others carried passengers, servicemen, and their dependents.

Tempers were slowly rising to a critical level on the part of the ADC crews. So, it was on this January 1952 night on alert at beautiful Hamilton Air Force Base, California.

Coolstone One and Two already had three scrambles behind them, and it wasn't even midnight yet. Two of the three remaining crews were airborne on their second scrambles, and the other crew on the ground with the Rock also had three behind them. Coolstone's call sign was Red 1, and he was ready to go. The vis had started to drop in the inevitable fog, as reflected by the telautograph and as observed by just flat looking out the window. The weather training at good old McFog came into good use here when it came to eyeballing the weather. The 25th Division pilots were very careful about observing the weather because the division commander had made his policy extremely clear about mandatory scrambles. "When the bell rings," he had said after calling all of the crews together, "that's me scrambling you, and I don't care what the weather is. The least I'll accept is running off the runway on takeoff if you can't see. The word is go and remember that. I'll promise you that those who don't go will wish they had. Is my policy clear?"

"Abundantly" was the aircrew's silent response. Coolstone and his fearless RO Two figured if they could see one light and were lined up, they could make it by getting on the gauges at rotation, with Two watching the radar real carefully, trying to keep the corner markers in sight. While he didn't tell Two, Coolstone figured that if you could just get lined up, light or not, the odds were good that you could make it. Anyhow, somebody thought you could and had obviously sold the boss on the idea, probably a blockhouse ops officer.

One positive thing that Coolstone had noticed about the Hamilton alert tour was that he was in better shape than when he first went down there. They had enough scrambles that the sprint out of the ops building, across the ramp, then onto the first line of aircraft was starting to redevelop muscles that hadn't been used for a long, long time. There was no way to make a 5-minute scramble without running as hard as you could from the minute the bell rang until you got to the aircraft. An added incentive was that if you didn't make the 5 minutes, the paperwork was horrendous. Several people had gotten lost while making the run in the fog, not an acceptable excuse to the boss at all.

The Rock went over to the pilot of the remaining crew on the ground and said, "Okay, we're all set up, and when I go, you probably should call out another crew. We're getting torn up tonight. We've intercepted two contract C-54s and a Navy P-2V so far."

"Yeah," said the Rock's fearless RO, "that P-2V was right on the deck. Man, we had to throttle right back, descend with a hard as possible port." Then he added, "but One had to take three cracks at it before he got it."

"Never mind," said the Rock, "if you had gotten the lock on before 300 yards, I might have been able to do something with it. All I got was a lot of conversation and a blank scope. He never gave me the dot until we were running right up this guy's tail."

"What's the matter? Didn't you have the gain turned up?" he asked Two.

"Lousy set," said Two, "and I think that black paint doesn't return too well anyhow."

"Oh, the cross I have to bear," Two thought to himself. "These converted day fighter pilots, they take it as a personal insult that there is somebody else in their airplane, and then if they're not pulling 7.3 Gs every flight, all the time, chasing one another, there seems to be some type of an emotional reaction that somehow ends up primarily on the backseater."

As they walked away from the other crew, Coolstone One whispered hoarsely to Two, "Never mind discussin' what we do when we're flying together. I won't say a word about you locking on to that cloud and running me in there with the throttle right back and slow as possible and all that jazz if you won't mention some of those very, very minor difficulties that I've experienced. OK?"

"OK," said Two. But they'd had this conversation several times, and neither one of them had been able to keep the agreement to the letter. But then, they had worked out pretty well together. Two recalled that One never did say anything to anybody about the night he had run them in on that flock of ducks, ducks that apparently were banded; in fact, One might not even have known it. Two knew it but hadn't bothered to mention it. They settled down with well-worn magazines and a cup of ersatz coffee and waited for the inevitable.

Sure enough, the bell rang, and the loudspeaker clicked on and said, "Red 1, scramble!" Coolstone One and Two were launched. They raced to the airplane, and as usual, Two won. But Coolstone was reducing the spread. He still remembered the time when Two raced to the wrong airplane. Coolstone never bothered to tell him as he saw Two go up the ladder and try to strap in. The Rock, however, went straight to the right airplane and began the engine start, to the startled surprise of Two. Coolstone never looked around as he got the engines started, checked in, and released the brakes, just as Two scrambled aboard. The Rock thought sure that lesson would slow Two down when they were racing on a scramble, but it didn't seem to.

They cranked up, checked in, and were given initial vectors. They taxied to the north end of the runway very carefully since the vis was really down, lined up, were cleared, engaged burner, and felt their way through the fog until becoming airborne.

Coolstone One cleaned up the aircraft and checked in with Sundance. "Sundance from Coolstone One, squawking normal, climbing through four angels."

"Roger, Coolstone, this is Sundance, understand. Continue climb to 15 angels, turn port 240, your bogie is at 10 angels, approximately 75 miles heading 085, speed 200 knots." And he added, "apparently into the San Francisco area."

"Roger," mumbled Coolstone, and then he mumbled to Two, "Looks like another contract carrier missing his ETA. I think those guys just fly east until they hit the coast and narrow it down after that. The crime is they never even know that they've been intercepted."

"How's the set look?" He asked Two.

"We're picking up a boat or two on the water. I think we've got a good one here," Two answered.

"I hope so," said One, "I want to get this guy, and I want to turn him in, and I sure want him to know that he's been intercepted."

Sundance kept them advised of the bogie's progress. They were placed several miles to the right of the target's track, and finally, at about 6 miles, Two picked up the target and began the conversion to a stern attack. As they steadied out on the reciprocal heading, paralleling the bogie's track, Two was able to lock on and gave One the dot. They stabilized their speed, then worked in very carefully, indicating about 160 with flaps and boards out, descending gently as they closed. One had the bogie's lights in sight, checked again to be sure that his were off, and moved on in.

Coolstone One could always tell when the range was getting critical because Two's commentary picked up pace considerably. Two was from Magnolia, Arkansas, and he normally had a drawl that dripped cornbread, but when they were within 2000 feet of anything at night or in the weather, his commentary picked up a staccato characteristic worthy of a New Yorker.

Coolstone One was able, as they moved to within a couple hundred feet to make out the horizontal stabilizer, and he positioned the aircraft just slightly ahead on the transport's right side. They identified it as a C-54/DC-4 type with large red letters painted on the fuselage. This indicated it was a contract airline of doubtful pedigree and even more doubtful ancestry. As they were stabilized, they could see people through the windows. It was a passenger flight.

Coolstone told Sundance the type of aircraft and the name of the airline. Sundance told them to break it off and gave them vectors for Hamilton.

Coolstone started a gentle starboard turn, added throttle, increased his airspeed, descending slightly, and then he said to Two, "what a shame, this guy doesn't even know we were here. I think I'll come back around and fly by them, just so they'll know they've been intercepted." Coolstone did a loose 360, climbing as he did until he was 5000 to 7000 feet above the bogie. He still had him in sight, and he started a descent in full mil from about 5 miles in the stern. By the time he got to the transport, he was slightly underneath it, slightly to the right, and pushing the mach. At this point, he plugged in the burner, pulled up sharply, and climbed steeply. He was sure the transport crew had seen him. He finally disengaged the burner at about 20,000 feet and headed for home.

"At least this time," Two told him, "they'll know they've been intercepted."

Sundance vectored Coolstone One and Two back to Hamilton, where GCA picked them up. Even though weather was calling it 100 obscured, with a quarter of a mile visibility in fog, the Rock gave it a try. He knew the fog was only a few hundred feet thick, and he also knew full well that if he didn't land at Hamilton, the rest of his night was going to be spent someplace other than where he wanted it to be spent and probably most of his day off too. They made the GCA to the north, and as they came on down the approach, Coolstone could see through the fog vertically, which gave him confidence. At least he could stay lined up with the runway until the last 300 or 400 feet.

He was on speed, on glide path, and on centerline when he finally entered the fog at about 200 feet. Just a short time later, he picked up the fuzzy green threshold lights and landed. As they were rolling out, Coolstone chuckled slightly and said, "By golly, that's one of them that knows he's been intercepted, and he'll think again before he misses his ETA that far."

"That's right," said Two, "we all ought to do that every time so that they know they're being had out there. Maybe the word will get around, and they'll think a little more about getting to the ADIZ on time."

When they got back to the Ops-ready room, Two filled out the intercept information card and asked One if he wanted to include the fact that they'd made a pass on the bogie. One said no, he didn't think so. They probably should leave that part out.

The pilot of another alert crew, overhearing the discussion, said, "What did you do, make a pass on him?"

Coolstone One said, "Sure, I made a pass on him. I wanted him to know he'd been intercepted. I'm sick of these guys coming in here in the middle of the night not paying attention to anything, and then we scramble our fannies off. I got up behind him, picked up a good head of steam, came down underneath, engaged the burner, pulled up in front, and held the climb until I was about 20,000 and came on home. There is no doubt in his mind that he was intercepted. He'll think about that a little bit the next time he's coming back to San Francisco."

"That's a darn good idea," said the other pilot. "When we get scrambled, we'll do the same thing."

"Did you call out a relief crew?" asked the Rock.

"No, I didn't," said the other pilot, "I decided since the scrambles drop off quite a bit after 1 or 2 o'clock, we'll probably get by okay. Why don't you and Two sack on out?" Both One and Two agreed with that assessment and spent the rest of the night trying to sleep in the lounge chairs that were placed strategically in the ready room.

The next morning after they were relieved, all of the outgoing alert crews decided to go up to the club and have breakfast before they hit the pad seriously. The club was on the top of the hill, as was the "O", so they had to make the climb anyhow. As they were going into the club, one of the crews spotted the headlines in a San Francisco paper that was showing through the grill of a vending machine.

He said, "Look at that." The group moved over to the vending machine and read the large headlines "Cigar-Shaped Objects Terrorize Transport Crews and Passengers."

Coolstone's hair began to rise on the back of his neck. He had a sneaking, horrible suspicion that he knew exactly what one of those cigar-shaped objects was. He looked at the other pilot. "Did you get a scramble after we sacked out?"

"Rog," said the pilot.

Coolstone One bought the paper and then read the front-page story, which said, in essence, "Two transports returning from overseas were harassed by cigar-shaped objects, belching green fire. The pilot of one of the airliners stated that the object passed his aircraft, going at least 2000 miles per hour, then climbed vertically until it went completely out of sight. The airline pilot stated he had never observed an airborne object moving that fast, climbing that fast, or climbing that high in his life. The pilots of both of the air carriers agreed in their description of the object. They also stated that there was a tremendous disturbance in the air which caused them to almost lose control of their large transports. Several passengers in each aircraft confirmed that the unidentified object passed the airliner on the right side at a tremendous speed. Some of them reported seeing portholes with grotesque faces lit by a strange red glow, and one of the passengers insisted that the beasts inside had domed heads, no hair at all, which could not have belonged to any being on this earth.

Coolstone One, and Two, and Three, and Four no longer cared for breakfast. The other two crews did not understand what the problem was, and the four of them went on in to eat. The remaining four stood silently, staring at the newspaper.

Two, Coolstone's fearless RO, finally said to the quiet group, "I guess they didn't know they were intercepted after all." Then added, "I don't believe any of us had ever better say a word about this as long as we live." A lot of head nodding met this sage advice.

Thereafter, whenever Coolstone read about an unidentified flying object, cigar-shaped, spewing green fire, he had a sneaking hunch that another bogie pilot didn't realize he had been intercepted.

Made in the USA
Las Vegas, NV
09 June 2024

90911744R00213